SHENANIGANS

SHENANIGANS

SARINA BOWEN

Tuxbury Publishing LLC

For my Jenn and Natasha. Thank you for all that you do!

ONE

I'M NOT WEARING PANTS

Charli

It's a beeping alarm that pierces through my hangover to wake me up.

At first, I fight it. I'm lying on my back in a plush bed that's way too comfortable to be my own. This isn't necessarily a problem. I'm a professional hockey player, and we spend a lot of nights in hotels.

Not *nice* hotels, though. It's the silky, high-thread-count sheets that provide the first clue that something is very wrong.

Also, I'm topless. And I have a hangover headache. But those two things happen occasionally, and neither one is too worrisome.

The alarm, though. It isn't mine, and it isn't my road-trip roommate Samantha's. Whose room is this?

I'd open my eyes to check, but it's awfully bright, and I'm so sleepy. I drift off for another moment.

Eventually, though, another mechanical beep pulls me back to the surface. This noise is familiar. It's the sound that Neil—Cornelius Harmon Drake III—makes when he's testing his blood sugar.

Wait. I'm in a bed with *Neil Drake*?

And I'm topless, too?

Shit.

My eyes spring open. The first thing I see is… the ceiling. It's really far away and very decorative. There's a line of goddamn gold leaf running around the border of the room. It's further confirmation that Drake is in this bed with me. He's the richest person I'll ever meet.

My head throbs in protest, and my mouth is dry. Hello, hangover.

"What the fuck happened here last night?" Drake mumbles from a few feet away. "Why am I not wearing my pants?"

"I am!" This comes out all raspy, as if I smoked a pack of cigarettes. I'm not a smoker, though. Then again, all bets are off this morning.

"You're wearing my pants?" Drake asks.

"No," I clarify, relieved to discover that my bottom half isn't as naked as the top half. "If we're taking inventory, I'd like to report that I'm wearing underwear and pantyhose. And also…" What is that thing near my foot? With my toe, I drag it upward until I can reach it. I pull one high-heeled shoe out from under the bedclothes.

We both snort at the same time. Apparently, I got in bed wearing my hose and at least one shoe. No shirt, though, which is going to be awkward in a moment when I get up.

Still, it's a relief. We got wasted in Vegas, but at least we didn't get wasted and screw each other. So whatever damage control we're doing right now, it can't be *that* bad.

I finally get up the courage to look over at Neil Drake, just about the same time he gets the courage to look at me. His hazel eyes widen. Mine do too.

He looks like he's been to *war*. He's still wearing his bowtie, but the tuxedo shirt underneath is open and missing half its buttons. His thick hair is all askew, like sex hair, even though I've established that no sex happened.

Well, no banging happened. But those missing buttons are ringing some bells with me. I think maybe I —

"*Oh shit,*" I whisper. I'm pretty sure I ripped those buttons off myself. Although I hadn't been able to get that bowtie off him.

"What the hell happened here last night?" he asks in a harsh whisper. His expression is so confused.

"Um..." *Think, Charli.* "We did some drinking after the awards ceremony. And after your fight with Iris."

"My fight with Iris," he echoes. His eyes squeeze closed with remorse.

The fight had been pretty ugly. Lots of shouting. I'd been eavesdropping from the living room, silently cheering Neil on whenever he landed a verbal blow.

Not that it's any of my business, but I can't stand his on-again-off-again girlfriend. They've been *off* for a while, but I think she came to Vegas to try to change that.

It hadn't worked. When she'd finally screeched her good-byes and had stormed out of this hotel suite, I'd smiled at the sight of her skinny ass as it departed.

"You got pretty drunk after that," I say to my tousle-haired companion. "Is your, um, blood sugar okay?"

Neil is diabetic. Before him, I'd never met anyone who has to monitor his own body chemistry to remain alive.

It almost makes him seem less like a carefree rich dude and more like a real person.

Almost. But not quite.

"I need to eat," he says. "Although we're supposed to be downstairs in, like, seventeen minutes."

"*Seventeen?*" I screech.

"Yeah, I like to sleep as late as I can."

Ugh. I sit up so fast that I feel nauseated.

Also, I'm still topless. Neil is now staring at my breasts.

"Oops." I grab them in two hands.

"Wow," he says, his eyes glazing over lustfully.

"Come on, now. You've seen tits before." I can play this off as a joke, right? We'll be laughing about this in a week. *Remember that time you flashed me your tits before we almost missed the team jet?*

But it's too soon.

"Charli," he croaks, his eyes still glued to my hands cupping my breasts.

"What?"

"I've seen *those* tits before. They look super familiar. Because we fooled around last night." He scrubs a hand over his face, somehow without breaking the stare-off he's having with my tits. "Hot damn."

"Whoa *whoa whoa*. First of all, tits are tits." This is a lie. As someone who's also fond of tits, I'm oversimplifying things. But now is not the moment for brutal honesty. "Besides, I don't remember it like that," I say carefully. "Maybe your memory could also fuck off right about now."

"That might be tricky. It might be hard to forget playing with those. They're pretty spectacular."

I grab the sheet and yank it up to cover me. "Hey! Is mind bleach a thing? Because I think you need some."

He grins suddenly. "My head is killing me right now. Like someone put an ax through it. But this is going to be so funny later, isn't it? I think I drooled all over your chest last night like a Saint Bernard."

"Stop! This isn't funny! What about Iris?" Honestly, Iris can die slowly in a pit of Las Vegas quicksand. (Is that a thing? It should be.) But if Neil feels guilty, then maybe he'll put our drunken encounter out of his stupidly handsome head.

Instead, he shrugs. "I told her we're never getting back together, right? That's why you and I got drunk. *God*, never sleep in a bowtie, though." He reaches up and unclips it.

I blink. "You wear a *clip-on* tie? You? With your Tom Ford tux?"

"The tux is Armani." He drops the tie onto the crisp white comforter. "The clip-on is something I bought just to irritate my uncle. But it's awfully handy. Saves time."

I just stare at the thing for a moment, because I'm having a bit of a flashback to last night. I'd been tugging on that bowtie to try to get it off him. Then I'd gotten frustrated and yanked the two halves of his shirt apart.

Then? I'd leaned down and licked his sixpack...

Holy, *holy* crap. I licked Neil Drake. And I liked it.

"You look like you just saw the devil." He snickers. "We were obviously in a weird, self-destructive mood. I never get drunk. And you never—" He stops talking suddenly. His mouth falls open in shock.

"I never what?" There's a lot of ways that sentence could end, and none of them are good. I've always been careful to *never* let on that Neil is the most attractive man I've ever met. I've never torn his shirt off, either. Or shown him my breasts.

His face is seriously confused. "Charli... you told me before that you don't fool around with *men*."

Oh. That's mostly true, especially lately. But really? That's what he finds so shocking here?

"But last night you... and I..." He swallows hard. "We were going to..." Then he lifts up the covers and looks down at his body.

His naked body. I can't see it right this second, but I saw it last night.

"I'm not wearing pants," he says again. "We were going to —" He's like a stuck record now.

"Okay, look." I clap my hands. "Time is wasting. Can we just get out of here, and worry about this later? Can I have the shower?"

"S-sure," he stammers. He's still looking at his dick, as if checking to see if it's still there.

"Close your eyes, please," I say primly.

Shockingly, he obeys me. He flops back onto the pillow and squeezes his eyes shut.

I dart out of bed and make a run for the bathroom.

TWO

PLAYING THE RICH ASSHOLE

Neil

I'm going to die of embarrassment. Or die of this headache.

Or both at the same time.

It's not the nakedness or the drunkenness that's killing me. I look good naked, and I rarely get drunk, because it makes my diabetes harder to manage.

And it's not the clip-on tie. I wear what I want. Fuck the haters.

But the details from last night are starting to cut through the fog in my brain. Charli's breasts woke me up for good. Those *spectacular* breasts that I've spent the last year and a half trying not to ogle.

Last night she let me, though. No, she actually *encouraged* me by whipping off her dress.

And I'd pounced. I'd been sloppy drunk for the first time in years. After we'd rolled around a little, I took off my pants while she tried to remove my tie and my shirt.

She'd been only partially successful. But eventually she gave up and kissed her way down my body.

I'd been in *heaven*, having guiltily jacked off to this very fantasy quite a few times. Then she'd—and I swear this actually happened, it wasn't a fever dream—put her mouth on me. Everything had been pure bliss.

But I'm a greedy bastard. I'd wanted more. So I'd grabbed a condom off the bedside table and tried to put it on, but...

I let out a loud groan of despair. Because unless I'm remembering a nightmare, I'd suddenly been afflicted with whiskey dick at just the wrong moment.

God, how embarrassing. I will never live this down.

Or maybe I will. Charli asked me to forget that it ever happened. And suddenly I'm on board with this plan.

Nothing happened. Not one thing. Not the whiskey dick or the blowjob. Okay, it's going to hurt me to give up the memory of my hand threaded through Charli's red hair as she—

Whew. My cock stirs at the mental image.

But no. I can't keep that in the spank bank if I don't want to remember what happened afterwards. So I have to delete the whole mental file, no? The breasts and the stumbling into the elevator. We'd been laughing like nutters. I'm pretty sure an elderly couple had exited the elevator early just to escape our howls.

"We gotta celebrate," Charli had said. And I'd agreed. We'd been celebrating our...

Whoa.

Hold up. That memory can't be right. Can it?

I leap out of the bed and cross the room, looking for evidence. Not that it's difficult to find. My belongings have been tossed helter-skelter on the desk in the way of a hotel drunk. And right there, beside the key card for this suite, is a certificate with a decorative gold border looping around the edges of the page.

A marriage certificate. With my name on it. And Charli's.

Holy fuck.

"Holy fuck," Charli calls from the bathroom. "What is this thing in my hair?"

I can't answer her, because I've lost all capacity for speech. Is there any chance this certificate is fake? Who'd marry a drunk person to another drunk person?

There's a crumpled receipt on the desk that answers the question pretty handily. It's from the TruLove Vegas Wedding Chapel, and the charge is for over twelve thousand dollars. It's itemized, because—as I learned in childhood—when you fuck up your life, there's usually somebody there to make sure you know the details of your self-destruction.

Wedding music: $57.50

Ceremony: $250

Flowers: $75

I glance around the room and find a bouquet of white roses on the floor near the bedroom door. So that charge tracks.

Deluxe Multi-stone Engagement Ring: $11,000

"Seriously," she calls. "What is this thing? Neil? It's heavy. Like jewelry. Help!"

At the sound of Charli's distress, I snap out of my stupor and cross to the master bathroom. When I open the door, I find that she's wrapped her body in a towel before summoning me. But I can still see cleavage.

I yank my eyes upward. "What's the matter?" My voice is outwardly calm, but inwardly I'm wondering if I can take care of this little marriage thing before Charli finds out. Or I investigate it, at least. So I know for sure if we're really—

Yeah, I can't even think it. Too crazy.

I concentrate on the problem at hand. Charli clutches a section of her hair, where there's an object imbedded in her red waves. It's in an awkward spot at the back of her head. No wonder she can't untangle it herself.

I reach up with shaking fingers and clear the loosest strands away from what turns out to be an eleven-thousand-dollar, multi-stone engagement ring. And by "multi-stone" they meant multiple *different* stones. It's like a rainbow parade in jewelry form.

"Holy fuck," I whisper. Somehow this makes it real in a way that words on a receipt don't seem to capture.

"What?" she snaps. "Did you just realize you're naked from the waist down?"

"That is the least of our problems," I mutter. "Just don't look at my dongle."

"Oh, sure. The same way you didn't just stare at my breasts? Fine. Is it out yet? OUCH!"

"Sorry. I didn't mean to pull so hard. But the last bit of hair was stuck between two stones."

"Two stones? Of what?"

"Nothing." I palm the ring, still in full-on panic mode.

"Neil, show me what was stuck in my hair."

"No." I put my hand behind my back with all the finesse of a kindergartener who's stolen a cookie.

"Cornelius!" The pitch of her voice is high and scared. "Show me. Because it felt like a..." She swallows hard.

"A what?"

"A ring. A damn ring. And I don't wear rings. Except I think maybe..." She takes a deep breath. "What did we *do?*"

I pull my hand out and slowly open it. We both look down, and then we both take identical sharp breaths.

"Wow," she says.

"I know," I grunt.

"That's *hideous.*"

"I guess you get what you pay for. It was only eleven large."

"Eleven...dollars?" she asks, her voice climbing in pitch. "Please say that's what you meant."

"Nah. Eleven thousand. We're in the tackiest city ever built."

"Oh my *God,*" Charli gasps. "What a waste of —" The sentence ends abruptly. "Shit. The ring isn't the real problem, is it?"

"No," I say quietly.

"Did we really...?" She looks up at me in horror.

"Yeah."

"Oh my God."

"Yeah."

"OH MY GOD." Her face flushes red, and her mouth flops open. "What have we *done?*"

Now I'm feeling the same panic that she is. I can't believe I got drunk and got... Urgh. Even *thinking* the "m" word makes me feel a little queasy. Charli clearly agrees. She's clutching the wall with one hand and her chest in the other. It's actually possible that the toughest girl I have ever met is about to fall into a dead faint. I brace myself to catch her.

Then, from the other room, my blood-sugar monitoring app starts pinging away to remind me to eat. The shrill sound seems to snap Charli out of her stupor. "Drake, order some room service before you crash."

"I'll eat granola bars. We've got to get out of here. Take your shower. I'm fine." I grab her by the shoulders and ease her toward the giant walk-in shower. "Go on."

She turns to give me one more dazed look before I head out of the bathroom. "You *do* know you're naked, right?"

"I'm aware. Just enjoy the view. You saw it last night already."

The door closes behind me.

"And we are legally *married* for fuck's sake!" I call out. There —I said it. Like ripping off a Band-Aid. I'll have to say it again to my lawyer on the way home to New York. Might as well practice.

I cross to my bag and pull out a granola bar and a bottle of fruit juice that will lift my blood sugar until I can have regular food. My system is probably haywire from the alcohol. Because I'm not usually a drinker, I don't have the tolerance for alcohol that other people have. If I had to guess, four or five drinks was all it took to accidentally get married.

A few gulps later, I've downed the juice. I'm just ripping the wrapper off the granola bar when my phone rings. I edge closer to it, wondering what else could go wrong.

Had anyone witnessed last night's fiasco? And if so, why didn't any of those assholes stop us? Maybe the whole team is laughing at me right now. God, are there photos?

But the caller is only Doc Herberts. I pick up the phone. "I'm fine! I'm eating. Are my numbers really that ugly?"

"Well, I've seen worse. But a couple of the guys said you'd been drinking. And then you missed the jet."

"I... what? We're meeting in the lobby at eight! It's a quarter to, at least."

He chuckles uncomfortably. "You're an hour off, Neil. Vegas is three hours behind New York. Are you sure you're okay?"

"I missed the jet?" I whisper.

"Seems so, son. Better stop teasing Anton about that time *he* missed the jet."

Anton. Oh, shit. "I'll never live this down. I'll never live *any* of this down."

I'd fucked up my personal life. But I'd screwed myself with the team, too?

"Take a breath. I'll let Hugh know that you're on your way back to New York as fast as possible. Call the travel office. They'll find you a flight."

"Right," I whisper. "Thanks for calling to check up on me."

"My pleasure," he says. "You always take good care of yourself and your condition. It's admirable."

That isn't really the word I'd use to describe myself right now, but I thank him again and hang up the phone.

Now I've got another problem to solve. Luckily, this one is easy. It's time for some Drake-family-style damage control. I hit another button on my phone and order up a private jet. Vegas is one of our larger markets. "I need it fueled up and ready to go in an hour," I tell the customer service agent. "No excuses."

Man, I am really embodying the role of Rich Asshole right now. That's something I try never to do.

But hockey is my whole life. I can't screw up the one thing that goes well for me. Even if I have to act like a rich prick, I'll do it in order to make it to practice this afternoon.

"Yessir, Mr. Drake. Whatever you need."

"Thank you." I hang up.

This is a terrible day, and it isn't even eight o'clock.

Oh wait, it is.

Fuck.

THREE

WAFFLES ON THE PRIVATE JET

Neil

An hour later we cross the tarmac to board a Drake jet. I motion for Charli to climb the airstairs ahead of me and then scoop her suitcase out of her hand as she passes me.

I get a frown for my trouble. Charli frowns a lot, actually. I've noticed she isn't comfortable getting help from anyone.

But carrying a woman's luggage is just the way I was raised. My father didn't spend a lot of time with me, but his lessons stuck, and that man believed in chivalry. So I am going to carry a lady's bag up a set of stairs if I can.

At the doorway to the jet, I'm met by an air hostess. "Welcome aboard, Mr. Drake. I'm Marsha. The pilot has informed me that we'll be cleared to push back momentarily. May I take your bags?"

"I'll stash them, Marsha." I open the baggage closet and do the deed, while Charli stands beside me wringing her hands.

"Is this a plane? Or a suite at the Ritz?"

I glance around the jet's interior. It's been a year or so since I've boarded one of our aircraft. Private jets are bad for the environment. And yet that's how my family makes their billions.

"I think we call this design the *Plaza*."

She snorts. "So I was close?"

"Yep." There's a lot of cognac-colored leather and dark wood paneling. This is a small plane, so there are two studded leather seats, each one twice the width of a normal airplane seat. They face a marble-topped table. Everything is bolted to the floor, including the plush Persian-style rug underfoot. Because Safety First.

After takeoff, the table will be set with crystal and china. "The design is a little much, right? But at least it's going to get me back to New York in time for practice."

Charli looks unconvinced. "Are you sure leaving Vegas was the right decision?" she asks. "Shouldn't we have tried to straighten this out at the county clerk's office?"

"In a perfect world, yes. But if I miss practice, I'll be fined."

"Do you even hear yourself?" she demands. "The fine probably costs less than this flight."

Charli is a smart girl, and unfortunately, she's right. "But it's the principle of the thing. Do you want to be late to practice?"

Slowly, she shakes her head.

"I didn't think so."

"I just hope you know what you're doing."

Marsha is watching this little drama play out, of course, so I have to be discreet. "I have a plan."

"That's such a relief," Charli says with a disbelieving eyeroll.

Honestly, it's hard to blame her. I don't know what the hell I'm doing, and she can probably sense my ineptitude, which is leaking from my pores along with stale whiskey.

"Once we reach cruising altitude, I'll be serving brunch," Marsha says, ignoring the tension in the room. "You can peruse the menu while we taxi."

"She needs us to take our seats." I nudge Charli toward the table. "Do you want to ride forwards or backwards?"

"Which one is safer?" she asks before plunking down in the nearest chair.

"Are you a nervous flier? There's nothing dangerous about this." I sit down opposite her.

"Oh my God. Are you trying to jinx us?" She leans over and knocks on the wooden wall panel.

"Easy now. I was just thinking that after all that's gone wrong today, it's time we catch a break."

"Okay, stop it." She knocks on the wall again. "Maybe that's how luck works in the Drake family empire. You have a little snafu, and then the world rights itself."

Marsha makes a strange choking sound which I assume is her trying not to laugh.

"But it doesn't work that way in the real world."

I roll my eyes. "Fine, but just so you know, I say this from a place of knowledge. Our safety record is unmatched, and in the event of an emergency, I could actually fly the plane myself."

Her eyes bug out. "Really?"

"Sure. You can't grow up in the Drake family empire and not know how to fly a plane. I was a qualified pilot at seventeen."

"You are such a freak."

I laugh for the first time all morning.

Charli is not like any of my other friends. My whole life, women have been trying to get closer to me. They want a trip on the jet. They want to join the Mile High Club. They think it's sexy. And if the planes don't appeal to them, the money does.

But not Charli. She looks vaguely revolted by this whole experience. She hasn't touched the menu that Marsha set down in front of us. She only grips the cool edge of the marble table as the plane begins to move, taxiing on the tarmac and then, after a few moments' delay, accelerating for takeoff.

"Breathe, doll. Everything is going well at the moment."

"Neil!" she snaps, and I chuckle.

The silly nickname was an intentional ploy to distract her.

I've been ordered to *never* call her "doll." That's how we met, actually. I mistook her for a member of the training staff, and casually called her doll, which is admittedly a patronizing name.

And she ripped me a new one.

Fun times.

"Now." I push the menu across to her side of the table. "Let's eat. I'm going to need a good meal to get us through this mess we made."

She sighs deeply, then picks up the menu.

Thirty minutes later I'm hoovering down a huge plate of eggs and bacon, while a waffle waits its turn on a fluted china plate.

"You're not eating," I say to Charli between bites. "How can you cure a hangover if you don't eat?"

She's seated across from me, a wedge of barely touched quiche in front of her. "Neil, there are two kinds of people in the world — the kind who eat their feelings, and the kind whose feelings eat them. I think I'm the latter."

My fork pauses on the way to my mouth, and I make a sad puppy-dog face, the kind that usually gets me out of trouble with women. "Hey, I'm so sorry."

"You said that already," she growls.

I have it so bad for Charli that her attitude only makes her more attractive to me. Even her growl is sexy. "I'm going to fix it. I promise. This is all my fault."

"It's not *just* your fault." She puts her head in her hands and takes a deep breath. "This is my fault, too. Last night I had a *lot* to celebrate. And things got out of hand."

She isn't wrong. Before we'd started drinking ourselves silly, it *had* been a fortuitous night. She'd just won a medal at the women's All-Star exhibition — a silver in the fastest skating competition. And my All-Star team had taken home a trophy.

I'd stood on that podium thinking I knew a thing or two about how to live my life.

Things began to deteriorate pretty quickly after that. First, I'd fought with my ex-girlfriend. I'd told her we were done for good. It had been inevitable, and I'd do it again, but it had left me feeling guilty.

And when my sister—Iris's bestie—had started in with her angry texts a half hour later, I'd just felt rage.

It's my damn life, right? I can date who I want.

That had been the battle cry that had led me to drink more than one pour—my usual amount. After that first whiskey, I'd just kept on going.

I really don't see why Charli is blaming herself. "Did you pour the whiskey down my throat?"

"No." She snorts. "But I probably egged you on. You were in a 'fuck Iris' mood. And I'm always in a 'fuck Iris' mood. So I didn't step in and tell you to slow down."

"Not your job," I grumble. "I'm pretty tired of people telling me how to live my life. And when you say you were in a 'fuck Iris' mood—" I use air quotes. "—Did you mean, like, literally? Or figuratively?"

I give her a cheesy grin, but the truth is I'm damn curious about what happened last night. Things are still not adding up for me—and not just the parts that I can't remember. Because I *distinctly* remember Charli's mouth on my dick.

But I spent the last year and a half thinking she wasn't into men. At all.

"*Not* literally," she clarifies. "I have never wanted to fuck Iris. She's too prim. I'll bet even her sex face is prim. Am I right?"

I shove another strip of bacon into my mouth so that I don't have to answer. Iris's sex face is definitely prim. She leaves her pearls on and only likes missionary. There's no way I'm telling Charli that, though. I'm a gentleman.

A confused one.

"Help me out, here," I try. "Didn't you tell me last year that you didn't do guys?"

"Well..." She looks guilty. "Those weren't precisely my words. I didn't say that I don't *like* dicks. I simply said that I would never ride a hockey player's dick. Do you hear the difference?"

"I guess I do. But —"

"You just *assumed* I meant all men. But I was just laying down some rules so that nobody would hit on me."

"But then you changed your mind," I point out. Last night I *know* she was about to saddle up and tango on my mango.

"Not necessarily." She gives her red hair a careless toss, but I can see the heat climbing up her neck. It's Charli's one tell. She blushes easily.

"Oh, so I just *imagined* the part where you tore some of my clothes off? And I'm being literal here. My tux shirt is history." And don't get me started on the dick-sucking. The sight of her lips wet against my —

Suddenly my underwear is too tight. I need to think about something else right now. Like the sight of my uncle's face when he hears that I accidentally got married.

Instant boner killer. He's going to scalp me.

"I was under the influence," Charli says with a scowl.

Even her scowl is pretty. I've been attracted to her ever since that first day when she yelled at me. And last night was a game-changer. I can't unsee that. I can't unwant it, either. I might have *gotten* it, too, except that my dick went to sleep before the grand finale.

I have so many regrets. I can't believe I blew my shot before I could, um, blow my shot. We're definitely going to revisit this question at a later date.

First I have a marriage to dissolve. And Charli still hasn't eaten her breakfast. "Is there something wrong with that quiche? If there is, I want management to know."

She gives me a withering look and lets out a sigh. "It's fine.

The peas are a strange choice, though." She reaches over and steals a strawberry off my waffle.

With my own fork, I grab a bite of her quiche. And, yup, the peas really are a strange choice. "Marsha?" I call out, and the flight attendant comes running. "Could you bring Charli a bowl of strawberries and a waffle?"

"Of course!" She picks up Charli's plate.

"Also? Could you send a memo to the chef that peas don't belong in a quiche? Like, ever?"

"Yessir. Right away, sir."

"*Neil!*" Charli yelps. "You can't do that. The man could get *fired* if some message comes down saying the heir to the Drake family throne doesn't like his cooking. *Jesus.* It's only a few peas."

"He won't get fired. Marsha!"

Her head pops out of the galley again. "Yes, Mr. Drake?"

"Never mind about the peas. I don't want to get anyone in trouble."

"Yessir. The waffle will be two minutes, sir."

"Thank you."

Marsha's subservient demeanor just makes Charli scowl harder. "How do they make waffles on a jet, anyway?"

"There's a waffle iron affixed to the wall right above the toaster oven. The batter is premixed in disposable cups."

She shakes her head like this is the dumbest thing she's ever heard. And maybe it is. We've always catered to the one percent of the one percent. My grandfather started Drake Enterprises in 1966, after retiring from a long and distinguished Air Force career. My father and uncle ran it after his death.

Four years ago, my father died at the age of eighty-one. Now my uncle runs the company, with the help of *his* son, who's almost twice my age. My mother, my sister, and I control some stock, two seats on the board, and half the family's charitable foundation.

That's how I happen to know how the waffles are made.

And that's why the flight attendant looks as though she'd offer up a limb if I asked her to spare one.

Honestly, being the heir to Drake Enterprises is mostly a pain in the ass. Every time I try to make a difference at the company, I get shot down. My board seat is only useful to me once or twice a year.

Today just happens to be one of those days.

When Charli's waffle shows up, she finds her appetite and gobbles it down. She doesn't even grimace when I prick my finger at the table to test my blood sugar, probably because she's seen me do it a dozen times before.

This month I'm calibrating a new insulin pump as part of a research project. It's finicky and time consuming. But I don't complain, because nobody wants to hear a rich guy gripe.

Charli isn't a complainer, either. That's part of why I like her so much. She knows the world is cracked and bitching about it is just a waste of breath.

Mostly. Occasionally she needs a good scream into the void. And then she's back to her default setting of *suck it up, buttercup.*

Although today we have a problem that neither of us can ignore. Charli is sneaking glances at me while mowing down that bowl of strawberries.

"What?" I finally ask her. It's my secret, fervent hope that she's sitting over there picturing me naked.

"What are we going to do?" she asks. "I still think we should have gone back to that county clerk and asked about an annulment. That's what they do on TV."

I wince. "Do you really want to go AWOL from practice?"

"Of course not," she grumbles. "But I don't want to be married to you, either."

"You're hard on a guy's ego, Charli."

She grins. "I've been told that before."

"I'll bet. Let's call my lawyer right now. He'll sort this out."

"That sounds expensive." She bites on her lip, and I'd like to bite it too.

"Listen." I lean forward on the table and nail her with a stare, which is, to my grave disappointment, the only thing I've managed to nail her with. "I know you roll your eyes when I throw money at problems. But there's no way around it, okay? I'm going to throw *all* the money at this problem and make it go away. And you're going to just nod and smile."

She scowls. "I hate it when you go all alpha rich guy."

"Even when it's going to make your life easier?" There's no way she can pay a lawyer. She can barely make the rent.

We both know she's going to have to eat her pride this time.

"I'll nod, but I won't smile," she finally agrees.

"Fine." I pull out my phone, place it on the surface of the table, and call Cassius Witherspoon, our family lawyer.

He answers on the second ring, because old money talks. My family has been his client since *his* grandfather ran the firm. "Neil," he says in his gruff voice. "What can I do for you?"

"I got a little problem," I tell him. "Something I need you to make go away."

"Who is it?" he asks. "A woman? Is this a paternity situation?"

Across the table from me, Charli rolls her eyes so hard that it might cause permanent damage. Then she collapses back against the leather upholstery, as if the first four seconds of this call has already killed her.

"Cassius, it's nothing like that. My friend and I pulled a dumb stunt last night in Las Vegas, and we need you to dissolve our..." I swallow hard. "Hasty drunken marriage."

There's a beat of silence on the other end of the line. "A Vegas wedding? How did that happen? Did you go to the clerk's office? If you didn't get a license, the wedding isn't legal."

"We, uh, went to the clerk's office." Now I feel like a seven-year-old kid who's been called to the principal's office. Only dumber. "Our friends were going to the clerk's office, so we went with them. And we bought a license as a joke."

"As a joke," he repeats slowly. "Did your friends get married, too?"

"No." I sigh. "They're getting married *next* time we're in Vegas. The license is good for a year."

My teammate Bryce Campeau and Petra, his sweetheart, have decided to have a small Vegas wedding when we play there in March. Last night they'd been preparing for it. Like normal, responsible adults.

Charli and I had been their loud, drunk friends who'd commented on everything and everyone in the room. We'd gotten a marriage license as a funny kind of Vegas souvenir.

But then I'd had another two glasses of whiskey. And woke up with a wife.

"You're *sure* you went through with it?" My lawyer sounds skeptical.

"Uh, yup. Got the witnessed certificate and the bill."

He sighs. "Okay, I have a couple of preliminary questions. Please tell me the name of your bride."

"Charli Higgins."

Another pause. "You married a man?"

Charli snorts. "Charlotte Fern Higgins."

"Aw!" I break into a smile. "You were named after two characters in *Charlotte's Web*!"

She gives me a death glare.

"Where are the two of you right now?" Witherspoon asks.

I look out the window. "Somewhere over the great plains, I think."

"Wait, you're not in Vegas anymore?"

"No way. I have practice this afternoon. I had to get back."

My lawyer groans audibly. "That was a mistake. If you'd gone right back to the clerk's office, you might have talked your way into a quick annulment."

Charli pales right before my eyes. "Oh my God. I knew it."

Shit.

"Well, we're on the jet," I say levelly. "We'll have to fix this another way. That's why we pay you the big bucks."

"One last question," the lawyer prompts. "Did you sign a prenuptial agreement?"

Charli and I let out twin snorts of laughter. "No," I say. "Have you *met* whiskey?"

"I had to ask." I hear the sounds of rapid typing in the background. "And the date of your wedding was…"

"Yesterday." I say.

"No, today," Charli corrects. "It was past midnight."

"We can still fix this, right?" I press. "Even though I'm not in Vegas? Should I call a divorce attorney? People who don't want to be married don't have to stay that way. It's a rule. Ask my father's first wife."

"Calm down," my asshole lawyer says. "Location matters in a courtroom. But let me do some digging and see what I can learn. By any chance could you get back to Vegas sometime in the next seventy-two hours?"

Charli buries her face in her hands, because she already knows the answer.

"I have three games this week, none of them on the West Coast."

"And you can't skip just one? This seems important."

"There is *no way* I can skip one. It's not high school! And Charli has four practices and two games this week, too."

"Fine. Let's talk about annulments versus divorces, anyway. Technically, you need grounds for an annulment but not for a divorce. I think your grounds for an annulment would be—"

"Inebriation," Charli offers.

"Yeah," the lawyer agrees. "And we'd throw in Neil's disability."

"Hey!" I argue. "It's not disabled. Usually it works."

"He means your *diabetes*," Charli corrects. "Not your penis."

"But we can also use the penis," the lawyer says. "I'm writing that down."

"Do not write that down," I roar. "Please just find out if we can get an annulment in New York."

"Right. I'll call you in a couple of hours," he says. Then he hangs up.

When I look at Charli, she's laughing for the first time all day.

"What?" I bark.

"Nothing," she says. Then she giggles.

"I knew he meant diabetes," I lie.

She braces her head in her hands and laughs until her shoulders shake.

FOUR

IF A UNICORN SNEEZED

Charli

Cornelius Harmon Drake III feels guilty. I can tell because he insists on dropping me off at my apartment even though it's in a far-flung corner of Brooklyn he's never seen before.

This is not okay with me.

"It's *way* out of your way. You might be late for practice," I argue. I really don't want him to visit my apartment. There's a reason that none of my friends have ever seen it.

My objections are shouted down, though, so I let him put my hockey bag into the trunk of a gleaming sedan. And when the female chauffeur opens the back door, I climb in and sink into the buttery leather seat.

"Liz, we're making a stop before I head to the rink. Charli, can you tell Liz your address?"

Oh boy. This isn't just a car service. It's Neil's *driver*. I tell her my address.

"What are the cross streets?" she asks.

Even when I provide the answer, she types it into the GPS. She's probably never seen that corner of Brooklyn.

I don't blame her.

"Okay, let's figure out our game plan," Neil says as the car heads east. "We'll need to talk to the lawyer again tonight. Or tomorrow. I could come into the diner after practice."

"It's hard to carry on a private conversation at the diner," I point out. I'm a waitress at the Orion in the DUMBO neighborhood of Brooklyn, which is a pretty good gig. The hours are early, and everything there costs a fortune. Neil and his teammates often come in for breakfast or lunch and leave me fat tips. "Although maybe you could use a plate of fried oysters. Just saying."

It takes a beat before he realizes I've made a dig at him. Oysters are supposed to make men virile. "*Charli!*"

"I'm sorry. But come on, you walked right into that one."

He scrubs a hand over his face as silence falls over the backseat. "This is a crazy thing to say, but I'm glad it was you."

I run that sentence backwards and forwards a few times before deciding that I have no idea what he's talking about. "You're glad *what* was me? The whiskey dick? The legal trouble?

"The whole mess," he says. "If I'm going to make an ass out of myself, I'd just as soon do it in front of you."

"Why? Because I'm so easy to impress?"

"No, dummy. Because I trust you."

Oh. That shuts me up for a second. I honestly have no idea what to say. Neil and I haven't known each other that long. The first time we met, he offended me, and I let him know it. Since then, he's been much more courteous. Friendly, even.

But I still don't know what to make of Neil Drake III. He grew up with more privilege than most people dream of. He's exactly the kind of person who made my teenage years hell at the fusty private school I attended on scholarship.

Neil and I are acquainted because our circle of friends overlaps. But I trust about three people in the whole world. On a good day. My heart is like a skittish kitten. It runs away at the first sight of danger.

Still, it could always be worse. "You're right, Drake. If I must be needlessly shackled to a man or ask him to remove the ugliest ring ever made from my hair, it might as well be you."

He gives me a sweet smile. Like I've just paid him the *best* compliment. And my inner kitten crawls a little farther under the sofa. Now is not the time to think sentimental thoughts about Neil Drake. I've got enough problems, and that was *before* I accidentally got hitched.

After a long ride, we eventually pull up in front of my dumpy apartment building. There's a check-cashing place on the ground floor. "Thanks for the ride," I say, my hand on the door before the limo even comes to a complete stop.

"Let me walk you up," he says, opening the other door.

"Not necessary." I hurry out, hoping he'll stay put.

No luck.

"But we've got to strategize." He's already lifting my hockey bag out of the trunk before I can get to it.

This is really not the time for chivalry, but I clamp my jaw shut as he follows me to the grimy door. I unlock it and start up the stairs. "What did you mean, strategize?"

"Well..." He steps over a dead bug on the stairway. This place smells of old kitchen grease, with top notes of urine. Neil is almost certainly disgusted. But his blue-blooded manners make him too polite to say so. "Are we going to tell management about this?" he asks. "They hate PR surprises."

"No way," I say quickly. "When I do stupid things, I like to keep it to myself. This is bad enough without telling Bess and Rebecca about it."

"It's not like I *want* to tell them," he argues. "And forget management. My teammates would never let me forget this."

I smile a little wickedly. "Is it terrible that I'm really curious which pranks they'd pull first?" I unlock my door, wondering if I can avoid letting Neil see the inside of my apartment.

Apparently not. He pushes open the door and then carries my hockey bag right into the cramped little space known as my living room.

And just when I thought this day couldn't get any worse, it does. My mother's cousin's creepy son is sitting on my sofa in his underwear, smoking a bowl. He's also pointing a remote control at a TV.

Except I don't own a TV.

"Robert? What are you *doing* in my apartment?" I bark. "DENNIS!" I yell. Robert and my useless brother often lurk around together.

"Hello to you, too. I'm watching wrestling. Your brother found a poker game."

My stomach drops for a whole bunch of reasons. "In Philly?"

"No. In the neighborhood somewhere. I don't fucking know where."

Oh no.

Oh, *hell* no.

Until this moment, I've held it together. But the minute Neil leaves, I'm going to lose my shit. I can already feel the scream building like a hurricane inside me.

Robert, that idiot, has no idea, either. He takes another puff and then passes his beady eyes over my breasts. "Have a seat, Charli." He pats the couch cushion beside him.

My couch cushion.

I feel like grabbing that TV—and the cardboard box it came out of—and hurling them both out the window and onto the avenue below.

But I don't do it. Not yet. Instead, I turn to Neil and thank him for bringing me home.

He shifts his weight, eyeing Robert. But he doesn't set down my hockey bag. Neil, being ten times smarter than Robert, can probably sense the fury radiating off me. Lord knows he's seen it before, occasionally directed at him.

"You know…" he says. "What if you got your stuff together and came home with me so we could do that thing?"

"What thing?" I'm not in the mood to play games.

"That thing we have to work on?" He gives a faint eye-roll at my refusal to get with the program. "We could have dinner together tonight, right? To discuss our project?"

He has a point. Why wait to discuss our problem? It's not like I want to stay here alone with Robert, and Neil is giving me a reason to leave. I make it a point to stay as far away from Robert's branch of the family as possible.

But this is *my* place, damn it. Am I really going to let him chase me out of it?

On the sofa, Robert lets out a tremendous belch.

Yup. I am. "All right," I say through clenched teeth. "Let me grab a few things."

I roll my suitcase into my bedroom where I realize the bed is unmade. It wasn't me who left it like that. Either my brother or Robert has been sleeping in my *bed?*

Someone is going to die. I just haven't decided who.

Hastily, I swap the dirty clothes in my bag for clean ones. I make sure I have everything I need for practice tonight. And I turn around and march right out of there again. Neil opens the door for me, and I leave without a backward glance.

Downstairs, Neil's driver is so well trained that she doesn't even blink when we return with the same number of passengers and the same amount of luggage as we left with a few minutes ago.

"Where to, sir?" she asks Neil.

"The practice rink, please. And then please drop Charli and all our luggage at my apartment building? Thank you."

We get back into the car. I'm grinding my teeth as the worst streets in Brooklyn begin to slide past the window.

"All right—who's that guy?" Neil asks.

I actually have to take a breath before answering, because nothing triggers me quite like Robert—or his evil father. "He's my second cousin. He's tight with my brother."

"Looks like he made himself pretty comfortable in your apartment."

"Yeah, I noticed that. We're gonna have a talk later."

Neil grins. "Can I watch?"

"No, you can't. I don't want any witnesses."

He snickers. "How come I've never met your brother?"

"Because he lives in Philadelphia? Or he's supposed to."

Last year, during my first season, my brother said he wanted to come into town and watch me play.

I'm not stupid. I knew he'd have some ulterior motive. But I'm not like the other girls on my team. I don't have a fan base of family members who use my comp seats every week to cheer me on. I spent my childhood getting passed around to various family members. Everybody's burden, nobody's joy.

I play hockey for myself. Just for myself. And it's usually enough, but I'd said yes to my brother. He'd shown up alone that time, thank God. I'd spent money I didn't have taking him out for Brooklyn pizza and beer.

That weekend, he'd made a copy of my key. "For emergencies," he'd said.

Pretty shortly after that, he began using his key whenever I was at an away game. It happens all the time now. I stopped telling him my schedule, but apparently, he can Google as well as anyone.

And I guess Robert joined him this time. Maybe other times, too. The thought of him in my place makes me want to howl. My apartment is supposed to be a sanctuary, but now it's a flophouse.

I'm so mad I could burn the place down.

But then I'd be in jail. And there's no hockey in jail.

My family is the worst, and getting out of Philly was my

life's goal. But now Philly comes to me all the damn time, and I don't know how to scrape them off.

"Look, I know you don't like to accept help," Neil says quietly. "But I could help you get him out of there if you need me to. Right now, if you want. Then we could change the locks."

"I'll change the locks later this week," I say, because I don't want Neil worrying about it. But a decent deadbolt on that door will cost me over two hundred dollars including the labor. I don't have that kind of cash.

"Or—here's a suggestion. You could find a different apartment."

"You know, I wondered how long it would take for the rich boy to throw shade on my place." I fake a glance at my watch. "Ten minutes. Not bad."

"But there have to be better options. Most of your team-mates live closer to the practice facility."

"It's not that simple, Neil. Most landlords want three months upfront. The security deposit, first month's, and last month's rent. And when I arrived in New York, I had zilch."

Less than zilch, actually. I'm still in debt, thanks to my idiot brother.

Neil nods as if he understands. But a billionaire really can't. "If things are better now, maybe you should try again? Maybe Bess will get you another modeling job."

"God, I hope so." I once made some quick cash modeling clothes for a sportswear company. But that was last year, and lately I'm always broke. Everyone thinks that professional athletes are well paid.

That's really only true if you're a man.

So my first weeks in New York were hard. Not only did I take the first apartment I could afford, I took the job with the quickest access to cash. For those first couple months, I tended bar at a strip club.

Yup, strip clubs are open at lunchtime. And when you're

topless while making drinks, the men tip pretty well. It paid the bills until I could afford to get the kind of job where you can keep your clothes on.

It had been a stupid risk, and I shouldn't have done it. I hope nobody finds out. Not even Neil.

Especially Neil.

"Maybe you can find a landlord who likes really ugly engagement rings," Neil suggests, a smirk in his voice.

"Not likely." I pull the ring out of my handbag and hold it up to the light. We both stare at it for a long time.

"It's kind of mind blowing," he says. "Someone's *job* was to design that."

"Right? One day the designer woke up and asked himself— what would it look like if a unicorn sneezed? And this was the answer."

Neil lets out a belly laugh, and I join in.

What a pity drunk me didn't have more sense. Eleven *thou-sand* dollars. That's just disgusting. Maybe I can get them to take it back.

Neil's poor credit card. Ouch. "Here." I offer him the ring. "You should obviously keep this, for whatever that's worth."

"No way." He pushes my hand gently away. "That's your party favor. Obviously, you picked it out."

"I did not," I argue vehemently. "There's no chance."

"Well, I sure as hell didn't." He laughs. "That thing is so tacky."

"Hold on," I bellow. "Did you just call me tacky?"

"No," he backtracks. "It's just... I don't have opinions about jewelry. So I wouldn't have made the choice."

I snort. "Here's a plan—how about we just assume the sales-person suggested it? Because I don't *think* you meant to imply that this gaudy disaster reflects a personal lack of taste on my part."

He gives me an amused smile. "Sure, wifey. Let's go with that."

"Thank you," I grumble.

"Was that our first marital fight?" he asks.

"Nope. Our first fight was when I said we needed to fix this in Vegas, and you said *don't be silly*. Then, if you recall, the lawyer agreed with me thirty seconds into that call."

"Okay, yup." Neil winces. "That's on me. But I'm not taking the fall for this ugly ring. Sell it. Or keep it as a reminder of why drinking is a bad idea. Whatever floats your boat."

I tuck the ring away and sigh. It should make a fine reminder. This is what happens when I let my hair down—bad, bad things.

Neil checks the time. "I can still make it this session. I'll give you my keys. You can take a nap before your practice."

"Thanks," I whisper. "Hey, look—let's not tell management yet? We can wait until the lawyer gets back to you, right? Just give us one day before we reveal ourselves to be idiots?"

"Fine." He tucks an arm around me, which shouldn't be a comfort but somehow is. "Maybe nobody will have to know that we fell out of the stupid tree and hit every branch on the way down."

"Every. Last. One," I agree.

FIVE

POSH INDUSTRIAL

Charli

The limo pulls up at the practice facility at one minute past three. Neil is *almost* on time.

"Here's my key card," he says, one foot out of the car already. "I just texted Miguel, so he'll let you go up. I'm apartment 613. Leave the card with him when you leave for practice, okay? Gotta bolt."

He tosses the card, and I catch it. Then the door closes after him with a well-engineered click.

I lean back against the leather and let out a long breath. The car slides onward toward his apartment building, which is only two blocks away on Water Street.

When we stop again, I hop out of the car before the driver can open the door for me. "I'll get the bags," I offer.

"I'll help," she says easily. "There's a lot."

She isn't wrong. I grab my own, and she takes Neil's. Miguel, the concierge of the Million Dollar Dorm—as we refer to the luxury renovated condo building where many of the Bruisers live—emerges to stack all the luggage on a trolley.

"Thank you," I say uselessly. The people who live in this

building are used to this level of service. They hand out fat tips at Christmastime.

Across the street there's a line of smaller, walk-up buildings where some of my teammates rent apartments. There aren't any doormen across the street, but the Bombshells are still grateful for the two-block walk to work and the below-market rent that the team owner charges.

I wish I'd taken one of those places. I'd tried to save money, and now I live in a dump, and I can't evict my brother's creepy pal.

Fun times.

"Raphael will help get these upstairs," Miguel says as I follow him into the glamorous lobby and across the marble floors to the elevator. "He'll be down in a moment."

"No, I can do it," I insist. "Can I just leave the trolley outside of Neil's door?"

"Sure," he says. "Have a nice afternoon, Charli."

Wow. He even remembers my name. "Thank you, Miguel."

It occurs to me that he probably makes more money than I do. My salary on the hockey team is about twelve thousand per year, and my waitress job pays about sixteen dollars an hour after tips.

I should ask if they have any openings here in this building. I'd look fine in a navy jacket with gold buttons. And I already know the names of everyone who lives here.

The elevator arrives, so I file that idea away for later.

On the sixth floor, I carefully steer the luggage cart out of the elevator, so as not to ding up the walls, which are papered in a paisley pattern.

I've visited this building before. My teammate Sylvie's boyfriend Anton has a loft apartment a couple floors below this one. So after I unlock Neil's door and enter the apartment, I'm expecting more or less the same space as Anton's.

But that is not what I find.

I roll the trolley through a generous foyer, and into a vast living space with impressionist paintings on the walls.

Yikes. I hope I can spend a couple hours here without breaking anything.

I carefully unload the luggage into the foyer, and then steer the trolley back into the hallway.

And then I go back into Neil's apartment and sit politely in a chair for two hours.

No, that's a lie. Who could resist snooping around a billionaire's bachelor pad? Taking my time, I walk slowly around Neil's luxury apartment. I'm not going to open any drawers, or anything. But I pace every inch of the shiny wood floors.

First, I tour the living room, which is the size of a soccer field. It's a corner unit, so the windows provide views from two directions—the cutest streets in Brooklyn with the Manhattan Bridge looming in the distance.

New York is prettier from up here. When you're down at street level, hurrying to work, things look a lot less romantic.

The apartment's interior is just as impressive as the view. Everything looks like it belonged to a Roosevelt or a Carnegie. It's beautiful, but not comfortable.

The super-formal-looking living room furniture consists of a big leather sofa with buttons all over it and a couple of stiff-looking armchairs. There's a bronze sculpture of a horse on the coffee table.

I didn't know Neil was interested in horses. Or maybe he isn't, but this is just something rich guys have.

Like I'd know the difference.

The room is so big that I don't notice the grand piano in the corner until after I make a complete circuit. There's also a formal dining table and six chairs.

Does Neil throw dinner parties? I can't quite picture it.

Things get a little homier in the enormous kitchen. It's fancy, but more inviting, with a table for three by the window, and a couple of nice stools at the counter. There's a gleaming metal coffee machine and a six-burner stove in stainless steel. The backsplash is laid with shiny mosaic tiles, and the countertops are concrete.

The style is what I'd call "posh industrial." I dig it. There's even a metal circular staircase in the corner that leads upward. Toward the roof, I suppose?

I don't climb up there to snoop, because getting trapped on the roof of a strange building is the only way this day could get worse.

I wander the rest of the apartment, passing an elegant half bathroom, where a rolled-up fluffy towel waits on the marble counter. I open a door, expecting a bedroom, but find a giant walk-in closet.

True fact? Neil's closet is nearly as large as the bedroom in my shithole apartment.

After exiting the closet, there's only one doorway left, so I head through it. And wow. Neil's bedroom is the nicest room of all. It's enormous, for starters, with a bed the size of a city block. The pretty views of Brooklyn are back, and on the wall opposite the bed hangs a nice but not outrageously large television.

This is also the only room in the place with hints of life. There's a *Men's Health* magazine on the bedside table. I can picture Neil reclining against the padded headboard, thumbing through that magazine, comparing the fitness gurus' sixpacks with his own perfectly sculpted, lickable—

Okay, nope. I am not picturing Neil Drake naked. That is a bad idea. I'm ashamed to say that even before last night, I'd often wondered what Neil Drake looked like naked.

And now that I know, I wish I didn't. Because he was a truly breathtaking sight.

With a shuddery breath, I poke my head into the en suite bathroom. It's ludicrously large, with a fancy walk-in shower and a deep, triangular tub—the kind you see in movies about billionaires.

So the bathtub is on-brand.

Although I suppose Neil could live in a three-bedroom apartment with a home gym and—heck—something bonkers like a bowling alley or a movie theater.

But nope. He lives in the nicest one-bedroom apartment I've ever seen.

On my way out of the bedroom suite, I take one more glance at the bed. The sheets look crisp and smooth. And as I pass by, it occurs to me that—at least for the next couple of hours—I'm actually Neil's legally wedded wi—

Nope. I can't even think that word, let alone say it.

I hurry back into the silent living room. I'm supposed to be napping. It's a great idea, because I need rest for practice later, and I need to shut off the worry loop in my brain.

I slip off my shoes and take a seat on Neil's weird sofa. I scoot back, leaning against the buttoned leather and it's... awful. Somehow, I'm reclining on the least comfortable piece of furniture I've ever encountered.

Who had decided that putting so many buttons under your ass would be a good idea? The buttons dimple the leather upholstery into a surprisingly firm, pot-holed surface. Not only is it too hard, but it's also bumpy.

I kick off my shoes and lie down on it anyway. A button digs into my cheek.

I close my eyes, but it's hard to sleep. The couch is partly to blame, but blurry memories keep teasing my consciousness. Even though last night I'd been very, very drunk, when I close my eyes, it comes back to me in little flashes.

A glimpse of Neil laughing at the county clerk's office.

The wedding chapel with its fake roses on every surface.

I'm pretty sure the wedding had been Neil's idea. It was supposed to have been a game. My drunk self had known this. But I hadn't spoken up, even when we'd been standing in front of the Rent-A-Reverend dressed like Elvis.

It's painful to think about why.

But the truth is, I'd done it because he'd chosen *me*. Drunk off his ass, of course, but it still mattered that he'd looked at me and had said *she's the one*. I hadn't been able to resist a starring role in his drunken caper.

I don't remember all the specifics, and Neil, with his unlucky metabolism, probably remembers even less. But I do remember how it had felt to be picked by the fancy guy all the women wanted. The sleek athlete who grew up in Westchester and Switzerland and Whistler and on Martha's Vineyard. A guy who knew what kind of wine pairs well with fish.

He'd smiled at me. Sloppily, sure. But at *me*. Not Iris. Not anyone else. Just me—the rough kid nobody had ever wanted. So I'd helped him make a huge mistake that would complicate our lives, just because I hadn't been able to turn down the compliment.

Nice one, Higgins. Way to go.

One of the sofa's buttons is poking my jaw. When I roll over, they poke my ass. I dig my bulky phone out of my back pocket. The top-of-the-line Katt phone all the Bruisers and Bombshells carry is as big as a slice of bread.

Since I can't sleep, I shoot off a text to my brother. *DENNIS! I don't ever want to come home again and find Robert. Take him and that TV and clear out of there by tomorrow morning.*

God, he'd better do it, too. Then I'll have a big decision to make. Do I change the locks and force a confrontation with the only family member I have who bothers with me?

I really don't know.

My Katt Phone beeps, but it's not my brother. The tone is the special sound reserved for management. My stomach rolls with dread, and I check the screen with great reluctance.

My fear grows when I see that the text is from Georgia, the publicist. *Holy crap!* What does she know? I tap the message with a shaking finger.

Hey Charli—can you bring your All Stars medal to practice

today or tomorrow? And if you could be a few minutes early, I'd love to get some photos.

Oh. Phew. *Sure. No problem*, I reply.

I get up and tiptoe into Neil's bedroom with the goal of stealing a pillow, but the giant king-sized bed beckons. I climb onto it, resting my head on a luxury goose-down pillow covered in a crisp linen case.

It's much more comfortable here. Maybe I'll be able to sleep.

But my stupid brain pokes me with the terrifying truth: I'm *married* to the man who owns this bed.

I'm his *wi*—

Nope. Still can't do it.

SIX

EGGPLANT JOKES

Neil

It would usually embarrass me to be even two minutes late for a video meeting. But today my timing was perfect. I'd slipped into the back of the tape room just as the session was starting, leaving my friends no chance to razz me for missing the jet.

And no chance to ask awkward questions about last night.

Sure, several heads turned to give me the once-over. My friend Anton's gaze had lingered the longest. *You okay?* he'd mouthed.

I'd nodded quickly. *Nothing to see here.*

Then the session had begun, with me sitting up straight in my chair and paying close attention. I'm the kind of guy who always shows up on time and does what's expected of him. Last night was an anomaly, and I need management to know that.

Let the healing begin.

The meeting is pretty dull, though, and after a while, I take a surreptitious glance at my phone. This must be how criminals feel after the heist has been accomplished—uneasy, like they're waiting for cops to show up.

Anyone could have seen us in that wedding chapel. Las Vegas was crawling with hockey journalists for the All-Star events. That's why I'm nervous. Anton used to frequently find himself on the gossip rags. I'd like to avoid the same fate, thank you.

Luckily, none of my new messages are from the publicity department. There are dozens of texts from my teammates, though, and these are almost as scary. If I was drunk enough to get married last night, who knows what else I did or said?

One mortification at a time, please.

I skim through a series of emails where my teammates razz me over missing the jet. *Dude, what happened?* Anton says. *I thought you were joking when we argued about the time zone.*

Well, that's embarrassing. But it's only Anton. He's done worse. For example, the team tells every rookie that he has to get a Brooklyn Bridge tattoo on his ass to prove his loyalty.

Anton is the only one who fell for it. He wears that sucker proudly now.

But I guess I can't feel too smug about it anymore. I'm the only one in this room who accidentally tied the knot in Vegas.

Not that I'll tell anyone. I don't want to look like a dumbass. And Charli would kill me.

When the video session ends, most of us head to the weight room. After a day spent in planes and cars, we need to move around.

So the room is crowded. I stretch, check my blood sugar and wait my turn on the bench press.

Castro refills his water bottle beside me. "Where did you go last night? I lost track of you after the clerk's office."

"Oh, here and there," I mumble. I unwrap a granola bar and shove half of it into my mouth. "You?"

"We played some blackjack. It was awesome. Beacon won a grand. And Heidi Jo won three grand."

"Of course she did." Castro's wife is a total shark.

"How's the hangover?" Castro chuckles. "Musta been brutal if you missed the jet."

"Yeah, brutal."

"Who were you drinking with?" Castro glugs his water and waits for an answer. Why won't he just let it go?

"Charli mostly," I say with a shrug.

His eyes widen. "Oh yeah, I remember you guys drinking whiskey at dinner. You and Charli. She missed the plane too, right? Did you guys...?" He wiggles his eyebrows.

"No way. No," I say awkwardly. "It's not like that with us." He doesn't have to know how close we came. Charli would *hate* to hear people gossiping about her, almost as much as she hated waking up next to me this morning.

Although, I didn't hate that part at all. I don't need the whiskey to want her, either. I'd do her drunk or sober, any time of day. I've always had the hots for Charli.

I thought there was no conceivable way she'd be attracted to me, though, so of course I never said anything. And now I have sketchy memories of tumbling into bed with her. Making out. Unzipping her dress...

"You okay, Drake?" Castro asks, poking me. "You seem a little dazed."

"I'm fine," I say quickly. "Long day, right?"

"Yeah," he says, giving me a sideways glance. "I love Vegas, though. Totally worth it. Did you hit the casino at all?"

"Uh, nope." I shake my head. "Not a fan of gambling."

"You're up, Castro!" the new guy calls, saving me from this conversation. The big defenseman—a recent trade from Chicago—trades places with Castro. "How'd you get home, Drake?" he asks, squeezing my shoulder. "Thought you'd miss the video session at least. Felt like a dick when I realized you weren't on the plane."

"No worries, Newguy," I say quickly. His real name is Newgate. But of course, we don't call him that. Not with the perfect nickname just dangling there in front of us. "It was easy enough for me to get a flight."

"He's not kidding," chirps Silas from the leg press. "Drake basically owns a whole fleet of aircraft."

A few guys chuckle, and I clench my jaw. Like I said—calling on Daddy's private jets is not a good look on me.

But it's my turn on the bench, so I shake it off.

The workout is just what I needed. An hour later, I'm sweating out last night's bad decisions on the treadmill after a quick upper body workout. I'm feeling much better about my life and ordering groceries via voice commands on my phone.

But then Georgia appears in my peripheral vision, and the team publicist is wearing a cautious frown.

Uh-oh.

I remove my ear buds without breaking my stride. "Hey, Georgia. What's up?"

"Do you have a minute?"

"For you? Sure."

She hits the STOP button on the machine, and my stomach sinks further. "Step into my office, please. We have a situation." Then she leaves the cardio room.

Oh shit. This is bad.

Two minutes later I enter Georgia's office to find Charli standing there, arms crossed, her green eyes full of hot fury.

"I'll get right to the point," Georgia says from her desk chair. "A journalist saw you two go into a wedding chapel last night. He left me a message asking if there was any exciting news in the organization."

"Well…" I chuckle nervously. "Do you see anyone excited here?"

"I'm sure not," Charli growls. "I already told her the truth, Neil. This is bad."

"Okay," I say, even though nothing is okay. "The two of us are speaking with a lawyer tonight. We're hoping to resolve this quickly."

"Right," Georgia says, fighting a smile. "Still, we have to decide our plan of attack. What am I telling this reporter?"

"Nothing," Charli spits. "It's none of his damn business."

"Saying nothing never works," I point out. "If it's a gossip site, they'll publish whatever they want. What if our statement just said—*Charli and Neil Drake are not a couple.*"

Charli's eyes cut to mine. For a split second, hers look guilty. But they quickly return to angry.

"Guys, I'm not sure you'll be able to contain this story," Georgia says. "Marriages are public information. I don't know how many days it takes the Clark County clerk's office to post them on their website, but sooner or later the marriage will be searchable."

"Oh, *no*," Charli gasps.

"Oh, yes," Georgia says. "I just checked, and it's not up there yet. But unless you guys failed to make it legal somehow, it will be."

Charli groans. "Can we just, like, give it a day? We really don't know what this lawyer is going to tell us."

"Sure," Georgia says soothingly. "Call me tomorrow morning. Can I ask if your teammates know?"

"No," Charli says immediately. "And we plan to keep it that way."

Our publicist sighs. "Fine. Steal all my fun. What good is the best gossip in the world if you can't share it?"

"Georgia," I warn.

"Okay, okay," she says with a smile. "I'm a vault when I need to be. Call me tomorrow when you sort this all out. I can't keep the journalist off our heels forever."

"I'm late for practice," Charli says. She looks panicked.

"Go," Georgia and I say at the same time. "It will be fine," I add. "We'll keep this quiet." I hope we actually can.

At home, I cook a really nice meal to soften Charli up. By the time she arrives at my apartment after practice, I've got marinated eggplant *and* a cauliflower gratin in the oven. I've got steaks ready to grill, and one piece of cheesecake chilling in the fridge.

"You didn't have to cook," Charli says, even as she eyes the vegetables through the oven's glass door. "We could have just gotten takeout."

"I was in the mood for a steak," I explain. "And it's just no good as takeout food."

"Why not?" She pulls out a barstool and sinks down onto it.

When I glance over at her, I lose my train of thought for a second. Because she's so fucking pretty. Even in an enemy T-shirt—the Flyers? *Please*. Even with her hair still damp from the shower. She's got luminous skin, a spray of freckles across her nose, and giant blue-green eyes.

I *kissed* her last night. I only remember the night in blurry snippets, but I'll never forget that I'd had my hands on her smooth skin. On her body.

I'd liked it. A lot.

She's blinking up at me, waiting for an answer, and it takes me another beat to dredge our conversation from the murky depths of my lust. "A steak has to be eaten right off the heat, or it loses its crust." I open the first package of meat and put the steak onto a plate. Then I grab my salt grinder and go to town. I do the same with the pepper grinder.

"If you say so," she says. "That looks like a lot of pepper."

"Shut up. I know what I'm doing."

She gives me a tiny smile. "I had no idea you could cook. If I had limitless resources, I'm not sure if I'd bother."

"I like it," I insist. Although, I have a lot of guilt over my *limitless resources*, as she calls them. I learned to cook because nobody else in my family ever did. "And nutrition is a big deal for me." Diabetes means watching what I eat. "It's easier to know what's in your food if you make it yourself."

"True. But where are you going to cook that?"

"On the grill, of course. Like real men do."

Charli snorts. "Where's the grill? On your super fancy oven?"

"No—on the roof. I have a Weber up there." I point at the spiral staircase in the corner.

"Get out of town!" she squeaks. "You're like a suburban dad."

"I know." I shrug. "It suits me."

"What else is on the roof?" she asks.

"Nothing. I didn't bother with furniture. Wasn't sure if I'd get to stay in Brooklyn, you know?" Not every rookie makes it. "Besides, the grill is actually against the building's policy. Don't turn me in."

"Me?" Her smile is amused. "Are you kidding? You're the rule-follower in this marriage."

I bark out a laugh. She's right. I *am* a rule-follower. But, man, the word *marriage* sounds so wrong. All day I've been having these moments of cognitive dissonance.

It's freaky to hear her say it out loud.

Charli must think so, too, because she changes the subject. "So how do you decide what kind of steak to make?"

"Well, I got you a filet mignon." I nudge the second package toward her. "And me a sirloin."

She glances at the label. "Thank you for buying me a steak I can't pronounce."

"Really? You can't say *filet*?" I say lightly. "Something wrong with your tongue?"

Our eyes meet for a split-second right after I say the word *tongue*. And then we both look away. I open the package and toss the filet on the plate for the salt and pepper treatment.

I need to stop picturing Charli naked.

I need to feed her dinner.

And I need to figure out how to unwind the mess we're in.

In that order.

A half an hour later, I've got Charli moaning. "Oh God, oh God." She lets out a dreamy sigh. "I didn't know it could be this good."

If only she'd take her clothes off and say that again.

For the moment, we're sitting at the table, enjoying a nice steak.

"It's like *butter*," she says, wiping her mouth. "This is the best thing I've ever eaten."

"That's what all the girls say when they taste my meat."

She reaches around the table and slaps my arm. "Don't ruin this sensuous experience for me."

"Have some more of the cauliflower," I offer, scooting the dish towards her. I'd heard some moaning over that, too. "You know you want to."

"I have to slow down," she says, plopping another scoop of it onto her plate anyway.

"You really don't. Go hard, baby. Go all night long." She kicks me under the table, and I chuckle as I cut another bite of my own steak.

"Linen napkins, though? You complain about your rep as the fancy guy on the team, but you don't fight the cliché very hard."

"Cloth napkins aren't fancy. They're better for the environment." I lift the wine bottle and top up her glass. I can't enjoy a good steak without a nice, full-bodied red. "Do me a favor, though, and don't mention the truffle butter at the rink."

"Deal," she says, sipping her wine. "I mean—I wouldn't want to piss off my truffle-butter dealer." She takes another bite.

It's very gratifying to cook for Charli. She looks super happy right now.

"It still blows my mind a little," she says. "Cornelius Drake III can *cook*. You even made *eggplant* taste good."

I put down my fork. "Charli, if you want me to stop making dirty jokes, you have to stop serving them up to me like that."

She laughs and covers her mouth. "Ten bucks says you bought the eggplant just to make that joke."

"No, ma'am. Eggplant is super healthy. You should have more of it in your diet." I give her a sleazy wink.

She rolls her eyes and goes back to her meal. "So, what's our plan? Is the lawyer calling at a set time?"

"He's sending over some papers, and we're supposed to call him after we receive them."

"Even if business hours are over? It's eight o'clock."

"Yeah. I guess his clients get into trouble at all hours of the day. He's used to it."

"And I'll bet he charges accordingly."

I smile at her over my dinner plate. "Trust me, he does. But don't worry about that, Charli. You promised you'd let me handle this."

"Because I have no choice." She takes a tiny bite of steak, like maybe she's trying to make it last longer. "But my experience with men who say, 'Trust me, Charli,' has not been great."

"I'm here to break your streak," I insist. "I'm going to make this right."

"Okay," she says warily.

It's time to bring out the big guns. "There's chocolate cheesecake for dessert."

She puts her chin in her hand and lifts those green eyes to mine. "Thank you for dinner, Neil."

"You're welcome, doll." I give her a wink.

"Still can't call me that," she grumbles.

"Not even while we're married?"

She scrapes the last of the cheesy cauliflower off her plate and eats it. "Not even then."

But she's smiling when she says it.

SEVEN

SKITTISH KITTEN

Charli

After dinner, I insist on tidying up Neil's kitchen.

I cannot believe he cooked that lovely meal for me. Of all the bonkers things that have gone down in the last twenty-four hours, a steak dinner shouldn't shock me the most. And yet it does.

When his white casserole dish is clean again, I dry it with a crisp dish towel and put it away in a pristine cabinet. The tiles glisten under warm lighting, and Neil has some music playing on an invisible stereo system.

This place is like a foreign country, where every drawer is tidy and even the bottle of dish soap is pretty. My belly is full of exquisite food, and I feel... almost optimistic.

Which is just crazy. Today was a disaster by any measure. Maybe I'm not as sharp as I thought, though, because a nice meal, a glass of wine, and a pretty kitchen have smoothed all my rough edges.

Apparently, my inner skittish kitten is easily bought off with treats.

Just as I'm closing the dishwasher door, a phone affixed to

the wall chimes. Neil answers it, and the concierge tells him that the lawyer's documents are on the way upstairs.

"Thank you," he says as I streak past him to reach the foyer. I open the door for a sweaty messenger in a bicycle helmet who's trotting down the hallway. He passes me his phone and asks me to sign. I scribble my initials and greedily accept the envelope he's brought us.

"Hey, I'll take that," Neil says from right behind me.

"Why? Are you going to mansplain the documents to me?"

"No, but—" He tries to take the envelope from me, but I duck under his arm and edge away.

That puts Neil in a pickle. The messenger is gazing hopefully at him. Neil lets me go and reaches for his wallet to tip the guy.

I'm not afraid to play dirty, so I slip farther way, heading into Neil's generous living room.

"Hand it over," he says, joining me a moment later. "I'd like to read it first. My name is on the envelope, isn't it?"

"So? This mess belongs to both of us equally." I'm eager for a solution, so I rip open the envelope and skim the cover letter. *Dear Cornelius, enclosed please find a summary of divorce procedure, and...* "Whoa!" I cry. "Your family wants us to sign a postnuptial agreement? Is that like a prenup for people who were too stupid to sign it before they got hitched?"

"Basically," he says with a sigh. "Charli, let me read it first."

"Hell, no," I say. "We'll read together. The first page is an introduction to New York divorce law..." I skim the letter. *There are several paths to divorce in New York, including a no-fault option. Depending on the path, a divorce could be accomplished in as few as twelve weeks, or it could take nine months. After you agree to the post-nuptial agreement, we will discuss your options...*

"Twelve weeks," I breathe. "Ouch."

"That's not *that* long," Neil says from over my shoulder.

I'm still skimming. "It also says that the divorce will be on the public record."

"So will the marriage," Neil points out. "We know this already."

This is upsetting, though, and I feel the urge to remind him again that we should have stayed in Vegas to try for an annulment. We might have been able to take care of this faster and more privately.

On the other hand, this whole mess would have been avoided if I weren't a weak and stupid person. So I keep my silence and turn the page, where it says POST-NUPTIAL AGREEMENT in big letters.

That's when Neil makes a sneak attack, reaching for the papers. I handily leap aside, just out of his reach. "If you want to take something from a professional athlete, you got to try a little harder than that."

"Charli," he says cautiously. "The appearance of that post-nup means my uncle is involved now. He probably put some ridiculous shit in there. I'd like to read it first."

"Neil, I said I'd let you handle the divorce, but I didn't say you could keep me out of the loop."

He sighs.

"Besides, I already know what it's going to say. When I divorce you, I don't get a penny. That's exactly as it should be." I skim the first page, but the text is dense, and there's a lot of legalese. I navigate over to the world's least comfortable sofa and sit down to read.

WHEREAS Cornelius Harmon Drake III is legally wedded to Charli Fern Higgins. This document sets forth the terms of their divorce. Upon divorce, the settlement of their affairs will proceed as follows. Charli Fern Higgins will receive a cash payment of $250,000...

I let out a choked-off shriek. "What the actual fuck! You never told me your family was *stupid*. Don't they know I'm divorcing your ass for *free?*"

"Charli, they *don't* know that. I'm warning you that document is going to be a tough read. And whatever they're offering you—it won't be worth it."

I stare at that number for a long beat. All those zeroes. I'd never take that money from Neil. How would I even look him in the eye afterward? But now that number is sitting here on the sofa between us, like a hand grenade.

God. I feel a flare of anger at Neil, even though I know this wasn't his idea. He's still reading, easing the sheaf of papers out of my hands and flipping to the next page.

He makes a noise of pure disgust and folds the pages in half, like he's shielding us both from what's written there.

"Hey! I was reading that."

Ignoring me, he makes a move to get up. I sense the window of opportunity closing, so I dive for the pages with the same one hundred percent commitment that I bring to each lunge for the puck.

And guess who's the number-two scorer on her team? It was Neil's mistake to try to be casual about his exit. Because I get my hands on those papers and clamp down with a vise-like grip. Then, with a forceful jerk, they're mine.

"Charli," he cautions, the tone of his voice uncharacteristically beaten.

"What?" I turn my body slightly away from him to protect my prize. He too is a professional athlete with top-notch reflexes.

He tries a different tactic. "Just don't read that."

"Why?"

"You're not signing it."

"Well, the financial part is garbage. But can't we just cross out that number? We can write in ten dollars as a joke. I'll let your family buy me a premium beer."

"Just don't," he whispers.

I glance at him over my shoulder, and he honestly looks distraught. A nicer girl would hand back the documents. But I'm not that girl. I'm the desperately curious one with poor impulse control. I flip open to a random page.

Furthermore, Charlotte Fern Higgins will not reside within three miles of Cornelius Harmon Drake III. She will not approach him nearer than 200 yards. She will not call, text, email or otherwise contact him in any method either extant or invented in the future.

"Holy. Crap." I read that paragraph three more times just to make sure I'm not dreaming. But it's right there in black and white. The Drakes want me so far away from their precious son that I'm not allowed to contact him at all. *"Invented in the future?"* I sputter as my famous temper ignites. "Who *knows* what future ways there might be for me to get at your fortune! Robots? Attack drones?"

"Charli, don't *read* it," he begs.

But now I have to. I skim the whole damn thing, and it's horrifying. "There's a paragraph whereby I agree never to give a quote to a journalist about *any* member of the Drake family, living or dead. There's one where I agree never to supply my likeness to any news organization for any purpose. So I guess if I win MVP this year, we can't take a *photo?"*

Wow. That's just *mean.*

On one level, I know this isn't really about me. But it's still cruel. These people want to write a fat check and then erase me from their son's orbit. "This doesn't even make sense. I could never comply with—" I wave the papers around. "—this atrocity. Do they even care that we work in the same building?"

"They don't," he says in a low voice. He parks his ass on the sofa, then plants his elbows on his knees and buries his forehead in his palms. "You know this isn't personal, right?"

I make an angry noise. I do know what he's saying, but this isn't my first brush with crazy rich people. "They're *terrified* of me," I say, as the realization dawns.

I'm not sure how I feel about that. I spent my teenage years trying to become so fearsome that I could incinerate everyone who'd bullied me with a single glance. I learned how to fight. I learned how to support myself, even in some pretty grim ways.

I learned how never to take any bullshit from anyone. And

definitely never to cry. I thought by now I knew a lot about how the world worked, and maybe I do.

But I've always been an outcast. The kid from the wrong side of the tracks who won a sports scholarship to the same prep school Neil's sister and ex-girlfriend attended. The girl nobody ever brought home to meet the parents. I'd been cast in that role since I was fifteen, and after a while, it wears on a person.

"This is not about you," Neil says quietly. "It's actually about my mother."

"Wait, what?" I'm totally lost. "Your mother?"

"Yup. It's an old family rift. Uncle Harmon always thought my mother was a gold digger, and my father was an idiot for marrying her."

I try to make sense of that. "Because she wasn't rich, too?"

"Possibly. She was also twenty-five years younger than my father and his second wife. My uncle doesn't need reasons to dislike people, though. He doesn't trust anyone. He never liked my mom, and ever since my father died, it's worse." He rubs his handsome chin. "He controls my mother's inheritance. Hers and Paisley's."

"Wait—but not yours?"

Neil's smile is thin. "The estate was set up in a complicated way. I got control of my share when I turned twenty-five. Paisley will, too. But my mother's money is under Harmon's control for life. He gives her an allowance, and she has to petition him for any unusual expenditures. She wants to sell her apartment and buy another one, and he's making her write a proposal. It's humiliating."

"Yikes." On one hand, I'm starting to get the picture—Neil's family is all twisted up about money, and it doesn't have a thing to do with me.

On the other hand... don't these people know they don't have any *real* problems? Jesus.

"I'm sorry you are tangled up in it, too," Neil says quietly.

"You can't sign this document. I can find another attorney to handle this." He flings the pages at the coffee table, where they land at the feet of the bronze horse.

One page goes skimming off the table, and I lean over to pluck it off the floor. I hadn't noticed this page before. It's separate from the post-nup. "Hey, what's this?" The letterhead is different, too. *The Drake Family Foundation.*

Neil takes the page from my hand and reads it, a deep furrow forming in his forehead. "Huh. I'd forgotten about this provision."

"What?" I let out a huge yawn. This has been the longest day. Literally, since I woke up in another time zone.

"When a Drake gets married, his spouse automatically claims a seat on the board of the family foundation..." Neil trails off, but he's still staring at the page. "So they're asking you to give up your seat voluntarily."

"I don't need any new hobbies, so that's an easy decision." I reach up and pat his cheek. The stubble scratches my palm in a satisfying way.

Okay, stop touching Neil. Bad things happen when you touch Neil.

He hasn't noticed. He's still staring at the paper. "You'd change the vote," he says slowly. "We'd control the foundation."

"So what?" I lean back, trying to get more comfortable on this awful sofa. My limbs are weary. I need this to be over, so I can go home to bed.

Then I remember Robert might be there.

Shit.

"The family foundation is partly a charity and partly a political vessel. My uncle supports certain causes to get the breaks he needs on Capitol Hill."

I yawn again so widely that my jaw cracks. That's how intrigued I am by Drake family politics.

Neil picks up the post-nup and tears it in half, loudly. Then he produces his phone and hits a button. I hear a dial tone.

"Evening, Neil," the lawyer's voice says through the speaker a moment later.

"Witherspoon," Neil barks. "We read this document. And I honestly can't understand why you bothered. Is this some kind of sick opening gambit?"

"No," he grunts. "This was your uncle's language. He's very adamant about most of these clauses."

Neil stares at the phone as if he could incinerate it with his eyes. "We're not signing."

"Think carefully before you make that call. Your uncle will use this against you."

Neil's head jerks back, like he's been slapped. "Really? You're his heavy, now? Did I piss off the Godfather? Am I going to wake up with a bloody horse's head in my bed?"

"Don't be dramatic," the lawyer rumbles. "I'm just reminding you that he'd do anything for his company. And your marriage threatens the family's hold on voting rights. So you can expect that he'll take action to protect his shares and his interests in the foundation."

"What kind of action?" I whisper. Because that sounds bad.

"He'll go after Neil's board seat," the lawyer says. "I'm just stating facts."

"Here's a fact," Neil spits. "You're fired."

The lawyer sighs. "You can't actually fire me. You know that, right?"

"I do know that," Neil clips. "But if you were my personal attorney, you'd be fired for insulting Charli like this."

"We offered her a quarter million dollars!" the lawyer booms.

"An insult that comes with two-hundred-fifty large is still an insult. Now go bill my uncle for your time and tell him to get fucked." Neil taps the screen, and the call is disconnected.

I let out a long breath. "Okay. Wow. You just fired the guy who was going to fix this!" My voice gets a little high and crazy. "We're still married, Neil! Maybe I should have just signed."

"No!" he thunders, rising to his feet. He steps around the coffee table and begins to pace the vast expanse of his living room. "No way. We're not signing that thing. I wouldn't lower myself to that."

"But what's the alternative?" I squeak. "You can't lose your father's company over this. It's not worth it."

"Isn't it? My uncle is a bully. He's been controlling my mother and sister for years."

"But how does this end?" I fret. "The lawyer made it sound like you could lose everything just because we got drunk in Vegas."

He stops pacing and turns to me. "No way, Charli. Even if I lose my seat on the board, I'll still keep most of my shares."

"Oh." I know nothing about Neil's strange life. "But that's still bad, right?"

He shrugs. "It depends on your point of view. My uncle hates me, and the feeling is mutual. I've been trying to get him to step down as my mother's trustee. I've been trying to make his company more ecologically responsible. I've gotten nowhere. But now that could change."

"Because of *me*? Not likely."

He stops pacing. He glances out the window, toward the Manhattan Bridge in the distance. His handsome face says he's thinking. Hard.

I find myself holding my breath, and I'm not even sure why.

"I have a plan," he says quietly. He turns around and pins me with his hazel-eyed stare. "I know how to win. I'll beat him at his own game."

"How? Lay it on me."

"We have to stay married."

EIGHT

MRS. CORNELIUS DRAKE THE THIRD

Charli

"*What?*" I gasp. "I could swear you just said we have to stay married."

"I did." He crosses his arms over his sculpted chest and looks down at me. There's humor in his appraising gaze. "You have to be my wife."

"What?" I shriek. "That's ridiculous."

"Exactly!" He grins.

My head begins to pound, because it's possible he's lost his mind. "This isn't funny, Neil. Do you hear me laughing?"

"I'm not joking. I'm finished with my uncle and his stooge of a son."

"Finished… how?" I ask. Because you can't change who your family is. If you could, I would have already done that.

"They think I'll just roll over and do whatever they ask. Because of the power and the money."

"It's always about the money," I agree.

"And it's not worth it," he says passionately. "I'm done. I just need a little help from you."

"What kind of help?" I'm so lost now.

He leans down, his hands on the coffee table, his arm muscles bulging. "My family sent us an offensive post-nup, because they're treating me like a child and you like a leech. But we aren't either of those things."

"Yeah, true," I admit. "But it's not really about me. They don't know me."

"But they know *me*. And they obviously think I'm dumb enough to pick up a conniving stranger in Vegas and sign away my life to her. Can you picture me doing that?"

"Uh…" I look up into his expressive face, and I'm not sure what to say. "No. Of course not. But if you'd asked me yesterday morning whether I thought you and I could accidentally get married, I would have said no."

His smile flashes and disappears so quickly that I wonder if I've imagined it. "Fair point. But this isn't the first time my family has assumed the worst and then tried to steamroll me. I can't do this anymore."

He casually picks up the sheaf of papers and tears the whole pack one more time down the center.

"Um, Neil? You also ripped up the *divorce* page, too. We need that one. I never agreed to stay married. You said you'd fix this."

"I know, and I will. But first I'd like to take a different approach. I want us to remain married for a short time without any kind of written agreement."

"But where does that leave us?" I ask, trying not to panic. That's just a ridiculous idea. Me? Married to Cornelius Drake III?

"I'll retain my own legal counsel," Neil says slowly. "I'll quietly ask some friends to refer me to a divorce specialist."

"Oh." I let out a sigh of relief. Now we're getting somewhere. "Won't that cost a wad and take longer?"

"Doesn't matter. We'll still be divorced by the end of playoffs season." He sits down beside me, propping his feet up on the coffee table, long legs bent. He's wearing shorts, so I can see the crisp outline of his thigh muscles above his bare knees. I try not to notice how close we're sitting right now. Last night I'd felt his skin on mine. We'd been *kissing*. That seems almost crazier than the hazy memory I have of blowing him. Dicks are nice and all, but I'd stared into those sparkling eyes and kissed him like my life depended on it.

My inner kitty-cat had forgotten to be afraid and had rubbed herself all over Neil Drake. And she'd *liked* it.

Shoot me.

"Look, it's a big ask." Neil is still talking.

"Hmm?"

"You're right that this will slow us down a couple of weeks. Because I want my family to believe that we're married for real."

"But *why?*"

"Two reasons. First, I need to show them that I can't be bullied, and also…" He points at the one sheet of paper that he did not tear in half. "That foundation seat. You're going to come to the next quarterly meeting and cast a vote."

I let out a peal of laughter. "A vote for what?"

"It almost doesn't matter. But when my wife joins this board, my uncle and my cousin lose their majority. We could vote down every single one of their priorities and advance all of our own."

"Will it solve your mother's money thing?" I ask. Because making a rich asshole cry actually sounds fun to me.

"Not directly. But that's my ultimate goal—to do a little horse trading. If he believes we're going to stay married, and he can *never* win another foundation vote again, he might sign over the trust to my mother and listen to one or two of my ideas."

"That's… complicated," I complain. "It was only a few hours ago when you said to trust you and that the divorce wouldn't be a problem."

"Hey." He picks up one of my hands and gives it a squeeze.

"If you don't want to do this, you can say no. I'll find a new divorce lawyer tomorrow and get him to file ASAP. Or you can do me this favor. For a few weeks, you and I will pretend to be married for real."

"But…" I'm having so much trouble picturing this. "What would that look like?"

He gives my hand another squeeze and then runs a fingertip across my fingers. "You'd have to wear a wedding ring. Not that Vegas monstrosity—a nice one."

"The trappings of heteronormative love," I say with a sigh. "Fine. But that can't be all."

"No, it's not. We'd have to show our faces together as husband and wife. We have to walk the walk, essentially. So no hookups or girlfriends…" He gives me a sideways glance. "Or boyfriends. Now that I know you like those sometimes."

I brush aside the question of my sex life with a wave of my hand. "So… essentially you're borrowing *my* freedom as leverage in order to gain your own freedom from your scary uncle?"

"Yeah, basically. Only for a short time, and only with your permission. But you helped shackle us together in the first place, loser, so we've got to untie that knot somehow. I just want to do it sneaky-like."

"Sneaky-like," I grumble. "You want me to lie."

"I'll do all the lying. Meanwhile, there will be perks."

"Perks?" I yelp. "I hope you don't mean sex." That's my guilty conscience talking, of course. I was *just* thinking about sex with him not two minutes ago.

"And people say I have the dirty mind? I was only thinking about shortening your commute to the rink. You can stay here. We'll be roommates for a little while, and you can walk to work in three minutes flat."

"Well, damn. I must be a real New Yorker now, because that short commute is a huge draw."

He smiles. "Yeah, you're legit for sure."

I mull this over for a moment. Staying in Neil's apartment for a little while would solve some problems for me. I could let my lease go and shake my brother and my awful cousin out of my space. *And* I could walk to the rink for every practice and every home game. "How long would I be here, do you think?"

"A month or two? Whatever seems comfortable to you once the divorce gets underway. But Charli..." His smile dies. "I'd need to ask you to go to a few events with me. And my family will do their best to be cold to both of us. We have to show our faces, or the ruse won't work."

"To your uncle and your mother?"

"That's right. And my cousin and sister, too." He makes a face. "The things that come out of their mouths can be pretty brutal."

"I can take it," I say immediately. I've been putting up with other people's shade for my whole life. "The food will be good, right? If I have to see your family, will there at least be more steak?"

"How about this." He leans closer to me, which makes it a little hard to concentrate. "Every time you come face to face with any of my blood relatives, I will make you another filet mignon."

"*And* the cheesy cauliflower?" Negotiation comes naturally to me.

"Sure. I'll throw in the cauliflower gratin."

"Cool, cool." I can't believe I'm seriously considering this. "People are going to find out, though. I mean—besides your family."

He looks thoughtful. "I guess that's inevitable. My family would try to keep it a secret," he says. "They don't even want people knowing that I'm a professional hockey player. My cousin actually said once that it was 'so blue collar.'"

"Seven figures a year is not blue-collar work."

He shrugs, like it's not worth arguing the point. "Georgia

made it sound like it's going to become public whether we want it to or not."

"But hang on—how far are we taking this charade? Will I have to play the little wife in front of our friends? I don't think I'm that good of an actor."

He smiles and then pokes me in the knee. "I think I'm offended."

"Really? Have you *ever* seen me cozy up to a man? Or a woman? Have I ever said: 'Gosh, I wish I could shackle myself to a man?'"

"No." He laughs.

"Besides, *you're* the one who recently got off the relationship roller coaster with your snobby girlfriend. Which part of our sudden, secret romance would you find believable if you were our friends?"

"The secret part," he says with another smile. "So secret that neither of us knew about it." We both snicker. "I guess we'll have to be out to our friends, then."

"We'd *have* to be. Our friends aren't idiots."

"Some of mine are," he says. "But not all of them."

"Agreed." Although, I can't believe we're having this conversation at all. Could we really fool anyone? Is there a less obvious couple anywhere in New York City than we are?

"There's one more thing I'd need from you," he says.

"Oh boy. What now?"

NINE

DRINKING FROM THE CUP OF BAD DECISIONS

Neil

I can't believe Charli is actually considering my harebrained plan. And I know she won't like this last detail, but I'm going to insist. "You have to let me find you another apartment when this is all over."

"*Why?*" she demands.

"Because..." How am I going to put this delicately? I'd always suspected that Charli lived somewhere unsafe. But God knows she doesn't want my help. "That apartment you've got now is not ideal. It's too far away. You'll be able to save some money living with me. You can shut off your cable bill."

"I don't have a cable bill." She crosses her arms.

"Fine. You'll save on rent and subway fare. You can save that money for an apartment somewhere nicer."

A furrow develops down the center of her kissable forehead. "I'm listening."

"Great. So, how about you let me pay the deposit on your new apartment when you're ready to move out of here? First and last month's rent, plus security."

"No way!" she says immediately. "That's silly."

"But you'd deserve compensation for your time and trouble."

Charli is at war with herself now. I can see it on her face. I hope she lets me do this—it would solve so many problems for her.

"I don't think I can accept," she says. "The minute you pay me off, then your uncle was right. I am a gold digger."

"Fuck no," I argue. "I'm not paying you to divorce me. I'm paying you to stay *married* to me for a few extra weeks. That's not creepy at all, right?"

We both laugh.

"Just think about it, okay? My family are going to be assholes. The post-nup was just an opening gambit. You should get something for your trouble."

"I'll think about it," she says quietly.

"Good. You'd be letting me solve this one little problem for you, while you'd be helping me solve a really big problem—which is that I don't have control over my own life."

"All right," she says slowly. "Exactly what do I have to do?"

"Just be my arm candy, baby."

She groans right on cue.

"Seriously—I have a gala for the Diabetes Research Fund coming up. I'd like you to go as my date."

"A *gala*." She pronounces the word the way other people would say *root canal*. "Like—ball gowns and tuxes?"

"That's right. You'll need to wear a dress and heels."

Her cute nose wrinkles. "Which night? I couldn't miss a game, Neil."

"Sunday," I say with a devious smile. Because Sunday is the Bombshells' night off, and she'll have no excuse.

"Crap."

I grin. "My wife would naturally attend the gala with me. And it's less stressful than a quiet dinner with my family. At a gala all you have to do is smile."

"Smile like a gold digger, right?" She sighs. "Fine. I'll borrow a dress from Sylvie or Fiona. I don't have time to shop."

"Don't even worry about that. I'll ask Vera to bring a few dresses over one night. She has to bring me a new tux shirt anyway."

"Vera?" Charli gives me the side-eye.

"My personal shopper."

"Oh wow." Charli laughs. "Is she going to dress me like an Upper East Side socialite?"

"Well, no." I can't resist pushing Charli's buttons a little. "She's going to dress you like my *wife*." And—whoa—it's still hard to say that. *My wife*. I feel like I'm in a role-play right now.

Charli's eyes widen. "And what does *that* look like, exactly?"

"I have no idea. That's why we need Vera. Trust me on this."

"Don't say *trust me*, Neil. It's practically a jinx at this point."

"Noted."

She rubs her forehead. "So when would this charade start?"

"Right now, doll."

Charli groans. "I have a couple of ground rules."

"Hit me."

"You can't call me doll."

"Okay, fine. I'll have to find another pet name for you, then."

"Yikes. I need veto power on the pet names. That is something I want in writing."

"Sure, doll. Go grab a pen."

She slugs me in the arm. "Don't make me regret this, Cornelius. You have to agree to the rest of my rules."

"That was just a little joke." I rub my arm. "Go on with your rules."

"No sex," she says. "That's just obvious."

"Is it?" I ask. "Personally, I think we're destined to finish what we started. But that will be up to you. No sex until you ask me for it."

"Fine." She rolls her eyes, as if that's a ridiculous idea. But I know better. "No whiskey, either."

"That's okay with me. I don't need whiskey to want to bang you. Heck, I'd do a better job without whiskey. A word of advice, though? If you're set on staying out from under me, better lay off the sauce yourself. I've noticed you like me a lot better with a couple of drinks in you."

Her cheeks get pink. "I'm off hard liquor for a while."

"Cool, cool. Whatever works for you, wifey." I give her a big smile.

"This is really a crazy-ass plan," she grumbles. "You're just lucky that I hate my commute enough to play along. I keep telling myself that this will be funny someday."

"Of course, it will." I wrap an arm around her. "It will be a funny story we can both tell our grandkids."

"You can tell yours," she says. "I'm never getting married for real. And I'm never going back to Vegas."

"Not even for the All-Star games?"

"Not even for that."

I'm pretty pleased with myself for brokering this arrangement until Charli asks a crucial question. "Where are we going to sleep? I'm not sleeping on this sofa."

"Right," I agree. "But neither am I."

"So you're sleeping on the floor?" She gives me a catty, appraising glance. "You wouldn't make your wife sleep on the floor, would you?"

"No, ma'am. A succession of nannies raised me better than that."

Charli laughs.

"We'll share the bed," I say confidently.

She gives me a look that's trying to be stern, but her cheeks flush, so she ends up adorable, instead. "Even if I help you with this... charade you're trying to pull off, we're still not having sex."

I shrug. "We agree that the marriage thing and the sex thing aren't a package deal. That's where we went wrong in the first place. We should have skipped the marriage and the whiskey and had all the sex."

Her flush deepens. "In an alternate universe, maybe that's what we did. But in this universe, you behave like a gentleman."

"Absolutely," I agree. "There's no universe in which I ask you to stay married to me as a ploy to get into your pants. I don't need deception for that. Sooner or later, you'll invite me back, anyway."

Her chin snaps up. "That is *not* happening, Neil."

"If you say so." I shrug once again, as if it doesn't matter at all to me. "But either way, I wouldn't dream of removing any of your clothing until you're onboard with the idea. So we're *sharing* the bed. And because I'm a gentleman, you can have the first turn in the bathroom."

Silently, Charli gets up off the sofa. With a straight back and her head held high, she walks toward the bedroom.

Her cheeks are bright red now. She must be thinking about last night, because she looks a little hot and bothered.

Unfortunately, my dick notices, too, after we're finally tucked into my extra-large bed. I shut off the light, and I'm all too aware of Charli nearby. And once again, the image of her crouched between my legs, her pink tongue running up and down my—

Nngh. Now I'm pitching a tent in my boxers and trying to ignore the scent of her minty shampoo from point-blank range.

Lying on my back, my hands folded on my chest, I let out a sigh. Two feet away, Charli lies in the same stoic position. The room is dark, and we're both lying quietly, staring at the ceiling.

Last night I had my hands on her body. And my tongue. I must have started sobering up by the time we hit the sheets.

Because although the wedding itself is a blur, I have flashes of memory for what came later.

Or to be more accurate, what *almost* came later.

"Neil," Charli whispers.

"What?"

"Stop thinking about it."

I smile in the dark. "How do you know what I'm thinking about?"

"You're a man."

The laugh escapes before I can stop it. "Really? You're stereotyping me?"

"Am I wrong?"

"Um…" That shuts me up. "Okay. Good night."

"'Night."

Once again, I close my eyes. I try that meditation where you relax every part of your body in turn. But one part of my body is not relaxed, and I find myself wondering if there's a meditation for killing a boner.

If Charli wasn't here, I'd grab my phone and check.

No, that's not true. If Charli wasn't here, I'd take myself in hand and solve the problem the old-fashioned way.

Fuck.

A few more long minutes drag by. Maybe when Charli falls asleep, the sound of her deep breathing will calm me down.

But she's not asleep yet. Eventually, I hear her let out a frustrated sigh. I'll bet she's feeling the same way I do right now.

At least, I hope she is.

"Hey," I whisper. And I swear I was going to make a joke to lessen the tension. But instead, I hear myself ask, "Why didn't you ever say you're attracted to guys?"

"Because I knew it would get weird," she says immediately.

I think that over for a second. "No way. It didn't get weird until you pulled off my underwear and put my dick in your mouth."

She groans. "What can I do to get you to stop bringing that up?"

"You could do it again." Like a ninja I raise my arms just in time to fend off the projectile headed my way. Which turns out to be my favorite throw pillow. I tuck the pillow against my horny crotch and roll to get a better look at Charli. "Aren't you a little curious, though? About how we'd be together?"

She rolls, too, but maintains a healthy distance between us. "Of course, I am. But it's the same kind of curiosity I feel about car chases in movies. It's dangerous, and I don't need to try it to know it's a bad idea."

We blink at each other for a long beat. "Now, hang on," I say, disagreeing, because I pride myself on being a decent guy. "I'm not dangerous."

"Sure, you are," she argues. "You're dangerous in the way that Pringles are dangerous. One of them is fine, but before you know it, half the can is gone. I have to keep my distance or risk forming bad habits."

I give her a cocky grin. "Did you just compare sex with me to a dehydrated potato snack?"

"Maybe I did. You're both kind of cute and a bad idea."

My laugh is loud in the quiet room. "So you *are* tempted. I knew it."

"So what if I am?" she counters. "Temptation is everywhere. You're an all-star athlete, Neil. Nobody has a lock on mind-over-matter more than you do."

"Maybe." I flop onto my back. "But thanks for admitting that I'm a temptation. My ego needed that. I didn't want it to be all in my head. If you're actually attracted to me, I'm perceptive instead of being a creep."

She snorts. "Let me state for the record that I never thought of you as a creep. But either way, this thing between us is just something we'll have to ignore."

"Easy for you to say. I'm the one with the *thing* between us."

I gesture toward my erection. "I've got the hots for you and a dick that's eager to prove himself after last night's disasters."

"Tell it to sit down."

"Fine. You're welcome to sit down on it."

"I walked right into that one, didn't I?"

"Yes, you did."

"But you know I'm right. This arrangement between us can't function if you're going to mope about sex and give me sad doggie eyes."

"Oh, please. I don't mope. And the only *doggie* you'd be getting from me is doggie style. But I'm a gentleman. So you'll have to ask nicely."

Charli laughs from her side of the bed. "Don't hold your breath."

"You sound pretty confident over there. But the evidence suggests that you can be as impulsive as I am."

"Not often," she insists. "That was your one big chance. Now you have to move on."

I fold my hands on my chest. "Fine. I get it. Having you stay here was my idea, right? So I will suffer in silence."

"This isn't so bad. I could be home right now in my skanky apartment, trying to get my brother to leave and fending off advances from my creepiest cousin." Her voice is flip, but I can tell those problems are weighing on her. "God, was this the longest day ever?"

"Yeah, it kind of was." I reach across and hook her pinky finger in mine. I squeeze it, like the most low-contact hug.

She squeezes my pinky back. "What were we even thinking last night?"

"We were *drunk*," I point out. "Drunkey drunk."

"We were drinking from the cup of bad decisions. You'd just fought with Iris, and in your inebriation, you decided that I was going to be your rebound lay."

"You still could be," I whisper.

She ignores this. "Is this really it for Iris? Or are you going to go back to her as soon as we're done scaring your family?"

"I'm *never* going back," I insist. "I don't know why she even showed up in Vegas. She hates both Vegas and hockey."

"Why did you date her, anyway?" Charli presses. "I never understood you two as a couple."

"I've known her since preschool," I say by way of explanation. But the truth is we *don't* make sense as a couple. It's probably why we broke up no fewer than eight times in six years.

"But why did you two cling to each other for so long? When you don't enjoy any of the same things? Was she great in bed?"

"*No*," I say immediately. "Ouch. Now I just sound like a dick. But we weren't sexually compatible. That was probably responsible for more than half of our breakups. I think I stayed with her too long because she understands me. She was never after my money. And she wasn't trying to bang a hockey player, you know? She liked me in spite of it. She loved me for me."

Charli is silent on her side of the bed. Very silent.

"What? She has her own family fortune."

"I'm not arguing that point," she says quietly. "But you shouldn't constantly try to *change* the people you love. She was always trying to mold you into her perfect image."

"You know…" I give her pinky another squeeze. "I had no idea you paid so much attention to my romantic life, Charli Higgins. That's a lot of analysis for a guy you claim not to like."

"Don't forget that I've known Iris since the tenth grade. And I notice everyone," she says primly. "It's my superpower."

"You notice *me*, Charli. And someday soon you can notice me again at very close range."

She changes the subject again. "Serious question—why *don't* you have a nice sofa bed? Or even a comfortable couch?"

"Because I hired a decorator and told her to just do up the place in a style that works with the architecture of this building, which is from the early 1900s. I handed her my credit card and told her I was too busy to weigh in on furniture."

Charli props herself up on an elbow and stares at me. "So...
you ended up with furniture that you don't actually like?"

"Like it? I *hate* it. There's a bronze horse on my coffee table.
Do you know how much it hurts to accidentally kick that thing?
And there's no room to put down a pizza."

Charli cackles. "Why don't you peel off a few of your
millions and fix it? Does your uncle control your decorator,
too?"

"No way. I can do whatever I want. But I hate waste. Just
because I don't like that sofa doesn't mean I have the right to
create more landfill. Rich people are the hardest on the environment."

"Um..." She's staring at me now. "You could probably give
the couch to someone who needs one."

"Who needs *that*? Those damn buttons make dents in my
ass. I never sit there. I spend all my time in the kitchen or the
bedroom."

"Huh..." she says slowly. "I'm sure you could give away that
sofa. That's what Craigslist is for."

"I thought Craigslist was for prostitution."

"That, and getting rid of furniture. I could find you a willing
taker in hours. You could start over with a comfy couch, and
even watch TV in the living room."

"There's no piece of furniture for a TV," I point out. "The
designer hates TVs."

"Maybe the designer hates you," Charli says. "She didn't ask
your opinion on anything."

"Eh. I didn't let her. I thought I didn't care what she picked.
I thought wrong."

Charli laughs quietly. "Fine, but if you got a sofa bed, I
could sleep out there. Maybe you wouldn't be tossing and
turning like this."

"I'm not," I argue, even as I roll over onto my side to see if a
different position will make me feel sleepier.

Nope. Still horny. Now my dick is pointing straight at

Charli, like one of those divining rods farmers use to locate water. "Besides, I can't have a sofa bed."

"Why? I could sleep on it, and you could have your bed back."

"Not really. If I had a sofa bed, then *I'd* have to offer to sleep on it whenever I had a guest—like you or my cousin Cyrena. So it's actually better this way. You can share the bed, and Cyrena always gets a hotel room."

Charli lets out a whoop of laughter. "You have an interesting view on chivalry. And yet it's fine to deceive your uncle into thinking we're going to stay married?"

She makes an excellent point. "I hate lying. I don't do it often. But this is bigger than a simple lie. This is a decision to finally take control of the situation. To prove that Mom and I aren't toys my uncle can kick around. It's time he understood that."

"Okay." She props her hands behind her head. "So I guess I'm spending some time on your million-thread-count sheets."

"And I thank you for it. Now let's get some sleep."

"Right on," she says.

I close my eyes. But it takes me a good long time to fall asleep.

TEN

MY ACCIDENTAL HUSBAND IS
SUPER HOT

Charli

The first bars of my alarm music cut through the silence of Neil's bedroom with a pounding drumbeat.

But I have fast reflexes, and I reach over to silence it immediately.

"No way," Neil mumbles beside me. It's all he has to say before beginning to breathe deeply again.

I listen to the sound of his slumber and take stock of my life.

On the one hand, I've made a mess of things. My bank account hates me because I took a week off from work for the All-Star event in Vegas. My family is still doing its best to bleed me dry. And this is my second morning waking up next to a man I married by accident.

When I shift my eyes to the left, I see his muscular, colorfully tattooed arm. There's a wireless insulin-delivery device stuck right there in the midst of the artwork. It's all black, about the size of a matchbox but with rounded edges. And somehow it makes him look even more like a badass.

My accidental husband is super hot. At least there's that.

Even better, I got a great night's rest in his luxurious bed.

Most nights I jolt awake three or four times. My subconscious likes to double check that I'm safe. There have been many nights in my life when I had cause to worry.

But in spite of everything that's gone down with Neil, I somehow knew he'd stay on his own side of the bed. I fell asleep confident I wouldn't wake up in the middle of the night with a man on top of me trying to start something.

That very thing has happened to me before. I've had a rough life, with several unstable living situations. That's why I lied to Neil and the other guys about my sexuality early on. They were strangers when I arrived in Brooklyn a year and a half ago. It seemed safer to take sex off the table.

Maybe it wouldn't have mattered, though. Neil's teammates have been surprisingly good to me. And Neil?

I sneak another glance at him. His aristocratic chin points toward the ceiling and long eyelashes graze his cheekbones. Sleep robs him of his cocky attitude. He sleeps with a serious expression on his face. Like there's something vital written on his eyelids.

Neil is a little more complicated than I'd thought. A billionaire who hates landfill? A private-jet mogul who worries about the environment?

And the man cooks a mean head of cauliflower. It's a lot to take in.

But I don't really have the time, so I slip out of the bed and avail myself of the limestone spa known as Neil's bathroom. The shower feels as luxurious as it looks.

Under the hot spray, I'm still thinking about Neil. If I'm being fair, I'd admit that my view of him is evolving. He was an ass to me the first time we met, and I've always assumed he was a spoiled brat.

It's that school he went to—Parkhurst Prep. It was just around the curve in the road from Miss Draper's School, where I went.

Both those schools are dead to me. I won a lot of hockey

games and got a good education in the woods of Massachusetts. But I was friendless there for three solid years.

High school was a long time ago now, but sometimes it's hard to leave that stuff behind. When I look at Neil, I see a hardworking athlete. But I also see his rich-guy smirk and his Parkhurst diploma.

It's confusing.

I shut off the water, because I'm turning into a prune, and I don't want to be late for work. Neil's towels are like fluffy white clouds. I didn't even know a towel could be so thick.

He doesn't wake up when I tiptoe through the room in a towel to collect my clothes. Or when I slip into the kitchen to guzzle water and put on my shoes.

I wash and dry my glass and put it back in the cabinet. I've had a lot of training at how to be a nearly invisible house-guest. I know how to make myself look small and less inconvenient.

This kitchen is unlike any other, though. Light shimmers through the window as I park my butt on a kitchen chair and tie my shoes.

I'd love to linger here on a quiet morning, drinking coffee. And for a moment, I contemplate making a pot before I leave. The machine is so shiny, and it would make this kitchen smell fantastic. Neil could wake up and pour himself a cup.

But that's so domestic, like a real wife would do.

I can't play house. I can't pretend this is my kitchen. I'm just a visitor.

And I'd better not forget it.

My shift at the Orion Diner starts at seven thirty, but the walk to work is even shorter than I'd thought, and I arrive fifteen minutes early.

"Charli!" Sal calls from the cash register. "Grab an apron,

baby doll. Table seventeen is shootin' daggers over here because I haven't brought out the coffee."

"Sure thing, Sal. But I'm clocking in early."

"Fine, fine."

For the record, Sal is the only man on Earth who's allowed to call me "baby doll." In his defense, he's about a hundred and forty-seven years old. His mother opened the Orion Diner just after World War II, and he's been running it for fifty years, according to a newspaper article on the wall.

The write-up came about when Sal hired some design students from Pratt to redo the interior of the Orion—keeping the fifties feel of the place but smartening it up.

And then he hired some cooking-school kids to give the menu a modern makeover.

Now Sal gets fourteen dollars for a plate of eggs or an avocado toast. And I get fat tips, because everyone loves the Orion Diner.

I tie on an apron and hustle the coffee pot out to table seventeen. They order complicated omelets and ask for a side of mesclun salad.

"Coming right up," I promise them.

"Keep the coffee flowing," is their parting shot.

Whatever. I'm happy to dart around the sunlit diner, topping up cups and taking orders. My first job after I landed in Brooklyn was a huge mistake, but this one is solid.

I'd found this place when my teammates had demanded that I come out for brunch with them. I never have enough money for restaurant food, but I'd given in that one time, because there are only so many times you can say no before people decide you're aloof.

We'd had a great brunch at table eleven. On my way out, I'd spotted the *Help Wanted* sign in the window, and I'd turned around to ask Sal for an application.

I've been working here ever since. This place is a mere seven-minute walk from the practice facility, plus I get a free meal during every shift. I could probably earn more at an upscale lunch spot. But Sal tolerates my scheduling constraints —no nights or weekends. I need those hours for hockey. Plus, he's a hoot.

"Good news," I tell him during a quiet moment between orders. "You can schedule me a half hour earlier in the mornings if you want to. I'm staying in this neighborhood for a couple months."

"Yeah, chickie! Did ya finally leave that dive out in East New York?"

"For now," I say, omitting the complicated details. But I'm happy to pretend to belong in a gorgeous neighborhood for a little while, anyway.

"Good call. How was your trip to Vegas, kid? Glam?"

"A little too glam. You wouldn't believe the hangover I caused myself."

"Oh dearie. I got aspirin in my desk drawer. Your girls are here, though," Sal says. "Just walked in."

I swivel my head to find out which girls he means. It could be any number of my Bombshells teammates. Sal refers to all of them as "your girls."

Side note—Sal is the only one allowed to refer to a team of fierce female hockey players as "girls."

When I head over to the circular booth in the corner, I don't find any hockey players. Instead, it's Rebecca, the team owner, Bess, an agent who helps Becca manage the team, and also Heidi Jo and Georgia from the front office.

And? Sasha, my coach.

"Wow, it's power hour," I say, sliding menus onto the table. "Three coffees, one ginger tea?"

"Thanks, Charli!" they say, and I hurry off to grab their cups.

The next table to sit down contains the Bruisers' goalie Silas Kelly and the other goalie—Mike Beacon—who's also brought his two-year-old son, Mikey.

"One booster seat, please, two coffees and two orders of the scrambled egg tacos," Silas says without a glance at the menu. "Thanks, Charli."

"Don't mention it."

This pattern holds. More of the Bruisers trickle in, and from their oversized orders I can tell they're having a meeting today before morning skate.

No man eats two eggs, two pancakes, and a side of sausage hash immediately before practice. That's just asking for trouble.

Lucky me, too. The Bruisers are great tippers.

On weekdays, you won't see many Bombshells in here during breakfast. They're at work. Women have to work to support their pro-hockey careers while the men's team are like pampered thoroughbreds with only one job—winning.

I'm pouring coffee like it's going out of style when I catch Georgia beckoning to me from the corner booth.

I grab a fresh pot and hustle over there. "Careful, ladies, Sal likes his coffee strong." I'd just refilled them five minutes ago.

"Oh, we've had plenty," Georgia agrees. "But Charli, I have news."

My stomach drops. "What? Oh no."

"Oh yes," she says. "*Sports Illustrated* has it." She thrusts her phone in my direction.

STANLEY CUP-WINNING PRIVATE-JET HEIR MARRIES FEMALE HOCKEY PLAYER.

"Omigod," I gasp. "I always wanted to be in *Sports Illustrated*. But not like this." I swallow hard. "I'm sorry. Wow. This is going to be a huge distraction, right? I'm really sorry."

When I glance up, I'm afraid to make eye contact with the powerful women at this table. I've just brought tawdry gossip to the team. And as I glance from face to face, I see nothing but...

Barely concealed laughter.

"This isn't funny!" I insist.

"Not funny at all," Rebecca says. Then she slaps a hand over her mouth.

"*My* definition of funny absolutely includes you and Drake getting bombed and accidentally married," Bess says with a toss of her red hair. "Who's with me, girls?"

"Sorry, toots," Sasha says. "Wait—does Drake have a pet name for you, too? Like pumpkin? Or love bug?"

"No, he does not," I hiss. "And he never will! This is just a... little mess. Temporary insanity."

"And a great excuse to go lingerie shopping!" Heidi claps. "And you know what? It's never too late to throw a bridal shower."

"*Oh yes, it is!*" I argue a little hysterically. "There will be no shower. No jokes. No actual marriage. Just some paperwork, eventually. In a couple of months. Neil is in charge of that. Just... forget you ever saw that article. I have to get back to work."

Trying not to panic, I return to seating customers and taking orders. But after I cash out table fifteen, I catch Silas and Beacon sneaking looks at me. "What?" I bark. "Did you need something more from the kitchen?"

"Got any wedding cake? Seems I missed my slice?" Beacon asks.

"Very funny," I grumble. "Here's your check." I slap it down on the table. "Please don't talk about this, okay? We're filing for divorce and hoping nobody really notices us."

Silas winces. "I don't know, Charli. I think it's too late. Look." He points at something over my shoulder.

Where there's a TV hanging over the counter. Oh hell.

I turn around slowly as my heart begins to pound. The TV is tuned to ESPN, where there's a photo of Neil in a suit in front of a private jet. *MARRIED* screams the graphic at the side of the screen.

"Oh my God," I breathe. "At least they don't have..."

My team headshot appears next on the screen.

"Nice picture," Beacon says gently. He puts his credit card down on the check.

"Thanks," I say, my throat suddenly dry. "But this still sucks."

"Hang in there."

Numb, I carry his card to the register and swipe it through the machine.

"Charli?" Sal says slowly. "I think I gotta ask this again. How was your time in Vegas?"

"I mentioned my hangover, didn't I?" The snap in my voice is really too much for an employee speaking to her boss. My temper has gotten me fired from more than one job.

But Sal just laughs.

Why does everyone find this so damn funny? I pull out my phone and text a warning to Neil. *It's out. I'm sorry. There goes your day.*

"Order up!" calls the cook from the kitchen.

I hurry to the order window to grab a plate of eggs and a stack of pancakes. After delivering them, I drop the receipt on the goalies' table. I can do this job without actually thinking about it.

That's a good thing, because I'm spiraling inside. I don't want to be famous for marrying a billionaire in Vegas. All our friends are going to laugh. The whole *world* is going to laugh.

Just as I'm finishing this thought, the door opens, and Bruisers winger Jason Castro flies into the room. "Guys!" he calls. "I just heard the craziest rumor!"

Oh *man*. Here we go.

Castro skids to a stop in front of me. "Uh, hi Charli."

"Hi," I say warily.

He grabs the back of his neck, and I watch the hockey player struggle. He doesn't want to be a dick. And yet his inner gossip hound is trying to claw its way out of his muscular body. "Is it true?" he blurts out.

"Yes and no," I say with a sigh. "On paper I'm married to Cornelius Drake III. But whiskey made me do it."

"Wow," he says. "I mean... we've all been there."

"Really?" I sputter. "You accidentally married someone as a joke—and then woke up to discover that it was legally binding?"

"Well, no," he admits. "Although I once got so drunk that I pulled a testicle out of my fly instead of my dick and then peed down the leg of my pants."

We blink at each other for one really awkward moment.

"Your mess was cheaper to fix than mine," I point out.

"Although a little more disgusting."

"Yeah. Um, well, let me know if there's anything I can do to help."

"Thanks, man."

I swerve around the diner delivering orders and dropping checks and pouring coffee. But all I can think about is how I just want to run away and hide.

Naturally, the door opens again to admit two more hockey players. And behind them come two more.

"Am I crazy?" Sal asks. "Or are you drawing a crowd?"

"I don't want to talk about it," I hiss. "But if they're here to stare at me and gossip, they'd better order the caviar eggs and smoked salmon, and tip twenty-five percent."

"Sounds fair." I expect Sal to be the one person in this joint who's too busy to stand around staring at me. But nope. He's giving me the kind of squint a man wears when he can't figure out what a woman is thinking. "Did you *really* get married?"

"Seems so."

His frown deepens. "This mean you're gonna quit on me?"

"No!" I yelp. "Do *not* put your *Help Wanted* sign in the window. I'm not going anywhere."

He wipes his hands on his apron. "But the TV said your man owns private jets."

"Don't believe everything you see on TV, Sal."

He hurries off to answer a ringing phone.

The door flies open one more time, and I almost don't

bother to look up. Does it really matter who else has arrived to gawk?

Except everyone in the room suddenly goes quiet. The silence is so deep that I have to wonder if we're being held up at gunpoint. But when I finally close the cash register drawer and lift my chin, I see Neil Drake standing just inside the door, hands on his hips like Superman, arms rippling, jaw ticking. He spots me and lifts his chin in a solemn greeting.

"Hi," I whisper stupidly. It's just hitting me that the whole world is going to know *why* drunk me couldn't say no to a sham marriage with Neil. Because when he levels that hazel-eyed stare at me, it's really hard to say cool.

"Morning," he says calmly.

"Your friends are..." I indicate the entire breadth of the restaurant. "Everywhere. I suppose you can just pick a table."

"No, I'm sitting at the counter. We need to talk."

"Right now?" I squeak.

Everyone is listening. You could hear a pin drop in here. Until Rebecca Kattenberger stands up with a smile on her face and starts a slow clap. And beside her, Heidi Jo pops up and joins in.

Then someone else starts clapping. And someone else. Until the whole damn room is applauding. Even Beacon's toddler in his booster seat.

I'm frozen like a proverbial doe on a dimly lit road as the car barrels toward her.

But not Neil Drake. He turns around, gives the whole room a regal wave, and then takes an elegant fucking bow like an Academy Award winner. Some people don't mind the spotlight, I guess.

I wish I were one of them.

ELEVEN

OF ALL THE BONEHEADED STUNTS

Neil

I take a seat at the counter and watch Charli hurriedly tap a few orders into the terminal. Her hands look shaky, and I know that look on her face.

It's *fear*. She's freaked out, and the attention she's getting this morning isn't helping. Unfortunately, it's about to get worse. ESPN and *Sports Illustrated* won't be the only media outlets that report on us. My family has baggage. And people love to write about that shit.

"Charli," I whisper. "I'm sorry about the article. And all this attention." She slaps a menu down in front of me, and I grab her hand before she can flit away again. "Hey. Are you all right?"

"Not really, no." She takes a shuddery breath. "I don't know if I can do this."

"Okay," I say immediately. "Do you want me to walk right over there to Georgia and tell her to call off the dogs? She could tell the media that it was all a joke and tell the world that we're getting a divorce."

Charli's pulse flutters in her throat, and her eyes look wild. "Would you really do that? What about your plan?"

"My plan doesn't matter," I say quietly. "If it's making you very uncomfortable."

She lets out a shaky breath. I'm still holding her hand down on the counter, and she doesn't pull it away.

My watch beeps. She takes a deep breath. "You need to eat, right? Is that alarm bad?"

"It's just a reminder, not an emergency."

"Oh. You want the usual?" She removes her hand from mine. "Two eggs, whole-wheat waffle, side of ham?" She grabs a cup and pours me some coffee, with a swirl of half-and-half, because she already knows how I take my coffee and what I want for breakfast.

"Yeah, of course. But only after you answer my question. Are you okay?"

Charli visibly pulls herself together. She drops her shoulders and straightens her spine. She takes a slow breath. "It's out there now, whether we put your plan into action or not."

"That's true," I agree.

"If we call off our deal, it doesn't make the hounds go away."

"That's hard to say. If we yell divorce, maybe we're less interesting."

She grabs a dishrag and wipes down the counter. "Man, how I would love to blame this whole thing on you."

"Go for it," I offer. "I really don't mind." It's not worth it to see her so stressed out.

"No, it is what it is. I can just suck it up for a little while, like I always do. We can still do this your way."

That's not what I expected her to say, and so I hesitate. "How about this—I'll start calling around before the game, interviewing lawyers. Just so we have options."

She taps my order into the terminal. "Isn't that when the thoroughbreds are supposed to be in their stalls resting?"

"Yeah, but I'm pretty sure I can manage a phone call or two between the massage and the catered meal."

She laughs quickly. "Do you really have a massage booked?"

"No. It does sound like a good idea, right?"

Charli just shakes her head. "Seven minutes until your meal comes out. I'll pour the waffle now." She gives me a fierce smile. Her game face is already back on straight. "Find that lawyer. But I'm cool, okay? Don't worry about me."

"All right."

She flits off, and I settle in and pull out my phone. There are approximately one billion text messages waiting for me. Seems like everyone I've ever played hockey with has reached out this morning.

Most of the messages are some variation on *Dude, no way!* Or, *Congrats, man!*

Then there's a grumpy three-word message from my cousin Fred—my uncle's evil minion. *Call me ASAP.*

Pass, thanks.

I also discover a message from my mother. *Neil, my love, what on earth is going on? I got a nastygram from your uncle, demanding that I talk sense into you. That's a fairly common occurrence so I didn't think anything of it. But this morning all my friends started emailing to ask who you married. MARRIED? I'm trying not to freak out, here. Call me when you can.*

Oh boy. I'm not looking forward to that call. Although Mom is on a beach in the Caribbean right now, so at least I don't have to deal with her questions in person.

"Hey, Drake." Sal—the owner of the diner—sidles up to the counter in front of me. "You really a billionaire?"

Well, shit. This is why I hate the media. "Not exactly," I hedge. "Why? You're looking for an investor? Got expansion plans?"

"Nah." He shakes his head. "Running one place is hard

enough. But if Charli married a rich guy, she'll quit the diner. Just tryin' to figure out when I have to start interviewing."

Yikes. "Don't do that, okay? Charli would *not* appreciate you looking to replace her. She likes this job."

"If you say so." There's skepticism all over his face. "If I married up, though, I'd be sleeping in. Just saying."

"Sal! Knock it off," Charli says, poking him in the arm. "We already talked about this. Neil—cook is plating up your eggs."

"Thanks." Charli knows that I need to dose myself with insulin before I eat.

"Sure thing, hubby."

With a snort, I open the app that's connected to my insulin pump and activate my breakfast dose. That done, I turn my phone over, so I don't have to think about all the people who want to grill me about this recent turn of events.

My breakfast lands in front of me a moment later. Charli is gone before I can even thank her. I stare down at two eggs scrambled just how I like them, a slab of ham, and a whole wheat waffle that's dripping with whipped butter but no syrup. There're a couple orange wedges on the side of the plate, because Charli knows that I enjoy them.

I pick up my fork and sink it into the waffle. If this is what it's like to be married, I guess it isn't half bad.

After breakfast, the crowd at the diner eventually disperses. As fascinating as my drunken foibles may be, my teammates and I have a playoffs spot to clinch.

I'm the last to leave. I pay my check—tip fifty percent—and push a key card across the counter to Charli. "Here. This is your copy, okay? Miguel and the rest of the staff know that you're staying with me. Nobody will give you any trouble."

She blinks. "Thanks," she says, slowly pocketing the key.

I stand up and tuck my wallet away. "I'll see you after practice, okay? Just text me if you need me."

"I'll be fine," she says.

"Good." I lean across the counter and give a surprised Charli a kiss on the cheek. "Take care of yourself."

Then I head outside, where I'm ambushed by my friend Anton Bayer. "There you are," he says, leaning against the wall of the diner. "Thought you were never coming out."

"Well, you know how newlyweds are," I deadpan, and he chuckles.

Together, we head down the street toward the practice facility. And I'm silently counting in my head. One Mississippi... Two Mississippi... Three Mississip—

"So," Bayer says.

"Two and a half seconds, man. That's how long you waited to pry into my private business."

He snorts. "How do you know what I was going to ask?"

"Because I've met you?"

"Okay, fine. But your first mistake was assuming you have private business, when the rest of us have already had to put up with all the team gossip. That's just what you get for hooking up with somebody in the organization. Ask me how I know."

He makes a few good points. When he and Sylvie started carrying on, it was all we could talk about.

"So Sylvie and I have a few questions. Did you two..." He clears his throat.

"No," I say immediately.

"You mean no like *no*, no? Or no, like, Charli would murder me in my sleep if I answered that question?"

"I mean *no* like *fuck off*."

"But Sylvie and I have a bet going!" Anton says.

"Oh, well. Why didn't you say so? It's more fun spilling my secrets if one of you stands to make twenty bucks."

"It's a hundred." Anton chuckles. "So did you, or didn't you?"

I let out a sigh. "Go fish, man. I'm a vault."

Anton cackles. "That means I win! You did obviously did it."

"You *don't* win, sucker," I bark.

Well, shit. As Anton's eyes grow round, I realize I just got played. Now he knows.

"Hold on," he says in a hushed voice. "Really? You didn't bang? Isn't that what people do when they get drunk-married in Vegas? What is the goddamn point of reckless behavior if you don't round all the bases?"

"We just…" There must be an exit ramp from this conversation. But I can't seem to find it. "We just didn't. There's drunk and then there's sloppy drunk, right? I overshot the target."

Anton stops walking and grabs my arm. His face is full of shock. "You're *kidding* me. You couldn't close the deal?"

"What if you didn't make such a big fucking deal about it," I say through clenched teeth. "It wasn't my finest hour."

Anton throws his head back and laughs. "Ohhhhh, buddy. I'm sorry. Does Charli know about you?"

"What *about* me?" I ask in a surly voice. We resume walking toward the practice facility.

"Does she know you've had it bad for her since the first minute you met? Does she know you get all hot and bothered whenever she smiles? Does she know your eyes are always pasted to her fine ass?"

"They're not," I grumble.

"Sure, but that's because you're a gentleman. In your head, you're undressing her half the time."

"You shut up."

He laughs. "Fine. But you did hook up, right? I didn't even know she was into guys."

That makes two of us. "That's private." Charli doesn't need me to gossip about her behind her back. I've already done enough damage.

I expect him to rib me some more, but that's not what happens. "Whoa, Drake—check it out."

Glancing up, I see two TV vans in front of the Brooklyn Hockey headquarters and a couple of cameramen standing around looking for something to film. I think that something is me.

"Seriously?" I groan. The only other time I've seen camera crews here was during the playoffs. "Is that about me? For real?"

"I think so, buddy."

"Hey! Cornelius Drake!" A reporter in a red tie steps out from behind his van. His cameraman swings around to focus on me. "Congratulations on a great showing at the All Stars."

"Thanks," I say stiffly, trying not to break stride. But there are still ten paces between me and the building.

"Tell us about your Vegas wedding!" he demands, flashing me a big smile to make this seem fun.

"Keep walking," Anton whispers. "I got this."

"How've you got this?" I have to wonder.

Anton spreads his arms out wide and shields me, like I'm a perp being led into the police station. "Drake is not taking questions at this time," he says theatrically. "The happy couple eloped, because they like their privacy."

I jog up the steps and pause at the top, turning around. There are two cameras recording everything I've done. Which is not much. I wink at the camera, because they came all this way. Then I turn around and pull open the door.

Anton doesn't follow me. "I'm Anton Bayer. Jersey number seventy. That's one better than sixty-nine. I also do some modeling, and I'm available for impromptu musical performances. Ask me anything."

The reporters laugh as I head through the door. I guess it's useful to have ridiculous friends.

"God, Neil!" Georgia squeaks as she hurries across the lobby toward me. "I tried to warn you that they were here."

"Wasn't looking at my phone," I grumble.

"I'm sorry. There I was frittering away the morning at the diner without any idea you were going to be ambushed."

"Don't mention it," I say. "It's not a big deal." At least I hope it's not. "How can we make this go away?"

Georgia chews her lip. "Getting married isn't much of a story, unless it causes drama for somebody else."

"Like the team. Or my family," I say slowly.

"Right," Georgia agrees. "The team doesn't care, of course. But your family is fascinating, Neil. Any girl who marries you is suddenly rich. Now that's a story."

I rub a hand over the center of my chest where tension is starting to gather. I think I oversold this gig to Charli. She's not used to this kind of tabloid nonsense. "We've gotta stick with *no comment*, okay? There's nothing I can say about my, uh, marriage that anyone wants to hear."

"All right," Georgia says quietly. "Both Mr. Drake and Ms. Higgins decline to discuss their personal lives, blah blah blah. The press will move on eventually."

"Thank you."

Anton steps inside, clapping me on the shoulder and steering me toward the tunnel leading to the practice facility. "Everything all right?" he asks as we hurry toward the players' meeting.

"It will be."

I'm unsettled, though. Until today, the coverage of my hockey career has largely ignored my family background. On the rare occasions that I've been asked to do lifestyle interviews, I always find a reason to say no. It's cool if they write about my stats, but please leave the private-jet empire out of it.

But now it's going to be harder to fly under the radar. And it should have occurred to me that Charli could be skewered in the media for marrying me.

Is that what a good guy does to the woman he's crushing on? No, it is not.

———

"Are they still out there?" I ask a few hours later.

"From this angle I can only see one news truck," Silas says, stretching his quads as he looks out the window.

"That's an improvement, right?" Anton points out.

"I guess," I reply from the stretching mat.

"So how did this happen, again?" asks Mitch, the newest trainer. He's got my ankle in his hand, and he's angling my leg back toward my body. "Was it, like, a drunken thing or what?"

"Hey," Silas says. "Don't ask, man. That's none of your business."

Mitch laughs. "Fine. But dude, I'm sorry. Of all the women you could wake up next to, it had to be that bitch?"

I yank my leg out of his hands and sit up fast. "Do not *ever* refer to a hardworking athlete as a bitch. Or any woman. Especially not my wife."

He jerks back a few inches, as if I'd slapped him. "But you're not really—"

"Not. Your. Business," I say through gritted teeth.

"Yo." Henry, the head trainer, whistles from the doorway. "Mitch, go wash a load of towels."

"What?" the kid whines. "I'm workin' on Drake."

"Not anymore you're not," Henry barks. "And mind your own business next time."

The kid hops to his feet with an irritated sniff and heads for the door.

Once he's gone, Henry kneels down on the mat and stretches me. "Sorry about that, Drake. I'll have a word with him."

"Thanks," I grunt.

But I brought all this speculation upon myself. And on Charli, too.

What have I done?

I don't make it home until around four. Charli's practice doesn't start for another hour, and it's a new thing for me to unlock my door and expect to find someone else in my space.

"Hi honey, I'm home," I call out as I step inside.

When I leave the foyer, it's true that I'm not alone, but the person sitting on my sofa is not the one I'm expecting.

"Mom," I say, startled. "You were out of the country."

"I was," she says archly. "But when you start receiving strange messages about your son's sudden marriage, it tends to change your plans. Joshua never brings me this kind of drama."

My half brother—from my mother's first marriage—has the benefit of not being a Drake, though. So he can marry whoever he wishes and nobody will say a word.

I fling myself onto an armchair. "Are you here to complain, too? Like one of Uncle Harmon's henchmen?"

"Ouch," she says, touching her cashmere-covered chest. "I would never take his side over yours. But please tell me you *didn't* really marry a stranger in Vegas?"

"She's not a stranger," I grumble.

"A girlfriend?" she asks.

"A friend. Harmon has nothing to worry about. But did he ask me? No. He just sent over the most humiliating post-nup ever written. He took the nuclear option, as always. So I'm fighting back."

My mom's expression is still grim. At sixty, she's a beautiful woman. And more than a little intimidating. "But you did marry her. And you're sure it's legal?"

Slowly, I nod.

"Of all the boneheaded stunts. Your uncle tries to paint you as the non-serious member of the Drake family. So what do you do? Get drunk and get married in Vegas."

I lean back against the chair and rub my temples.

"How's your blood sugar?" my mother asks immediately.

"It's fine. Getting yelled at might destabilize me, though."

She reaches out a high-heeled boot and kicks me with it.

"Nice try. But I'm not done yelling at you."

"I figured."

"Your uncle is losing his mind. If that girl decided to screw you, she could endanger this family's voting majority."

"She won't," I argue, but my mom has a point.

"Harmon will use this against you. He and Fred could muster the votes to oust you. And then with you off the board, I wouldn't be able to secure a seat for your sister."

"I'm aware." I've already done this math.

"We've spent the last two years trying to convince your uncle that we're capable of managing our own resources. So what the hell are you doing?"

"I thought I'd give marriage a try."

She groans. "This isn't you, Neil. You don't play games. What are you hoping to accomplish?"

"It's my life, Mom. I can get married on a whim, if I want to. And I can stay married if it suits me."

She blinks. "Neil, did you get a head injury in Vegas?"

"No!"

"Lord." My mother rolls her eyes theatrically. "She must be a hellcat in bed."

As if I knew.

"Is she the reason you finally gave Iris her walking papers?"

Now there's a tricky question. "That's something that needed doing a long time ago."

"No kidding. I wondered if you got married to let Iris know she should finally move on."

"Mom! That sounds like an extreme way to break up with someone."

"It's the only thing I can think of. Honestly. This impulsive behavior isn't like you."

She's right. I like to party. I'm a fun guy, but I'm not impulsive. I care too much about my athletic performance to be a wild man.

But that's what I became that night in Vegas. Turns out there was a wild man inside me just waiting to get out.

And drunk logic is still logic. The blotto me had a reason for marrying Charli. I was trying to make a statement, even if I picked a damn foolish way to do it.

If only I knew what statement that was.

TWELVE

MEET THE PARENTS

Charli

Scrolling through story after story about me and Neil, I try to stay calm. They're just gossipy headlines, right? The only people who care about someone else's marriage are people who lead uninteresting lives.

That's what I'm telling myself, anyway.

I put my phone away and watch the subway stops go slowly by. I'd thought I could skip this trip today. After my shift at the diner, it had been a pleasure to stroll up the street to the Million Dollar Dorm and wave my new key in front of Neil's door.

It had opened with a satisfying click, and I'd let myself into Neil's pad for an hour of relaxation in peace and quiet.

My Zen mood had lasted about ten minutes until I'd checked my bank balance. That's never a very relaxing activity, but I hadn't been prepared to see a strange check written on my account for three hundred ninety-nine dollars.

My heart had leapt into my throat. The only checks I write are to my landlord. There's no way I could have spent four hundred bucks and forgotten.

The banking app provided images of cashed checks, and I'd

focused on the name of the recipient. In a messy hand was written, *POGO APPLIANCES.*

I'd recognized the name. It's a store a couple blocks away from my apartment, and I've never been there. With my heart in my mouth, I'd zoomed in on the signature, too. Someone had scrawled *CHARLI HIGGINS* there.

What the...?

Then I'd remembered the TV that Robert had been watching, and I'd wanted to vomit. It had been bad enough when I'd imagined he'd been making himself at home in my place, but things were so much worse than I'd thought. He'd obviously found my checks and helped himself to my bank balance.

I'd heaved myself off Neil's uncomfortable couch and headed for my apartment. The subway ride isn't helping with my rage. I barely earn enough money to keep ahead of my credit-card payments. And the whole reason I have credit-card debt is because of Dennis.

Right before I'd left Philly, he got in what he calls a "tight spot"—meaning, he lost too much money at another poker game. It happens a lot. That time I went four thousand dollars into debt because the game runners were going to break Dennis's legs if he didn't pay up.

I'd taken out a cash advance on my credit card, and I'm still trying to earn that money back. Lord knows Dennis isn't going to.

But now he and I are going to have a chat, and he is not going to like what I have to say.

If Robert is there, he won't like it either.

When the train finally pulls into New Lots, I'm practically bursting with anger. I jog the three blocks to my crappy little building and pound up the stairs. Even though I've only spent one full day in Neil's luxury pad, the assault of stale food aromas seems worse than it was before.

This place is such a dive. I can't believe Neil walked in here with me yesterday. But what's one more humiliation this week? It barely scratches the top ten.

My key turns in the lock, and I push the door open.

On the sofa, my brother startles. Then he hits the pause button on a remote control.

"Dennis," I snarl. "What the hell are you doing?"

He has the good sense to look guilty. "Just hanging out, Charli. I shoulda called you."

"You think!" I let the door slam behind me. "Nice TV. Where'd you get it?"

"Robert bought it."

"Uh-huh. And you said—hey it's no problem if you put a TV in my sister's place? *She won't mind?*" The volume of my voice escalates on every sentence.

He flinches. "I knew it was a little rude. But you know how he gets."

"Where is he?" I poke my head into my bedroom, where the bed looks thrashed. But there's nobody there.

"I dunno." Dennis shakes his head. "He went out."

Not trusting him, I poke my head into the tiny kitchen and the even tinier bathroom, where there are unfamiliar hairs dotting the shower stall.

Hot rage courses through my veins. I'd spent most of my life underfoot, staying with whichever relatives weren't sick enough of me and Dennis to send us packing. Once in a while, my mother would turn up to announce that she'd "started over with something good." She'd haul us to another unfamiliar apartment with another unfamiliar boyfriend.

And the cycle would start all over. Until we'd inevitably be dumped on one of her many siblings "just for a spell."

It's a miracle I survived my childhood. It wasn't until my teenage years that hockey scholarships allowed me to move on to shared dorm rooms at prep school and then college.

I'd *never* had my own room until this apartment, dumpy as it is. But Dennis and Robert couldn't keep their grubby hands off it.

In my bedroom, I crouch down in front of the plastic file box where I keep my bills and my banking stuff. Sure enough, there's a carbon copy of a check written to the appliance store for the TV.

There's one more check missing, too.

Shit.

I stomp back into the living room and stand over Dennis, my hands in fists. "Did you happen to notice how he paid for that TV?"

Slowly, Dennis shakes his head. But he looks guilty.

"You turned the other way when he ransacked my stuff, took my checkbook, and helped himself."

"Shit," Dennis says flatly. "I'm sorry."

"YOU'RE SORRY!" I shriek. "How does that help? Does he have a key?"

Dennis puts his head in his hands. "I think so."

"*Fuck.*" I kick the cheap sofa, which does nothing but make a dull thump. "You are fucking spineless, you know that? You let him walk all over both of us. Unless the whole thing was your idea?"

"No, Charli! I swear." Dennis shakes his miserable head. "I thought it would be harmless to come here a couple of nights. See if New York is a good place to get a job, ya know? I didn't think he'd steal."

"You didn't *ask*," I snarl. "You do everything the cowardly way. I'm so tired, Dennis. Grow a backbone and own your own bullshit for once."

There's so much more I have to say on this topic. I've tried for years. *Get it together. We could help each other. We could be a team.*

You're my only real family.

Pretend like you love me.

Because—against all odds—I love you.

But today I bite back most of the things I want to say. I've said them already. I've seen this show before, and I know how it ends.

There's nothing to do but cut my losses. Again.

"Dennis," I say quietly. "I'm giving up this apartment." I am, too. I've decided on it this very second. "I'm paid up through the middle of February. After that, this place is gone. If anyone is here after Valentine's Day, that person is trespassing. The landlord will call the cops."

"Where are you going?" Dennis whispers. "Did you get kicked off the team?"

"*No!* Bite your damn tongue. I'm moving in with a friend for a little while. In a better neighborhood. He, uh, needs a roommate, and it's a good commute."

"Oh," my brother says heavily.

"Valentine's Day," I repeat. "Tell Robert that the party is almost over."

"All right." He sighs. "Sorry."

"I'll bet you are." I turn my back on Dennis and head back into my room. On the floor, there's a mattress and box springs that I bought. Aside from the sofa in the living room, which I bought off Craigslist, I didn't invest in any other furniture.

Good thing. Because I'm going to have to leave everything behind. I have no way to get them to Neil's place and nowhere to put them even if I could.

I march into the kitchen and find my box of trash bags. That's what I have to pack my clothes in. So classy.

But sometimes a girl just has to move on.

And now is one of those times.

It's mortifying to get out of a cab with four trash bags and two boxes in front of the Million Dollar Dorm.

But Miguel, everyone's favorite concierge, doesn't even blink at my tawdry luggage. He rolls out the shiny brass luggage cart and calmly stacks my bags on its velvet base. "I could just make two trips," I say, because I don't want the help. I gave my very last dollar to the cabbie, so I can't even tip him.

"Just stack it up here," he says quietly. "And you can fetch it whenever you're ready."

"Oh, okay?" I say, getting the feeling that I've missed something. "But I have a key to Neil's place, so I can take it upstairs now. He's probably home already."

He nods stoically. "Mr. Drake is at home. And his mother is visiting."

"His *mother*," I echo. I glance helplessly at all my worldly possessions in trash bags and a cardboard box advertising cheap vodka.

I want to die.

"You can fetch this later, if you wish," Miguel repeats. "I would put it in the package room for you."

"Oh God, *thank you*," I gasp. He's saving me right now. What a guy. "I owe you big. Thank you so much."

He nods once.

"Neil's mother," I breathe. "On a scale of one to ten, how terrifying is she?"

At first, I don't think he's going to answer. He's too discreet, and I'm putting him in a terrible position by asking. I don't even live here.

"She's an eight," he whispers.

Gulp.

"And a half."

"God. Really?" I hiss.

Instead of answering, he marches toward the elevator to summon it for me, pressing the button firmly.

Either button-pushing is a service that rich people enjoy, or he's trying to get rid of me. It could really go either way.

"Thanks again!" I call as the elevator arrives.

He gives me a salute as the doors close.

I fluff my hair in the reflective brass doors as the car

ascends. I'm wearing jeans, damn it. But at least they're my *good* jeans.

I'd happily skip this meet-the-parent thing entirely. But I have practice in an hour, and my Brooklyn Hockey ID is in Neil's apartment. So *this* Mrs. Cornelius Drake is about to meet another Mrs. Cornelius Drake whether I want to or not.

The elevator doors burp me out on the sixth floor before I'm ready. I unlock the front door and hear Neil's voice and then footsteps approaching the foyer. "Hi," Neil says with a tight smile. "My mother is here."

"Oh, is she?" I ask in a clear, sweet voice. "How lovely."

Neil quirks an eyebrow. I must not be a very good actor.

"Come and meet her," he whispers as he removes my coat. "She has a lot of opinions, but she's seventy-five percent harmless."

I drop my voice to a whisper. "That means she's twenty-five percent deadly. Got it."

With a chuckle, he slips his hand into mine, as if that's something we do.

And I realize this is it—our first big performance.

I'm so not ready.

Nevertheless, Neil draws me toward the living room. "Charli, this is my mother, Paloma. Mom, this is Charli. My wife."

Breathe, I remind myself as I smile at the woman who's perched so regally on the world's most uncomfortable sofa.

"Hello, darling," she says with a forced smile. Her eyes are the same hazel as Neil's. But not as warm.

"Hello," I echo. "You look just like your daughter." The resemblance is downright uncanny. Like Neil's younger sister, Mrs. Drake has honey-gold streaks in her brown hair, aggressive cheekbones, and the cunning hazel eyes of a sly fox.

Now they widen in surprise. "You know Paisley?"

"We've met," I say carefully. "Boarding school." *And I've been avoiding her ever since.* "I went to Draper on a sports scholarship," I explain. "She was on the soccer team, if I recall."

Might as well get that out there—I was the scholarship kid that never fit in. But at least we won the Northeast Hockey Championship two of the four years I was there.

"Where are you from?" Mrs. Drake asks.

Another fun question. "Philly. Not the nice part, either." This comes out sounding a little curt. It's a reflex born of having people judge me.

"I see." She tilts her head, as if analyzing this new bit of information. "And what do your parents do?"

"What parents? I haven't seen either one in years." I probably wouldn't even recognize my father. But I keep that detail to myself.

"That could change," she says airily.

"Not likely." I don't even know why she'd say such a thing.

"Charlotte," she says, and I wonder if she googled me, or if my real name was just a lucky guess. "People behave strangely around money."

"I really wouldn't know."

Neil chuckles. He sits down on a sort of chaise thing that looks more comfortable than it is. Then? He tugs my hand until I'm seated on his thigh, like a little girl visiting Santa at the mall.

We are the least convincing couple in the world, as I predicted. It's a nice thigh, though. And when he parks a warm hand on my lower back, I enjoy the calming presence.

"Money makes everything weird," Paloma says.

"You must be right, because Neil's uncle burst a gasket over my sudden appearance in Neil's life."

There's another small sound of amusement from Neil. And his thumb traces a lazy arc across my back, which I really should not be enjoying.

"Indeed," Paloma sniffs. "Neil's uncle had his sense of humor surgically removed sometime before puberty. And his son is just as bad."

Interesting. "They sound like a lot of fun. Remind me not to invite them over for cocktails the next time Neil and I are entertaining."

This is the first time in my life I've ever used *entertaining* as a verb. I sound like a twat right now. I flick a glance at Neil, to see how I'm doing. He grins at me.

"It's their loss, really," I continue. "I make a nice margarita."

His mother gives me a fox-like smile. "You'll have to meet them both, though. By virtue of marrying my son, you're the newest voting member of the Drake Foundation board of directors."

"So I heard. But I don't know anything about the foundation, so I plan to vote for anything that Neil votes for. Unless he votes to have mushrooms on pizza. Those are a hard no."

I'm rambling now, because playacting doesn't come easily to me. But Neil's mom doesn't seem to mind. "Perhaps there's a charity you'd like to support," she says. "A cause that's meaningful to you personally. If you think of something, send me the details, and I'll do any necessary research."

"All right." I lick my lips nervously. I really need to get out of here, and I have the perfect excuse. "Sorry," I say, standing up suddenly. "If you'll excuse me, I have to get to practice. And I'm sure you'd like to visit with your son."

I escape to the bedroom. That had not been an easy few minutes. I'd never wanted to meet Neil's mother, and I sure as hell never wanted to meet her as his *wife*.

Jesus. This was never going to work. I should just tell Neil that our charade is a non-starter.

Then again, I just told my brother I was giving up my apartment.

Shit.

I get down on the floor and do a series of cat and cow yoga stretches, ending up in down dog. It calms me a little bit. I can hear the murmur of Neil's voice in the living room, and it calms me down even further.

Standing up, I grab my ID and my gym bag. As I cross the

apartment, headed for the door, my body language tries to convey how busy I am. But not too busy to stop and give Neil's mother a smile that attempts to look presentable. "It was lovely to meet you Mrs. Drake."

"Call me Paloma," she says. "Will I see you at the Ones and Twos benefit?"

"That's the diabetes fundraiser I mentioned," Neil says.

"I believe you will," I say as cheerfully as I can. Not that I'm looking forward to it.

"What will you be wearing?" she asks.

"*Mother*," Neil warns. "Charli doesn't have to clear her wardrobe choices with you."

Her smile is feral. "Of course not. But I'm sure she wants to look lovely by your side. It's not easy being a Drake. People will tear her down just for sport."

"I have no doubt. But it's handled. Thank you. Now I've really got to run." I grab my coat.

Neil follows me into the foyer. "Shall we dine out tonight, sweetie? There's a Turkish place on John Street that I like. And I'm leaving on a road trip tomorrow, so it's kind of our last chance for a while."

"Sure," I agree quickly. "Can I wear jeans? And can you wait until eight? You might need calories before then."

His eyes warm. "It's fine. The place is casual, and I'll snack. But Charli? Didn't you say you had to take your All-Stars medal to the rink for pictures tonight?"

I freeze, my coat half on. "Oh, sh… sugar."

Neil smiles after me as I run for the bedroom to find it in my suitcase.

When I return, he's standing just shy of the foyer, in view of his mother. He catches me there, straightening my coat and smoothing the collar down, as if I'm his pet.

Then? He leans in and kisses me softly at the corner of my mouth.

I forget how to breathe.

"Goodbye," he whispers before taking a step backward. "Have a good practice. Mow 'em down, wifey."

I give him a look that's so flustered he laughs. "Thanks," I stammer. And then I get the hell out of there, because practice starts very soon.

What a stressful half hour that was, I decide as I jog down the sidewalk after a short elevator ride.

Luckily, my five-minute commute to the rink is pretty sweet. I only have to jog a few seconds before I'm turning the corner onto Hudson Avenue, in view of the Brooklyn Hockey headquarters.

This fake marriage thing has its ups and downs, that's for damn sure.

THIRTEEN

THINK AGAIN

Neil

That evening I text Charli the address of the restaurant. And when she walks in at eight, I'm already waiting at a table.

She looks agitated, and it's not hard to guess why. "How was practice?" I ask as she slides into her chair. "Did your teammates give you a hard time?"

"Practice was crazy, and the girls were relentless." Her gym bag lands with a thunk beside her chair.

I push a little dish of roasted chickpeas toward her. "My teammates were pretty damn nosy, too."

"I bet. Mine were awful." She pops a chickpea into her mouth. "They were *full* of questions."

She lifts her green eyes to mine, and for a second, I can't remember what we were talking about. This happens sometimes when Charli gives me her full attention. I get a little lost, thinking about how much I need to lean in and kiss that sassy mouth.

"You don't have to worry, though. I said as little as possible," she says.

"What did you give 'em?" I ask, helping myself to another bean. "Did you tell them I woke up in a clip-on tie?"

"No!" She looks scandalized. "I'm not sharing *any* details."

"Nothing?" I don't even understand. "How'd you get away with that?"

"Like I always do. By refusing to answer questions about my private life and changing the subject. That almost made it worse, you know? The first time they get me alone, they'll pounce. But I know they'd never sell pictures to the tabloids, or anything."

"Eh, don't worry," I say, looking away to break the spell she has on me. "The media will forget about us in a blink. The news trucks were gone, right?"

"Yes," she agrees, laying her napkin in her lap.

"So... What did your friends want to know?"

"You don't want to hear it," she says as a waiter drops off a glass of red wine along with an appetizer tray full of stuffed grape leaves and hummus. "Oh, wow. This looks amazing."

"Dig in." I grab a stuffed grape leaf.

"Isn't this yours?" She points at the glass of wine in front of her.

"Nope. I ordered it for you." I rarely drink unless it's a very special occasion or I'm eating a perfect steak.

"Oh." Her cheeks turn pink. "Thanks. You're going to spoil me."

I shrug, although spoiling her is exactly my goal. Charli should feel a little spoiled for putting up with my bullshit. "Dish, girl. Who is giving you shit? My money is on Fiona. Oh —and Sylvie. Because Anton is hounding me."

She smiles into her wine glass. "Of course, they're the ringleaders. I have a long history of not sharing, though. I'm a tight-lipped friend."

I nudge her knee under the table with mine. "Is that so?"

The chuckle she lets out is low and sexy. "I'm not a sharer. What can I say? Maybe you picked the right fake wife."

"Of course, I did." She glances up quickly, and I feel like someone socked me in the solar plexus. Bringing Charli to a candlelit restaurant was probably a mistake. It puts me in the mood to crank up Barry White's "Love Serenade" and *take it all off*, as the great man said. "What do they want to hear, anyway?" I take a gulp of cold water. Maybe it will cool me off.

"Mostly they want to hear about your dick."

I almost spray the table. "What?" I choke. "Really? Who asked about my dick?"

"Why? Do you want a list of interested parties for after the divorce?"

I blink. *"No,* Charli. I was just trying to picture..." *A whole room full of women hearing that I couldn't close the deal.* "I thought a women's locker room would be, uh, less raunchy than ours."

"Think again," she says. "It's probably worse."

"Huh. Here I was picturing beauty tips and hair-braiding."

Charli rolls her eyes. "Nice. A sexist joke for the little woman. That's the thanks I get for my discretion."

"So you *didn't* describe my manhood to all the Bombshells?"

"Please. You know I wouldn't do that. Besides, I wasn't taking notes."

"Good thing," I mumble, shoving a stuffed olive in my mouth.

"Neil." Charli peers at me over her wine glass. "The fact that we passed out before we could make even *more* bad choices is honestly a blessing. You aren't still obsessing about that night, are you?"

"A little," I admit.

"God, why?"

Isn't it obvious? "First of all, there's the missed opportunity to add you to my list of very satisfied customers..."

Charli looks heavenward.

"And then..." I hesitate, because there is such a thing as oversharing with your crush.

"What?" she demands.

This is something I don't talk about if I can help it. But she asked. "Vascular issues can be, uh, a side effect of diabetes."

Charli blinks. "No way."

"It's true."

"Oh, for sure. But you do *not* have vascular issues. You are the healthiest person I know. Any guy who drinks half a bottle of whiskey is going to peace out before or even *during* the action."

I busy myself with some hummus on a wedge of pita bread. "I don't usually drink hard alcohol, so I wouldn't know."

"Oh, Neil." Charli's grin starts small, but then takes over her whole face. And she's so pretty when she smiles. "As someone who has had more than her share of disappointing sex, I can *assure* you it's common. Possibly epidemic, especially among the losers I encountered during college."

"Huh." There's a lot to unpack in that statement.

The waiter picks that moment to set a huge platter of food between us. "Here we are. Döner kabob, which is lamb and beef. Also, chicken kabob, grilled meatballs, grilled octopus, pilaf, and baba ganoush."

My mouth waters. "Thank you."

He walks away, and Charli's eyebrow practically disappeared into her hairline. "Wait. You ordered for both of us? Is that what husbands do?"

"Yes." I pick up my phone and prepare my insulin dose. "Ordering for you would be sexist, sure, if I hadn't ordered a variety of things for you to sample. So you can learn what you like for next time."

She looks down at the succulent dishes before us. "Fine. I'll allow it. But only because this looks so flipping good."

"Go on." I tap an insulin dose into my phone. "Try everything. The white rice is all for you, though. I don't eat it."

"Roger that. Octopus isn't really my thing, either. And I'm still not so sure about eggplant."

"So you've mentioned."

Charli *giggles*. Actually giggles. I didn't even know she was capable of that.

It doesn't last long, because we fall on the food like hungry lions. As it turns out, Charli loves Turkish food. (Although, who wouldn't.) And I enjoy feeding her. That's honestly why I ordered for both of us—so she wouldn't just choose the cheapest thing on the menu.

Together, we eat a lot of shish kabob. "I've got to slow down," Charli says, sitting back in her chair. "But it's so good."

I puff up a little hearing this, although all I did was bring her to a restaurant to let someone else cook for her. "You finish the lamb," I urge, because I can tell it's her favorite. "Or take the rest home for lunch tomorrow. I'll be traveling. Which reminds me..." I dig out my wallet and pass a shiny new credit card across the table. "This is for you."

She picks it up and squints at the front, where her name is engraved. "What's this for?"

"Expenses," I say lightly. "While we're living together."

She slides it back onto my side of the table. "There aren't any expenses. I don't need this. And you'll be pleased to hear that I decided to let go of my apartment in East New York, so I can find something better."

"I *am* pleased to hear that." But I am also stubborn. "Take this," I insist, pushing the card back toward her. "I'm out of town a lot. We'll be like ships passing in the night. But we still need to eat, right? And I buy expensive food for my low-carb diet. So when it's your turn to shop, just use the card and hit up Whole Foods for the good stuff, okay? Don't over-think it. If you don't get around to shopping, that's fine. But just tell me so I can pay Belle Pepper's Delivery Service to do it."

Her expression is scandalized. "You *pay* someone to buy your groceries?"

"You bet. I'm getting home from Minneapolis on Friday evening, and I'll be hungry. So will you, right?"

"Fine. I'll do some grocery shopping," she says quietly, fingering the edges of the card. "Text me your list."

"Thank you. I appreciate you doing me yet another favor."

She gives me a wizened glance over her wine glass. Like she's onto me. "You need anything else while you're gone?"

I shake my head. "Just enjoy the quiet. My meds will be delivered on Thursday, but Miguel stores them for me."

"Speaking of meds..." Charli sets her wine glass down on the table. "Doc Herberts pulled me aside after practice today. He wants to add me to your monitoring team."

"Oh. Sorry." I guess I should have anticipated this. "You can tell him no. The doc watches my numbers, as does Bess." She's my agent, and she lives in the same building.

"I said yes, because I thought it would look bitchy not to." She pulls out her phone. "But if this app beeps, I'll probably just panic. I mean—I can barely keep myself alive, so it freaks me out a little to be responsible for your continued existence."

This makes me smile. "Honestly, it's not a big deal. The app will blow up your phone if I go too low—which means I need glucose. A bad low makes me sleepy and half responsive. But then I drink some juice and I'm fine. In theory, I could lose consciousness and die. But I'm super careful, so you don't have to worry."

"Okay." She doesn't sound convinced. "Your family already hates me for marrying you. I don't want to be the one who gets in over her head and accidentally kills you off."

"There's nothing to it. If I go low, just find me and pour some glucose gel into me. Worst-case scenario—you call 911. But none of that will be necessary. Diabetics existed even before apps were invented, you know? It's a lot of babysitting, if you ask me."

"Okay." She gives me a faint smile.

"You want dessert?" I can't eat it, but she could.

"No way," Charli says, patting her tummy. "I couldn't possibly. Let's get out of here."

I lift a hand to ask for the check.

After dinner, we walk home. Charli does a hilarious impression of her teammates arguing about whether it's bad luck to change the order you tie your skates before a game. "These girls are all smart. But they are superstitious as hell, and sometimes I wonder if they're putting me on."

"Dude," I say gravely. "Screw with that kind of thing at your peril."

"But it doesn't make *sense!*" she yelps. "If superstition mattered, you'd win every game. And nobody can do that."

"Maybe you're to blame," I point out. "Because you're the nonbeliever."

"Seriously? You too? I don't think I would have drunk-married you if I knew you were into the superstitious woo-woo stuff."

I spot a guy hauling ass down the sidewalk towards us, and I wrap an arm around Charli, pulling her into me on instinct. "Hey, watch it," I caution the man. "Where's the fire?"

"Sorry," he mutters before hurrying off again.

Then I realize I'm still holding Charli close. I release her, of course. But it felt so natural. Like we were just a regular couple walking home from dinner.

Weirdly, I don't hate this idea as much as I would have expected. Although Iris kind of broke me. After putting up with all her drama, I told myself I never wanted to be in another relationship. Casual hookups have been my speed for the past year. It works for me.

Or it used to. But it's just dawning on me that my crazy plan to stay married to Charli for a while means no more hookups.

That's going to blow.

But not literally.

"By the way," Charli says, bringing me back to reality. "I hastily packed up my apartment today."

"Into several trash bags and a box," I add. "Miguel delivered them after my mother left."

Charli groans. "Classy, right? Sorry."

"Who cares? At least you got out of that shithole. The landlord should have paid *you* to live there."

She makes a noncommittal noise. "I'll have to start looking around in a few weeks. It's hard to find an apartment."

"I wouldn't know."

She looks up at me. "Wait. How *did* you find your place? People say nobody ever moves out of that building."

"They sometimes do."

"So you just got lucky? Because apparently Tank and Bess had to buy their place in one hour or risk losing it."

I hesitate, because the story suddenly seems a little outlandish. "There was no luck involved, actually. I had my realtor call everyone in the building and offer them a premium price to move out. The previous owner of my unit wanted to move to Manhattan. So I paid him an extra half million to leave."

Charli makes a gagging sound. "You paid a half million *dollars* more than it was worth?"

"Not exactly," I say defensively. "Having that place was worth that much to me."

"God, rich people are weird."

I poke her in the hip as we wait for the light to change. "You like me anyway."

"Says who?"

I chuckle. "Need any help hunting for a new apartment?"

"From you? No."

I just laugh.

Everything is copacetic until bedtime. But once again, falling asleep in a bed with Charli is hard.

Literally.

She's lying beside me, smelling like freshly washed hair and pure girl.

I keep my eyes trained on the ceiling, where I can't catch a glimpse of her bare shoulders with all those freckles I'd like to nibble. And I can't see the press of her breasts against the fabric of the soft, stretchy tank top she sleeps in.

Although I can see it in my mind. And since I have a great imagination, I can also see my hands lifting that tank over her head...

Okay, nope. This is torture. I'm going to lie here in a state of distress every night, losing sleep.

My game might even suffer. If coach asks me why I'm so distracted, I don't even know what I'll say. *My fake wife's real tits are driving me insane.*

But this is what I signed up for. There's nobody to blame but me.

The tent pole in my pants would embarrass me, except that Charli is already breathing evenly beside me. She's drifting off to sleep, while I lie here struggling to calm myself down.

It's going to be a long night.

FOURTEEN

NIGHT, KITTEN

Charli

As I often do, I wake up suddenly, as if someone just shook me from a dream. I lift my head to get my bearings. I'm in Neil's bed, and it's still dark.

Quiet and safe, I tell myself. *Everything is fine.*

Except... hang on. Neil is missing. I'm the only one in this bed.

That's odd.

I lay still for a moment, listening to the relative silence of his apartment. This is still New York City, so the silence isn't complete. I can hear the distant sound of a truck rumbling down a nearby street.

But when the truck's engine noise dies down, I hear another sound. A brief moan.

Still half asleep, I sit up in bed. Dr. Herberts had startled me with his request to put me on Neil's blood-sugar patrol. What do I know about Neil's metabolism?

I slide off the bed and sleepily try to discover where he's gone. I start for the kitchen, but the door to the en suite bathroom is slightly ajar and light spills from the gap.

Then I hear the shower. Who takes a shower in the middle of the night?

When I spy Neil's naked body through the cracked-open door, my breath seizes. He's in the shower all right—water raining down on his muscular back, one colorfully tattooed arm braced against the tile wall.

His other hand is wrapped around an ambitious erection. Which he's stroking. Rhythmically.

All the air whooshes from my body. *Lorrrrd.* In my twenty-four years, I've never seen such an erotic sight. My eyes are everywhere at once—on his muscular ass as it moves each time he thrusts. On the powerful flex of his forearm as he strokes. And on his grimacing face as he reaches for his own pleasure.

I'm sort of lost in my own shock until he straightens up suddenly. I freeze, panicked that he's about to turn around and catch me staring.

But that's not what happens. He reaches for my bottle of conditioner, squirts a white stripe of it onto his hand and then goes back to stroking himself lustily. "*Fuckkkk,*" he groans.

The sound of his voice raises goosebumps on my body.

And then Neil lets out a deep gasp, throws his head back, and paints the wall with his release, while I tremble and stare. He groans, his stroke slowing, his forehead coming to rest against his forearm on the tile.

I exhale shakily—like a person who just stepped off a roller coaster. And somehow I find the self-control to back away from the door. I scoot quickly toward the bed and slide back in, face down, heart thumping.

My nipples are hard, and my body feels loose and hungry. I press my nose into the starchy-clean pillowcase and try to slow my pulse. I shouldn't be so turned on right now. And I definitely shouldn't have watched.

Get a grip, Charli. I can't lust after my fake husband. That's just bad news.

Luckily, Neil takes a good ten minutes to finish his shower and dry himself off, while I lie still and play dead.

But the eventual sound of his footsteps padding across the carpet toward the bed makes my heart flutter again. The mattress is such high quality that I barely feel it depress under his weight. It doesn't matter, though. I sense him over there. The sound of his satisfied sigh brings my goosebumps back. And the heat of his body reaches mine—even if it's only imaginary.

And now I have a *very* detailed mental movie of Neil Drake III stroking himself. And I know the gravelly sound he makes when he comes.

Damn it all. I may never sleep again.

———

"Morning," Neil says cheerfully seven hours later.

"M-morning," I stammer, walking into the living room where Neil is seated in the middle of the rug, looking edible in nothing but a pair of sweatpants.

"You look a little wrecked," he says, having no idea that the sight of his happy trail is making my mouth dry right now.

"Uh…" *Pull yourself together, Higgins.* "Mornings, you know?"

I'd been awake for hours last night listening to Neil sleep, fighting off the craving to roll onto his side of the bed and climb onto his hot body.

Meanwhile, he wears the relaxed smile of a sexually satisfied guy who got a better night's sleep than I did. "That's why I pack ahead of time."

"Pack?"

"For my road trip." He points at his suitcase near the door.

"Right. Road trip," I echo. "Don't you need to put a suit on?" Preferably immediately?

"Yup. Car comes in fifteen. You finished in the bathroom?"

Finished. Bathroom. Nnngh. When I'd brushed my teeth a few minutes ago, I could swear the air had still been scented with my conditioner.

I swallow hard. "All finished."

"Cool." Neil reaches out to stretch his hamstrings one more time, before hopping up to get ready to leave. "Make yourself at home, doll."

"*Neil*," I argue reflexively. "We agreed you wouldn't call me that."

"I was teasing, wifey. But I still need a good nickname for you, don't you think?"

"Not really," I grumble, too tired to play along.

"We'll workshop it. Have a great game on Friday, if I don't catch you beforehand. Flights out of Chicago tend to get delayed."

"Have a great trip," I manage.

"Thanks!" On his way out of the room he stops, pulls me into a quick, hard hug and then walks off, nonchalant.

I let out a shuddery breath and wonder what the hell is wrong with me.

With Neil gone, life gets a little easier. Staying alone in this apartment makes me feel like a queen. The first night I play some music on Neil's kickass sound system while I eat leftover Turkish food on a comfortable stool at the kitchen counter.

Afterwards, I retreat to Neil's bed, propping myself against a decadent pile of dove-gray pillows, and turn on his TV. I tune into his game against Minnesota to check the score.

And there he is, charging after the puck, passing back and forth to Castro. Deep in the first period, the score is 1-0 in Brooklyn's favor.

Neil is a talented winger who averages just under one point a game. Last year there'd been an article describing his skill as a sniper, giving him the nickname "magic hands." His teammates had teased him about it for days.

He's a dedicated player. Almost as dedicated as I am. It's the one thing we have in common.

There's an offsides call in the game, and play is stopped. The camera zooms in on Neil's face as he gets into position for a faceoff. His expression is earnest and watchful, his eyes clear.

And sexy.

He's also sweaty.

Fuck.

I've spent the whole day trying not to think about last night, how devastating Neil is when he's turned on. And now I'm watching his game in his bed thinking lustful thoughts about him.

Who's the creeper now? Me. That's who.

I change the channel. In fact, I change it several times. But it's hard to concentrate on a police drama or a singing competition when there's a hockey game on.

My phone lights up with the Bombshells' group chat.

Fiona: OMG Neil! Great goal! His wife must be so proud!

I groan, but I'm already grabbing the remote and turning back to the game so I can catch the replay.

It really was a great goal—he'd shot it from a wicked distance at a tricky angle. I watch the play in slo-mo and listen to the commentators chattering about Neil's speed and form.

Yup. Great form. Unfortunately, I know more about his *form* than I ever have before. And I'm a big fan.

On the screen, his teammates pat him on the butt and congratulate him. Giving up the pretense of watching something else, I settle in to watch the game. Brooklyn hangs onto their 2-0 lead until they give one up in the third period. But a win is a win.

There are only seconds left on the buzzer when I hear the chime of a different buzzer. It's the doorman, calling upstairs. That's odd. I pause the TV to get up and answer it.

"Sorry for the late interruption, Mrs. Drake," Miguel says. My brain hops the tracks for a moment, because I can't believe he's referring to me. "It's *Higgins*," I insist. "I'm not... changing my name." The correction comes out sounding a little sharp. But I can't have people referring to me as Mrs. Drake. That's just crazy talk.

"Apologies, Ms. Higgins," Miguel says carefully. "But there is a messenger here with documents for Mr. Drake. Can I send him up? He needs a signature."

"Yes, of course," I say quickly. "And thank you again for your help yesterday. You saved my butt."

"It's my pleasure," he says smoothly before disconnecting.

I grab Neil's bathrobe off the back of the bathroom door and throw it on as I head for the foyer. I open the door for the messenger, and he barely spares me a glance. "Sign here, please."

When I hand back the pen, he waits a beat. I realize that he's waiting for a tip. But I do not have any cash. Like *none*. I'd spent the last of my cash tips on groceries earlier. I'm broke until payday tomorrow, and even then, I won't be able to make a withdrawal until my deposit clears.

After an awkward moment, the guy pockets his pen and turns away, miffed.

I get it. This is a luxury building. At nine thirty on a Wednesday night, a typical resident would eagerly hand over a fat tip to receive... whatever is in this thick envelope.

What is in this thing, anyway?

I carry it back to bed with me, tucking myself in while still wearing Neil's bathrobe.

It smells like his aftershave, and I should probably take it off. I have got to stop thinking about how good Neil smells and how hot he is. Lustful thoughts are like a deep crevice—if I fall in, it will be tricky to claw my way out.

I pick up my phone to text my husband. *First of all congrats on that fab goal! Very exciting. IDK if you were expecting any deliveries but a messenger just showed up with a fat envelope for you. Let me know if I should do anything with it.*

I toss down the phone and get ready for bed, having done my wifely duty. I don't expect an answer, because the Bruisers will be busy celebrating their win.

The phone rings when I'm tucking myself in again.

"Hi, babycakes," he says right into my ear. It sounds weirdly intimate, but maybe that's because I'm in his bed.

"Babycakes?" I ask with more snark than I really feel. His voice is sexy. It just is.

"I'm still trying out nicknames," he explains. "I can't keep calling you 'wifey.'"

"No, you really can't. Nice goal, by the way."

"You watched my game, huh?"

My cheeks heat. "I've already seen everything on Netflix. I thought this envelope that was delivered might be important. There's no name on it, just an address." I reel off the street number on Park Avenue.

"Eh. That's from the Drake Foundation. Probably a list of the charities my uncle wants to fund."

"Do you need me to open it? Why would they send you something when you're out of town?"

"They sent it *because* I'm out of town." There's more bitterness in Neil's voice than I've ever heard before. "It's just more politics."

"You need me to do anything?"

"Nah. I'll deal with their bullshit when I get back."

"Has he done anything else?" I hear myself ask. "Will he really try to punish you just for marrying me?"

"He might, sugarpop," Neil says calmly. "But I don't care anymore. I'm tired of playing his games."

"Well, that's a drag. I was kind of hoping the packet was from our new lawyer. How's that coming along?"

"I interviewed two lawyers," Neil says. "Didn't like either one. But I promise this is at the top of my list. What we really need is a recommendation. Do you know anyone who's divorced?"

I snort. "Sure. Every member of my extended family who ever got married. But those guys use the kind of lawyer that hangs billboards on the highway. Not exactly the smart, discreet person you're looking for."

Neil laughs like I'm joking.

"Hey, you didn't text me your shopping list," I point out.

"You're right. You want me to just have some stuff delivered?"

"No, I'll handle it." If I'm going to mooch off this man for a while, the least I can do is fetch the groceries. And I'm definitely mooching off of him, because I am broke as fuck. "Just tell me what to buy. As far as I can tell, your diet is brown rice, avocados, veggies, and steak."

"That's fairly close, but I'll send you a list. Oh, and don't forget about your appointment with Vera on Friday. She's bringing over some dresses for the benefit."

"Oh," I say in a flat voice. I'd managed to forget about the damn benefit. "Right. Vera."

"I'll text you the details again."

We hang up. He texts me back right away, but it's not a calendar notification.

Night, pumpkin.

Night, sugar face.

Night, kitten.

Ooh! The last one works right? I think I found it!

I send back a gif of a roaring tiger.

See? he replies. *It's a keeper.*

I'm smiling when I put my phone down on his bedside table. Then I roll onto my side and try not to think about how the bed smells like him.

It won't lead me to a restful night of sleep, that's for damn sure.

FIFTEEN

A BAD BOY LIKE NEIL

Charli

The next day I do Neil's shopping after work. Sure enough, his list is all lean proteins and whole grains. He specifies brand names, and I try not to look at the prices.

But nobody should pay $22.99 for a piece of fish. That's just wrong.

When the three-digit total comes up at the checkout, I hand over Neil's credit card. There's no way I would shop here for myself.

That evening when I go to practice, the girls are still clucking around me like hens. None of them is satisfied with the vague things I'd told them about me and Neil.

"So," Samantha says as I'm drying off after my shower. "Are you still married to the hottest billionaire hockey player in the world?"

I sigh. "Yup."

They all titter.

"Do you have to run off now?" Fiona asks. "We're heading over to the Colorbox for manicures."

I hesitate. The Colorbox is a nail salon that Rebecca Rowley

Kattenberger owns. That's right—she owns two major league hockey teams and a nail salon. She is a study in contrasts.

"Well, the Bruisers are traveling," I admit. "I'm staying at Neil's place alone."

Fiona hoots, and everyone else in the room is staring at me with hearts in their eyes.

"No kidding?" Sylvie squeals. "You moved in with him?"

"Don't get excited. It's just temporary," I say quickly. And I suppose I can't avoid explaining the situation. At least partly. "I'm having some trouble with my apartment. Neil thinks I should find a better one. He's offered to help me. And in return, I'm attending a couple of functions with him."

Sylvie's eyelashes flutter. "As his date?"

"Yes."

"As his *wife?*" Fiona presses.

"Sort of. Didn't I tell you it's complicated?"

"You don't tell us *shit*," Samantha says. "It's why we keep asking you questions. And we won't stop until you spill."

I was afraid of that.

"Come get your nails done with us," Fiona says. "The Colorbox is a goddamn confessional. You won't even feel a thing."

"She's right," Sylvie adds. "When you're getting a hand massage and a chocolate-covered strawberry, it's easier to tell the truth."

"Wait. Chocolate-covered strawberries?" I ask.

"Get it, girl!" calls Samantha from across the room. "This is what you've been missing."

"I'll be there," I promise. "Give me fifteen minutes."

First, I have a quick meeting with Dr. Herberts, which was my idea, because if Neil ever has trouble in the night—with his diabetes, not his erection—I need to know what to do.

Doc gives me a quick rundown on how the monitoring app works, and then I'm on my way out the door with my gym bag slung over my shoulder.

But as soon as I step outside, a bulky form looms in my peripheral vision. Luckily, I have street smarts and an athlete's reflexes, and I leap out of the way before he can block my path.

"Jesus. Calm down. It's just me," says my cousin Robert gruffly.

That is *not* a comfort. Anger rises through my chest as I glare up at him. "You are literally the *last* person I need to see right now," I growl. "You *stole* from me!"

"Simmer down. You and I are due for a talk." He crosses his arms and leans against the side of the brick building. "And you're gonna wanna hear what I have to say."

"*Unlikely.* Unless you've come to give me back my cash and the extra blank check you lifted. Where's Dennis?"

He shrugs. "Went back to Philly like a pussy when his sister told him to scram."

"But you didn't," I hiss. "Better get gone, or the cops will toss you from that apartment. I'm out of there." Not that I've actually made the call to my landlord yet. But Robert doesn't know that.

"Dennis said that," he says mildly. "But you and I are not done with that place. Don't give it up."

"Too late. It's a hole, anyway."

"It's trashy," he agrees with a dark-eyed smirk. "Then again, so are you."

My stomach plummets, even though I've been called worse. In fact, I've been called worse by people more closely related to me. Nothing Robert says should matter, but it does. His branch of the family tree is the worst of the bunch. I hold my breath as he pulls a piece of paper out of his pocket, unfolds it, and hands it to me.

It's a paystub. *My* paystub. As soon as I see it, I go cold inside. The name of the business is listed up top—*Bad Boy Enterprises*. It's the parent company of the strip club where I'd worked for a few weeks. Anyone with a Google search bar could make the connection.

I swallow hard and wonder what this means. That job is my biggest secret, not because I'm actually ashamed of it, but because of the morality clause in my contract with the Bombshells. I thought I'd gotten away with it. Nobody has ever connected me with that job.

Until now.

At least I've got excellent control over my emotions. My moment of horror and shock is well hidden. "*This* is your smoking gun?" I ask with a casual head toss. "A paystub? So what? I worked at one of these bars for a couple of weeks. As a *bartender* by the way. Not as a dancer. Not that it's any of your business. I don't have the first idea why you think this is important."

"Don't be dense," he grunts. "Your name is in the fucking newspaper this week. You and that rich boy?"

My lungs collapse. "You shouldn't believe everything you read."

"Honey, I *know*. *You* married to a billionaire?" His laugh is mean. "That's rich. Just because you get your picture taken with a fat cat in Vegas don't make you a queen. You're still just a slut from Philly. We both know it."

I see where he's going with this, and I really don't want tomorrow's headline to say that Neil Drake married a stripper.

Robert is already tucking the paystub into his pocket with a smug grin. "Help me, Charli. I need a favor."

"Seriously?" I demand. "Dennis put me into debt with his gambling. I have no money. You already took it. I literally have no cash until payday. I spent the last of it on some groceries."

"Not my problem." He shrugs. "I need you to make the next rent payment on that apartment. Call your landlord back and tell him you want to keep the place a little while. I'm trying to pull a few things together. I need a place to crash while I do it."

A nauseous wave rolls through me. I have no idea what "pull a few things together" means. But it's nothing good.

My mind whirls while I try to decide how to play this. I'm not naïve. Nobody negotiates successfully with a blackmailer. On the other hand, I have a couple of things going for me. First, I've got no binding lease on that apartment. That's why I rented the dump in the first place—it's low commitment. I could pay one more month's rent and then stop when I'm ready.

Plus, I don't need much time to get out of this pickle. Neil and I will be divorced. In a couple months, my brief stint at the strip club will cease to interest Neil or to the Drake family empire.

Then I call Robert's bluff. I'll tell him that it doesn't matter who knows about that job. It might even be true—the Bombshells management has proven that they don't scare too easily.

"Okay," I decide. "I'll pay next month's rent after I get my paycheck." My bank account will hate me, of course. "But if you *touch* my money again, it won't matter. The rent check will bounce. Can't get blood from a stone."

He gives me a menacing grin. "That's a good girl, Charli."

"I don't want your praise. I want you out of my sight before I change my mind."

"Fine." He gives me an even sleazier grin. "Enjoy chumming up to your bigshot friends." Then he finally goes.

Everything inside of me sags. I hate Robert. I hate my family for being such assholes. I'm so flattened by him that I almost turn right around and go back to Neil's place instead of heading for the Colorbox.

But Fiona is already texting me, wondering where I am. I point my feet in the direction of the salon and give myself a pep talk. *Keep marching, Higgins.* One foot in front of the other. Minute to minute, day to day. Game to game.

That's how I've always survived. Looks like today won't be any different.

The salon is lit up, and through the windows, I see my team-mates draped over the pedicure chairs and the sofas.

After I push the door open, I feel a little bit better. These people are my real family. So long as I don't get booted off the team, I belong with them.

"Charli!" Fiona calls from one of the manicure tables. "Pick a color and get over here."

I'm not really in the mood to sit still for a manicure. But then I remember that I promised to go with Neil to his benefit on Sunday night, and all the women there will probably have killer nails.

A frisson of anxiety runs through me at the thought of standing beside Neil in a ballroom. Did I really think I could pretend to be his *wife?*

What a ridiculous idea. No wonder Robert didn't believe it.

I select a demure shade of rose polish that won't be too garish against my pale skin and give it a shake. Then I sit down in the chair beside Fiona.

"Hello," says the manicurist. She sets a shallow bowl in front of me and gently guides my fingers in for a soak. "Let me finish Fiona while you soak."

"Thank you."

"Jersey number?" she asks.

"Fifteen."

She picks up a clipboard and marks me down. The only reason I can come here at all is that Rebecca provides us with one free manicure and pedicure service each month, including a generous tip. The people who work in this salon are always happy to see us.

I'm usually too busy to enjoy the perk. I've only been here three times in two seasons.

"All right," Fiona barks. "Tell me the real story. What the hell is going on with you and Neil?"

I let out a sigh. "It's exactly what everybody thinks. We got drunk. We got married. We woke up horrified."

"Whoa." Fiona looks up into her manicurist's eyes. "Dani, this conversation is in the vault."

Dani blinks. "I didn't hear a thing. But I hope she keeps talkin'." She gives me a grin. "This is the *best* gossip! I finally got the good table."

I just sigh.

"Can't you get, like, an annulment?" my teammate Samantha asks from the chair on my other side.

"If we'd stayed in Vegas, maybe," I explain. "But now we have to get a divorce."

"Bummer," Fiona says.

"Seriously," I agree. "I truly believed I'd be the only member of my family to never get divorced. But here we are."

My teammate Angelica pipes up from the pedicure chairs, "I can't really picture you married to a man."

"Join the club," I say. "I can't really picture me married to *anyone*."

"Oh, I can," Sylvie argues from her pedicure chair. She's the most romantic among us. "You're fun, you're loyal. You're super-hot."

"Especially when you do your face," Fiona adds. "Wait—did you do the makeup magic that night in Vegas?"

"Yeah. So?"

A low murmur passes through the busy salon.

"That explains so much," Sylvie says. "No man can resist your skills. You did *my* makeup the night that Anton and I hooked up, right? And now we're planning the rest of our lives together."

"Mmm-hmm," Samantha says. "I see a pattern here."

"You guys are bonkers," I mutter as the manicurist begins to work on my cuticles. "And is this really what we should be talking about tonight? We have a game tomorrow. We could be strategizing."

Every woman in the room gives me the side-eye. Someone snorts.

"Take it easy on her, girls. She never comes in here." Fiona lays a manicured hand on mine. "Honey, we never talk shop when we sit in these chairs. This is a gossip-only zone."

"Now you tell me," I grumble.

"So what's Neil like?" Sylvie asks. "We're dying here!"

"Hey, now. I already told you there was nothing between us. And I wouldn't spill even if there was."

"But what's he *like*?" Sylvie presses. "What's with that fancy pad? That place is only a one-bedroom, and it still manages to be bigger than every other apartment, except for Silas and Delilah's."

"Oh." It's not gossip if you're just talking about furniture, right? "His place is great and also terrible. I'm afraid to touch anything because it's probably priceless. And the sofa is too uncomfortable to sit on. That's why we watch TV in bed."

Everybody titters, and I realize that if me watching television with Neil is entertaining, they must just not have a better scandal to chew on tonight.

"Okay, that's dumb," Samantha says. "Wouldn't a bad boy like Neil light the bad furniture on fire and start over?"

"That's not Neil," I say immediately. "He's a bad boy the way nachos are Mexican food—some of the toppings are familiar, but it's still not the real thing."

The whole room erupts with laughter.

"She's right," Sylvie says, coming to my defense. "He's the guy who walks around after the party, making sure all the beer bottles get into the recycling bins."

"He's a surprisingly good dude," I agree. "He's just not *my* good dude. Recent evidence to the contrary notwithstanding."

"I can *totally* see you two as a couple," Sylvie says.

"You are the only one," I mutter.

"Oh, I'm not," she says with a sly smile.

"What does *that* mean?"

She just shakes her head. "I think you two deserve each other. You deserve somebody who will never do..." She waves a hand in the air. "...whatever it is people did to make you so angry. And he deserves somebody who isn't a bullshitter like that awful ex of his."

"What *was* the deal with Iris?" Samantha demands. "What a drip that girl was. Why did she show up in Vegas?"

"Who knows?" I say. "Although, I overheard their fight. Iris was trying to tell him that their separation had been long enough. She said she loved him. And he went all Taylor Swift on her ass. *We are never never getting back together.*"

Honestly, Neil had been uncharacteristically blunt. I'd wanted to cheer. And afterward I'd offered to get him drunk.

The rest is (sordid) history. And that is why I'm sitting here having my fingernails painted in a tasteful color.

As punishments for drunk stupidity go, I've seen worse, I guess. "Thank you," I tell the manicurist. "That is beautiful."

I'm not even lying. It is beautiful. But we all know that it just isn't me.

SIXTEEN

YOU HAVE TO STROKE IT

Neil

Before we go wheels up in Chicago, I take a call from Vera the stylist. "How's my favorite athlete?" she asks playfully. "How's married life treating you?"

"Um, great." Although every time someone asks me that, I feel like a dickhead. Lying all the time is not that much fun. Who knew?

"Your tuxedo shirt is all ready to go. But your wife didn't send me any dress measurements, aside from height and weight. So I'm bringing a lot of different styles for her to try on."

"Oh, sorry," I stammer. "She's probably very busy."

"It's fine," Vera says in a bubbly voice. "Not everyone enjoys measuring her own bust, you know?"

I chuckle along. But I'm asking Charli to step pretty far outside her comfort zone. What if Vera starts asking her a bunch of personal questions? How badly could this go?

We hang up, but I feel uneasy. When our jet reaches the gate at La Guardia, I'm the first one pulling his bag out of the overhead compartment.

"You want to share a car?" Tank asks me.

"Sure," I say, even though I was about to sprint for the taxi line alone. If Vera and Charli are locking horns, I'd like to get home as soon as possible.

"Take me too!" Anton calls as we file off the plane.

"And me!" Newgate calls. "I'll drop you guys off on the way to my place."

"Sure," I say. "But hurry."

Luckily, we snag a minivan yellow cab and pile inside.

"Can't wait to get home to see my girl," Anton says as we approach Brooklyn. "You guys coming to the game tonight?"

"I am," Tank says. "Bess will want me to hold the baby while she takes some pictures."

"I'll go," Newgate says. "I don't have plans. And Drake is in, right, bro? Gotta watch the little woman play?"

"Um…" Am I going to Charli's game? I've been to Bombshells games before, and she's been to one or two of mine. But our schedules rarely line up, so it hadn't occurred to me. "What time does it start?"

"Ask your wife!" Tank snickers.

I can't, though, because I've already sent her two unanswered texts since we landed. *Everything okay with Vera? Or are you throwing darts at our marriage certificate?*

Radio silence.

So I'm a little unnerved when the taxi finally pulls up in front of our building. I'm the first to grab my suitcase out of the back and hoof it into the building.

"See you at the game, Neil! I'll save you some popcorn!" Anton calls.

I slap the elevator button without stopping to give him a snarky response. And two minutes later I'm stepping off onto the sixth floor and hurrying toward my door.

When I step inside, there's nobody in the living room. But Charli's voice floats out from the bedroom. "You have to stroke it," she says. "Make it soft and *lush*. Ooh, that's it!"

"Like this?" Vera asks. "Ohhhh, yes! *Wow*. Oh baby."

"*Just* like that. *Yes!*"

I don't know whether to be really turned on or really confused. I hurry toward the bedroom, where Charli and Vera are both staring into the full-length mirror on my bathroom door.

"Curve it more," Charli says. "And then blend it out."

Vera strokes something against her eyelid. It's... makeup? That makes sense. I think. But I've suddenly lost about half my brain power because Charli is standing before me in nothing but a corset, lace panties, and high heels.

A *corset*. It's made of lace, and it curves saucily over her perfect ass.

I make a noise like "*nnngh*," because how could I not.

Two heads swivel in my direction, and both women straighten up in surprise. "There he is!" Vera hoots. "Welcome home, big guy. I brought over your tuxedo shirt."

With Charli facing me now, I lose even more of my executive function. Her breasts are trying to spill out of the corset's cups. And her eyes are done up in a way I've only seen a couple of times before—with a sultry dark outline that says, "Do me right now, Drake." Her lips are tinted in a bitten color that I just want to taste.

"Fuck me," I whisper to myself. "It's good to be home."

Vera titters. "Say hello to your wife. I'll wait in the living room. Charli has one more dress to try on, and I want to see that shirt on you!"

She hurries out of the bedroom, closing the door and leaving us standing there staring at each other. Charli's cheeks are tinted a bright pink color and not because of makeup.

"This is a warmer welcome than I was expecting," I admit.

"Neil." She rolls her eyes. "I honestly didn't mean to greet you in..." She waves a hand in front of her delicious chest. "Whatever this is."

"That is a goddamn miracle. That's what that is." I take a step toward her. "Can I have a closer look?"

"Not a chance," she says, taking a step backwards. "Let me just put on this last dress."

Yeah, I really should have been here half an hour ago.

"Try on your shirt." Charli waves toward a tuxedo shirt hanging on a metal clothing rack that Vera must have rolled in here.

"You're asking me to strip down," I point out, setting down my suitcase. I toss my suit coat over the end of the bed, and I start in on my buttons.

"That is not what I'm asking." She leans forward (*nnnghh!*) as she steps into a copper-colored dress, then hastily pulls up the fabric, hiding that lingerie miracle from view.

I make quick work of my shirt, tossing it aside. And let's just say it's a good thing poor Vera isn't trying to take my measurements today, because my trousers are suddenly too snug.

Charli slips her arms through the dress's silk armholes. "Would you, um, zip me?"

"Of course. Although I'd rather unzip you."

"Behave," Charli hisses.

I do. Mostly. But first I slip one palm up Charli's back, gathering her hair in my hand and giving it a little tug as I hold it up and out of the way.

Her breath hitches, and goosebumps break across her skin.

My chuckle is deep and dark as I slide the zipper upward through the silk.

"Thank you," she says quickly.

"You're welcome." I put my hands on her bare shoulders and turn her gently around. "Just for the record, I don't mind coming home from a road trip to find you wearing lingerie in my bedroom."

"I got distracted," she sniffs. "Vera and I got to talking about eye techniques."

"With… makeup?" I clarify. "I didn't know you were a makeup guru."

"There's plenty about me you don't know," she says huffily.

"Now put on your penguin shirt. I have to show Vera this dress."

I grab the shirt and follow Charli out of the bedroom. My tongue is practically hanging out. The copper dress dips low in back, and I just want to run my hands all over her exposed skin.

"Wipe off your drool, slugger," Vera says immediately. "That isn't the right dress for her."

"It's the neckline, right?" Charli does a twirl. "This bias cut isn't doing me any favors. And the color is too flat with this hair."

I've never heard Charli talk about fashion before. I didn't know she spoke girly-girl. "I like the dress," I say sadly. "I think it's a winner."

"You'll like the blue one better," Vera says cheerfully.

"Okay. Can I *see* the blue one?" *And the naked moments in between the dresses?*

"Sure, you can. On Sunday night," Charli says. "Vera, a little help with the zipper?"

"I got it," I volunteer.

But Vera is already reaching for it. "It's been fun fitting you, Charli. You have such a great eye. Thanks for the browbone contouring tutorial."

"Anytime." Charli flounces toward the bedroom, and my eyes follow her with an internal whimper.

"Ouch," Vera says after sitting down. "Why do you still own this sofa?"

"That's a fair question." I button the tux shirt, note that it fits fine, and then unbutton it again. "I hate the sofa, but I can't stand to create landfill. Also? I hate shopping and I travel a hundred nights a year."

"Huh," she says. "Why don't I call Housing Works for you, and they'll come and pick it up. You'd get a fat tax deduction."

"Sure? Does your store sell couches?"

"No, sir. You'll have to go to an actual furniture store. Charli would enjoy picking out a new couch."

"She probably wouldn't have time for furniture shopping, either," I reason.

"WRONG!" Charli calls from the bedroom. "I would happily pick out a comfy sectional. And a coffee table that you could actually put your feet on. Maybe a pouf, too."

"What's a pouf?" I ask. "Wait—I don't want to know. Just surprise me."

"Okie doke," Vera says. "Now I'll get my dresses together and head back to Manhattan. I'll put the blue one on your card, Neil."

"And the corset?" I ask, feeling hopeful. "And those fuck-me heels?"

"They *aren't* fuck-me heels!" Charli shouts.

"Are too!" I shout back. I know this because tonight I'm going to be lying in that damn bed thinking about them, wishing someone would fuck me.

Specifically, Charli.

"No comment," Vera says. "I'll show myself out so you two can get reacquainted. It's been a long week apart with that road trip, no? I can only guess what a couple of newlyweds will be up to!"

She'd be right if I had anything to say about it.

Charli emerges from my bedroom a few minutes later, fully dressed in athletic pants and a Bombshells jacket. "I have to leave early for my game," she says. "Georgia wants to have a PR meeting beforehand. Can't imagine why. She already got her All-Star photos."

"Who are you playing tonight?"

"Albany," she growls. "And they're annoyingly good. Solid defense, plus a dangerous sniper."

"You guarding her?" I ask.

"Of course." She leans down to tie her shoes.

"This should be fun." I chuckle. "Hope my seat is right down in front."

Her head swings up. "You're coming to my game?"

"Sure. That's a thing fake husbands do, right?"

She gives a slow blink. "You don't have to, though. I wouldn't be offended."

"It'll be fun," I insist. "It's *hockey*. Duh."

"Okay. Your night off, your choice." She shrugs, picking up her gym bag. "Look, I shopped yesterday afternoon. Let me show you something." She beckons, and then trots into my kitchen.

I follow her like a hungry dog. Although food isn't really what's on my mind.

"See? Your food is here, and I put my things in this drawer." She opens one of the fruit crispers, and I see a couple of apples and some off-brand milk.

The rest of the fridge seems to contain everything on my list. "Thanks?" I'm still a little confused.

"And this is my shelf," she says, opening a cupboard and pointing to a jar of cheap peanut butter and grocery store bread.

I grab the peanut butter and read the label. "You like this stuff? It has added soy oil and sugar. It's not even organic."

"*Neil.*" She grabs it, shoves it back into the cabinet, and opens the adjacent cabinet. "Don't panic, fancy boy. Yours is here."

Indeed, my peanut butter is waiting there. But we still have a problem. "Charli, I didn't mean for you to shop twice. I doubled up on my stuff for both of us. You're supposed to eat whatever you want and put it all on one bill."

"No way." She closes the cupboard firmly. "I can't afford your highbrow stuff, Neil."

When she turns to go, I catch her hand. "Wait a sec. We're not done."

She stares down at our joined hands, then looks up at me. "I don't want to be late."

"I know," I whisper. "But I'm only saying this once. The food in this kitchen is yours to enjoy. I don't want to be bothered segregating the fridge. I'll probably eat your apple or something and then worry the entire Bombshells squad will come for me in my sleep."

She snorts. "Not on a first offense. Touch the oranges, though, and I can't make any promises."

"Ah. Good to know." I give her hand a squeeze, and let it go. "The deal was that you save some money by living here. It's room and board, Charli. Just like college, but with a hotter roommate." I lean against the counter and flex my pecs conspicuously.

She rolls her eyes. "I really have to go, poser. It's game night."

"Knock 'em dead, kitten." I take a step closer and wrap her into a hug.

Charli goes still, and I realize belatedly that we don't do this. *Oops.* But she feels good in my arms.

The truth is I *did* miss her when I was away. This whole fake marriage thing is messing with my head.

I pull back, my hands on her shoulders, and she blinks at me, her eyes wide, her cheeks pink. "You're still wearing the sexy makeup," I point out.

"Until I sweat it off," she whispers. "It won't be sexy then."

"Says you," I whisper back. "Sweating can be *very* sexy, if the timing is right."

Charli's lips part, and her flush deepens. Her shoulders relax under my hands. She licks her lips, and my gaze drops to her mouth. I want to taste her again. I want to savor it this time.

"Got to go," she says abruptly, taking a step to the side. "Toodles, hubby."

She darts out of the kitchen. The front door opens and shuts, and then she's gone.

I stand there like a dope for a beat longer, just staring at the space where she stood before.

SEVENTEEN

WE'RE SOLD OUT

Charli

I walk into the conference room for the pregame PR huddle, expecting to see all my teammates there. But there's only Coach Sasha and Bess Beringer, who helps manage the team. "Wait. Am I in the wrong place?" I ask.

Georgia hustles in behind me. "Not at all," she says. "We need to chat with you for a second."

Oh no. What the hell is wrong? What did Robert *do* to me?

My mind whirls, and I numbly take a seat at the table. I start practicing my speech. *I was just a bartender. Just for a couple weeks...*

"Charli, we just wanted you to be prepared to do the press conference tonight."

I search my brain for understanding and come up blank. "After the game?" I clarify. "But we don't know yet who will score."

"You will," my coach says with a laugh. "You'd better try, anyway. Because I know you, and if your personal life is all you've got to talk about, I fear for those reporters."

"What reporters?" I ask. Our postgame press conferences

are a joke. Sometimes there's only a single journalist there, plus the family members of a few players.

"We're sold out, Charli," Bess says.

"Of *tickets*?" I clarify. We usually play in front of a half-capacity audience.

Bess actually presses her hands together and rolls her eyes toward the ceiling. "O Lord above, may there come a day when my players aren't surprised if we sell out. And if it could happen in my lifetime, I'd be very grateful."

Sasha snorts, and Georgia grins.

"What are you trying to tell me?" I demand. Something's happened, and I am in the dark.

"We sold out of tickets," Georgia says slowly. "Tonight's game will be very well attended. So the postgame press conference should get more attention than usual. And we'll want you to participate, no matter how the game goes."

I finally understand what's going on. And I do *not* like it. "This... The record attendance is because of *me and Neil*? What the actual fuck?"

"This is a good thing," Sasha says quickly. "It's going to be a great game between two stellar teams. And several thousand people are going to discover how much fun women's hockey is."

"Right," I say slowly, because my brain is still playing catch-up. The women in this room think this is a *good* thing. A positive development.

And I just want to smash things.

"You're going to get a lot of playing time," Coach Sasha says.

"I always get a lot of playing time," I point out. "I work hard for it."

"Of course," she says with a smile. "But you'll be starting tonight for sure. We're going to give the crowd what they want."

"Are we?" I yelp. "Because it sounds like you're telling me that somehow marrying a rich dude just made me *twice as inter-*

eaating as I was before. In case you were hoping my game has also gotten twice as flashy since last weekend, I'm going to have to burst your bubble."

"Easy," Bess says with a smile. "We are already fun. We are already fascinating. We are already ass-kickers. Now we just have a few more people to watch us."

"Fine," I grunt. "Can I warm up now?"

"In a second," Georgia says. "Later, in the press conference, I'm going to need you to be full of sunshiny gratitude that all these new fans came out to watch tonight."

Oh boy. "Sunshiny gratitude is not my default setting," I point out. "Tell me exactly what to say."

"Just think—if you score a goal or hold off their sniper for a shutout, this gets easier," Coach Sasha points out.

"Okay." I take that in. "But what if we lose? What if the game goes badly? What the hell am I supposed to be sunshiny about? I mean—I'll say we'll work hard and do better next time. But it's gonna be a pretty short interview. You won't even want me there."

"Oh, yes we will!" Georgia sing-songs. "You have to talk about Neil. Just for a moment."

"I *can't* talk about Neil!" I squeak. "I can't lie to a room full of people about our relationship."

"Don't lie," Bess says. "Yes, you two eloped. Yes, you met right here in this very building. Yes, he's hotter than a Texas day in July. See how easy this is? And if we give this information at the press conference, we're controlling the narrative."

I let out a groan. "You are using my personal life to sell more tickets."

"No, we're *not*," Bess argues. "We didn't ask you to marry Neil. And we didn't alert the media. But they are here anyway, and they are hungry. So you'd better feed them some badass hockey. Because that *is* our job."

I hate it when other people are right. "Fine," I clip. "I will win this game and then I will be sunshiny and make sure everyone loves women's hockey."

"Atta girl," Georgia says. "It's a bit of a pony show," Georgia says. "But it's your pony show."

I take a deep breath and remind myself that my sham marriage is something I've agreed to. I'm going to stay with Neil and save up some money so I can scrape off my awful family and live in a nicer apartment.

Meanwhile, I have a game to win. "If I score a goal, I can talk about that instead of my screwed-up personal life, right?"

"Works for me," my coach says. "Better get changed, then."

I realize the meeting is over, so I make a break for the door.

———

I'm stretching my hamstrings on the bench in front of my stall when the dressing room door bangs open, and Samantha comes through. "Omigod, that crowd is *amazing!*" she gushes.

"Isn't it?" Fiona agrees, tying her skates with quick fingers. "We were born to play in front of that crowd. This is everything."

I grit my teeth and drop into a forward fold, limbering up my back and checking the double knots on my skates at the same time. "We played in front of a crowd at the All-Stars game," I point out to my captain.

"Sure," Fiona agrees. "Where—as you pointed out—the men probably got up to take a piss during the women's events."

I had said that. Sue me.

"Charli, let's go," Fiona says, standing up. "It's time for warmups. You'll see that crowd, and you'll realize this is a good thing."

"I'm still stretching," I grumble.

"You nervous?" Scarlet asks, clipping her goalie mask into place.

"No," I say quickly. "Just trying to take it all in."

After a few more stretches, Coach tells us that it really is time to go. I head for the door and push it open, my teammates on my heels.

On the other side of the door, I'm greeted by a rubber-coated ramp and a few rubber-coated stairs leading down to the rink. The Bombshells' suite of locker rooms is the nicest in the league. But it's bizarrely on the second floor, so we have to descend carefully.

Eighteen months ago, the Bombshells' dressing rooms were built on top of the men's facilities. As usual, women's hockey was literally an afterthought. Even now, we play on the Bruisers' ice when they're done with it at the end of the day.

Nobody wants to hear me say these things aloud, though. We're supposed to be filled with gratitude at the opportunity to be professional athletes.

And mostly I am. I know Rebecca started a women's hockey franchise that is almost guaranteed to lose money for several years—and maybe indefinitely. I *know* I'm one of the fortunate twenty-three women who gets paid (a paltry sum) to play here.

It's just that everything in my life works like this. I grew up sleeping on relatives' sofas and was *grateful* they didn't turn me over to the state. I went to a fancy private high school where I was snubbed by the other girls, but I was very *grateful* to get a top education for free, so long as I kept helping them win hockey games. Ditto college.

I've been an afterthought my whole life. Just once I'd like to be somebody's first choice.

I reach the bottom of the stairs, and the ice door is closed. But hell—I can already hear the crowd through the door. They are *loud*.

Okay. Well. That is pretty wild. I open the door just a crack so I can peek through. And the view causes my breath to stutter in my chest. It's a sea of lavender out there. The Bombshells' fan shop must be picked clean. The crowd is packed with women and also little girls. So many little girls. Some of them are holding lavender pompoms.

"Isn't it wild?" Sylvie says from behind me. "Bess said they did a rush order of merch. It was printed in the Bronx this morning. Hundreds of sweatshirts and jerseys."

"Jesus." Even the topmost row is full.

"Listen up, chickies!" Coach Sasha says. "I've got their game roster, and Reba Hastings isn't on it."

I let out a whoop. "That is good news." She's Albany's dangerous sniper, so this game just got easier.

"Thought you'd enjoy that," my coach says. "I wonder if she's injured."

"Don't tell me," I grumble. "I'd rather not know." It's not like I sit around praying for other women's misfortunes, but I'm pretty happy not to be blocking Hastings tonight.

Coach looks at her watch. Then she steps past me and opens the door. "All right. Let's have a big night."

A tone sounds, signaling the start of warmups. Fiona is the first to step out on the ice.

The crowd *roars*. It's deafening.

"It's a big night here in Brooklyn!" the announcer says in a cheery voice. "Packed house for the Bombshells. Warmups last fifteen minutes. Then we'll have the national anthem sung by Grammy-award winner Delilah Spark…"

Christ. Georgia and the management team pulled out all the stops tonight. I guess the future of women's hockey in Brooklyn will depend on how the game is received by our five thousand new fans.

Cool, cool.

When it's my turn to step onto the rink, I push off and keep my head down. I lengthen my stride to activate my muscles.

The crowd roars, and a ripple of something like excitement rolls through me. I guess I'm not immune.

I take a nice, easy lap and try to tune it out. If I let this bullshit change my game, I'm sunk. When I skate past the penalty box, I see a familiar face out of the corner of my eye.

Neil's sitting beside a bunch of his buddies. They're all decked out in... are those Bombshells jerseys? And every guy is holding a shiny, printed sign. *Let's go Bombshells*, and *Brooklyn Hockey Strong*.

Good lord. The production values are pretty high around here tonight.

I skate a little faster. *Don't screw this up, Higgins*, I coach myself. *Head in the game*. Fiona sends me a pass. I easily flick the puck toward the net, and the crowd roars.

Well, that's trippy. What are they going to do if I score an *actual* goal? Set off fireworks?

Warmups end way too quickly. As I make my way back to the bench, I notice that some of the fans are holding signs, too. One woman's says: *Go Bombshells! (And BTW, does Neil Drake have a brother?)*

"Are you shitting me?" I growl. "Are the fans here for us or for Neil?"

"Who cares," Fiona says, making room for me on the bench.

"I care!" I turn slowly around, looking at the faces in the stands. Then I face my team, and my voice goes high and squeaky. "Do you realize what this means? Do you see what's going on here? The Bruisers play in front of fifteen thousand fans every night. But I had to *drunk-marry* one of them to draw an audience!"

I expect their faces to fall, because my anger frequently lands badly. But Fiona only beams. "We have this chance to show the whole world how awesome women's hockey is. They showed up and bought tickets, Charli. They paid to watch this game."

"Hell, I'd play *topless* if it meant selling out every night," someone else says.

I just groan. "Guys, we *have* to win this thing. We have to dominate. The only thing worse than packing a stadium for the wrong reasons would be losing in it."

"Acknowledged," Fiona says. "We can beat Albany."

My attention turns, as it should, to the opponent's bench. None of them are gazing around at the fans. Their heads are bent together in consultation. They want to win this thing, too.

"All rise for the national anthem!" the announcer calls.

I place my hand on my heart. Even through my chest pad I can feel its rapid thud.

Please, Lord. Let me put up a good showing tonight. I know I shouldn't care that everyone is watching this screwed-up Philly chick hit a puck with a stick.

It's just that everyone is watching.

Note to self—a big crowd fires everyone up. Even your opponent.

The game is a dogfight right from the first puck drop, and Albany is feisty. The first period is a blur whereby we fight to keep the puck in our offensive zone.

I'm skating backward at high speed, listening to Scarlet's chatter from the net as if my life depends on it. "*Samantha—man on! Close it in, girls. Clear it out! Move, Charli!*"

The benefit of having a tough opponent is that there's really no time to think about all the other bullshit in your life. If you don't keep your head in the game, you won't be in the game for very long.

I get in there and fight for it. I get my stick on the puck and move it where it has to go. But it's rough sledding, and by the time my first several shifts are done, a few patterns have emerged.

First, Albany doesn't miss their sniper as much as I'd hoped. They've doubled down on defensive clout and sheer grit.

Second, Albany has replaced its sniper with a hellion. A very small hellion, but still.

"Steady on," Coach Sasha says over my shoulder. "And watch out for number twenty-seven. Seems like the new girl is just getting started."

I take a drink and follow the play. Number twenty-seven is surprisingly fast. But she's small, and she looks young. I'm not all that worried.

That proves to be a mistake. She resembles a mosquito in a camping tent—all that buzz, *right* in your ear. No matter how frequently you swat at her, she dodges you. Every time I get the puck, the little freak runs me ragged.

And then? That bitch strips me with a poke check so fast that I barely see her stick move. And she rips a shot right between my legs.

I hear Scarlet curse as she dives for it.

The crowd makes a noise of grave disappointment, and the lamp lights.

"Nutmegged!" my scrappy little opponent cackles.

"Shi—shkabob!" I scream.

Another Albany player skates past me. "I wonder what your husband thinks of that?"

On an ordinary night I would have chirped right back. I've got a million comeback chirps in my repertoire. Cross me? I will colorfully insult your skating, your team mascot, your face, your mama, *her* mama, and your mama's mama.

But a chirp about my marriage to Neil? That's a new one. I've got nothing.

We set up for another faceoff and the period grinds on. Number twenty-seven gets more irritating. Behind that cute little button nose lies the heart of a piranha on speed. She's everywhere at once, and her bite is sharp.

I've faced all kinds of players. I know how to adapt. But number twenty-seven picks apart my game. One by one, my usual tactics fail, like bowling pins falling over in slow motion. She manages to slip past me time and time again.

Then she picks me off. She fires a wrister past Scarlet's shoulder and the lamp lights.

The crowd groans. Loudly.

Very, very loudly.

"All right. It happens. Get it back," Fiona says, giving me an extra-long glance as she skates past.

She's right. We've been here before. It's only a small failure.

But as I set up for the next faceoff, it occurs to me that *this* failure will be written up in a dozen more places than usual.

That ugly thought slows me down. For a split second, I've let them get inside my head. And it's just long enough to slow my reaction time as the puck drops.

I flub a pass, Albany grabs it, and they shoot *again*.

Scarlet saves it this time, but we're still down 0-2, and it's probably all my fault.

When we troop back upstairs for intermission, it's very quiet during Sasha's speech. "You can do this," she says, her voice deadly serious. "You've beaten this team more than once. Sure, it feels a little different out there tonight. But this is *your* game. This is *your* house. You have everything it takes to come through on the other side."

In my head I know she's right, but my heart isn't convinced.

I play like crap as the second period commences. Every time number twenty-seven zooms in my direction, I feel doomed.

At least my teammates are faring better. Samantha puts one in the basket eight minutes into the second period.

"That's it, babies!" Sasha crows. "Now do it again!"

I fight on, but everywhere I turn, my mosquito is there with her stinger. She's in the corner when I'm scrapping for the puck. She's in my face when I'm defending the zone.

She's just *there*, and it's making me insane. She's fucking smiling at me, and I want to choke something.

So I trip her, instead.

The whistle blows immediately. Of course, it does.

"Not so fancy now, are you?" she says, getting up off the ice. "Can't wait to read about your loss tomorrow in *Sports Illustrated*."

Gah! My hands itch to push her down. I actually tilt in her direction.

"Nope," Fiona says, cutting me off. "Nope nope nope." My teammate gives me a nudge in the direction of the penalty box, where the official is holding the door open.

Fuck.

I skate toward the box, feeling beaten. I already know I'm too far inside my head. I know exactly how I'm fucking this up, but I can't seem to get a handle on myself.

The bench hits my ass, and I resign myself to two minutes of watching my teammates try to fend off a power play. Everyone on the ice is skating hard, but I swear number twenty-seven gives me a snide smile as she whizzes by.

Someone thunks loudly on the plexi behind me, and I tune it out. But then it comes again, two heavy bangs of a fist. I turn around, and there's Neil, his earnest eyes staring seriously into mine.

My heart drops a little further, because I'd forgotten that Neil was part of the crowd of people watching me screw up.

He presses his cardboard sign to the plexi. I don't see the shiny face of another *Go Bombshells* sign. Neil has flipped his around and scrawled something on the back.

For a second, I'm confused. Neil's message is not the upbeat PR message I was expecting. It's not a *You got this!* Instead, it's a question.

WHO'S STRONGER?

That's it. That's the whole message.

I glance up into Neil's hazel eyes, and he holds my gaze for a long beat. Then he lifts his chin toward the game, and I turn around to look.

There's number twenty-seven buzzing Fiona. She's such a little, infuriating skater. Quick as lightning.

But strength and speed don't always pair up, do they? And I'm starting to take Neil's meaning. There's no mass there. Only flash.

Huh. Okay.

"Ten seconds," says the official.

I stand up. And I can't help but glance over my shoulder one more time. Neil is still watching me. He doesn't try to say anything. He just winks so quickly I'm not sure I didn't imagine it.

Then I'm stepping onto the ice and powering toward our net, where Albany has swarmed, looking for an opportunity to score.

I bulldoze my way into the action. A sweaty Fiona passes me the puck, and I move it out of our zone, pushing forward.

Here comes number twenty-seven, looking for a poke check. This time, I don't try to outsmart her. I use my body to hold her off the puck until I can pass to Samantha. It's not flashy. It won't make a good headline. But it gets the job done.

We're still in this. The game is only half over. I need to stop freaking out and play a boring, dependable game of hockey.

So that's what I'll do.

EIGHTEEN

PINT-SIZED TORMENTOR

Neil

My blood sugar drops at the end of the second period.

"Dude, your phone is beeping," Castro says, nudging my knee with his.

"Right. Thanks." I dig into my pocket for my glucose tabs and stick one in my mouth.

"Weren't you eating this?" my teammate nags me, tapping the forgotten packet of trail mix in my hand.

"Who could eat?" I say, dipping my hand in for a couple of nuts anyway. "This is such a close game."

Leo Trevi chuckles on my other side. "Relax, man. Charli is pulling it together."

He's not wrong. As I crunch on some nuts and dried apples, Charli skates like a woman possessed. It took her a while, but she finally found her center, especially against that little demon who keeps trying to piss her off.

They're both in a corner now, and I forget to chew as they fight for the puck. Charli makes herself into a human cage, with a wide stance and shoulders that won't budge. She boxes number twenty-seven out and then passes the puck around the boards to Samantha.

"YEAH BABY!" I scream. I stand up and pound on the plexi. "That's the *way it's done!*"

My teammates crack up.

"It's a good thing you don't come to all her games," Leo says. "You've already developed, like, several nervous ticks in the past hour. I swear you were less invested in our Stanley Cup final last year."

"Oh, please. It's just this matchup," I argue. "It's so *tense*, am I right?"

There's more laughter.

I shove the nuts into my pocket, because rabbit food just isn't doing it for me tonight. "Does anyone have some more popcorn?" *Or maybe a sedative?* Someone hands me a box of popcorn, "Thanks." I shove some into my mouth. The truth is that I am a little worked up. I need the Bombshells to win so badly in front of all these people.

It would make Charli so happy. And she deserves that, especially after the hard week she just had. Heck, she deserves it anyway.

But the victory won't come easily. The game grinds on. I gasp when Brooklyn gets lucky with a sloppy goal in front of the net, but then I gasp again when an erratic shot from Albany pings off our post and goes into the net.

By the end of the third, we've fought our way to a 3-3 tie, and I'm eating my feelings while they set up for an overtime period.

"You make marriage look like hard work," Anton says, elbowing me from the seat behind mine.

"Oh, it is," I grumble through my popcorn.

"If they win, are you getting victory nookie?" Castro asks.

"Wouldn't you like to know," I growl.

"We all would, actually," Anton says.

I'm not even listening anymore, because the team is back.

Charli's expression is pure determination as they set up for the first overtime faceoff.

"Let's do this! Let's put this game to bed!" Anton calls, clapping loudly.

The puck drops, and our girls win it. They make a couple of decisive passes, and I realize I'm leaning forward in my seat with both fists clenched. The women play by the same sudden-death overtime rules that we do, so all it takes is one goal to end the game. Overtime is exhausting, though. You're playing on shaking legs and an empty tank.

"Come on, baby!" I yell as Charli whips past me. "Bring it home!"

"He's totally in it for the victory sex," someone murmurs.

But my attention is one hundred percent spoken for as Charli faces off against her irritating little opponent for the millionth time. Charli is trying to keep her off the puck, while Samantha and Fiona try to make a play.

The puck is knocked loose by an Albany player, and as it shoots toward Charli, I forget to breathe. I press my hands against the plexi and yell, even though she can't hear me. "Don't foul her!" A powerplay is the last thing we need right now.

Charli hunkers down and gets the puck on her stick. Her tormentor tries to take it, but Charli doesn't budge. She's looking for an opening and not finding one.

Meanwhile, her opponent is elbowing the shit out of Charli's ribs.

"Foul!" I call. "Open your eyes, ref!"

Then — *Shit!* She trips Charli, who goes down hard.

"*FOUL!*" I scream. "Assault and battery!"

"Oh, so you're one of *those* hockey fans, now," Newgate says, taking the popcorn out of my hand.

"Did you *see* that bullshit?" I yelp.

The whistle shrieks. *Finally.* And the ref calls the foul.

"Yes! Fuck! Get in that penalty box, you bad thing." I wave my hand toward the box that the official is opening now.

"Oh my God, sit down," Heidi Jo says, grabbing my shoulders from behind and guiding me back into my seat. "It's bad form to go Hulk Smash on a player who weighs ninety-five pounds in her gear."

"She has it coming," I grumble. "I've put up with her bullshit all night long."

"You have, huh?" Someone snickers.

Nothing can distract me, though, from the next two minutes of on-ice action. The Bombshells make a series of careful, accurate passes in their offensive zone, playing keep-away from their opponent who is desperate to send the puck whizzing away from the crease.

"Come on, come on," I mutter as the seconds tick down. "You can do this."

Charli receives a pass from her winger but then ships it to Fiona. She's still exercising caution. But this moment is for brilliance. For risky behavior.

Fiona makes a move, and several thousand new Brooklyn fans lean forward in their seats. A pass and a shot. I hear the clink of the puck hitting the post.

"Shit," Anton mutters as an Albany player scrambles for it.

"Get it back!" My voice is hoarse from yelling.

Charli is already there, lunging for the puck, neatly poking it away from her opponent and turning toward the net.

"SHOOT!" I scream as Charli does exactly that. With a flick of her forearm, she lifts the puck off the ice and jams it into the upper corner of the net.

The lamp lights, and the arena erupts into loud cheering. We're all on our feet yelling. Or at least, I am.

Charli's teammates pile onto her in a giant group hug and then hoist her off the ice.

I exhale for the first time in hours.

Thirty minutes later, the thrill of watching Charli get her goal still hasn't faded. I'm standing in a crowded corridor outside the women's locker rooms. I don't make it to a lot of Bombshells games, but it seems like there are a lot more people milling around here than usual.

My view of the dressing room door keeps getting blocked. Finally, I spot a flash of ginger-colored hair when the door opens again. She glances around, her eyes widening at the sight of so many people.

I wave, but she doesn't notice. "Wifey!"

Her chin snaps in my direction. My first thought is that she'll probably kill me for using that nickname in a room full of people. But a smile blooms on her face. Scoring the winning goal might just do that for a girl.

We've definitely attracted attention, and the crowd parts for her to reach me. Charli doesn't notice the stares. She just comes running.

I do the natural thing—I scoop her up into my arms. She fits perfectly against my chest, and I hug her fiercely. "That was…" I don't even have the words to explain how exciting that game was.

Also, the scent of her freshly washed skin so close to mine is a little distracting.

"So fucking cool," I babble. "Seriously—you took 'em *down*."

Charli's clear eyes are smiling at me from close range. We're nose to nose. I want to kiss her so bad. Her gaze drops to my lips, and…

Click click click. The sound of a camera's shutter interrupts my train of thought.

She hears it, too, and wiggles out of my arms. "Crap. If I see a picture of myself on a news site tomorrow, it had better be of my goal. Not—" She waves a hand between our bodies. "—this. I'll have to break someone in half."

"Now, hang on," I argue. "If the photo is on *Sports Illustrated*,

I totally take your point. But if it's a post on TMZ about how hot we look in our matching jackets, that would fly, right?"

She rolls her pretty eyes at me. *"Somebody'∂* better write about that goal."

"Then you'd better get to your press conference." I step back, letting her pass. Because tonight is not about me.

"Right," she says quickly. "You don't have to stay."

"Actually, he does," Georgia says, appearing out of nowhere.

"Why?" I argue. "It's the Bombshells' big night."

"I know," she says, taking my elbow. "Nonetheless, you're going to *atten∂* the press conference like the doting husband that you are. I'll put you against the back wall."

"Fine," I say, allowing myself to be led into what is a very cramped and crowded press room. "This space is too small," I point out.

"That's strategic," Georgia whispers. "We don't like to throw pressers in a big, empty room."

Charli and two of her teammates make their way toward the dais, while Georgia tests the microphone. "Good evening! We're just waiting one more minute for Coach Sasha Marshall, and then we'll get started."

A guy swivels around in his seat and points his phone at me. "Neil Drake! Was it love at first sight for you and Charli Higgins?"

Uh-oh. I'd better tread carefully. Then again, the truth never hurts. "Nah," I say loudly. "She *hate∂* me."

The room erupts in laughter. When I glance at the dais, Charli has a wry look on her face, but Georgia is smiling.

"How come?" the reporter asks.

I plow ahead. "Well, I was having a low-blood-sugar episode, and feeling a little loopy, so I came upstairs looking for some juice. I mistook Charli for a member of the staff and—this is the worst part—I called her *∂oll*. Yup. It was a dumbass thing to say, and I apologized many times afterward."

Laughter echoes off the walls of the room. I guess the press likes my story of being a dumbass.

Coach Marshall has appeared now, and she's making her way toward the front of the room. I turn my body toward her and start to clap.

The applause catches on, saving me from more ramblings. The reporter who'd questioned me also turns his attention toward the front of the room.

Does he realize I only gave him Charli's side of the story?

Of course, mine is more complicated. I shouldn't have called her *doll*, because there's nothing doll-like about Charli. She's feisty and sharp. Prickly, not warm.

But when you break through all those defenses, there's nothing better than her smile or the sound of her quick laughter when a joke lands.

It's been a year and a half since we met, and I live for those moments.

Maybe if I hadn't screwed everything up in Vegas, I would have had a real chance with her someday.

Now I might never know.

NINETEEN

TEN OUT OF TEN

Charli

Neil and I are brushing our teeth in his grand bathroom under soft lighting. There's a fluffy wool rug underfoot that warms my toes. Fresh towels wait beside us, because Neil's housekeeper was here this morning. When I had come back to the apartment smelling like fried eggs and waffles, Neil's gleaming home had smelled of lemons and lavender.

It still does.

Neil spits toothpaste into the sink and rinses his mouth. And I do the same. The casual domesticity of this moment ought to relax me. Instead, I'm all stirred up inside.

"What?" Neil asks, wiping his mouth.

"What what?" I grab my hand towel, which is so thick it almost doesn't fold properly.

"You're sneaking looks at me in the mirror."

Oh God. It's probably true. Neil is wearing a pair of blue-and-white checked boxer shorts and nothing else. That's half the problem. His colorful sleeve of tattoos glows brightly in the expensive lighting. I'm intrigued.

But something else is what's really distracting me. "You never told me what happened that first day."

His eyes meet mine in the mirror. "What first day? You mean the infamous moment when I called you *doll?*"

"Yeah, that. You never told me you were having some kind of *attack.*" All I'd seen that day was an entitled prima donna. The story is different if he'd literally been about to pass out.

Neil shrugs, like this isn't important. "Kind of dumb to call random women a derogatory name, even when you're loopy. It didn't seem like an important detail."

"I think it is." Damn it. I'm still staring at the honey-gold expanse of his muscled chest in the mirror. I drag my eyes to my own reflection, where I'm *also* wearing a pair of blue-and-white checked cotton shorts, plus a little blue tank top that I sleep in.

"We're twinsies," I say, by way of changing the subject.

This backfires, because it invites Neil's gaze to sweep over my body in the mirror. "Are we, now?"

"It's the shorts," I point out.

He leans on the counter with both hands and grins at me in the mirror. "Wifey, I like the shorts. I like how short they are. You have killer legs."

"Erm, thank you?"

"I had a great time at your game tonight," he says. "You were fun to watch."

Oh boy. Neil probably has no idea that this line of conversation is far more seductive to me than compliments about my legs in these shorts. "Thank you," I say quietly. "It was a really special night."

He carefully folds his own towel and sets it back onto the counter, while I rinse my mouth one more time. "The guys asked me if I was in it for the victory sex."

"What?" I almost choke as I spit out the water. "And you told them...?"

"I said—Charli wants me, but she won't admit it. You should see the way she looks at me in the bathroom mirror."

"Neil!" I swat at him with my towel.

He catches it of course, his eyes glittering. "Joking, kitten. I didn't say that."

"Good," I say stiffly.

He grins. "It's true, though. And who knows? This could be the night you break down and beg me for it."

"It won't be," I assure him.

He lifts his chin. "Huh. That's interesting."

"Why?"

"Well, you said tonight won't be the night. But that implies there *will* be a night."

"No." I swallow carefully, but my eyes make another unbidden circuit of his chest. "I didn't imply that."

"I think you did." He pats the marble countertop. "This looks sturdy. I could put you right here. We could do a naked victory dance."

"Neil!" I squeak. And then I flee the bathroom, because I like that idea way too much.

His chuckle follows me into the bedroom, where he turns off the lights. He slides between the sheets, and the sound of his skin against the cotton does nothing to quiet my pulse. "Let me know when you're ready," he says playfully. "My dick and I are open for business."

I groan. "This is about saving face, right? I'm sure all your equipment works, Neil. Gold star."

He laughs in the dark. "I *know* it works. And I'm not in it for the reviews. Although I know what you'd be saying—*ten out of ten, would ride again.*"

I groan. But that's exactly what I'm afraid of. I could become addicted to Neil. It wouldn't just be the sex, either. It would be the whole package. That hug I got after my game tonight, for example. Another thing I enjoyed way too much.

The way he feeds me.

The way he listens when I talk. I like it all too much.

"It's not easy sleeping next to you," he whispers.

"This was your idea," I point out.

"I'm well aware. Maybe you should warn me in advance—how sexy is that blue dress you're wearing on Sunday, anyway?"

"It's a *ten out of ten. Would drool again.*"

He groans, and the sound of it doesn't make falling asleep any easier. Not one bit.

———————

I don't see much of Neil for the rest of the weekend, because we both have Saturday night games, and I work long shifts at the diner, too. On Sunday afternoon, I treat myself to the most expensive haircut of my life. I refuse to look like a rag doll in front of Neil's family.

When it's time to check out of the salon, I take Neil's credit card out of my wallet, but I can't hand it over. He might have paid for that fancy dress I'm supposed to wear tonight and those sexy shoes. But he doesn't own my head. I take out my own card, instead, and pay for the haircut with money I don't have.

Pride is a bitch sometimes. It really is.

Then, well before I'm ready, it's Sunday evening, and I'm shaving my legs for a dressy benefit that I really don't want to go to.

"Are you done in the bathroom?" Neil calls through the door.

"Oh, *hell* no." I haven't even gotten to my makeup yet.

He snickers. "People warn you about marriage, but I never listened."

Honestly, I don't know what that man even needs the bathroom for. He looks fantastic from the moment he rolls out of bed in the morning until the moment he closes his eyes again at night.

"I can give you fifteen minutes," I offer. "You can shower

and shave while I have a cup of coffee. Then you have to vacate the bathroom and the bedroom, too."

"You are a hell of a negotiator, but I'll take that deal."

Satisfied, I throw on his bathrobe and exit the room.

"*Hey!*" he complains. "Stealing my robe wasn't included in the terms."

"You'll live," I snap.

The truth is that I'm nervous about this thing tonight. I don't like eyes on me, but lately they've been everywhere. The postgame press conference, especially Neil's bit, are making the rounds on sports blogs and social media. And while I'm excited that the clip of my winning goal was retweeted five thousand times, the scrutiny makes me break out in hives.

Not literally, though, which is a good thing, because I'm about to show some skin at this benefit.

In the kitchen, I pour a cup of coffee and contemplate my makeup. I want to look devastating, but also classy. It's a fine line.

Makeup is a hobby of mine. I'm good at it, which only goes to show that my talents lie in very impractical places. No woman ever got rich playing hockey or creating a perfect smoky eye.

"All yours," Neil says, emerging in nothing but a towel, his tux on a hanger. "And by the way, you look exceedingly fuckable in my robe. Just saying." He winks.

"I'll accept the compliment," I tell him. "But please let the robe know that it won't be seeing any action tonight."

"The robe is sad," he says, giving me a puppy-dog face.

Ignoring that, I step past him to reclaim the bedroom and fabulous bathroom.

For a moment I'm tempted to put on my dark green dress I bought on sale at Macy's last year for a Bombshells benefit. It has a flattering body-conscious shape, without showing any skin. But I wear it to literally every event that requires a dress.

Including a certain drunken night in Vegas. So the green dress needs a night off.

That leaves me with the exquisite blue silk designer gown that Vera brought over. I run a hand down fabric that slides between my fingertips like water. I'll never wear another dress like this, because it cost a staggering amount. More than three month's rent. So it's now or never. If I'm honest, I can't wait to see Neil's reaction to this version of Charli—the one who's pampered and dressed in blue silk.

Just because I'm not going to sleep with him doesn't mean I'm immune to flattery.

I put on a pair of silk stockings that Vera brought me, plus the strapless bra Neil referred to as a corset. I don't even want to know how much these extras cost. There's no way I'll ever be able to repay him.

Now it's makeup time. But for all Neil's moaning about me hogging the bathroom, I'm quick with the brushes, and my shoulder-length hair doesn't require more than an additional smoothing. That's what expensive haircuts are for, I guess.

Lastly, I unzip the blue dress and step into it. The fabric slides over my skin like a cool breeze. The color is a deep jewel tone that screams money.

As I step into the sexy pair of heels, I realize this is *it*. My short, dramatic time as Mrs. Cornelius Drake III will peak tonight, and very soon it will end forever. This is my Cinderella moment, before I go back to the pumpkins and the rats.

Before exiting the bedroom, I say a silent prayer. *Lord in heaven, if we could just get through this without any embarrassing gaffes, I'd really appreciate it. I'll even* try *not to think so many lustful thoughts about Neil. Emphasis on try.*

No guarantees. That man looks spectacular in a tux.

Amen.

TWENTY

EYES UP HERE

Neil

I'm speed-reading the agenda for tonight's program when my bedroom door opens.

Lifting my gaze from the celebrity bio I'm supposed to memorize, I open my mouth to tell Charli that the car will arrive at any moment.

But then I forget how to speak. Charli stands before me in exquisite blue silk that clings to every one of her curves. Her skin is luminous against the fabric, which drapes across her cleavage in a way that teases me to the edge of distraction. The spray of freckles across her chest and shoulders only make her more interesting.

And maybe this is a weird thing to obsess over, but Charli has incredible arms. They're strong but shapely, and they crop up in some of my best dreams.

"Jesus Christ," I rasp. "It's going to be a long night."

She clears her throat, which probably means that I'm staring. "Eyes up here, sailor."

"Sorry," I slur, dragging my eyes off her body. But it doesn't help all that much. She's done something dramatic to her eyes.

They look enormous. Not to mention that her lips are a kissable rose color. "Wow, Charli. You really know how to torture a guy."

She puts one hand on a cocked hip and arches her eyebrows. "We're trying to torture your family, no? Do you think I've missed the mark? Is it too much?"

"*Noooooo,*" I say quickly. God forbid she change out of this heavenly creation. "Great dress. All the other women will hate you."

She pushes off the door jamb. "They already do, because you're my date."

The door buzzer rings, so Charli sashays past me on long legs and answers it. "Hello? Um, okay? Thanks." She hangs up and spins around. "Your mother's driver is on his way upstairs to fetch us. Does he think we can't find the curb?"

"There's honestly no point in guessing my mother's intentions. Is my tie straight?"

She takes a couple of steps toward me and adjusts it, while I struggle not to look down her dress. She smells like lemons and sex.

Or maybe just lemons. I'm obviously projecting.

Shake it off, Drake. Shake it off. "Before we go, there's something else I need you to wear." I pull the ring from my pocket. "There's no way in hell my new wife would show up to a gala without a ring on." I open my fingers to show her the ring in my palm. It's a two-and-a-quarter carat diamond surrounded by a pavé of eighteen other diamonds.

"*Neil.*" She gasps. "Where did you get that? Is it real?"

"It was my grandmother's. My grandfather bought it for her on their twenty-fifth anniversary to replace the tiny stone he'd proposed with." And then I remember something else about this ring. "He bought it in Vegas, if you can believe it. He was in the doghouse for spending their anniversary away from her."

My father told me that story when he gave me the ring. *Keep this for a special girl,* he'd said. Until this week, I'd honestly forgot I had it. There's a safe in the back of my closet that I never open.

Charli takes a step backward. "I can't wear that! It's a family heirloom."

"That's exactly why you should wear it," I argue.

"It probably won't fit me," she argues. "And I'll just look like I'm playing dress-up."

"Try," I beg. Then I take her hand in mine and slide it onto her ring finger.

Charli takes a breath, and I realize we're standing very close together, and this is a strangely intimate thing to do. "It fits," she breathes. "That's crazy."

It *does* fit. Perfectly.

"Question," she says in a low voice. "Shouldn't this be your sister's? Isn't she going to *murder* me if she thinks you gave it to me? And… is it insured? I never wanted to walk around with a luxury car on my finger."

"Paisley has a closet full of jewels from my grandmother. This is the only piece that came to me. And of course, it's insured."

She blows out a breath. Then I hear a knock at the door. "Why are we riding to this thing with your mother?" she asks. "Is my outfit being vetted? Is she going to send me back upstairs to change?"

"Hey." I put both hands on Charli's bare shoulders. This is a mistake, because her skin feels like silk, and it's distracting. "My mother likes to stage-manage me. So once a year I let her. There's a red-carpet moment when we get there."

"A red carpet? Why?" I see a flare of panic in her eyes. Then she takes a breath, and it disappears instantly.

"Marketing," I grumble, stepping back to open the door for Mr. Stoats, the driver. "They have to oversell this event, so that patrons feel good about coughing up two grand a plate."

Charli's eyes widen, but I can't tell if she's surprised about the benefit's ticket cost or by Mr. Stoats. He's standing in the door now holding out a full-length white mink coat. "Good evening," he says. "Mrs. Drake sent this upstairs for Mrs. Drake."

"Why?" Charli asks bluntly.

"It doesn't matter," I hurry to say. "You can wear your own coat if you wish."

Her gaze darts away from the giant fluffy white thing and toward my closet, as if considering her options. "Well, fine. I'll borrow your mother's coat. She's probably worried that mine is a rag. Which it is."

"We'll leave the coats in the limo anyway," I say, taking the coat from Mr. Stoats and draping it over Charli's shoulders. I pull the lapels together and force myself not to lean in and kiss her throat.

I'm sporting a semi in my tuxedo trousers, and I'm on my way downstairs to spend the evening with my fuckable wife who won't let me fuck her and...

My *mother*.

God. Why did I think this was a good idea, again? Type 1 diabetes hasn't killed me yet, but tonight's benefit just might.

"You look beautiful, darlings!" my mother croons as we settle into the limo. "Charli, that dress is smashing. Vera has outdone herself."

I inwardly wince at the shape of that compliment. As if Vera were even ten percent responsible for how Charli looks in that dress.

But Charli doesn't appear to care. Her back is as straight as a goalpost and her ivory chin is held high. "Thank you," she says quietly. "You look lovely as well."

"The white mink looks divine against your hair," my mother continues.

"Thank you for letting me borrow it," Charli replies dutifully.

"My pleasure, darling. Formal wear in the wintertime is such a challenge."

"Indeed," Charli says so sweetly that she may as well have been snatched by aliens. "It's a good thing we have dead animals to keep us warm."

My mother blinks, and I hold back a snort of laughter. My hand steals across the leather seat to find Charli's. Her smooth fingers close over mine and give a conspiratorial squeeze.

I love that. I lace my fingers through hers and settle in. I can tell Charli is outside her comfort zone, but she's still one hundred percent herself.

She's doing this all for me, and I'll never forget it.

Charli asks my mother a polite question about the foundation, which is a smart move, because my mother begins talking and doesn't stop until we've almost reached the midtown venue.

"How was your game last night, darling?" she asks as we finally roll down Lexington.

My snort escapes this time. "Well, we *lost*. Badly. And it was my penalty that allowed Boston to score the winning goal on us. So you could say I had a bad night. But thanks for asking. Charli fared better, though. If you won't watch my games, you could try hers."

"You know hockey isn't my thing." She smooths her own fur coat as the car rolls to a stop.

I hold back my comments, as always. Although I've spent the last decade wondering why my family doesn't care that I'm better at hockey than at running a corporation. "Hey, Mom?" I ask as the driver circles the car to open the door for her. "You didn't put Iris at our table, right?"

Charli stiffens beside me at the mention of my ex.

"The gala is her event, Neil. She planned it. She can sit wherever she wants. If she feels that table number one is her right, why would I argue?"

Fuck. I rub the back of my neck and wish I could rip off this bowtie. "It just seems obvious that my ex and my *wife* should not be seated on either side of me. Put Iris with the celebrity and put me at table two."

My mother makes an irritated sound and steps out of the car. She pastes on a smile, and a million flashbulbs go off at once.

"Tell me what to do," Charli whispers beside me.

I put a hand on her knee to stop her from getting up. "We're not getting out quite yet."

The driver closes the door, proving my point.

"Why are we still here?" Charli asks.

Sometimes I forget how much of my life is a stupid charade, and it depresses me to explain it. "We're A-list guests, so we arrive second to last. The car has to make a circuit of the East Sixties before he'll stop and let us out again."

"Who arrives last?"

"The celebrity speaker."

"Oh. That's bonkers, Neil." She picks up my hand, which has been absently stroking her knee through the silk of her dress.

Oops.

"You're going to pucker the fabric," she chides. "If they're going to take my picture, I'd like to at least look like I tried."

"Sorry," I say quickly, moving to withdraw my hand from hers.

But she holds tightly to it. "One more thing…"

"What? And I apologize in advance for whatever dirty looks we get from Iris tonight."

Charli waves a dismissive hand. "I've always been invisible to Iris."

She won't be anymore, though. "What were you going to say?" I curl my fingers around hers, surprised that she's letting me hold her hand. Maybe she's getting into character.

The car glides around a corner, and I'd honestly rather

spend the evening talking to Charli in the back of the limo than at any damn benefit.

"It's funny," she says, turning to gaze out the windows at the lights of Manhattan. "I thought you and I grew up with zero in common. But it's not exactly true. Because nobody ever came to watch my games, either."

"Yeah, sure. You're right. We're twins like that."

"And the thing is?" Her pretty face swings around toward mine, and I experience a jolt of longing. It's the fierce look in her eye that always knocks me flat. Charli has a fighter's energy, and it's so fucking sexy. "It took me a while to figure out that it was better this way."

"Hmm?" I stroke the soft skin of her wrist with my thumb. "What's better?"

"Focus, Neil. The fact that nobody came to my games was a *good* thing. Hockey was all mine. There was nothing else in my life that didn't belong to someone else first. Not clothes, not shoes, not a single book. That's not your life—I get that. But Neil, when I went to Draper, I saw what those hockey parents were like—all the pressure and the expectations. You didn't have that, and that's why you're a star. You had to find the drive inside yourself. And look where it got you? All the way to the top."

Her sharp gaze has finally burned off my lust-fueled haze, and I realize she has a point. "I never thought about it like that."

She pokes me in the ribs. "Neglect can be a gift. Trust me on this one."

"Okay, I will."

She pats my hand. "They're serving food at this thing, right?"

"Absolutely. There will be a seated dinner, followed by speeches during dessert, followed by dancing."

"Dancing," she repeats. "Really? I thought I'd already counted all the possible means of humiliation."

I laugh. "Your job is to hang onto me and look smitten.

Shouldn't be too hard, right?" I give her a cheesy wink, and she smiles. "The celebrity guest is Justin B., and —"

"Wait. *Really?*" She sits up straighter. "Justin B.—as in Justin Branaman, the front man for Tears of the Stag?"

"That's the guy. He's a type 1 diabetic."

Charli lets out the kind of girly shriek that I'd always assumed she despised. "Omigod! This night just got so much more interesting. I love that band!"

And now she's giving me the exact kind of smitten look that I wished she showed me all the time. "You are hard on my ego, Higgins."

She reaches up and pats my cheek with a smooth hand. "Someone should be, Cornelius. And that someone is me."

TWENTY-ONE

DRUNK LOGIC

Charli

When we arrive—again—at the venue, I see a lot of people on the sidewalk. And several photographers. There's even a damn velvet rope holding onlookers back.

"This is ridiculous," I say to calm my thumping heart.

"Truth," Neil says with a sigh. "Are you ready to take this off?" He slides the fur coat down my bare arms. "Unnngh, Charli. This dress should be registered as a lethal weapon."

"You can borrow it anytime you want. You're the one who paid for it."

He lets out another sigh as the driver opens the door.

Neil hops out first, offering me his hand from the sidewalk.

For once I'm grateful that chivalry exists, because gracefully exiting a limo in three-inch heels isn't easy. I set my feet carefully onto the pavement and then rise, hoping not to stumble.

Come on, Higgins, I coach myself. *You can stop an attacking forward with nothing but your wits and a snarl. A party full of snobs should be less stressful.*

It isn't. I wax on a fake smile and try not to look shell-shocked as multiple flash bulbs go off at once. I grip Neil's arm and allow myself to be led toward the open doors.

"Ms. Drake, who are you wearing?" someone calls out.

"Um…" My mind goes blank, even though I'd been told to expect this question.

"Tell him you're wearing *me*," Neil says out of the corner of his mouth.

The joke catches me by surprise, and I let out a belly laugh. Then he leans over and smacks a kiss on my cheek.

A thousand bulbs flash at once.

We proceed inside, where a hundred heads swivel to see who's arrived. I have to remind myself to keep breathing. The diamond on my finger feels heavy. I have never seen so many rich people assembled in one place. They mingle in clusters in the vast lobby of an old men's club. A heavy crystal chandelier overhead makes all the women's jewelry sparkle.

When I glance at Neil, he looks completely relaxed. "Good crowd tonight. Should be a nice paycheck for the foundation. There's some schmoozing over cocktails, and then we get to sit down and eat dinner."

"Yes, dear."

He flashes me a grin. "Now we're talking."

"If sir wants an obedient wife, sir will have one," I say with a straight face.

He sighs. "If only you weren't kidding."

For the next half hour, though, I am an obedient wife. I flash a megawatt smile at each donor who approaches to speak to Neil. And I say little more than "It's a pleasure to meet you." I've never been anyone's arm candy before, and it isn't all that difficult.

Neil is very popular and recognizable to everyone in this room. They wait in groups for a moment of his attention. Expensive fragrances fill the air, and the women's dresses are pops of color against the dark grays and blacks of menswear.

Vera is a genius, I realize as Neil leads me from cluster to cluster of well-wishers. The personal shopper had said that jewel tones were in fashion, and she was not wrong. My blue silk shimmers in the soft lighting.

"You holding up okay?" he asks me quietly.

"I'm fine," I assure him. "You do your thing, and I'll stand here looking ravishing."

"A-plus job with that, wifey." His throaty chuckle vibrates just behind my breastbone. Then he reaches for another hand to shake.

Billionaires must be born knowing how to schmooze. Neil doesn't seem to mind it. I'm literally hanging on his arm, wondering when food will be served.

"Excuse us," Neil says to an older man who wants to keep chattering at him. "I must find my wife a drink before we're seated for dinner."

"Congratulations on your marriage," the old coot says. "I remember my newlywed days." Then he aims his gaze directly at my breasts. "Those were some fun times."

Neil growls quietly, steering me away. "Sorry about that. The small talk is almost finished. Promise. They just opened the ballroom doors. We'll go in to dinner soon."

"Yes, sir. My tits and I are at your service."

He snorts. "If only."

Smiling, I glance up to take in the next smiling donor who's vying for Neil's attention. But it's a shock to find an icy stare pointed back at me, instead.

I don't even need an introduction to know who this is. Nobody else would look at me like that—like I was a piece of dog shit stuck to the bottom of his shoe—except for Harmon Drake, Neil's uncle.

"Evening, Neil," the man sniffs.

"Evening, Uncle Harmon. I'd like to introduce you to my wife, Charli."

The old man's lip actually curls with disdain. "Evening," he grunts, looking everywhere but at me.

Neil sighs. "Charli, this is Harmon."

"It's lovely to meet you, sir," I say with forced warmth. I will not let this asshole get to me. I curl a hand around Neil's waist and move even closer to him. I'm practically squishing my boob against his jacket, but it's worth it to see the old man look even more uncomfortable. "I want you to know your nephew is my whole world," I say loudly. "It's an honor to join your family."

The guy reddens with irritation, which gives me perverse pleasure. Neil grins so broadly that I'm half afraid he'll laugh and blow my cover.

That's when Neil's mother hurries over to us. I don't know if she's drawn by the need to smooth things over, or by morbid curiosity. It could really go either way. "I see you have all met," she says.

Harmon ignores her. He turns his grumpy stare on Neil and drains his scotch. "We have two items of unfinished business, son," he says.

"I'm not your *son*," Neil says immediately.

I broaden my smile another millimeter and wonder if I'm about to experience a Drake family brawl.

"Noted," the grumpy billionaire says. "If you were, you would have signed the post-nup."

"Really?" Neil scoffs. "That document is a piece of trash." He rubs my back in a slow circle, still calm, even though we're drawing a crowd of rubberneckers.

"That document protects your heritage," his uncle snaps. "What you both fail to understand is that I run a company that employs thousands of people. It's my job to always think of the worst-case scenario. Something could happen to you in that dangerous sport you insist on playing. And if you're not able to vote your shares, your next of kin has the power to do so. And right now, that's *her*." He gives me another lip-curled glare. "Your hasty marriage affects my ability to run the company."

Oh my fucking God. I can't let that go. "Look, sir, that was a very careful explanation—good enough for a five-year-old, or even a girl from South Philly."

The old man's glare swings in my direction. But I'm not scared of him. I plow ahead. "But if something happened to Neil, then the real problem would be that *something happened to Neil.*"

Neil's hand goes still on my back.

His mother claps a hand over her mouth.

"...If Neil were in a coma, would you *really* be fretting over which waffle maker to install in the latest private jet model? Because that's the definition of pathetic."

A deep silence follows my little outburst, and the old man's face turns red. Very red. I brace myself for some kind of explosion.

Instead, he looks right at Neil, as if I never existed. "The second item of business is a packet I sent you. Don't miss it."

At that, he turns and walks away.

I exhale, and Neil turns to me with a cheery smile. "That was super fun. How about a glass of champagne?"

"Okay?"

With an arm wrapped around me, he steers me toward the bar. "Have I mentioned how good you are at this fake-wife thing?"

"Really?"

"Really."

Neil finds me a very yummy glass of champagne to sip. I hold it with my wedding-ring hand. As I raise and lower it, the soft lighting glints off the diamond. I can feel eyeballs on me as Neil leads me through a maze of tables set for ten people each.

He stops at a table right in front of the stage, pulling out a chair for me. "Madame, this seat will have an excellent view of the stage. Clap loudly when I make my introduction."

"You have to speak?"

He shrugs. "Only for a moment."

I'm about to sit down when I see his ex, Iris, just ten feet away. Her dress is a column of emerald silk, asymmetrical, and very beautiful. But she's staring at me with laser eyes. "Uh-oh."

"Ignore her. At least my mother switched the seating around."

This means that Iris is at the neighboring table instead of ours. But that doesn't stop the dagger eyes as I sit down.

We're no longer in high school, I remind myself. *Iris's opinion doesn't matter.* That's my new mantra. Although I never was very good at meditation.

Our table fills up rapidly, which is a nice distraction. I'm introduced to an internet billionaire, a talk-show host, and a journalist.

Neil's mom and sister are seated at Iris's table. That's fine with me. I don't need their drama.

The tech billionaire starts a conversation with Neil, and I pretend to listen. Really I'm just staring at the enormous diamond on my finger. It's heart-stoppingly beautiful. *Well done, Earth.*

Dinner is served in several courses—first a creamy leek soup, followed by a filet of salmon with mushroom risotto. And the good food makes me feel more relaxed.

"I didn't know rice could taste this good," I say with a sigh. "This stuff is magic."

"Don't tell me," Neil says. His plate has a portion of salad. "I don't eat white rice. The glycemic index is too high."

"That is a tragedy." I fork up another bite of cheesy goodness. "Now here's a question—do they serve dessert at a benefit for diabetes?"

"Depends on your definition," Neil says. "Last year it was a tiny no-sugar-added cheesecake or a dish of raspberries."

"I will temper my expectations."

Neil gives me a warm smile, and once again I relax. *This is just a minor adventure,* I remind myself. *A strange little journey. Might as well enjoy it.*

When dessert is served, I choose the tiny cheesecake and Neil goes for the fruit. I'm startled to see Iris take the stage and adjust the microphone.

"Good evening, ladies and gentlemen. My name is Iris Montclair, and as a board member of the Ones and Twos Foundation, I'd like to thank you for your participation tonight."

There is a polite round of applause.

"She's on the board of your family's charity?" I whisper.

Neil shrugs. "It's her day job, such as it is. Planning this event is, like, three quarters of the work."

A number of brief yet boring speeches follow Iris's introduction. Raising money for charity seems to involve an endless stream of thanking people.

But it's all good, because I have a fresh glass of champagne and the promise of a close-up sighting of Justin Branaman.

Neil's mother reaches out from the neighboring table and pokes her son in the arm. "You're next." And at the next polite smattering of applause, he rises from his chair and strides up to the stage as if he were born to this.

I suppose he was.

"Good evening." He spreads his arms in a dapper welcoming gesture. "My name is Neil Drake, and in a roundabout way, it's my fault that you're here this evening. Years ago, when I was still a teenager, my father started this foundation, looking for a cure. He wanted to save other parents from the worry and pain of looking after kids with diabetes. He also started a second foundation with the goal of curing my hockey addiction. But that one flopped."

Neil gets a quick laugh.

"Thank you for coming together tonight to do what you can for type 1 and type 2 diabetes. And it's my absolute pleasure to introduce our keynote speaker for the evening, Mr. Justin Branaman."

Two or three hundred people—including me—applaud wildly as a long-haired man carrying a guitar strides onto the stage.

Neil shakes his hand and thanks him for coming.

"My pleasure," the rock star says in his gravelly voice. "I'm a big hockey fan myself."

I let out a loud squeal of excitement. Oops.

"I'm a fan of your music," Neil says. "And apparently so is my wife."

Another laugh rolls through the room, and I feel my face begin to burn in embarrassment.

Neil hands the mic to Mr. Branaman, gives the audience a grin, and heads off the stage.

"I was diagnosed with diabetes at the age of fourteen," the singer says. "And it was a big shock. I spent a lot of time worrying about becoming the school freak, you know?"

The audience chuckles. It's pretty hard to think of a Grammy-winning rock star as an outcast.

"I was caught up in the drudgery of daily injections and blood-sugar sticks. I was angry. Even then, I was composing songs, but they weren't any good. Not a lot of words rhyme with insulin."

I giggle. Loudly.

Neil slides into his chair and puts an arm around my shoulders. "You really dig this guy, huh?" he whispers.

When I glance at Neil, his hazel eyes are just inches away. He's so close that I can feel the heat of his body.

Just like that, the man on stage fades into unimportance. Neil is every bit as interesting to me as the rock star standing ten feet away. But I can't let him know that. "He's kinda yummy," I say under my breath. "Girls appreciate a guy who can sing."

"Why?" Neil whispers back.

"Because they feel their feelings." I'm barely an inch away

from him now in an attempt to stay quiet. "A guy who's singing is allowed to be emo. It's a rule."

His handsome smile appears, so close that I could kiss him without moving. "Emo, huh? I wouldn't have thought that was your type."

"Don't tell anyone," I whisper. "I have a reputation to uphold."

Those beautiful eyes dance, and I'm in danger of falling into them. I force myself to look away and listen to a rock star make a speech.

"...I was focused on all the wrong things," he's saying. "I was worried about being a cool teenager when I could have easily been a *dead* teenager. That's just the way teens work. But the people in this room know better. And we can *do* better. Diabetes still kills more than a million people every year. That's way too many. Like many of you here tonight, I'm dedicated to educating young people, curing diabetes, and saving lives."

He has to stop for a wave of applause. The crowd loves him. "Nice event, husband," I whisper to Neil. "Well done."

"You won't want to hear this, but it was all Iris's doing." I make a face, and he smiles. "Also? I'm going to need you to dance with me in a minute."

"Already?" I whine.

"It's almost time. But I'll take it easy on you. No dips, no flips. Only a few twirls."

"Not funny," I grumble under my breath.

Justin Branaman brings his speech to a heartfelt close, and the room applauds wildly. "Thank you very much. And now I thought I'd kick off the dancing with a song I wrote for my second album. I sure hope you enjoy it."

He puts the mic on a stand while the lights change. A curtain goes up, revealing a seven-piece band. The rock star takes a moment to tune his guitar. Then he nods at the drummer, who begins a four-beat count with his sticks.

Then they all begin to play.

"Okay, this is it." Neil stands up, giving my hand a gentle tug. "Come and dance with me."

I rise, even though I'm confused. "But there's nobody dancing yet."

"Yep. That's the point. It's our job to get things started. Come on, beautiful. They'll only stare for a second."

Oh man. I let him lead me around our table toward the dance floor set up in the middle of the room. As we pass Iris, she gives me a look that could curdle milk. And it occurs to me that she was probably hand in hand with Neil for the first dance last year.

Maybe this makes me a terrible person, but her jealousy galvanizes me. I lift my chin and swing my hips as I follow my smokin' hot accidental husband onto an empty dance floor. I put one hand on his hunky shoulder and slide the other one against his palm. The rock on my finger glimmers like a beacon.

Then I lift my eyes to his and give him a big, sexy smile.

"Fuck me," he says, beginning to move. "You're a knockout. Every man in this room is drooling into his decaf coffee right now." He turns me slowly, his bright eyes never leaving mine.

"Or maybe they're drooling over you? You clean up nice, Drakey. I'm sure the women *and* the men have noticed. And they're all plotting my murder."

Neil chuckles. Then he pulls me closer, and my heart does a shimmy in my chest.

Jason B. starts to sing. The song he's chosen is called "So Far Away." I love it for the way his voice is so achingly beautiful, but I can't say that I'd paid much attention to the lyrics before tonight.

I need you here. Need you now.
Tried to tell you. Show you how.
But you hold yourself away.
So far away.
I want your love. I said as much.
You won't give in. Afraid to love.

And you hold yourself away.
So far away.
A spoonful of sugar. A drop on my tongue.
I want the whole damn thing, but you're stingy with love.
So far away...

It's a sad song, but with a dead-sexy beat. Neil holds my gaze the whole time we're dancing. I glance away to try to break the stare-off. But when I glance at him again, he's right there, waiting for me.

"Charli," he whispers.

"What?"

In answer, Neil closes his eyes. But his thumb slowly rubs my lower back.

I shiver. The Academy Awards committee should really be here to watch. He deserves an award for this performance. I hope his grumpy uncle is watching, because anyone looking at Neil right now would be a hundred percent convinced that his marriage to me is as sturdy as the Matterhorn.

Bravo, sir.

The singer hits a high note. And this seems like a very sexy song all of a sudden. Neil opens his pretty eyes and studies me at point-blank range. Then he leans in.

I stop breathing, but he doesn't kiss me. No, it's worse than that. He makes a deep, sexy sound and nuzzles me, his face brushing against mine.

All my nerve endings leap to attention. "Neil," I gasp. "You can stop now. People are already convinced."

"What people?" he whispers. "Nobody is watching us anymore."

I glance past him and note that he's right. The dance floor is crowded with other people now. "Then what are you doing?"

"What I've always wanted to do. Let's face it, wifey. We

didn't end up wasted and half-naked together in a hotel room by accident."

"Yes, we *did*. That is exactly what happened. You can't really be suggesting that we did that on purpose."

"It was drunk logic," he says. "But that's still logic. Everyone knows drunk logic comes from a place of deep-seated desire."

"What? No. It comes from deep-seated stupidity."

His smile grows wider, and I feel it like a heat wave. "You know I'm right. Every time I look at you for longer than a second, you get all hot and bothered."

"I do *not* get hot and bothered," I insist, even as I feel quite hot and very much bothered. At the same time.

"Keep saying that." Neil chuckles. "You even snuggle up to me in bed, did you know that?"

"That's crazy talk. And even if I did, I can't be held responsible for what I do when I'm unconscious."

"That's too bad, because I like the unconscious you. And the silly, drunk you who doesn't hold back."

But I *do* hold back. I'm a champion holder backer. It's my superpower, and it keeps me safe.

Neil makes it tricky, though. I have to look away from his beautiful eyes. "What is your point? You'll never convince me that you *meant* to buy the world's ugliest wedding ring and marry me at two in the morning in Vegas. If you argue that was part of your life plan, I call bullshit."

His fingertips trace the small of my back, and I break out in goosebumps. "Part of me must have thought — on some level — that it was a fabulous idea."

"Which part and which level? I bet I can guess."

I make the mistake of turning toward his smile again, and it is goddamn dazzling. "Sure. Sex had something to do with it. But that's not the thing that makes you really uncomfortable."

"By all means go ahead and mansplain my feelings to me."

Missing the irony, he does exactly that. "I know you're

attracted to me, and you don't feel like admitting it. But your real problem—the thing that makes you crazy—is that you actually *like* me. That's gotta drive you nuts, right? It's always hard to change your opinion of someone. But it's even harder for you, because you try so hard not to care enough about anyone or let them get inside here." He actually taps one finger on the bare skin of my upper chest.

And my goosebumps double.

Even worse, he's exactly right. I don't want to deal with my feelings for Neil, and I shouldn't have to. If I hadn't gotten drunk-married to him, we wouldn't even be having this conversation. "Please get out of my head. I have very good reasons for all the things I do."

"I know it," he whispers. "But here's the thing—I have really good reasons for all the things I do too." He gazes down at me, wearing a very serious expression. His hooded eyes drop to my mouth.

He's about to kiss me. I can feel it. And I'm going to let him. I want it—

The song ends. The crowd around us applauds loudly.

"That one goes out to Neil Drake and his new bride!" announces Justin B. "Congrats, man. Mazel tov."

The spell is broken. Neil—ever the gentleman—lifts his chin and gives the man on stage a friendly wave. The singer takes a bow and walks off stage just as the band launches into an instrumental dance tune. All around us, bodies begin to move to the beat.

Thank goodness. That was almost a disaster. I need a moment alone to shake it off. "I've got to…" I reach for an excuse to run away. "Touch up my lipstick."

Without waiting for a reply, I step back and then slip between two older couples happily jitterbugging.

It's not exactly graceful to ditch your new husband on the dance floor. But I do it anyway. My emotional kitty-cat needs a moment under the sofa where she's safe.

I grab my clutch purse off the table and head for the grand lobby, which is quieter and at least somewhat less populated than the ballroom. "Excuse me," I ask a uniformed man who's gathering discarded cocktail glasses from the bar and loading them onto a tray. "Is there a ladies' room nearby?"

"There's that one, which looks busy." He gestures down a hallway, where I spot a line of women waiting. "But there's another one up there and straight down the hall." He points up a grand, curving staircase. "Nobody knows about that one."

"You are a treasure. Thank you." I straighten my back and stride up the fancy staircase, clutching the curved bannister as if I belong here.

It's quieter upstairs. My heels sink into the sumptuous rug. My heart rate slows down, and I pull my phone out of the clutch to check the time. We've only been at this event for ninety minutes?

Unfrickingbelievable.

Wandering down the corridor, I find a door marked *Damsels* and roll my eyes. But if it's empty, I don't care what they call it.

Pushing open the door, I see a cluster of furniture upholstered in pink tweed. The sitting area has lit mirrors and a vanity with a supply of tissues. On the opposite wall another door leads to what I assume is the business part of the bathroom.

Before I can push through it, I hear voices.

"I can't believe he would *do* this to me! It's so humiliating."

That's Iris's voice. *Shit.* And Paisley answers her. "I'm sorry, babe."

"She's not his type at all! Little tramp from nowhere. Just like all the rest of his trash that he used to run to every time we broke up."

A gasp lodges itself in my throat, and it stings like anger. Self-preservation is the only thing that holds me back from giving her a piece of my mind. I'd like to, but I'm here for Neil.

He'd asked me to play the role of the nice little wife for an event that's important to him.

I won't blow it for him.

"That girl has no idea," Iris rants. "She's just a hobby for him. She'll figure out soon enough that he doesn't really care. There's nobody Neil really cares about except himself," she whines.

"Iris," Paisley says, and I expect her to defend her brother. "Don't cry or I'll have to redo your mascara. Here. Have a glass of water."

That's it? That's all Paisley has to say in defense of Neil? My heart thumps, and I know I should walk away before I get caught listening.

"You know what really burns me?" Iris goes on. "I spent three months of my life busting my ass to make a half a million dollars for this charity. But it only took that girl one night in Vegas and a bottle of tequila to take Neil for millions of dollars."

Holy shit. I'm burning up with fury. And she's not even done.

"That *whore* is wearing your grandmother's ring! She's not even pretty. She's a hockey player for fuck's sake. They fight dirty."

My jaw unhinges at this bit of slander. That's it. I'm done. You can't insult hockey like that.

I push that door open and walk in. "No, ma'am. I've got to correct you there. In hockey, if we have a problem with you, we say it to your face."

They both freeze, staring back at me in shock.

Paisley recovers first. She lays one manicured hand on the marble countertop and gives me a cool stare. "Are you going to go running to Neil and tell him we were gossiping about you?"

"Please," I scoff. "Of course, you're gossiping about me. How is that news? You did it in high school, too."

Her eyes narrow. "If you don't like the gossip, then maybe you should keep your mitts off my brother."

That's when I run out of comebacks. Because I know it doesn't matter how pretty my dress is, or whether I used the right fork at dinner. To these women, I'll always be *that* girl—the one who's shown up somewhere she doesn't belong.

They'll never understand that they have it all wrong. I'm not after Neil's billions. What I'd wanted that night in Vegas was even more pathetic. I'd wanted his approval. Just a little taste of what it might feel like to be someone's first choice.

My throat is starting to close down, but I lift my chin a few degrees and manage to get the last word. "It wasn't tequila, by the way. I used whiskey."

Then, lungs bursting from trying to hold in a scream, I leave the bathroom.

TWENTY-TWO

BIG PLANS. SO BIG.

Neil

I'm in the center of the lobby, leaning against the pedestal of a marble statue of Zeus, and looking for Charli.

Where has my dance partner run off to? Did I fuck up that badly? Has she left the party?

Finally, I spot her walking briskly down the grand staircase. Her legs look a mile long in those heels. *God*, that dress. I want to remove those little shoulder straps with my teeth.

As she gets closer, I notice her fierce expression. She doesn't even see me; she's just motoring down those stairs like she'll turn into a pumpkin if she tarries.

I set my club soda down on Zeus's pedestal — sorry, man — and step forward to tag Charli's hand before she can pass me. "Hey, wifey. Where's the fire?" When she turns, I have my answer — it's in her eyes. "Are you okay?"

"Of course." But the flush on her face tells a different story.

I catch her other hand, too, because she looks like someone who might do a runner. "What's the matter? You look a little angry."

"That's standard issue on this model," she says, her voice

breathy. But her eyes flick toward the staircase as if she's worried that someone is following her.

My sister and Iris come into view at the top of the stairs. They pause to lean on the railing and take in the view.

Shit. "Did something happen?"

She gives her head a shake and then looks me in the eye. "Nothing I can't handle. It's just part of the game, Neil. I'm playing my role as you asked me to. It's just a little messier than I expected it to be."

"Now hold up. Was somebody mean to you?"

Her laugh is bitter. "Does it matter? I'm a big girl."

I slide her hands a little farther into mine. "Actually, it matters very much. This arrangement was supposed to be an inconvenience, but not a trial. Nobody is allowed to be mean to you. Was it Iris?"

She flashes a smile so fast I almost miss it. "I don't know if that makes you a genius, Neil."

Probably not. "She's at the top of the stairs right now. Do I need to have a talk with her?"

"No," she says immediately. "Not on your life. I will *not* be rescued from Iris. She just…" Charli sighs. "She can't wrap her head around us as a couple. But can you blame her? I knew we'd make the least credible couple in New York City."

"That is *bullshit.*" I stroke the back of her hand with my thumb, and my grandmother's ring winks up at me. It looks beautiful on Charli's hand. I suppose I should find that shocking, but I'm kind of over my shock now. "When I look at you with your flashing eyes in this incredible fucking dress, I feel very, *very* credible."

"You don't have to flatter me," she insists.

"I'm not. I never lie to you. Not now, not ever."

She blinks. And I know what I have to do. "Credibility, here we come. Brace yourself, I'm going in."

Her lips part in surprise as I pull her closer to me. Then I tilt my head down and do the thing I've spent a lot of time trying not to do.

I kiss her. It's no polite peck, either. I slip my arms around her waist and take her mouth under mine, slanting my lips across her softer ones.

Charli makes a bitten-off sound, like she's not sure that just happened. Then her mouth softens like butter beneath mine.

Hell yes and hallelujah. I deepen the kiss, my hands full of silk, my heart full of wonder. And it's not just me. Charli clutches the lapels of my tux and melts against my chest.

For one perfect minute, she's mine. I slide my tongue over hers in the world's briefest victory lap.

But we're in a crowded room, and Charli hates a spectacle. I locate my self-control and ease the kiss to an agonizing end. I'm left looking down into Charli's hazy blue-green gaze.

"Why did you do that?" she whispers.

"To demonstrate our credibility. And because it was amazing," I whisper back.

"I noticed. But still."

"Don't overthink it. We're going to do it again. Preferably three minutes from now. But I need you to leave with me."

"You want to leave *now?*"

"Yeah, now. And I don't just want to leave, I want to *leave with you,* and give you an even more thorough demonstration somewhere more private."

"Oh." She gives me a slow blink.

"Unless you love this party so much you want to stay?"

"I don't care about the party. But we can't just..." She trails off with a guilty expression.

"Says who? We can do whatever the hell we want," I counter.

"Well, we *shouldn't,*" she corrects.

"But we're going to, right? The way you're gripping me right now says you can't wait."

Charli looks down at her hands on my body, and then hastily relaxes her grip. "Damn it all."

"See?" I press.

"Stop it. You're just being smug."

"You like it." I grin right into her freshly kissed face.

"I do *not*."

"Yeah, you do. But you have to pretend you don't, right? You pretend you're not attracted to me. You pretend you don't have a clue how we ended up working out some unacknowledged tension in Vegas."

Her gaze goes shifty, and she crosses her arms in front of that perfect chest. But she doesn't argue.

"You think it's some kind of moral failing to feel anything for me. Like you can't stay angry at the world if you're drinking a glass of overpriced champagne or taking a ride on my cock."

She makes a sound of outrage. "Cornelius Drake," she sputters. "That is *not* what a man says when he's trying to get in my panties."

I lean in close to her ear. "You're not wearing panties," I whisper. "But if you were, they'd be drenched. Because you want me, even if you hate saying so."

She exhales shakily. "That is the bossiest, most obnoxious thing anyone has said to me in years."

"Good dodge, kitten. Because I didn't hear you refute it."

She bites her lip and makes a sound of outrage. But she doesn't move away from me. We're toe to toe.

I reach up and stroke her cheek. "Can we leave, then? Fighting with you is always fun, but I have other plans for you and me."

"Plans?" she asks weakly.

"Big plans. So big."

Her eyes glaze over. I put my hands on her shoulders and gently turn her body until she's facing the exit.

"There's the door," I whisper, standing directly behind her. "All you have to do is walk through it." With those stilts she's wearing, we line up perfectly. I run my lips over the shell of her ear. "Is tonight the night? You should know that I have never wanted anything more."

Her breath stutters. She turns her head a fractional degree, and I hold my breath.

"We'll see," she whispers.

We'll see. Such a Charli way to answer. So cagey. But I'm starting to understand why she needs to be. It's not manipulation—it's self-preservation.

Charli doesn't have to save herself from me, though. I just haven't found a way to prove it to her yet.

"Go on," I whisper. "I'm right behind you."

She reaches back to grip my hand like she might like to choke it. She marches forward, anyway. I'd do a fist pump and whoop for joy, if I didn't think she'd hate it.

Quickly, we head outside. It's wintertime, and she's not wearing a coat, so she shivers immediately. "There's a cab," she says, pointing up the street.

But I have a better plan. I put two fingers in my mouth and whistle. Fifty yards down the block, the headlights of my mother's limo illuminate. The sleek car pulls out and approaches.

The driver gets out and hurries around to open the door. "Evening, sir. Departing early?"

"Yeah, Stoats. Home to Brooklyn, please. It's just the two of us."

"Yessir. There's an accident on the Manhattan Bridge. The Midtown Tunnel looks okay, or we could try the Brooklyn Bridge."

"Don't care," I grunt as he opens the back door. "Actually— pick whichever of those things will take the longest."

Charli reddens at this directive. Then she climbs into the car without a glance at Stoats and sits primly on the long seat, pulling the white mink over her shoulders.

I climb in after her, and the door shuts with a click. "Finally." I sit down on the other seat, along the rear of the car. "Come here, please," I say to Charli as I open a panel of controls. I flip a switch, and then I hit another button that pairs the stereo to my phone.

"What are you doing?" she asks from too far away.

"Shutting off the driver's speaker. What are *you* doing? Because it looks like you're not coming here." I pat the leather seat beside me.

She gives me a suspicious glance and holds her ground.

We're at an impasse, but I'm not giving up yet. "Listen here, kitten—last time you had trouble with my clip-on tie. So I'm going to solve that problem for you." I unclip the tie and toss it into the cup holder.

Charli doesn't say a word, but she's watching me with a bright, sharp gaze. She's pulled the fur around her body, her long legs splaying beneath the hem. There are fashion models who'd give a kidney to look half as sexy as she looks right now.

Music pulses through the interior of the car, and I hold her gaze. The craving I feel for her is both strong and familiar. I know she feels it, too. But this has to be her choice.

"My last tux shirt is a rag now, because you literally tore it open. So how about I help you with that step, too?" I reach for the button at my throat and undo it. Since that's fun, I do the next button as well. And the next.

Charli forgets to play it cool. She licks her lips and swallows roughly. Then she says two magic words: "Keep going."

"Yes, ma'am." If Charli wants a striptease in the back of a limo, I can work with that. I find the beat of the music with my shoulders as I shrug off the tux jacket. I toss it aside like a stripper, which wins me a tiny smile.

Then I begin working down the rest of my shirt buttons. Slowly. While we thread through stop-and-go midtown traffic. And Charli watches me with a hungry gaze.

Maybe another guy would feel ridiculous leaning back against the leather and slowly, sensuously unbuttoning his own shirt. But I am here for this, tapping a foot in time to the music, and slowly spreading the halves of my shirt to reveal my chest.

By the time I begin to caress my pecs, it's no longer a joke. I'm hella turned on. Our gazes lock, and Charli's eyes are dark and hungry. I slip my hand over my abs and then even lower. My cock is hard and tenting the fabric of my trousers, so I give it a squeeze. Charli's lips part. She takes a slow breath.

"Come here, beautiful," I say again. It's now or never. Indecision flashes through her eyes.

The moment stretches for an eternity, and I brace my heart for rejection, because she might just leave me hanging here, ever the fool.

"Fuck it," she whispers suddenly. She launches herself at me.

I would hoot with laughter, if I weren't so busy gathering her up in my lap and finding her mouth with my own. We come together in a hot kiss, and I groan against her lips.

I'm burning up for her, and I can't wait to show her how much. Her kiss kicks the door open and invites me in. Our tongues slide together, and Charli moans.

This is happening. Right here, right now.

TWENTY-THREE

ALL MY WORST IDEAS

Charli

If I made a list of all my worst ideas, mauling Neil in the back of a limo would be right at the top.

But I just can't seem to stop. The white-hot focus of Neil's kiss is a rare and beautiful thing. And beauty in my life is in short supply. It's always hard for me to let go and take what I want.

Iris and Paisley called me a tramp. But they got it backwards. This isn't normal for me. I rarely have sex, because I can't afford to show my unfiltered self to anyone.

Yet here I sit in Neil's lap, kissing him like the world's about to end. I'm hungry for his taste on my tongue. The scent of his cologne is like opium.

The wilder our kisses grow, the more I want. And don't even get me started on his strong hands, which take a slow tour of every curve on my body. His fingertips trace down my back, sliding over silk, which in turn slides over me. I break out in goosebumps from the sensual assault of the lush fabric against my skin.

Then those hands coast over my ass, stopping to give me a dirty squeeze, before they skate around my hip and down my thighs and under my skirt. He shamelessly wedges a hand between my knees, forcing me to relax and make room. I moan against his tongue when his fingers drag a line up my inner thigh.

His touch lights me up as brightly as the midtown buildings we're cruising past. The city passes like a movie we've muted in the background. It barely seems real.

There's only Neil's touch and the scent of his hair as he breaks our kiss to lick his way down my neck and between my breasts. Meanwhile, his clever hands tease my stockings off my hips and down my body.

My dress is ruched up around my waist. The word *tramp* rattles once more inside my brain, before it's chased away by the whine of my zipper as Neil slides it down my back.

I grab his head in two hands and yank it toward me again. I need his mouth. I need the sweet joining of his tongue against mine to keep my ragged thoughts at bay.

He kisses me deeply. Twice. Then I lose his mouth, but it doesn't go far. He's right at my ear, whispering instructions and encouragements. *Here. Lift your hips. Yes, baby. Unzip me. Fuck.* And finally, *lie back.*

The world tilts, and I find myself eased onto a cloud. The white mink coat has been draped across the long seat, and now I'm lying on it. I'm naked, except for the strapless corset bra that offers my tits to Neil like two dishes of fruit on a platter.

Neil leans down to feast on them. I shiver as his hand strays down my tummy, teasing my hip, and then finally, *finally* finds the place where I'm so needy for him.

I make an unseemly noise as thick fingers slide between my legs. Moaning, I spread my thighs to accommodate him on the narrow seat, and the motion rubs the soft fur against my bare skin.

This is easily the most sensuous experience of my entire life.

"Fuck, I need you," he rumbles. "I'm fucking starved for it." His mouth dips between my breasts, and my hand fumbles into his open trousers. He groans as my fingers close around his thick cock. I pump my hand up and down his length, enjoying the heat and friction of his hardness against my hand.

But it's the wrecked look on his face that I appreciate most. No matter how badly I'll regret this later, I'll never forget the expression he's wearing right now. Like he can barely stand how lucky he is.

And I know just how he feels. I yank his trousers off. He angles his hips against mine with a sexy grimace, and I'm so wet that I can feel myself leaking onto the shaft of his cock.

"Baby," he murmurs. "Fuck." All his smooth talking is gone now. He sinks down onto my body, knocking my hand away, diving into another wet kiss.

Our tongues tangle. The car accelerates, and the hum of the engine blurs through the music. I sink into the fur, my fingers in Neil's hair, one of my legs wrapped around one of his so he can't get away.

"Charli." The word is a prayer against my lips.

He'd been so smug. He'd said I'd beg him for it. I'd told him it would never happen.

I'd been wrong. "Please," I beg. "Now."

That's all I need to say. Neil produces a condom from somewhere and gears up without breaking our kiss. I don't even have time to second guess myself. A moment later he nudges thickly inside me with a happy groan.

As he bottoms out, I have to bite my tongue to keep from crying out in bliss. I slam my eyes shut and tilt my hips to take more of him, to get even closer to his hard body and the heat of his smile.

He takes both my hands in his and raises them over my head. I'm truly, deliciously caught, like a fly that finally stops struggling in the spider's web.

I'm Neil's tonight, whether it's a good idea or not. It doesn't matter anymore. Nothing matters, except his kisses and the throbbing pace he sets as he begins to move inside me.

TWENTY-FOUR

I WANT TO SPOIL YOU

Neil

I've tried so hard to prove to Charli that I'm not the selfish jerk she thought I was.

But tonight, I'm exactly that guy—the one who can't even wait to get home before fucking her. The guy who has to have her in the limo, because he's afraid to let this moment slip through his fingers.

But, God, the way Charli's body rises to meet mine on every stroke. And the way she's staring at me with a lust-filled expression, as if I invented pleasure. It could break a man.

Many women have charmed me, but few have challenged me—until this one, with her giant green eyes and her fierce gaze and her strong grip as she breaks free of my hands and tugs me by the hair down to kiss her again.

I pick up the pace, because I can't help myself. I feel wild, and Charli's hot kisses do nothing to rein me in. She strains against me, as if reaching for something just beyond her grasp.

"Let go, sweetheart," I murmur against her lips. "I've got you."

"Neil," she gasps, as if I've said something surprising. Her knees grip my hips, and she sighs with frustration.

"Give in," I rasp. "I'll catch you."

And I want it to be true. I want to make her feel what I'm feeling. I want her to need this as much as I do.

"Neil," she whispers, and it's more like a prayer this time.

I slow my roll, nudging her hips with mine, savoring the slide of our sweat-slicked skin. Our gazes lock, and there's fire behind her eyes.

"I can't last much longer," I say between kisses. "You undo me. You always have."

She gasps again. Her brow softens, and her eyes lose focus. She arches her back on a sigh, and her chest heaves. Then she finally pulses beneath me, sweetly whimpering as her eyes flutter closed, as if she can't bear to let me watch her come apart.

It's so beautiful that I can't look away, and I can't hold back. With a groan and a curse, I piston my hips and release all the pent-up need I carry around for her. My soul quakes as I kiss her lips. She bites my lip, and it hurts so good.

Then, at last, stillness.

Charli pulls me down with a clumsy tug, and we lay panting on a fur coat as the car accelerates once again.

"Look," she croaks.

I turn my head to see what she's seeing. And the lit-up Brooklyn Bridge passes like a dream over our heads.

It's not easy to regain one's dignity in the back of a limousine. Charli looks dazed as I gently help her back into her dress and stuff her stockings into my pocket.

"And to think you weren't sure about borrowing this coat," I whisper, tucking it around her shoulders, where it will hide all our sins. "You'll look perfect when we get out of the car, and I'm the one who looks like an animal."

She gives me a wry smile. "Serves you right."

The car glides to a stop before I'm ready. I worry that once we've arrived, Charli will build a fresh new wall between us.

Inevitably, the driver opens the door. "Thank you, Stoats," I say calmly while I exit the car without a glance at him.

I lift my chin, wrap an arm around my girl, and walk her toward the doorman and into the building.

"How was your evening?" Marco asks as we pass by.

"Remarkable," I say with as much dignity a man with a used condom in his pocket can muster.

Charli's cheeks are scarlet as the elevator doors glide shut. "Well. That party didn't end the way I planned," she murmurs.

I'm too smart to gloat. I just pull out my key and kiss her cheek. I let her into the apartment, and, after helping her out of the mink and hanging it in the closet, I bend my knees and scoop her up into my arms.

She lets out a little shriek of surprise. "What are you doing?"

"Taking you with me." I head for the kitchen.

"Neil!" She squirms in my arms. "What the hell?"

"I have to be careful," I explain, pacing over to the refrigerator. I open the door and grab a bottle of Coke. "Hold this, please."

Charli takes the bottle out of my hands. "What's this for?"

"In case my blood sugar dips during round two. Gotta have some sugar handy."

"*Neil.*" She wriggles, so I tote her into the bedroom and drop her onto the bed. "Why are you carrying me around like a caveman?"

"Because." I toe off my half-untied shoes. "If I leave you alone for too long, you'll start thinkin' up all the reasons this is a bad idea, blah blah blah…"

"Well, it is," she murmurs, removing her heels and setting

them carefully on the floor. Then she removes my grandmother's diamond ring and hands it to me. "I'm not like you. I can't just decide to be a hedonist."

"For one night?" I challenge. The ring is heavy in my palm.

"I'm not done dazzling you."

"Oh please, I think you already proved you're a sexy beast."

Grinning, I open my bedside table and drop the ring inside. Then I sit down behind Charli, tucking my chin onto her shoulder. "That's flattering, baby. My ego is satisfied. But this isn't about me." My heart thumps as I nuzzle her cheek. "I want to spoil you a little. You deserve it."

She shivers.

"Put this on." I rise to grab my bathrobe and hand it to her. "And I'll show you what I mean." Then I leave the room.

TWENTY-FIVE

REALLY HIGH PRODUCTION VALUES

Charli

When Neil disappears, I take a long breath. I'm in way over my head. I've given in. I've done everything I promised myself I'd avoid.

That man ravished me on the backseat of a luxury car, and I encouraged him.

What the hell has come over me?

Carefully, I unzip the blue dress and step out of it. It's wrinkled from our shenanigans in the limo. But I give it a good shake, and the silk is such high quality that I can tell it'll be okay.

I wonder if I'll ever have a reason to wear this dress again. Probably not.

I take good care of it, hanging it carefully in Neil's closet. I put on the bathrobe he left me, not because it smells tantalizingly of Neil's aftershave, damn it, but because it's cozy.

The Tantalizer in Chief emerges from the bathroom a couple minutes later, wearing nothing but boxer shorts and humming to himself as if this is all perfectly normal. He carries his suit over to the closet and hangs it up.

Then he departs again, heading for the kitchen this time. He returns a few minutes later with a tray in his hands. There's a bowl of grapes and two pink-tinted, iced cocktails tinted with lemon wedges cocked on their rims.

"I'm not drinking anything more tonight," I protest.

"No problem, kitten. This is a hydrating beverage—cranberry and soda. Now come along." He crooks one infuriating finger in my direction before carrying the tray past me and into the bathroom.

I admire his muscular body as he goes. *Grrr.* Maybe if he'd put some clothes on, I could think straight.

"Charli!" he calls. "Come snack with me."

"I wonder if that's a euphemism," I whisper. I follow him, because the moment he first kissed me tonight, I seem to have lost all self-control.

In the bathroom, he's run a deep bath in his giant corner tub. There's music playing over the speakers. He's up to his chest in foaming water, a drink in his hand. The other glass is waiting for me on the tray, which rests on the tiled surface at one end of the tub.

It's like the visual definition of decadence.

"Hop in," he says, cheerfully.

I hesitate for only a second. I'm treating tonight like the blue silk dress—something to enjoy once before hanging it in the closet as a memory.

I toss the robe aside and walk naked toward the bathtub, stepping in carefully. Neil makes an unsubtle noise of approval. Ignoring him, I sink into the warm water, holding back a groan.

My plan was to sit as far from Neil as possible, but the tub has a seat for two people, plus a deeper area where you put your feet, so I end up next to him anyway.

God. I'm such a pushover. "I bet this is how you charm all the girls."

In answer, Neil sets down his drink. He pulls me onto his lap, gently settling me against his sturdy chest.

"As a matter of fact," he says, his voice low and rumbly in my ear. "This bathtub has never had two occupants before."

"Why not?" I can't resist asking.

He lifts the other glass off the tray and hands it to me. I take a sip, and the cool fizz of the fruity soda tickles my tongue.

"Not sure," he says, smoothing my hair away from my face. "Never had the urge to invite anyone in here."

"I'm surprised," I say, arguing out of habit. "Both you and your tub were designed for decadence and seduction."

He chuckles. "You just *love* to paint me as the playboy. The party boy. The sensualist." He proves my point by kissing my neck slowly. Then he wraps an arm around my body and strokes my tummy with slick fingers. "And maybe you're right. But you also think that it's just a rich guy's attitude."

"Of course, I think that." I lean back against his shoulder and try to prevent myself from purring. "Look at us right now."

He chuckles. "Oh kitten, I *am*."

"Laugh it up. But I can't really afford to let go very often. That's just the way it is."

Neil lifts one wet hand to my shoulder and massages the muscles there. "But here's the thing," he says quietly. "You say you can't afford to let go. But I feel like I can't afford *not* to. None of us knows how much time we get. I don't mean to be dark, but people have been telling me how easy it is to die from T1D all my life."

"You're not going to *die*," I say quickly. What a horrible idea. "Not soon, anyway."

He uses one strong arm to shut off the water, and the room gets quieter.

"No, baby." He leans in and kisses my jaw. "I'm very careful and very healthy. But our time on Earth is finite, and I just happen to understand that a little better than most guys in their twenties. It makes you cautious. And sometimes it makes me live scared."

The idea of Neil Drake living scared gives me actual goose-bumps. I wouldn't think that was even possible.

"So I fight that by living each day to its fullest. I refuse to die with regrets." His firm hand gives my shoulder another squeeze. "That's why I'm a party boy when it suits me. Not afraid to get naked in the limo. Not afraid to stay up late. And not afraid to leave everything I've got on the ice during a game. Not because it's easy, but because it's worth it."

"Oh," I say softly, my head spinning. Neil really needs to stop saying smart, thoughtful things. It's messing with my head.

So is his touch. Those slick, wet fingers are traveling slowly across my torso. It's *so* nice.

"I know that letting go is hard for you," he whispers. "That's why I'm honored that you gave that to me. *Twice*. Once in Vegas and once tonight."

My goosebumps double. I tuck my cheek against Neil's bare chest and try to hang onto my composure. He's right. Letting go is hard for me. Sometimes it's excruciating.

Although, when I'm old and gray, I'll always remember this night. I'll always remember the way Neil made love to me on a fur coat and then held me in the bathtub.

Those aren't things a girl can forget. Even if she might want to.

The water makes a gentle lapping sound against the tub as Neil rubs smooth circles onto my back. Eventually, his water-slicked hand makes a pass around my rib cage, until he's cupping my breast. His thumb circles my nipple seductively.

Then he does it again. Slowly, he kisses the nape of my neck, sucking gently. He plays with my breasts until I have a new set of goosebumps for an entirely different reason.

"Is this you showing me how to have fun?" I murmur.

"Nah. Preaching's done for the night, Charli. This is me being a boob man. And your tits are spectacular."

I snort-laugh against his collarbone, because *that's* the Neil I know well. But I stop laughing pretty quickly as he takes my chin in hand and kisses me.

For a long moment, my heart wants to resist. Neil's kiss is so... intimate. His bright eyes are right there, boring into mine. I'm conscious of every inch of my skin that's touching his.

Neil somehow slides my drink out of my hand and turns me in his lap. He kisses me again, and there's no place to hide. So I thrust my fingers into his thick hair, and dip my face to kiss his strong neck, laving my tongue across his hot skin.

His sudden moan is loud and hungry. My resolve weakens. Again. He pulls me upward for another impatient kiss. He clasps me against his body like he needs me to stay. Like he wants me to feel the way his cock is hardening again between my legs.

As if I could miss it. As we kiss, our bodies slide together, dripping wet, steamy skin on skin. Just like that, Neil has broken down my defenses.

The longer he kisses me, the less I care.

Eventually, morning comes. It always does.

For the second time, I wake up topless in a bed with Neil Drake III. In fact, I'm still cuddled up next to him. His hand is a pleasant weight on my hip, and one of his big feet is wedged between mine.

In the cool light of a Brooklyn morning, I am a little stunned at everything that happened. I did the nasty with Neil Drake. *Twice*, and with great enthusiasm.

It's less surprising that Neil is so much fun in bed. I knew he would be.

But intimacy—even the fun kind—isn't something I have experience with. I can't toss my hair and write this off as an unexpected night of frivolity.

Now, whenever I look at Neil, I'll remember every detail of

those slow, searching kisses. And that thing he did in the tub with the ice cube against my nipple.

And the way he bent me over the bathroom vanity and fucked me while watching in the mirror with hungry eyes.

And the way we ate those grapes in his bed, our damp hair on the pillows, music playing on the rich-guy, invisible stereo system. The best night of my life had been set to a sound track, like a movie with a beautiful set and really high production values.

Then... more of those kisses. Who knew I even liked kissing that much? Not me. It had always made me feel too vulnerable.

Hell.

I glance at Neil, and his sleeping face gives me an unfamiliar melting sensation in my tummy. His hair is mussed, and his lips are parted in slumber.

I'm used to seeing Neil as a sexy beast, but sweet, sleepy Neil is hard on my heart in a whole new way.

His eyes blink open, and he smiles at me. "You watching me sleep, wifey?"

Guilty, I look away. "I was just wondering what time it is."

His hand leaves my hip so he can squint at his smart watch. "Eight thirty. Do you have to work?"

Slowly, I shake my head. His head lands on the pillow, and his smile returns, sexy this time. "Good, I have big plans for you."

"You do?" I ask carefully. Because my plan is to go somewhere Neil isn't and quietly freak out.

"Oh yeah. A decadent night deserves breakfast in bed. Otherwise, we're doing it wrong."

My stomach rumbles obligingly. "That sounds nice."

He reaches over and plays with a lock of my hair. "Totally. I need food and coffee, and then I need a small favor from you. I have a plan." His grin turns wicked.

"What kind of favor?" I ask warily.

He laughs, and then, like sexy spatulas, his arms lever

beneath me and slide me close. "Last night you were down with every single dirty plan I made for you. If you want to pretend otherwise, though, you go ahead."

My bare back makes contact with his hard chest, and I feel a shimmy in my nether regions.

This is all very bad news. Those hours of effort I'd expended resisting Neil? They were wasted. I'm basically a light switch he can turn on or off just by touching me.

"Don't be smug," I complain. "Just tell me your big plan."

"Well…" He kisses the back of my neck, and I squeeze my lips together to avoid a whimper. "…I'd like to measure my living room."

"Um, what?"

"Focus, kitten. If I'm buying a new couch, I need to know what size the place is."

"Extra-large," I point out. "They haven't invented a sofa that won't fit into your living room."

"Good to know. But I don't want to screw up the couch twice, you know? You can hold the other end of the tape measure. We should measure the old couch, too."

"Fine," I agree. "Just as long as you don't try to have couch sex on it. I don't need those buttons embossed on my butt cheeks."

Neil cracks up, and his fine abs contract against my body. "What would they say in the locker room?"

"Let's not find out."

He chuckles. "Okay, here's the plan—you start the coffee, and I'll order breakfast sandwiches from the deli. And we have breakfast in bed."

"Okay," I say, scrambling for the edge of the mattress. I need a moment alone to gather my wits, and he's just given me an excuse. "I get the bathroom first."

"Of course, you do." I can feel his heated gaze on my bare body, but I refuse to turn around to acknowledge it. "What kind of egg sandwich do you want?"

I have never felt more naked than I do right now, as I cross the room toward the bathroom. "Surprise me."

After a two-minute shower and a moment with my toothbrush, I make coffee in the kitchen. Wearing a Bruisers T-shirt that I stole from Neil, I'm prepping two mugs when he calls out from the bedroom, "Breakfast is on the way!"

I pour milk into the mugs and take a deep, cleansing breath. So what if I slept with him? I don't have to make it weird. Just two adults having a romp. People do it all the time.

Not us, though. Until last night on the seat of a damn limousine. Part of me can't believe that happened. And other parts of me want to do it again.

With one more steadying breath, I carry the mugs into the bedroom. Neil has donned a pair of flannel pants and nothing else. Reclining against a mountain of pillows, his computer propped on his rippling abs, he looks like a dream.

My blood fizzes again, and my pulse kicks up a notch. Who even needs coffee? I'm buzzing on post-carnal endorphins and a good night's sleep.

"Aw, thanks, wifey." Neil takes a mug and gives me a big, happy smile. "Now sit your sexy ass down beside me while I google furniture sizes."

I take a sip of my coffee and hesitate. Neil and I need to have a talk, but all I can do is stare at his incredible chest.

The door chimes, so I set my coffee down. "I'll get it!"

"I tipped him already," Neil calls after me as I leave the room again.

I float toward the front door, reminding myself that this is temporary. The food deliveries, the fluffy towels, the giant shower with three heads, the fancy coffee and the incredible sex.

Sometime soon the clock will strike twelve, and I'll turn into a mouse again.

That's just the way it is.

After egg sandwiches with cheese and bacon, we measure the living room. Neil writes down the measurements in fastidious handwriting in a small notebook. When he sets the notebook on the corner desk, I realize I never gave him the couriered envelope that had arrived when he was traveling.

"Hey," I say, trotting over to the desk and finding the envelope. "This is what I signed for while you were gone." I offer it to him.

"Oh, thanks." He takes the envelope and tears a corner off. He slides his finger into the opening and then... stops.

He sets it on the desk again.

"Do you want me to give you some privacy? I don't want to crowd you if that's personal."

He blinks. "No way. I'm not ignoring this because it's private. I'm ignoring it because I'm in a really good mood right now, and I don't want my uncle to tank it."

"Oh." My heart flutters. "What if it's important?"

"It won't be. Because I decide what's important." He pulls me into a hug. "I have a game tonight."

"I know," I say against his chest. "Aren't you supposed to be at morning skate?"

"It's optional. I skipped it."

"Really?" Neil is always such a hard worker. "Do you skip the optionals?"

"I did today. Seems like a good decision so far."

I swallow. Hard.

"So here we are, with a morning off together." He runs a hand up my back. "And you seem jumpy."

"I'm not jumpy," I say, because arguing is a reflex. "But we need to talk."

"About last night, kitten? It was amazing." I wait for another smug comment about his performance or my willingness. But it doesn't come. "What do you want to talk about?"

I peel myself out of his arms, because I have to at least pretend to be dignified. "We complicated our lives again," I explain. "It's messy."

"Well, I hear what you're saying," he says softly. "But last night it seemed pretty simple. And I have no regrets. Do you?"

As if that's an easy question. I *will* regret this. But right this moment, he's watching me with those warm, hazel eyes, and I can't bring myself to shut down that soft look he's giving me. "No, I don't regret it. It was a little harmless fun. Between..." I hesitate. "Friends."

He laughs suddenly. "Hurt you to call us friends, did it?"

"No," I lie. If I admit that Neil and I are friends, I have to admit that I was wrong about him. I'm not good at admitting I'm wrong.

He lowers his voice to a sexy growl. "I told you we'd end up in bed again."

"Friends don't say *I told you so.*"

"Touché." He grins. "You enjoyed yourself, wifey. And I'm willing to bet you could enjoy yourself a whole lot more before our little situation ends."

Our little situation. He means our marriage. I can't decide if this euphemism is a kindness or a copout. "Probably," I say primly.

"Probably," he repeats, a smile in his voice. He smooths a hair off my forehead. "Like I've said before, you're hard on my ego."

I doubt that's true, but it's beside the point. "So this is a short-term thing. A little fling," I clarify.

"It's not that little," he says, wiggling his eyebrows.

"Neil! I'm trying to set some ground rules here."

Then he hugs me, damn it. I'm a tough girl, but affection —
when I allow myself to enjoy it — is my Achilles heel. "A short-
term fling," he repeats. "I can work with that."

I lean into his warmth in spite of myself. And I wonder
when the regret will start to kick in.

It's coming for me. It always does.

TWENTY-SIX

LIKE SHIPS PASSING IN THE NIGHT

Charli

It turns out that two professional athletes who are married to each other don't actually spend that many hours together. Neil travels at least half the week, and my team has traveled the last two weekends.

When Neil first asked me to stay with him, he'd said we'd be like two ships passing in the night. He would've been right—if ships also spent each fleeting moment ripping each other's clothes off and banging on every surface of the apartment.

Well, not every surface. We've never once resorted to that awful couch.

Still, I can barely believe my own behavior. Sometimes when Neil's not around, I'll stop whatever I'm doing and remember one of our crazy moments together. I'll picture his heated gaze as he rolls over in bed to kiss me. Or the groan he makes when I drop to my knees in the shower to suck him off—

"Charli?" Sylvie nudges me with her elbow. "Are you okay?"

"Yep," I say quickly.

"You zoned out. Want a cocktail before we pick a table?"

She points across the hotel ballroom. "That bar in the corner doesn't look too overrun."

"Sure," I mumble, following her across the carpeting. It's a Sunday night, and we're attending a charity event—Brooklyn Hockey Casino Night. Members of the public and hockey players mingle and play cards. The chips are real, but every dollar goes to the Boys and Girls Clubs of Brooklyn.

Nate and Rebecca sure know how to throw a party. The place is packed. We get in line for a drink, and I find myself gazing out over the crowd again, looking for Neil. I haven't seen him in four days.

"Can't find him yet?" Sylvie asks.

I turn back to her with a frown. "Who? I was just looking around."

She rolls her eyes. "You don't fool me at all."

That's disheartening, because I am really good at fooling myself.

"There he is, by the way," Sylvie says, nudging me. "Neil just sat down at a blackjack table by the window."

I turn my head like a lost dog looking for her master. And there he is, smiling at a teammate, peeking at the cards the dealer has just set in front of him.

"Here," Sylvie says, pushing a glass of red wine into my hands. "Now I'm going to find my man, just like you're going to find yours. And please give him a big fat kiss so your teammates can all stop arguing about whether or not you two are practicing for a gold medal in naked bobsledding."

"*Naked bobsledding?* What the hell kind of a metaphor is that?"

She shrugs. "I can't pretend to understand what's in your brain, so I guess you don't have to understand mine. I love you anyway, though." She leans in and gives me a kiss on the cheek. Then I watch as she saunters through the crowd toward Anton.

I take a sip of my wine and make a slow circuit of the big room, pausing here and there to watch my teammates play a hand, and clapping for Samantha when she has a great roll at the craps table.

But I'm really just stalling. I'm headed for Neil, whether it's a good idea or not. And when someone leaves the seat next to his, I drop my pretense and hustle over there to take it before anyone else can.

"Good game last night, boys," I say, nodding at Neil's teammate across the table as I slide into the empty seat.

"Thanks, wifey," Neil says as I slide into the chair. "Long time no see."

Newgate watches with a smirk as Neil leans in and gives me a chaste kiss on the cheek.

What Newgate can't see, however, is that Neil's hand just landed on my knee. And his fingertips are already busy stroking my inner thigh in the space between my tall boots and my short skirt. "I heard you guys beat Albany again with Sylvie in the net."

"True story," I say, pulling a stack of chips out of my purse. The Bombshells were given our chips, so I don't have a financial stake here.

I'm playing for pride only. My usual currency.

"You any good at blackjack, wifey?" Neil asks casually as his thumb takes a slow tour of my thigh.

"Not a huge gambler," I say lightly. "But once in a while it's fun."

Gambling is a pretty big problem for my brother. He's always sure that he's right around the corner from a huge win. Honestly, I don't understand where he gets the optimism.

"Place your bets," the dealer says.

I nudge a chip onto the better circle. Neil nudges two chips. "Oh, so it's going to be like that?" I put a second one down to match Neil's bet.

The dealer gives us each two cards. I've got a six and a seven. Neil has a nine and an eight. Newgate crows over his two face cards. The dealer gets a five.

Neil brings his naughty hand up onto the table to take a sip of his drink. As he sips, he waves his hand sideways to decline another card.

I tap the table for a hit and get a two.

Newgate beats the dealer, and I mentally wave goodbye to my two chips.

I bet one chip for the next hand and decide to get my kicks a different way—this time it's me with a hand on Neil's thigh. I watch my cards—they're better this time—and I take my fingertips on a slow, teasing journey of Neil's leg.

He wins the hand anyway. Bastard.

But I don't let up. I keep playing while carrying on a conversation with the woman sitting to my left. All the while, my hand massages Neil's thigh so slowly that nobody will notice.

When I win a round, I use both hands to collect my winnings.

Then? My hand goes back under the table where I wedge it between his legs.

Right in the middle of telling a joke to the table, he squeezes his powerful thighs together, trapping my hand in place.

I wiggle my fingers closer to his crotch. With my free hand, I tap the table for another card. Honestly, I didn't know gambling could be this fun.

Even more surprising—I never knew I could be so sexually attracted to anyone. So free with it.

In college, friends would sometimes ask me about my sexuality. My running joke was that I was a celebritysexual. I dreamed of having a threesome with the stars of the *Hunger Games* movies—Liam Hemsworth and Jennifer Lawrence. Josh Hutcherson would have been welcome, too.

Sex with real people never seemed as interesting to me. Real people were unpredictable, if not downright scary. Sex was often less fulfilling than I expected it to be.

But with Neil, I'm a natural. Or at least he makes me feel

that way. He has some serious skills, and I'm the lucky beneficiary.

That must be why it's so good between us. He's flipped a switch inside me, and now all I think about is the weight of his body on top of mine and the heat of his kisses.

Newgate wins a hand, and the dealer shuffles. I stop torturing Neil for a minute to sip my wine and keep up the pretense of being someone who isn't horribly distracted and hoping it's almost time to go home.

"Kitten," Neil says into my ear. "You're evil."

I want to point out that he started it, but his teammate is watching with curious eyes from across the table. "Of course, I remembered to send in your dry cleaning," I say loudly. "That's what good wives do."

"Yeah? I can think of some other things," he says grumpily, and his teammate snickers.

I smile sweetly at Newgate and place my bet.

Then I put my hand *right* on the fly of Neil's trousers. I can't stroke him, because the angle is odd, and people would notice. So I just press gently.

And wow. *Hello there, sir.*

Neil grunts.

I glance at the cards on the table. The dealer has a six. I have a jack and an eight, and Neil has the same hand. *Interesting.*

The play circles the table, heading for us. At the exact moment the dealer looks to Neil, I close my hand around his cock.

He jerks, tapping the table. "Oops…um…"

Too late. The dealer hits him with a card—a five. He's bust.

"Dude," Newgate says. "Why?"

Neil sighs as I win the hand with my eighteen. "Check, please," he says. "Gather up your winnings, wifey. Come and get a drink with me."

Biting my lip, I scoop up my chips.

Neil stands slowly, buttoning his suit jacket very carefully, a grumpy frown on his handsome face.

"Sorry." I cackle as we walk away. "What do you want to drink?"

"Come here," he grunts, grabbing my hand. "There's something I want to show you." He heads for an exit in the corner. We step out into a narrow corridor, and Neil frog-marches me to a door marked *Billiards*.

He pushes it open. The room inside is dimly lit and—

Actually, I have no idea what it looks like because Neil pushes me up against the door and seals his mouth to mine.

And it happens. Again. I lose track of everything except the knowing press of his kiss. Forgetting myself, I moan against his tongue.

A pair of big hands grabs my butt and lifts. My skirt hikes up, and I wrap my legs around him.

He bucks his hips, his hard cock rudely grinding against my panties. "That's what you do to me," he says against my mouth. "All the fucking time."

I nip his lip instead of answering, but I'm in the same boat. My attraction to him is both a revelation and a curse. Of all the people in the world, I had to discover a sexual affinity for *Neil Drake*?

Why, lord? Why?

In all my twenty-four years I've never been obsessed with anyone, and I'd liked it that way. Then came Neil with his chiseled good looks and his skillful kisses. And now we're so familiar with each other's bodies. He knows exactly how to push my buttons. The familiarity is a drug in and of itself.

"Baby." He breaks our kiss so he can suck on my neck. "I missed you so much."

My inner kitty-cat rolls over on her back and purrs, the little traitor.

Neil cups my breast and tweaks my nipple, and I wrap my legs even more tightly around his body,

"I have a condom," he whispers. "And you're wearing this short little skirt."

Just the idea makes me wet. "This is a bad idea," I reply. And I don't just mean having sex in a strange room where we might get caught. I mean all of it—the fake marriage, the sneaking around.

The constant, addictive sex.

"I'll be quick," he pants, setting me on the pool table. "And so will you."

He isn't wrong.

And here I am tugging his zipper down. I don't even know myself anymore.

He tugs my panties down and then suits up, the condom wrapper shoved into his pocket, his trousers hanging down around his thighs. I brace my hands on the cool felt behind me.

Then it happens—Neil fills me with a heady thrust. We both gasp at the same time. And when I lift my chin, I see my own wonder reflected back at me in his bright, astonished eyes.

TWENTY-SEVEN

DATE NIGHT

Neil

We get away with our pool-table moment, crazy as it is. Nobody walks in on the frantic quickie that leaves us panting and staring into each other's soul.

Afterwards, I fantasize about it for days.

Nobody has ever wrecked me quite like Charli does. She doesn't like to talk about herself. She's cagy — except during sex or when we're lazing together in bed. Those are the only times I feel like we're speaking the same language.

In all my years of dating Iris on and off, I never once had the urge to move her in. But having Charli close by is an unexpected pleasure. Slipping into bed beside her makes me happy. Even when it's late and we're both tired, we'll usually turn on a game and burrow under the covers together.

I could fall for her. Maybe I already have. I think I started falling on day one, right in the middle of that lecture she gave me for calling her *doll*.

I don't know how Charli feels, though, or what to do about it. She's been asking me how our divorce is going. That makes the conversation trickier, especially since there hasn't been a lot of forward progress.

To make matters worse, I've screwed things up with the Family Foundation. I'd warned Charli that the upcoming meeting would be important, but I'd never opened that packet my uncle had sent me.

Which I now regret, seeing as my damn uncle changed the meeting's date.

My mother is pissed off at me, too. "He won't budge, Neil," she huffs. "This is a disaster."

We're on the phone, so she can't see me scowl. "That asshole." I kick an exercise ball in anger, and it ricochets off the wall of the gym and then hits me in the crotch. "Ouch."

"What's the matter?"

"Nothing," I grumble. "Just another error."

"You're full of them lately."

"Thanks, Ma. You always know what to say." I roll my eyes. She can't see that, either.

"What do you want from me? I tried. But your uncle did everything according to the bylaws. If you'd opened that packet sooner, you would have understood what he was up to. And you could have fixed this before the deadline."

"Thanks for that reminder."

I shouldn't be short with her, because she's right. Several weeks have passed since that packet of documents was delivered. And I've spent all my time on three things: winning hockey games, traveling, and spending time with Charli. I haven't had a moment for paperwork.

It's been a *great* month. But I missed the con my uncle had pulled—as president of the board, he changed the date of our quarterly foundation meeting to coincide with one of Charli's away games. She'll be on a bus to Boston on the Friday afternoon when the board is meeting to vote on next quarter's charitable activities.

I hadn't registered my objection to the new date within

ninety-six hours' time. Which means my side of the family can't wield our new majority like a cudgel, and I won't be able to force my uncle to change the terms of my mother's trust.

"Neil, I think your wife should support you on this," my mother says. "You can ask her to change her plans and be there for you."

Oh, hell no. "She doesn't have *plans*, Mom. She has a game."

"At four in the afternoon?"

I want to scream. "It's an away game. She'll be on a bus to Boston. They'll leave at two. The game is at seven."

"What if we flew her up there right after the meeting?" she asks. "We could have her at Teterboro by... six. Wouldn't that work?"

I'm ashamed to say that I've already done this math. And of course, it doesn't work out. "You can't just jet in and arrive at the rink when they're singing the national anthem. You have to be there with your team. This is Charli's career. She can't treat it like a hobby."

"How about a sick day?" she suggests.

I'm betting Charli never took a sick day in her life. "Look, I'm *sorry*. Maybe this is God's way of telling us not to fuck with Uncle Harmon."

It had been a stupid idea in the first place. I should have known his evil ass would outmaneuver me.

"There's always next quarter," my mother says with a sigh.

And now I feel like a giant dick, because there won't be any next quarter.

Then my mother twists the knife. "I sent you and Charli an email with several party venues today. Did either of you get a chance to look at them?"

I pinch the bridge of my nose. "No, we haven't had a chance. Like I said, there's just too much going on in our lives to plan a party right now. It makes, uh, more sense to do this in the summertime."

By then we'll be divorced, of course. And my mother will stop asking.

I can't believe I'd thought this lie was a reasonable idea. Our charade has accomplished nothing, except for me being an ass to my family and making Charli uncomfortable.

"I'll plan the party by myself, then," my mother says, sounding snippy. "You can't get married and expect nobody to acknowledge it."

"*Mom.*" I hold back a groan. "I have to go. We'll talk about the party another time. For Christ's sake, don't book anything without speaking to me."

She says a stiff goodbye, and I carry my phone back into the locker room where my teammates are horsing around together. Newgate is trying to recruit people to go with him to a party, but he's having a hard time.

"Did I mention there will be *Sports Illustrated* swimsuit models there?" he asks, upping the ante.

"Look, Newguy." Leo Trevi puts a hand on his shoulder. "I know this is difficult for you young bucks to understand. But some of us already found the perfect woman, and we're happy going home to hang out with her."

"Yeah, it's date night," Mike Beacon says.

"For me, too," Silas agrees. "Delilah just got back into town."

Newgate's gaze swings to me. "And Drake? None of us can figure you out, man. Are you married for real, or is this just a phase?"

I chuckle uncomfortably as the whole room turns to hear the answer. Even though I'm close to these guys, I haven't confided in my teammates at all. For very good reason. "It's complicated."

And that's an understatement.

"Huh." Newgate puts his hands on his hips. "Does that mean you're in or out, tonight? It's going to be awesome."

"Sounds like fun," I lie. "But I guess it's date night for me, too, since the Bombshells have the night off."

"I'm stoked!" Anton agrees, shouldering his bag. "Sylvie better be waiting for me at home. Naked. In our bed. It's been a long week."

He's not wrong. We got back from a road trip last night at eleven. I climbed into bed beside a sleeping Charli and passed right out. She was gone when I woke up.

"What are you doing for date night?" Newgate asks.

"I kind of need to buy a sofa," I tell him. "And I thought Charli and I could go look at them."

The whole room erupts with laughter. "Wait, wait. How long have you guys been married?" Castro asks. "Thirty days, or thirty years?"

"Jesus Christ, you really *are* an old married guy now!" Tank says, slapping me on the shoulder. "Welcome to the club, man."

"Laugh all you want," I tell them. "But I finally got rid of the couch you've all bitched about. The charity picked it up this week. And we can't watch hockey in my apartment until I have somewhere for you assholes to sit."

"We can't watch TV in your apartment until you actually get a TV in that big-ass living room of yours," Trevi points out.

"I'm working on it. But I need some guidance. Where do you shop for a couch?"

A silence falls over the room. Newgate shakes his head. "See this?" He loosens the towel from around his waist and flashes his cock at me. "It's called a dick. The fact that I have one means I don't shop for furniture."

"You must be very proud," I deadpan. "I guess I'll just google it, then."

"Don't you have people for this?" Castro asks.

"Yeah, but the decorator bought that first monstrosity, so I thought I would go it alone this time." I pull out my phone to google furniture stores in Manhattan, but I text Charli, instead. *Big idea! Let's go buy a couch tonight. You down?*

My phone rings a moment later. "Hey," she says, a little

breathless. "Long time no speak. I didn't even hear you come to bed last night."

"It was late." I sit down on the bench so I can give her my full attention. "We're having dinner later, right?"

"If you still want to," she says.

"Of course I still want to. How was your day off?"

"Glorious. Except Sylvie talked me into a manicure and pedicure. So I squandered a perfectly good hour and a half getting my toes painted."

"Huh. Can't say I've ever tried it. Would it kill your buzz if we went sofa shopping?"

"That could be fun," she says. "That big empty space in the living room is finally getting to you?"

"Definitely." I sigh.

"What's wrong?" she asks. "You sound tired."

It's weird how she can pick up on my mood in a two-minute phone call. "Nothing's wrong. This is the way I always sound when I get off the phone with my mother."

She laughs. "Yeah, been there. By the way—your mother emailed me about party venues. And I have no idea how to put her off."

"I heard. I'm dealing with it, I swear. So where are we going to buy this sofa? I need guidance. You have any ideas?" Charli isn't exactly a sure bet. Like me, she's got other things going on in her life that are more pressing than home décor.

"Oh! I know just the place," she says.

I grin, because I love how she always surprises me. And then I make plans to meet her in Manhattan.

After we end the call, I'm about to head out, but Newgate stops me. "Did your old lady know where to shop?"

"She did," I say with a smirk. "Guess you were right."

I wonder what Charli would do if she heard him call her my *old lady*? Probably throw down her gloves and try to rip his face off.

It's anyone's call who'd win that fight.

TWENTY-EIGHT

CAYENNE

Charli

Running a few minutes late, I hurry through the streets of SoHo until I see the Crate and Barrel store rising up in front of me. It's all lit up inside. I push through the front door as excited as a kid on Christmas.

I love this store. I used to walk past it every time my prep-school team played a certain school in suburban Boston.

The only time I'd ever gone inside, I'd found a coffee mug on sale for just five bucks. It had been glazed in a sunshiny yellow, and I'd bought it with the last money in my wallet.

The following summer had been the last time I ever stayed at my aunt Regina's place. She'd been mad at me for finishing the peanut butter, and had thrown my yellow mug against the wall and smashed it.

Just another fun day in the extended Higgins family.

Inside the store, I skid to a stop in front of a collection of dishes. *Inquire about Our Wedding Registry*, a sign reads.

Clearly, I'm in the wrong department.

I spin around and head for the escalator. It delivers me upstairs where the furniture lives. As I slowly arrive on the second level, I spot Neil standing in the midst of a big expanse of furniture, a thoughtful expression on his handsome face.

Just that first glimpse of him hits me like a ton of bricks. Even if I hadn't seen his face, I'd recognize his posture. Or his gait. Or the way his too-long hair curls to the left at the nape of his neck.

Then he turns and catches sight of me, his eyes lighting up. *God*, that smile. A fizz of warmth bubbles up inside me. It's disconcerting, yet lately I feel it all the time. I pick up my pace, because I can't help myself. My emotional kitty-cat leaps forward and practically climbs his leg.

Goddamn it. I've got it bad for my fake husband. This is such a disaster.

"Wifey," Neil says with a grin. He meets me halfway and puts both hands on my shoulders. The weight of his touch makes my inner kitty purr. "Nobody warned me there were, like, a hundred different kinds of sofas."

"You need me to set up a playoffs bracket?" I ask with a smirk. "Does this get easier for you if I translate it into hockey terms?"

"Someone's a smartass." His hazel eyes flash. Then he leans down and kisses me, right here in the living room section at Crate and Barrel.

The room seems to tilt. It's been four or five days since I've seen Neil, and I've missed this. That's how addictive his kisses are.

He steps back too soon, smiling at me. "It's date night."

"So you said." I glance away, because his smile is so brilliant it almost burns.

"Let's buy a motherfucking sofa!" He turns to survey the choices. "Now tell me which one of these looks the most comfortable. And how do we narrow it down?"

After a moment's perusal, I am ready to agree that there are an intimidating number of couches. "Let's break this down—

fabric or leather? Leather costs more, and it's not very eco friendly."

"Let's try fabric this time," he says. "But the color can't be too light. I don't want to worry about my friends spilling beer on it."

I don't know why this makes me smile. "You are a very practical billionaire. Let's talk about style now. That one is mid-century modern." I point at one with slim wooden legs that would look right at home on *Mad Men*.

"Pass," he says. "I like 'em big and fluffy. I'm a boob man, remember?"

I roll my eyes as he chuckles.

"Come over here." He takes my hand. "That sign says *The Lazy Sunday Collection*. Now we're talking." He leads me to another group of slightly different configurations of a generously sized sofa in two different colors—nickel and cayenne. "Still so many choices, though."

"Your living room is *huge*," I remind him, pointing to the longest one. "You could handle the ninety-six-inch couch easily."

"Oh baby, *yes*. More is more where inches are concerned. Am I right?"

This stupid joke manages to crack me up, because I'm inexplicably happy right now. Watching Neil pick out a sofa is the most fun I've had since… Well, since the last time I let him get me naked.

"Whoa!" he says, walking over to one model. "Check this out! There's an extra deep section for your feet."

Sure enough, he's found a huge L-shaped couch with an extended chaise at one corner. "That's fun."

"Right? Baby, our butts belong right *here*." He sits down on the sofa and pats the cushion beside him. "Come, kitten. Test the sofa with me."

I sit down beside Neil as if we were a real married couple looking at furniture together.

He wraps an arm around me. "Is this a big improvement, or what?"

"Huge," I admit. "Although anything in this store would be."

"Good pick, wifey. I like Crate and Barrel. And I love this couch. Wait—we gotta test the footrest part." He toes off the shiny slip-on shoes he's wearing and kicks his feet onto the chaise.

"Neil, are you wearing Gucci loafers? That's very on-brand for you."

"They're comfortable. And so is this couch. See?" He scoops me closer, so we're both in range of the chaise. I obligingly lean over and untie my shoes so I can join him.

"Are you wearing Doc Martens? That's very on-brand."

"Shut up." I kick my feet up beside his. And now I feel even more like a wife out testing furniture with her hubby.

Freaky.

Neil extends a hand and moves his thumb up and down.

"What are you doing?"

"Practicing changing the TV station. I need a TV in my living room. Screw the decorator. That means I need a TV console table..."

"It's possible you're getting a little carried away now."

"Am I? I remember someone telling me recently that a rich asshole like me could have any furniture he wanted. Pretty sure those words came out of your mouth." He kisses my jaw. "Or do I have that wrong?"

"*Neil.*"

He chuckles. Then he kisses my hair.

And there it is again—that fizzy feeling inside my chest. I can't let myself get used to this. I don't know how long it takes for furniture to be delivered, but I'd lay odds that we'll have filed for divorce by then.

"Which color are we getting?" He picks up a metal ring with swatches on it. "Nickel is just a nice word for *gray.*" He flips to the other square of fabric. "How about cayenne?"

"Hmm." Cayenne is a deep red-orange. Like a nicely aged red brick. "I like it."

"Me too! Wait—" He reaches behind his back and pulls out a throw pillow. "Do I need fuzzy pillows like this, too?"

"If sir wants fuzzy throw pillows, sir shall have fuzzy throw pillows."

Neil snorts. Then he waves a hand in the air.

"What are you doing?"

"Calling the nice sales lady over. She's going to sell me a couch."

I stand up and put my shoes back on while Neil greets the salesperson.

"Patricia, I think I found the one. How quickly can I have this kind of Lazy Sunday sofa, in cayenne, delivered to Brooklyn? I'm willing to pay a rush fee."

Of course he is.

Neil asks me where I want to eat, and I pick that Turkish place again. I've been more or less dreaming about the food since last time we went there.

"I ordered for us last time," Neil says, tossing down the menu after a single glance. "But I wouldn't want to assume what the lady wants to eat."

"You are so progressive." I put my menu down, too. "But I want the same things as last time. Do it up."

He gives me a smug smile and places the identical order, right down to the glass of wine he chose for me last time.

The food is just as good tonight. Maybe even better. After eating a giant portion, I finally make myself slow down. "God, I needed that," I say with a happy sigh.

Neil gives me a slow smile from across the table. "You're a fun dinner date, wifey."

"Thanks, hubby."

But then his smile fades. And he's fiddling with his napkin in a way that isn't his usual cocky billionaire manner.

"Something bothering you?" I demand.

He looks up with a sheepish expression on his face. "I have a little problem, which probably has no solution. You know how I gave you a date in March for the quarterly meeting of the foundation?"

"Yes. It's on my calendar. Why?"

He props his handsome face in his hand and sighs. "My uncle moved the date. As the chairman, he can do that. I could have objected, but the time for me to do so has passed."

I have a sinking feeling. "Moved it to what?"

"A Friday afternoon at four."

"*Which* Friday?" I pull out my phone.

He reaches across the table and covers my hand. "I already looked, Charli. You'll be halfway to Boston when this meeting convenes."

"Hell." I drop the phone on the table. "What does this mean? I don't get to vote?"

He shakes his head. "The bylaws say there's no absentee voting. Which means we can't strong-arm Uncle Harmon into negotiating with us on the other things we want from him. Not this quarter, anyway."

Whoa. "What do you mean, *this* quarter. When's the meeting after that one?"

He winces. "June."

"*June!*" My temper flares. "You said our divorce would be final by then."

"It can be," he says quietly, smoothing the napkin on his lap once again. "I made that promise, and I'll keep it. Unless you want to try to make that June meeting."

"*And?*" I pick up my wine glass and take a sip to cover my reaction. This can't be happening. He did *not* just ask for a three-month extension.

"If that was the new plan, we, uh, couldn't file until after the meeting." He worries his butter knife on the tablecloth.

"And the divorce would happen...?"

"August. Or, well, September."

I might break apart from confusion. A few minutes ago, we were two people out on a fun date. But now it feels like a setup. Is he wining and dining me to get another shot at family politics? "How long have you known about this?"

He shrugs like it doesn't matter. "A few days? A week? I asked my mother to try to get the meeting date changed back. She couldn't."

The waiter drops the check on the table, and I watch Neil slide his Amex Black card onto the slip of paper. And I don't think I can survive being Neil's fake wife until the fall. Three extra months of holding his hand at Drake family functions. Three extra months of pretending this is my life. Three extra months of rolling over to curl up against him in bed.

Only to walk away after all those moments of lighting up each time he smiles at me.

"No," I blurt out. "I would have showed up and voted with you. I wanted to help you. But this last-minute change isn't my fault."

"I know," he says quickly. "Forget I mentioned it."

"I have a *game*, Neil," I say, my mind racing. "I can't just call in sick. My games are just as important as yours are."

"Did you hear me argue with that?" he asks, one eyebrow cocked.

"No, but..." I let out a deep sigh. "You want me to make a sacrifice. Otherwise, you wouldn't have brought it up in the first place."

"Not true," he says, his frown deepening. "I told you about it because we have a partnership here..." He waves a hand back and forth between us. "No matter how unusual. And we're *friends*, right? Am I still allowed to assume that?"

"Yes," I say softly. But that doesn't make it better. We

should have stayed friends, because sleeping with him is messing with my head.

When it comes to Neil, I keep making the same mistakes over and over again. I've got to stop. Right now, preferably. I've got to keep a cool head.

I push back my chair. "Dinner was excellent. Thank you for coming back here with me."

He tilts his head to the side. "Don't do that, Charli."

"Don't do what?"

"Get all polite on me. I thought we were past that."

"Should we be?" I demand. "This was always just an arrangement. What do you think will happen when it's over? *All* the politeness. Nothing but politeness. And that day is coming soon. Whether you're ready or not."

TWENTY-NINE

I CAN EXPLAIN

Neil

Well, shit. The moment I brought up the meeting next quarter, I knew I'd fucked up. I should have kept my mouth shut. We were having a good time.

Now Charli is closing up like a clamshell over there—her face unreadable, her body pushed back from the table. She's running scared.

I'm a damned idiot.

"Hey," I say softly. "I know this game we're playing is temporary. But I didn't mean to ruin our fun." *Not yet.* "This thing with my uncle is a setback. But you don't have to feel weird if my end of this bargain doesn't work out. Hell—you probably think I'm about due for a few setbacks in life anyway, right?"

I expect her to agree, but she just shakes her head. "I *don't* think karma owes you a kick in the teeth, Neil. I swear. But we made everything complicated. And then we made it *more* complicated. At some point, we have to make it less complicated. We might as well start now."

Then she stands up and plucks her coat off the back of the chair.

Oh no.

I rise too, and the waiter comes running over with my receipt. I add the tip, sign, and hand it back in mere seconds. But Charli is already on the move. I don't catch up with her until she's ten paces down the sidewalk outside.

"Wifey," I call, rushing after her. "Don't ditch me. That's in the handbook, too."

She slows her pace and sighs.

"Don't panic," I say, catching up to her. "Please? I don't expect you to throw yourself on the sword to defeat the Dark Lord. And you and I were having fun tonight."

She stops and turns to me. "Yes, we were. I was, anyway. But fun isn't going to get us out of this mess. And I have no idea what will."

I search my brain for some way to disagree, but I come up blank. I take Charli's hand in mine and rub my thumb over her palm. We start walking again, more slowly this time.

She lets me hold her hand, at least. That's always my way in with Charli. Her words never cut me a break, but when I touch her, she can't resist me. And she can't hide it.

Then I realize I do have a crumb of good news for her. "Guess what? I finally hired the right divorce attorney, by the way. And the lawyer needs to meet you before I file."

"Why does he want that?"

"*She,*" I say, my mouth curving into a smile. "Why did you assume it was a man. So sexist, Charli. Wow."

She tips her head back and laughs. "Okay, that was a setup. Cheap shot, Drake."

"Maybe." But I got her smiling again, and I am covered in victory. Making Charli smile is one of my favorite hobbies. Along with feeding her.

And making her moan.

"Why does she need to meet me?"

"Oh—to make sure you understand your rights. And to discuss the filing. That's why I liked her. She was unsettled by the idea that you don't have your own representation. She's really invested in thinking through all the issues and making sure we get the resolution we want."

"That's nice," she says. "But the resolution is pretty simple, no?"

I hesitate. Because it turns out to be a little less simple than I'd thought. And if I explain this to Charli right now, her head will probably blow off. "Just meet her for coffee, okay? She'll tell you exactly what's going on. You'll like her. I hired her because she gets us."

"Okay. Sure."

I rub my thumb over her palm again. "Thank you. I'm trying to do right by you. I hope you know that."

She lets out a heartbreaking sigh. "I appreciate that. Even though I know you're still hoping the night ends with you getting your dick sucked."

I bark out a laugh. "I don't know whether to plead guilty or not, wifey. Because I'm pretty much always angling to get my dick sucked by you. I think about it whenever I'm not playing hockey. And I'd probably think about it then, too, if the lack of focus weren't potentially fatal."

"Lucky for you, I've discovered my inner easy chick."

"Babe." I stop walking, and since I'm holding her hand, Charli stops, too. "Nothing about you is easy. Not one thing. But I like it that way. My whole life, people have given me the benefit of the doubt, even when I don't deserve it. But not Charli. She makes me *earn* it."

She opens her mouth and then closes it again. "I don't know whether to take that as a compliment or not."

"Oh, it absolutely is." I raise a hand to her cheek and stroke the soft skin there. "You are not like other women. Being Charli doesn't always look easy. But you know your own mind, and you are endlessly fascinating to me."

Her lips part, and there's a softness to her expression that I rarely see. Her pretty face is upturned and vulnerable.

The temptation is too great. I lean in and kiss those sweet lips just once. But I make it a good one. I tilt my head and try to show her how much I care. She's not the only one who's caught off guard by how well we click.

Firm hands land on my chest, and when I soften the kiss, she murmurs against my mouth. "What the hell am I doing with you, Neil?"

"I have a few suggestions," I whisper.

That's when we hear someone pounding on the plate glass window right behind us. Both our heads swivel to see Anton Bayer slapping the glass, his girlfriend Sylvie waving at us beside him.

Yup, I've managed to stop walking right in front of Elixir, a dark, appealing cocktail bar and a frequent hangout of my teammates who live in this neighborhood.

"Shit!" Charli squeaks. She looks up at me, and the fire is back in her eyes. "Nice going, slick. Now we're going to be everyone's gossip of the week. *Again!*"

I know I shouldn't, but I have to laugh. "Sorry. But you were looking up at me with those sexy eyes and I could swear you were practically begging me to kiss you."

She growls. "Doesn't mean it was a good idea."

"You like this place?" I hook my thumb toward the bar. "We could have a cocktail and face the gossip like champs."

"I've never been. Too pricey for me."

"Not tonight it isn't. You get the married-to-an-idiot discount. My treat. Come on." I put a hand on her back. "Let Sylvie get it out of her system. This way you can control the narrative."

"My life used to be boring," she grumbles as I steer her into the dark, chic bar. "And I *liked* it that way."

"Sure, you did." I lean down and whisper into her ear. "And you just *hate* coming home from practice to find me waiting in bed wearing nothing but a boner and some fun ideas."

Charli actually shivers as I make her remember how last Monday night went down, before my road trip. I'd made a pot of chili, but I didn't let her eat any of it for a good hour and a half after she'd arrived home. We were too busy getting busy. Every time with her is better than the last. And it's kind of a miracle that we've kept our secret this long. These days, you can probably read the sexual satisfaction on both our faces.

But I don't get to gloat anymore, because Sylvie grabs Charli by the hand and steals her away, leading her toward a table in back where Bess Beringer and another of Charli's teammates are waiting.

"Hey—want a fancy cocktail?" I call after Charli.

"Yes, she does!" Sylvie barks over her shoulder. "The blood-orange margarita. Four of them!"

And just like that, I've completely lost control of the evening.

At least Anton, Tank, and Newgate are waiting at the bar, grinning at me.

"Hey," I say, my voice grumpy.

"Hey," Anton says with a laugh. "You sly dog."

"We're not discussing it. And what happened to date night? You guys are here at the bar together. Your women are over in the corner. And you're not even watching hockey." This bar is too chic to have a TV.

"It's still date night," Tank argues. "I'm paying a babysitter so my wife and I can pretend we're still young and fun." He grins.

"Besides, we just checked the scores," Anton says. "Detroit is beating Minnesota. Tampa is pounding Carolina. And speaking of pounding, the night is still young. Sylvie and I will be finishing it off in high style, probably on several different surfaces in our apartment."

"TMI, man." I catch the bartender's attention and order

myself a light beer and four special margaritas. Charli is a fan of citrus, so it's all good.

I watch the young man's hustle as he stirs up four drinks the color of a tropical sunset. He slides my beer across the bar, and I leave him a nice tip. That's when I notice my teammates hunched over Anton's phone. They're laughing about something. "Castro's a sore loser." Anton snickers.

"Loser at what?"

"The pool!" Newgate says with obvious glee. "There was a lot of money riding on whether or not you and Charli have been mashing. You cost him four hundred bucks."

"Four hundred?" I think I'm offended. "He bet that much against me?"

"Bet against *what?*" Charli's voice says icily, and we all glance up. She and Sylvie are *right* there, probably to collect their cocktails.

Oh shit.

"There was a pool," Newgate says, oblivious.

"About me and Drake?" Charli yelps.

"Apparently," I say quickly. "I didn't know."

"How did you plan to settle it?" Charli demands, eyes flashing.

"Excellent question," I say, turning to my friends. "Because if I look out my bedroom window and see one of you assholes with a periscope, someone dies."

"Easy." Anton holds up both hands in a sign of surrender. "We hadn't worked that out yet. So thank you for that PDA on the sidewalk. Makes life easier. I just won fifty bucks."

Charli lets out a noise of rage, and her face is bright red. She lifts two cocktails off the bar and takes a big gulp of one of them. "Men are revolting. It's crass to make bets on a woman's sex life. We'd never do that."

Beside her, Sylvie's eyes pop wide. She clamps her mouth shut and slaps a hand over it.

"You sure about that?" I ask Charli, whose eyes narrow with even more fury.

"I can explain," Sylvie whines.

"God, you'd better," Charli growls. "Grab those two drinks, get your ass back to that table, and start talking."

Watching them walk off, I almost feel bad for Sylvie.

I wave at the bartender. "Probably going to need a couple more of those margaritas. Our girls look a little feisty tonight."

"Say the word," the guy says. "And good luck."

I might need it.

THIRTY

LIKE BOXERS IN A RING

Charli

"A pool?" I demand, plunking down on the banquette. "That's just mean."

"It isn't," Samantha insists, taking her margarita and giving it an appreciative glance. "We just want you to have fun. Besides, it's a small pool, because it was hard finding anyone to take the other side."

"*Was* it? Because I would have bet against me all day." I slug back another gulp of my drink. "Sleeping with him is just stupid."

"I used to tell myself that about Tank," Bess says cheerfully. "Being stupid turned out to be the best decision I ever made."

"You guys have been circling each other for a while," Sylvie says.

"Yeah, like boxers in a ring," I point out.

"There is a *fine* line between hate and lust," Samantha says. "And Neil Drake is a catch, Charli. Those tattooed arms..." She sighs.

"Hear that?" Sylvie says. "Your friends know what's good. And it is, right?"

"It is *what?*"

"*Good,*" she says, lowering her voice. "He is a *hottie.* And he's really into you."

"He is not," I insist. "But I am very convenient." It hurts to say that out loud. I'd been trying to think of our fling as a short string of stolen moments before real life intervenes again. But tonight it feels ugly.

Part of me feels *used.*

The other part of me just wants to be used again all night long before it's over.

Bess tilts her head, watching me with soft eyes. "Neil doesn't care about convenience," she says. "He cares about you."

"Maybe a little," I concede. "But that doesn't make it into the big deal you all seem to think it is."

"Hmm," Bess says. "Nobody is tougher than you, Charli. It's very useful at the rink. You're an amazing defensewoman. But you play defense when you're off ice, too. Nobody gets past your guardrails. Neil must have done a lot of work to get through to you."

"Maybe," I hedge. Although, all he has to do to get through to me lately is take off his shirt. "It doesn't matter. We're still getting divorced. He wanted me to help him with some things with his family, but now that's all gone to hell. So probably he'll get that divorce done *fast.*"

Samantha, Sylvie, and Bess all make eye contact. It's a little unsettling. "What?" I demand.

"New pool!" Samantha says, grabbing her phone and tapping on the screen. "Will Charli and Neil get divorced? Bets in five-dollar increments, please."

In my pocket, my own phone buzzes with a text on the group chat.

I sigh. "You people are insane. This is *not* how successful marriages begin."

"Not for most people," Sylvie concedes.

"But you two are *not* most people," Bess argues. "You're

both driven, smart, a little intense. You each deserve somebody who's really dynamic."

"I have a good feeling about this," Samantha says.

"I am *surrounded* by crazy people," I complain. Then I drain my drink. "But at least you have very good taste in cocktails."

They all laugh, but I feel dark inside tonight, and I don't think tequila can fix it.

Still, I try. Neil sends us another round, and the alcohol begins to soften my sharp edges. After Bess leaves, my teammates try to hound me for sexy details, but it doesn't work. I'm a very private person.

Besides, I don't think I could really explain what it's been like these past few weeks. Sex has never come easily to me. But now it does. Neil smiles at me. Reaches for me. And I respond. Just like that.

Our fling is just like this cocktail—astonishingly expensive, goes down sweetly, instantly intoxicating, and guaranteed to cause a hangover.

The hour grows late, and my teammates are tipsy. They lean in, chins propped on the table, confessions flowing as freely as the margaritas.

They love talking about sex. I've heard all kinds of dishy little details about Sylvie's antics with Anton and Samantha's one-night stands.

But talking about sex with Neil would be like cutting myself open and exposing my own beating heart. I couldn't possibly explain what it feels like when he rolls on top of me and stares into my eyes. Or the way his neck muscles strain when he's about to come.

I would never gossip about the times his watch beeps when we're deep into it. Literally. He grabs the glucose drink off the night table, pounds it, and discards the can without even breaking the action.

To me, it's not just sex. It's true intimacy. I didn't even know I was capable of it.

Another thing I didn't understand—and this is my deepest, darkest secret—is how it feels to be held by him right afterward. We always collapse together, hearts pounding, toes uncurling. Our limbs are a sweaty tangle. The covers are half off the bed. Neil likes to stroke my arms and kiss me absently while he comes down.

It makes me feel safe. And it's my new favorite thing in the whole world.

Sleeping with him is the biggest mistake I've ever made in my life. Because now I know how good it can be.

And that pisses me off. Greatly.

We close down the bar, and then I'm riding the elevator back up to Neil's apartment, hanging on his arm. It isn't sexual. I'm kind of tipsy.

"Almost there," he says with a chuckle.

He's stone sober, having kept his intake to a couple of light beers and a club soda.

I've ruined date night. I hadn't meant to, but I'd panicked when Neil told me about his uncle's manipulations. And then I panicked some more when my friends started up with their gossip and their betting pool.

"I'm so grumpy," I say as Neil leads me into the apartment.

"This too shall pass," Neil says gently.

"My friends are crazy," I say after I brush my teeth.

"So are mine," he agrees, steadying me in case I wobble as I try to put on my sleep shorts.

I'm already sobering up. I'm too wary a person to even get drunk properly.

"I've never made so many mistakes in such a short period of time," I complain as I tuck myself into bed.

"And it will still be okay," he says, putting a glass of water on the bedside table.

It *won't* be okay, though. I don't believe him, because I'm so confused.

I used to be good on my own, but that's gone now. Neil makes me want impossible things.

Rolling onto my side, I face away from him. But Neil cuddles up next to me and starts kissing my shoulder.

"You're not supposed to boink a drunk girl," I remind him. There's no need to confess that I'm not actually drunk.

"I'm not boinking her. I'm smooching her neck."

My phone vibrates with another text on the group chat, and I sigh.

"You need to get that?"

"No. There must be nothing good on TV. My friends have nothing better to do than gossip about us."

Neil nibbles on my earlobe. "It sucks to be mad at your friends."

"It does," I agree. "And I'm mad at you too. As soon as that couch shows up, I'm sleeping on it."

"Uh-huh," he says, running his fingers through my hair.

"I'm serious!"

"Yeah, okay." He sits up. "I can't stop you, even if I'd like to."

"But why not?" I sit up, too. "How does this end? We've got ourselves into a ridiculous situation. We don't even make sense together."

"That's not true at *all*." He waves his arms around. His gorgeous arms. "We make all the sense. But every time I say so, you pick a fight."

"I do not."

"Yeah, you do."

"Stop." I put my head in my hands. "You're not listening. And I'm not feeling very articulate right now. I blame the tequila."

"*Charli*." He sounds exasperated. "We make the same amount of sense whether we're drunk or sober. I don't think they've even invented a liquor strong enough for you. You need some kind of top-level truth serum shit to stop lying to both of us."

"Lying?" I yelp. "I don't lie!"

"Yeah, you do it every day," he says, leaning in, meeting me nose to nose. This is what I get for picking a fight in his bed. It's too easy for him to get in my face. "You lie every time you pretend you don't like me. Every time you won't look me in the eye after I say something nice to you. That's what lying looks like."

"Not true," I say, choking a little bit on the words. "We have chemistry. So what? It doesn't mean any more than that."

I see something unexpected flash through Neil's eyes. It's *pain*. Then he closes them. "You drive me insane. You're the most stubborn woman I've met in my entire life."

That's not even an insult because stubbornness has kept me alive. "True," I say gruffly. "And it's nothing you can change."

"That's *exactly* what I'm afraid of," he snaps. He looks as angry as I feel. Like he might explode.

"What the fuck does that mean?" I holler, as my heart rate doubles. Weirdly, I feel more in control of my life right this minute than I have in weeks. Fighting, at least, is familiar. I've done it all my life.

"You're someone I could *love*, Charli! But you make it impossible by hiding yourself from me."

My heart detonates, because that's a horrible thing to say. *I could love you, if you were a little less difficult.* It's the same message I heard from my mother every time she'd drop us off at another relative's house. *You're too wild, too loud, too young, too old, too needy.*

"And you're a bossy fuck!" I shout. "You think you know what's good for me! You don't know a thing."

Neil sits back, his face red and angry. "Yeah? If I don't know what's good for you, it's only because you won't share. You never show me the dark stuff."

"I don't *owe* you that! I don't owe you a damn thing! I

played my part, and I spoke my lines, and I even gave you my *body*, and nothing is enough, is it? That's how it works in your world. You get more than anyone else, and you just keep wanting more."

He makes a noise of pure anger, and even that doesn't shut me up.

"This is *your* idea. Your mess! You keep changing the rules! If you wanted a girl who'll do whatever you say, you should have drunk-married someone else. I hear Iris is available."

Fury tightens his eyes, and his jaw flexes. My oldest reflexes kick in, and I brace myself for violence.

When it comes, it's not what I expect. Neil leans forward suddenly and takes my mouth in an angry kiss.

For a moment, I'm so stunned that all I can do is experience it. The taste of Neil is familiar now, in a way that always undoes me.

But I can't let him wreck me like this. Not when I'm too emotional to survive it. I put both hands on his hard chest, planning to shove him away.

And then I don't. Instead, I kiss him back so hard that it might leave a bruise.

With a huff of rage, he nips my lip. I retaliate by breaking away to run my teeth down his neck. His skin is so smooth over all that muscle. I run my tongue along the place where my teeth just traveled.

"Mark me." His voice is a dare. "You know you want to."

My nipples harden, and it pisses me off. "You don't know what I want!"

"Yeah, sure I don't." He snorts.

Goddamn you! I want to scream. But you can't scream and suck on someone's neck, which is what I'm doing. I'm marking him. Once he put that idea into my head, I wanted it just like every other damn thing he's ever suggested.

He groans when I bite the juncture of his neck and shoulder. "Fuck, Charli. Harder."

I stop, of course, because I'm not in the mood to take orders. I need space. The familiar clean scent of his shampoo makes me ache.

Strong arms wrap around my torso, and the craving hits me so hard that the only way to save myself is to push him off me. Before it's too late.

I do the exact opposite thing. I soften my body into the hard cage of his embrace. It's a tactic to make your tormentor think you've given in. Then you bide your time for a few beats and take him by surprise.

That's the way it's supposed to go, anyway. But Neil makes a sound that short-circuits my brain as his mouth travels down my jaw—it's a broken groan. His hands grow supple against my back.

I lose my own battle as Neil rolls me onto my back and kisses my neck.

The throat is one of the most vulnerable parts of the body. I know how to protect mine. But as soon as Neil's stubble grazes my heated skin, I lift my chin and offer myself up like the loser I've become.

My traitorous nipples are like pebbles now. Neil doesn't miss it, either. He makes another bitten-off groan that rattles my heart. His broad hand skims up my tummy, cupping my bare breast inside my tank. His grip on my flesh grows possessive, and I feel myself get wet because of it.

I want to weep from anger and confusion. I shouldn't do this again.

I shouldn't *want* to. "This is the only way you know how to win an argument," I hiss.

"You fight dirty," he says. "Why shouldn't I?"

I don't, I try to say. But it comes out as a whimper.

You're breaking me. Right in half.

Neil keeps pretending we're a couple. Taking me to dinner. Shopping for a couch. It suckers me in the same way a mirage in the desert lures thirsty nomads.

The worst part? He doesn't even know he's being cruel.

Giving me all this sweetness—but temporarily.

Just a fling.

Before we get divorced.

So he should stop sucking on my breasts the way he's doing now.

He should stop looking at me like he cares. I've seen that look before, and it always betrays me.

I toss off my tank top, anyway.

Then I kick my shorts off the bed. When he covers me with his bulky heat, I run my fingernails down his back a little too sharply.

In answer, Neil grabs my hands and pins me to the bed. He uses a muscular knee to nudge mine apart, before filling me with his cock in one sudden thrust.

I suck in air as my body responds shamelessly. The feel of him is always overwhelming. Every time.

He doesn't give me a chance to acclimate. He moves right away, setting a pace that's half lust, half punishment.

I bury my face in his neck and take it. No—I revel in it.

Like we both knew I would.

THIRTY-ONE

PRACTICING MY I'M SORRY SPEECH

Neil

I wake up the next morning face down in the bed. It's awfully quiet in this room, and before I'm even fully conscious, I feel regret pooling in my stomach.

Call me hopeful or call me stupid, but I stretch out an arm, hoping to find Charli's smoother one. I find only cool sheets.

Regret hardens into dread.

Last night I'd fought with the person I care about most. I'd been impatient. I'd pushed.

Hell, there had been panic in her eyes, but I hadn't shut up. I'd just kept arguing my position.

She'd said, *you're not listening*. So I'd talked some more.

And then I'd tried to make it all better by jumping her like a beast. Like a horny, bossy dick. We'd had epic sex. It had not been the answer. Charli had accused me of always pushing for more from her.

I'm so damn guilty. *Goddammit.*

My head actually throbs. I feel hungover—but not from alcohol. It's the sour taste of remorse.

I did *everything* wrong last night.

So I guess I'm about to spend the day apologizing. I sit up fast, looking around. There's no sign of Charli anywhere. Her clothes aren't on the floor where we tossed them. And when I listen, the apartment is completely still.

Shit! My heart kicks with the certainty that she's gone. Really gone. There's no evidence at all that she was here.

Sliding off the bed, I trudge into the bathroom. I relax a little. Her makeup kit is on the counter, tucked up against the wall, as if it's trying to stay out of the way. Her toothbrush is perched on top of it.

I let out a breath. *Okay, dumbass. She's just gone to work early.*

It's only seven o'clock. I'm not due at the rink for two more hours. I can either pace around the apartment practicing my *I'm sorry* speech, or I can get outside and move my body.

Easy decision. I hastily put on some running clothes and shoes and tuck my phone into my arm band.

February is pretty cold in Brooklyn. There's a fierce wind, so after about five minutes on the waterfront, I'm regretting all my life choices.

I'm still an asshole, but now I'm a cold one. And where's Charli? She's probably at work.

I have to know, so I turn my freezing face away from the river and pick up my speed, heading for the diner. It takes five minutes to get there. The bells on the door announce my arrival, and Charli glances up. She swallows nervously but puts on her mask of indifference so quickly I'm not sure it wasn't my imagination.

The place is quiet, because it's still early. Only two tables have customers, and the counter is empty. I take a seat on one of the stools.

A moment later, my wife slides a menu in front of me. "What can I get you?" she asks politely.

Shit.

"Charli," I rasp. "I'm so sorry. Are you okay?"

She swallows. "I'm fine, Neil. I'm always fine. Coffee?" She plunks a mug onto the counter and pours, like nothing happened. As if last night didn't wreck us both.

She adds the cream.

I take a slow breath. Getting angry won't help. Besides, I'm only angry at myself. "Would you do me the kindness of letting me apologize? I wouldn't ask, except it's dead in here right now, and it's game night, so we won't see each other all day and night."

With a sigh, she sets down the carafe. "I'm a big girl, Neil. I was in a difficult mood last night. There's nothing you need to apologize for."

"I disagree," I say quietly. "Christ. I didn't even use a condom."

Her eyes widen suddenly, like she can't believe I went there. She checks over both shoulders before leaning closer to speak to me privately. "Like I said, I'm a big girl—who also has an IUD. Because nobody has time for cramps on game day. So you don't have to panic that you put an accidental kid in your accidental wife."

"Whoa!" I've fucked up *again*. "Hang on. I'm not panicked. Having kids with you doesn't scare me half as much as it scares you."

Her eyes widen even further. "Thanks for the update, but then *why* are you sitting here apologizing for last night?"

"Because I wasn't *nice*. You said, 'I can't do this anymore.' And my response was to do you anyway."

"Listen." Red circles appear on her cheeks. "I have been a *very* willing participant every single time, stud. That is not our issue. What works in bed doesn't work in life, however. But I *swear to Christ* this is not the time or the place for this discussion."

"I know," I whisper, looking straight into her green eyes. "But I feel bad about how I acted. You deserve my full support and all the kindness in the world. I didn't show that to you last night. I threw a tantrum, and I regret it."

She blinks. "Okay. Wow. Well..." She looks flustered. "I wasn't winning any awards for patience, either. Why don't we just forget about it?" She moves, as though she intends to walk away.

I catch her hand before she can go. I lift her palm and kiss it. "I never wanted to hurt you."

She looks down at where her hand is snugged against my mouth. "Same," she whispers eventually. "But Neil..." She sighs. "I need to get off this carnival ride."

My heart constricts.

"Please give me that lawyer's contact information, so I can get this ball rolling."

I force air into my lungs and take a breath. I want to argue. I want to make my point that what happened last night has nothing to do with our weird legal situation. But she doesn't need any more arguments from me.

Defeated, I pull out my phone to find the lawyer's information. "Got a pen?"

Charli straightens up and pulls a pen from her apron pocket.

My watch beeps. It's the sound of my blood sugar dropping.

She makes a noise of surprise then grabs a small glass and fills it immediately with fresh-squeezed orange juice. After placing the glass in front of me, she turns to call through the kitchen window. "Sal, can you rush me an order? We need two eggs scrambled, a whole wheat waffle, and a side of ham. ASAP."

"You got it!" he calls back.

"Ten minutes or less," she says to me. "Will the juice hold you?"

"Yes," I say, my face hot. The care she's showing me right now just makes me sad. "Thank you."

I expect her to say, 'don't mention it,' or some dismissive thing. But she doesn't say a word. She studies me with sad green eyes, puts her order pad on the counter and pushes it toward me. "I'll call the lawyer today."

"Okay," I croak.

I drain my juice and pick up the pen, writing out the lawyer's name and phone number and email address.

Several minutes later, a perfect breakfast lands on the counter in front of me. I eat every bite and linger over my coffee. I watch Charli buzz through the room, talking to everyone except me.

Twelve hours later, the buzzer sounds for the end of the second period.

We're down by one goal, but by all rights the score should be worse. Beacon's genius between the pipes has saved us too many times to count.

No thanks to me.

I'm fucking up all over the place. Toronto has had possession about seventy percent of the time, because every time the puck touches my stick, I make poor life choices.

"What's the matter, man?" Castro looms over me. "How are your numbers?"

I glance at my smart watch. "Numbers are fine. They're actually perfect. I'm a fucking mess, but it's not my blood sugar."

Castro lifts his chin. "What's the deal? Is it, uh, Charli?"

I lean back on the beach, my head against the locker cubby. "She's slipping away from me. I can feel it."

He lets out a low whistle. "That's what's got you so twisted up you can't find my passes? *Dude.* What happened since last night?"

"We had a fight, I guess. After we left the bar. I didn't handle it well. Now she's upset. I spent the whole day replaying it in my head, trying to figure out how I can get through to her."

Castro winces. "Did you fight over the damn betting pool? That was supposed to be harmless fun."

"It wasn't the pool, jackass. Although I'm still a little sore you'd bet against me."

"Hey—that wasn't a comment on your skill level. That was a vote for you letting that fish go. She put the prick in prickly. I didn't want to see you get burned."

I groan. "You assumed I'd fuck it up?"

"No way. I assumed that *she* would. That girl doesn't trust people, Drake. I don't think she can."

And just like that, he names my greatest fear.

"How serious is this thing for you, though?" he asks, sitting down beside me.

"Who knows? We had, uh, a temporary arrangement. Until our divorce." I run my hand through sweaty hair. "The problem is that I want more than just a hookup with her. I want a chance. But I didn't say that up front. And every time I try to renegotiate, she doesn't want to hear it. Then there's the whole issue that I'm currently divorcing her."

"Women hate that."

"Yeah." I can't even crack a smile at Castro's joke. "Maybe we could have had a shot at something real. But it's hard to ease a girl into the idea of dating you when you're also divorcing her. She feels used, I think."

"Women hate that, too," Castro points out.

"Yep. I spent the whole day trying to figure out how to convince her that I'm one of the good guys."

"We're all the good guy in our own story," my teammate says. "And some people just can't function as half of a team. I know because I used to be one of them."

"But you're not anymore," I point out. "You and Heidi Jo are a great team."

"We are," he agrees. "But I had to *choose* to trust her. I had to *decide* to take on that risk. You can't make Charli do it. You can talk until you're blue in the face, but if she's not ready to jump, you can't make her."

"Charli has her reasons," I say tightly.

"Oh, I don't doubt it. And I get why you like her—she's sharp and independent. The tough-girl thing is sexy. She's like the complete opposite of Iris."

"Tell me about it."

"But, dude, Iris would have waited her whole life for you to pop the question. And she'd never leave your side. She was stuck to you like hockey tape. It was easier."

"That's *not* what I want in a woman."

"I get that." Castro pokes me in the knee. "My point is that Charli is wild and free and gives no fucks what anyone thinks. But maybe she *can't*. Maybe the thing that makes you want her is also the reason she can't be tamed."

My chest tightens with renewed dread. "She's not a *mustang*, Castro."

"Isn't she?" he asks quietly. "She'll either put on the bridle or not, man. All you can do is ask her to hold still."

Well, that is damn depressing.

Coach stops in front of me, and I look up into his irritated face. "Is Castro straightening your shit out? Or do I have to take a crack at it?"

"I've got this, Coach." Castro slaps my knee. "Drake is all twisted up about a woman."

"Aw, hell," Coach says with a shake of his head. "Not another one. What I need is a bunch of monks who can skate. Stop thinking about girls and get back out there. We can still win this thing, if you get your heads out of your asses."

"Yes, Coach," I say. Sitting here thinking about Charli isn't exactly getting me anywhere.

"She doesn't *exist* for twenty more minutes of play," Coach announces.

"Yes, Coach," I drone. "She's gone from my life."

That's probably true, anyway. There's very little I can do about it.

After some stretching and a quick pep talk, we head out

again and play a better period of hockey. We tie it up before the buzzer, but then lose in overtime.

"Still worth a point," Crikey says as we both get dressed beside our lockers later. "Good hustle in the third, Drakey."

"Thanks," I grunt. I did have good hustle in the third period. But now that it's over, I'm back to worrying.

When the boys decide to hit the Tavern on Hicks, I don't go with them. I head home instead.

Dread curls in my gut when I see that my apartment is dark. It's possible Charli may already be sleeping. I tiptoe through the place, so as not to wake her. But when I enter my bedroom, the New York City glow is bright enough to show me an empty bed.

Fuck. I flip on the lights, toss my suit jacket onto the bed, and head into the bathroom.

Her makeup case is gone. Her toothbrush is gone. Everything.

She's left me. It's true. I find a note on my bedside table.

Neil—I'm sorry. But I need to go. I'm staying with friends. The lawyer is squeezing me in tomorrow. I'll let you know what she says.

You take care,
C.

Shit!

She's left the ring on top of the note—the ugly one from our wedding. That makes me even angrier. I open the drawer and drop the ring inside, where it lands with a clunk next to my grandmother's ring.

I look down at the two of them—and it's a study in contrasts. One sparkles with an icy beauty. Diamonds in platinum. The other is a cheap shade of yellow gold and has too many gemstones. It tries to dazzle but fails.

That is what I offered Charli—a cheap mockery. A drunk groom. An ugly ring.

That's not how I feel about her. Yet here I stand, blaming her for misunderstanding me. Frustrated that she can't look beyond all my awkward flailing and assume that I have her best interests at heart.

Fuck. I tried to tell her, but I did it all wrong. Now she's gone, leaving nothing but a two-line note about meeting the lawyer.

I crumple the note in my hand, like the sore loser Charli accused me of being, and I throw it into the trash bin.

Then I fish it out and recycle it, because even when my heart is breaking, I still care about the planet.

THIRTY-TWO

PUT IT ON NEIL'S TAB

Charli

Seated on a sofa with Fiona and her girlfriend, Aly, I watch the Bruisers lose.

"That's a damn shame," Fiona says, clicking off the TV. "Drake struggled tonight. I wonder what's eating at him." She gives me a sideways glance.

"Ooh, burn," Aly says.

"Please," I say. "Don't you think it's a little presumptuous to assume that I ruined Neil's game?" Although my heart thumped with the same dark question as I watched him screw up over and over again during the first two periods.

"I don't think it's presumptuous at all to assume that he'll miss you," Fiona says. "Want another glass of wine?" She tips the bottle toward my glass.

"I'm still nursing this one," I say, holding my glass aloft.

She pours the rest into Aly's glass, and the two of them chat me up for a while longer, even though it's a school night, and Fiona will have to face down a horde of children tomorrow at work. She's a P.E. Teacher for the New York Public School System.

"We know some nice girls," Aly says. "Maybe it's time to cast your fishing pole in the other pond again. Want me to set you up on a date?"

"That's awfully nice, but I don't think so," I say. The idea of dating anyone right now hurts my heart. "I'm good. Besides— women have always found me as undateable as men."

"Nobody is undateable," Aly says with a wink. "You just need to find your other half. The person who appreciates all your eccentricities."

Oh boy. It hurts to hear that. Because only one person has ever told me that he liked the way I challenged him and that I was *endlessly fascinating.*

Fiona sighs, and when I glance at her, she gives me a tiny smile and then shakes her head. But she doesn't say it out loud, which makes her an excellent friend.

"Look, I need a new place to live more than I need a guy," I announce. "I'm going to text a plea to the group chat."

"And I'll ask around school," Fiona says with a yawn.

I'm keeping them up late. "You guys, it's nice of you to babysit me, but I'm okay. And I know you need your sleep."

Fiona yawns again, climbing off the couch. "Sad but true. You know—Sylvie probably went to Anton's tonight after the game. You could sleep in her bed."

"But she might be out at the bar with the team," I say. "We don't know for sure."

Aly gets up, too. "But if you wake up in the middle of the night because that couch is killing you, maybe you should make the move."

"I'll be fine," I tell them. "Sweet dreams!"

Keeping out of their way while they get ready for bed, I wash all our wine glasses in the kitchen. I can't believe I'm someone's houseguest. *Again.*

Eventually, holding hands, they retreat to Fiona's room, where the door closes with a soft click.

I shut the lights off and sit back down on the sofa, where I can hear the soft murmur of my friends' voices behind the bedroom door as they settle into Fiona's bed.

The sound of their conversation makes me feel hollow inside. I lie down, wondering if I'll be able to sleep at all. It's always been hard for me to relax in a strange place. Especially when I feel unsettled.

It's safe here, I remind my stuttering heart. *Everything is fine.*

Still, when I stretch out on the sofa, my view out the living room windows is… the Million Dollar Dorm. Lying on the sofa in a third-floor apartment gives me a perfect view up to the fifth and sixth floors.

Neil's living room is dark. He's probably out at the bar with friends. But eventually he'll go home and head to bed, closing his bedroom door with another quiet click.

He'll stretch out on the big bed that smells like his luxury aftershave and clean linens. When I close my eyes, I remember how it felt to lie beside his big sleepy body. How relaxed I became listening to him breathe.

My whole life I've been categorizing places as either safe or dangerous. Curled up by Neil's side, I had never felt so safe. I had never been so well cared for.

But looking into his hazel eyes when he smiled at me? That had been scary. I never knew a man could make me feel both safe and terrified.

That's why I had to go. Who could live each day like that — waiting for his smile to fade? Waiting for our arrangement to end?

When he'd casually brought up the idea of staying married for another three months, I'd lost it. I'd felt like a death row prisoner who'd been granted a temporary stay of execution.

It's hard to celebrate when you still feel dread.

I guess I finally found something I'm not strong enough to conquer. It's the tremble I feel in my heart whenever I wake up next to Neil Drake III.

I'm bleary the next morning at the diner. I can't stop watching the door, wondering if Neil will walk through it.

He doesn't, and I try not to care.

I need to stop thinking about him. Today won't be the day, though, because I'm going to meet his lawyer. When I'd called her office yesterday, her assistant had said she was booked solid all week. But when I'd pressed, she'd put me on hold and then returned to book me into Ms. Moss's coffee break today.

So, to Sal's distress, I have to leave halfway through my shift.

"You're not interviewing somewhere, right?" he asks, wringing his wrinkled hands.

"No way, Sal. We've been over this. I'm *not* quitting this job."

He frowns at me. "But you got that fancy husband now. I thought he'd hook you up with a desk job."

"Really?" My smile is wry. "As if you could see *me* in a desk job?"

The old man eyes me thoughtfully. "I can, baby doll. I can see you doin' a lot of things. I guess it's lucky for me that you can't see it, too."

Sal needs to get his eyes checked.

The lawyer has asked me to meet her at a coffee shop in midtown. But when I get there, the place is more like a fancy cafe. There are elegant men and women everywhere, and I feel underdressed in my waitressing uniform.

Figures.

It's hard to say which patron is the lawyer. I scan several grey heads, but nobody tries to flag me down. I ask the host where I might find Ms. Moss, and he points toward the last person in the room that I'd expect. She's beautiful, with thick, long hair, bedroom eyes and a lowcut blouse showing off a gorgeous diamond necklace.

I guess untangling other people's fuckups pays pretty well.

Lifting my chin, I approach the table. She glances up from something she's reading on her phone. "Charli?"

"Yes, ma'am." I reach out a hand to shake.

"You ma'amed me?" she says, looking taken aback. "Do I look that old?" She gives my hand a firm shake. "Actually, don't answer that. Have a seat instead."

"Um, thank you." I sit down in the chair and try to look relaxed. I'd never met a divorce attorney before, and I wish I hadn't.

"Coffee?" she asks. She waves down a waiter without waiting for an answer.

"Thank you." How much could coffee here cost? I hope not much. There's about sixteen dollars in my wallet.

Ms. Moss orders two cups of coffee, "And a plate of those cute little sandwiches. Thanks." She turns her attention to me. "I'm sure you know that Neil Drake hired me to dissolve your marriage."

"Of course," I say quickly. "We, uh, never meant to get married. And I believe we could have tried for a Las Vegas annulment. But we had to hurry home."

She nods quickly. She talks quickly, too. A true New Yorker. "I don't know exactly how they do things in Nevada, but I had to explain to your husband how it works here in New York. You both meet the residency requirement, but there's the issue of the six-month waiting period for a no-fault divorce—"

"Six *months?*" I gasp, panic rising inside my chest. "Neil didn't tell me *that!*"

The lawyer holds up a hand. "Don't panic, honey. Let me finish. If you want to get divorced immediately, I have a workaround."

My heartbeat tries to settle back into the normal range. "Okay. I'd love to hear it."

"First, I need to remind you that most parties to a divorce get their own representation."

I shake my head. "I can't afford it. Neil said he'd take care of the whole thing."

"Okay." She tightens her lips. "It seems I'm going to be your lawyer, then, not his. Only he'll be paying the bills."

"Why?"

She leans forward in her chair. "You can't get a no-fault divorce. So that means one of you has to sue the other for divorce. And you need to claim cruelty or inhumane treatment by Neil."

"I *what?*" My voice is pitched two octaves higher than usual. "Say that again?"

Her serious gray eyes take me in. "The only way to get you a fast divorce is for one of you to claim that the other was cruel. I know that sounds terrible, but the standard for cruelty in a marriage that's only a couple weeks old is pretty low. Has Neil ever yelled at you?"

"Um... not unless you count smack talk over darts at the bar." My head is spinning. "Are you serious right now?"

"I am," she says firmly. "You can have a divorce, but you need to claim that he yelled at you, and that it was frightening. Now, if you were married for twenty years, the standard is different. He'd have to beat you senseless with a pipe."

I sit back in my chair, mouth open. "That's madness. Neil would never hurt me."

The waiter picks that moment to set a cup of coffee down in front of me, in a beautiful, delicately scalloped cup. He also sets a plate of tiny square sandwiches down between us.

Ms. Moss waits until he leaves before she takes one of them. "Cucumber and smoked salmon. Will you have one? I love them."

"Tell me about this cruelty thing again," I say. "Isn't there any other way?"

"There isn't," she says. "You have to accuse Neil of cruelty if you want a fast divorce."

"But he's not," I stammer. "He's not a cruel person. I don't want *anyone* to think that he is. Aren't divorces public information?"

She tilts her head from side to side, as if considering. "The grounds for divorce are supposedly sealed. Although the details have been known to leak when the filing is recorded."

"So... some reporter could end up writing that Neil was cruel or inhumane to me?"

"It's possible," she concedes. "But he said you two want this divorce to happen fast. My plan would be to file your complaint at four twenty-seven p.m., in anticipation of the four thirty deadline, in the hopes that no reporters are lurking about in the vestibule when the clerk opens the file."

"And what if there are reporters there?"

She shrugs. "Maybe they won't pick up on his name when the clerk reads it out. Maybe she has a soft voice. We'll hope for the best."

Oh boy. Hoping for the best is not a strategy. My whole life is proof of that. I can already picture the gossip blogs posting some story about him, trying to make a link between hockey players and domestic violence.

They'd put Neil's face on it. He could even get in trouble with the league.

I shiver. "This is madness." I ignore my coffee and pick up a tiny sandwich and shove it in my mouth.

She smiles. "Delicious, right? I love the crunch."

Maybe this is all a weird dream. Maybe I'm still asleep on Fiona's couch. "Okay—tell me this. Why should I be the one who has to sue? Can't he sue me?"

She stares. "You'd rather be the cruel and inhumane spouse? Whatever for?"

"Because..." I swallow hard. *Because I'm already the bitch in this situation.* "Because nobody cares what I do. But people write things about Neil. His family is scrutinized."

"I don't see how that's your problem," she says, her cool grey eyes boring into mine. "But to answer your question, the law works either way. Neil has volunteered to fall on this sword for you. He said he promised to get the divorce done, and this is the most expedient way of doing that. Would you like me to draw up the documents?"

"Um…" My head is spinning. Can I really do this to Neil? Can I turn him into an *abuser* just to expedite my freedom?

"Look," the lawyer says. "I can see on your face how much you hate this. Honestly, it's a pleasure to deal with two people who don't actually hate each other. But you're in a sticky situation, hon. And Neil Drake is trying to help you get out. He has a pile of cash so high that nobody can even see over it. That's probably why he doesn't mind this route. He was very clear. 'Do whatever it takes,' he said. And when a man wants to take responsibility, I say you should let him."

"I should let him," I repeat dully. "Okay. Fine. You should go ahead and draw up those papers." I've complicated my own life, as usual. And now Neil's. I'm essentially homeless again. And there just isn't enough air in this cafe. I need to get out of here.

I reach for my wallet and dig out a ten.

"Oh honey, don't. I'll put it on Neil's tab. He can afford it."

He can, and so people always put everything on Neil's tab.

When I go through with this divorce, I'll be doing the same thing.

But worse.

THIRTY-THREE

IT'S NOT ALWAYS YOUR TURN

Neil

"How is she?" I demand of Anton.

"She's fine," he says, handing me a light beer.

I throw some money down on the bar. "Can you be a little more specific?" I press. "Did she look happy? Tired?"

"Dude," Newgate says, putting a hand on my shoulder. "Let the man sit down before you interrogate him."

Anton chuckles. "Yeah, we need a table. Hey—Newguy, grab that one." He points towards a booth that's opening up, and our teammate moves toward it.

We're in Philly, where we just eked out a win. No thanks to me. It's pushing midnight, but the hotel bar has beckoned to us.

I go to follow Newgate, but Anton stops me. He puts my money back in my hand. "You don't always have to buy."

"It's not my turn?" I shrug.

"Nah, you take too many turns. Come on, let's sit down and have a little chat." He nudges me toward the table.

I sit down opposite him and take a sip of beer. My body is tired, and my nerves are fried. I've spent a long week wondering if Charli is okay. But when I text her, I get only terse replies.

Anton had happened to mention that he saw her last night, so now I need answers. "Okay, tell me what you know," I demand.

"Charli is doing all right," Anton says slowly. "But I can tell it bugs her to be crashing on Sylvie and Fiona's couch. I tried to sit on the floor to play cards, and she made me take her chair." He rolls his eyes. "A man doesn't let a woman sit on the floor, you know? But a man doesn't win arguments with Charli, either, so…"

Oh, I know. "What else? Does she look tired?"

"Don't we all?" Newgate asks. "You sound like a crazy stalker right now, by the way. She's a grown woman. Can't she take care of herself?"

"She wouldn't be in this situation if I hadn't screwed up her life. She wouldn't have given up her apartment…" God, everything is such a mess.

"Yeah, the apartment thing is tough," Anton says. "They've been trying to find a situation for her where somebody needs a roommate. But no nibbles yet."

I nudge his foot under the table. "Isn't it about time you and Sylvie moved in together? Then she could take Sylvie's place across the street."

"Whoa!" Newgate hoots. "You're going to marry off poor Bayer, so your ex has a place to live?"

"They are stupid in love." I point my bottle at Anton. "I don't want him to be like me. Don't fuck it up, man."

Anton laughs. "Take a breath, cowboy. As a matter of fact, Sylvie and I have big plans to move in together. I'm buying the studio from my cousin, but we need to do some renovations. So that means me staying with Sylvie for a while before she can give up her place with Fiona."

"Well, fuck." I set down my beer. "I'm happy for you. That's big—you're buying a place together."

He beams. "We sure are. And an architect is helping us convert that loft into a real bedroom. The place is a little small, but we want to keep our spot in the building."

"Nice," I say, forcing my smile. "Congratulations."

A short while ago, I thought I didn't want what Anton has. I ended things with Iris because I wanted freedom.

But I was dead wrong. I don't want freedom, I want Charli. But now I've screwed things up so badly that she'll never take me seriously.

I pull out my phone and google *apartments for rent in Brooklyn.* "Hey, Newguy? How'd you find your apartment?"

"Some broker found it for me. I shoulda asked more questions, though. The location is all right, but the neighbors are noisy. Kids, man." He shakes his head. "Why do people have those?"

I'm not listening. I'm zooming in on the part of Brooklyn where Charli would most like to be. There are plenty of listings, but most of them are way over Charli's budget. She said she needed to pay about twelve or fourteen hundred dollars.

The cheapest thing I see is a studio in a nice condo building for three grand a month.

"Hey, Bayer?" I put my phone down and look up at Anton. "Do you think you and Sylvie could help me with a little white lie?"

"Uh-oh," he says with a smirk. "This sounds like a bad idea already. What would I be lying about?"

"What if you and Sylvie told Charli that you knew a guy who knew a guy who had an apartment to sublet for cheap?" I really think I'm onto something here. "Only, I'd be that guy."

"You have an apartment to sublet?" Newgate perks up. "Can I see it?"

Anton rolls his eyes. "He doesn't really have one, dumbass. He wants to rent a place for Charli and then let her live there cheap."

"Oh." Newgate scowls. "That is a terrible idea. Women are

too smart for that shit. If you're trying to get out of the doghouse with your girl, I don't think that's the answer."

"He's not wrong," Anton agrees. "You can't ask Sylvie to do that. When Charli learns the truth, she'll assume Sylvie wants her out."

"Oh, shit," I grumble. "Okay, yeah. I'm sorry. That's a bad idea."

"Just man up and offer to help her," Newgate says.

"You think I haven't? She doesn't want my help." I pick up my beer and take a swig. "It's so frustrating. I just want to help, and I don't want her to worry. But if I wade in, she assumes my motivations are impure."

"Well, *are* they?" Newgate asks. "I'd think with my dick, too, if that redhead was in my bed on the regular. She looks like a good time."

All my muscles lock up at once.

"Dude," Anton says, putting a hand on my chest. "Newguy meant it hypothetical-like. But wow, man. You've got it bad for this girl. Does she know?"

"Yes," I grunt.

"Are you sure?" my best friend presses. "Just because I can practically see you pawing the ground to get back in there, doesn't mean she understands how deep she's gotten under your skin."

"I guess," I say, playing with the label on my beer. "But she's a tough girl to impress. She doesn't want my money. She liked when I cooked for her, though."

"Well, there you go." Anton shrugs.

"I'm in Philly. She's in Brooklyn," I remind him.

"Bummer. You'll figure it out." He slaps my shoulder. "Can we get more beers now? This time it really is your turn."

I get up and head for the bar, where I order two more beers and a club soda for myself.

And I wonder if I'll ever figure out how to tell Charli that I need her more than I've ever needed someone in my life.

THIRTY-FOUR

A SOBER OFFERING

Charli

The next few days are rough.

Hunting for apartments is demoralizing. Nobody comes through with a *roommate wanted* situation. And I still don't have enough cash to handle things myself.

I know that Neil would help me with the deposit. He's probably *expecting* to help. But I don't want to ask him. So I keep calling landlords only to be told that decent apartments are out of my reach.

Or, in many cases, they're rented by the time I can even inquire.

"I swear I'll get off your couch soon," I promise Fiona and Sylvie.

"Don't worry," Sylvie says, popping her head out of the bedroom where she's changing for practice. "We've all been there."

I know for a fact that she hasn't. And sleeping in places where I don't really belong is basically my life story.

To make matters worse, I have two voicemails from my

brother asking me to call him. I'm still paying for a horrible apartment that I can't return to.

This is madness. How did I end up in this position?

The doorbell rings. "I'll get it!" I call. The least I can do is answer the buzzer. "Hello?"

"Hello Ms. Drake, this is Miguel from across the street."

"Yes?" Why is the concierge ringing this apartment? My imagination goes straight to tragedy. Maybe something is wrong with Neil...

"I have a delivery for you. Can I come up for a moment?"

Oh. "Sure. I'll meet you halfway." I hang up the phone, buzz him up, and exit the apartment to meet him on the stairs. What did I leave in Neil's apartment? A T-shirt? A hairbrush?

It's a little cold to send the doorman over with it. Neil must be really pissed at me for doing a runner.

I catch up to Miguel on the second landing. "Hey, thanks for —" He's holding a casserole dish covered with foil. "Uh, thanks for whatever that is."

He smiles. "My pleasure, Ms. Drake." He hands it over and then fishes a card out of his pocket. "And this goes with it."

"Okay, thanks. I, uh, appreciate it."

"My pleasure," he says. Then he turns and trots down the stairs at a fast clip.

I push my way back into the apartment a minute later, both hands full of the casserole dish.

"Huh," Fiona says, after I set it down on the table and pull back the foil. "I've heard of men sending flowers... But *cauliflower* is an interesting interpretation of the brief."

Sylvie giggles. "Smells amazing. Is that a *gratin*?" She gives the word the same French pronunciation that Neil uses.

The scent of cheese wafts up, and my stomach growls. "Okay, wow. This is a dish he made for me before. I'm not sure why he sent it, though."

"Read the card?" Fiona says. "And you'll share, right?"

"Of course." I open the envelope and pull out a single sheet of stationery. It says *Neil Drake III* in fancy script at the top. And Neil has written:

Charli—

I miss you, and when I was cooking today I thought of you. I'd love to make you another steak to go with it. But if you want that, you have to call me. Because a steak deserves to be eaten right after it's grilled.

Cauliflower can travel, though. Bake this at 375 for forty minutes before you eat it.

— N.

"Damn. Remind me why you can't stay married to this boy?" Fiona asks.

I stare down at the casserole feeling sad. But also hungry. "Neil never *intended* to marry me. You can't spend the rest of your life with a guy who only proposes when he's out of his mind."

She points at the cheesy dish. "This is a sober offering. And the kind of gift that true love is made of."

Just the sound of the L-word makes me feel a little shaky. I don't know what I'd do if Neil looked at me and said *I love you*. Nobody ever has.

"He feels a lot of guilt," I point out, laying the foil over the top and sealing the edges. "This is a guilt casserole."

"Perhaps," Fiona allows. "But we're going to eat the heck out of it after practice."

"That we are," I agree. "Let's put this in the fridge and head over there."

It feels good to skate hard. Sweat has always been the best way I know to shut off my worry brain and take a breath.

"You're on fire today," Coach Sasha says as I guzzle water on the bench. "I want to skate you with Everly for a couple of scrimmages. If it goes well, I'll pair you together against Philly. And maybe Boston, in the following game."

"Boston," I repeat. "Right."

It's the game that conflicts with the Drake Foundation meeting. We lost to Boston earlier in the season, and I've been looking forward to the rematch.

I shouldn't feel guilty getting on that bus. It's not my fault Neil's family is bonkers.

I shouldn't. But I probably will.

After the scrimmage, I take a shower and stretch my muscles.

"I'm running home to turn on the oven," Fiona says, shouldering her gym bag with a wink.

"Good call! 375. I'll be out in a few."

She leaves, but then reappears a minute later. "Hey, there's a guy out in the hallway who wants to speak to you."

I'm instantly alarmed. "What does he look like?"

"Tall, dark hair…"

Oh shit. I know this place is pretty secure, but my mind instantly jumps to Robert.

"Nice smile," she adds. "Cute New York accent. Brooklyn Bruisers T-shirt."

"Oh. Thanks." Nobody would call Robert cute. It has to be somebody else. "Tell him I'll be there in a second."

When I emerge from the training suite a minute later, there is indeed a hottie standing there. And I recognize him. "You're Jimbo, right? The equipment guy for the dudes?"

"Yeah, that's me. I heard you were looking for a place to live. And I got a buddy who's trying to sublet his place while he's away overseas for a year."

"Really?" My heart leaps. "Tell me more."

He grabs the back of his neck and looks at the floor. "Well, it's, uh, thirteen hundred a month. Condo on Jay Street in a highrise building."

"Wow." Except I saw a listing over there on *Apartments.com*. And it cost more than three grand. "Who is this buddy, exactly?"

"Just, uh, a friend of a friend. I grew up in Brooklyn. I got a lot of friends." He shifts his weight awkwardly.

"And what kind of work does he do that keeps him overseas for a year?"

Jimbo actually cringes. "He's in, like, private security."

"Private security," I echo. "Let me guess—I'm his only customer, and his name is Cornelius Drake III."

"Hell." Jimbo lifts his gorgeous brown eyes. "I told him this would never fly."

"Because I'm not an idiot? Yeah, you tell him that I read the listings, too."

Jimbo grins. "I'm not telling him anything. You go ahead, though. Sounds like the two of you need to talk."

I blow out a breath. "I hope he at least bought you a drink or something for this bit of stupidity."

"Hoagie sandwich." Jimbo shrugs. "Lying isn't really my thing, but it seemed like he was trying to be nice."

"Yeah," I say on a sigh. "Men are such weirdos, Jimbo. What was he going to do if I wanted to meet the guy?"

"I got no idea." He shrugs again. "Put on a fake mustache? You should pretend to take him up on it just to find out."

"Fun idea." I hold up a hand, and he high-fives it. "But I think I'll pass. Enjoy your sandwich. I have to run."

"Night, Charli." He gives me a smile, which is, as Fiona said, nice. And then he leaves me alone.

"So let's review," Fiona says, her fork poised above the rectangular pan of cauliflower gratin. "This man baked you a dish you enjoy. And he is trying to make sure you have some-place safe to live. But he doesn't want the credit. And you still think he doesn't love you?"

"Yeah, wow," Samantha says. "That's an interesting take, Charli." After hearing about the casserole, she invited herself to dinner. She also brought two dozen chicken wings, and Sylvie made sangria.

So now I guess it's a party. We're all standing around the counter that divides Sylvie and Fiona's kitchen from their living room. Each of us has a fork, and we're eating it right out of the pan.

Don't let anyone tell you that hockey players aren't classy.

We aren't, but we will still fight you over it.

I take another bite of Neil's cheesy masterpiece and sigh. It's so good.

"Why don't we trust Neil, again?" Sylvie asks, picking up a chicken wing.

"We don't trust a lot of people," I grumble. "Especially billionaires who make us feel special and then make us feel used, all within the same half hour."

"If you weren't married…" Fiona pauses to take another bite of cauliflower from her corner of the pan. "If you were dating, would it be different? Would he be easier to trust?"

I don't even hesitate. "Of course he would. If he'd just asked me out…" I try to picture Neil casually asking me out, and I really can't. "Maybe it would be different. I didn't even know he had a thing for me until I woke up married to him."

Sylvie slaps her hand on the counter. "Men! So clumsy. So terrible at showing their feelings."

I think that over for a second. "I'm pretty bad at it too, though. I don't let people get close to me. Hell, I called Neil an asshole the first time we met. Would *you* ask me out?"

There's laughter, but then Fiona shakes her head. "Neil did it all backwards. But what if he really loves you? He keeps trying, Charli. Are you going to cut the boy some slack?"

They make it sound so easy. But every moment I spend with Neil is so charged with lust and longing that I don't know how to take things slowly. I don't know how to unwind the knot in my heart.

The buzzer rings, interrupting my thoughts. "I'll get it," I volunteer.

"Someone else must have heard about the cauliflower," Sylvie jokes.

But it isn't another dinner guest. It's Miguel again, and he has *another* delivery for me. "We've got to stop meeting like this," I say as I meet him at the door.

That wins me a small smile. I definitely owe this man a tip. "Let me get my wallet," I say.

"It's covered, Mrs. Drake." He hands me a manila envelope. "Good night."

"Goodnight, Miguel! You're a prince among men."

He actually turns and winks, and I feel like I've won a prize.

My good humor only lasts for as long as it takes me to open the envelope. The documents inside are from the law offices of Moss, Baker and Moore. *Summons and complaint in the matter of Higgins vs. Drake.*

Gulp. These are my divorce documents. Shit just got real. With a real feeling of deja vu, I scan the cover letter of another legal document. *Blah blah blah, dotted line...* All they need from me is my signature.

And my soul. When I start flipping pages, looking for the clause I'm dreading—the lawyer's grounds for divorce—I find it on page two. It's worse than I'd guessed. *Verbal abuse. Unsafe and improper to continue the marriage...*

Oh my *God.* I'm supposed to sign my name to these lies? What does that make me?

"Charli?" Sylvie says softly. When I raise my head, I find all three of the women are watching me. "Is everything all right?"

No, it really isn't. I got married by accident, and the only way out is to paint my husband as a terrible person. "Divorce is really complicated," is all I can think to say. "Don't ever get divorced."

I take a deep breath, and it's shaky on the way out. My phone rings, and when I grab it out of my pocket, I see Neil's name on the screen.

I answer, because I'm not *that* big of a coward.

"Don't panic," he says immediately. "I know it sounds harsh."

"Harsh?" I yelp. "It sounds like you should be arrested. You could get in trouble with the league. Don't they sanction players who are involved in domestic violence? They ought to."

His chuckle is dry. "I don't think it will make you feel any better to hear this, but I'm pretty sure you need to be arrested to get their attention."

He's right—I do not feel better. "Is that really a chance you want to take?"

"Yes," he says firmly, "if it makes things right between us."

I blow out a breath. "I have no idea what to do. I don't know how to make this decision. I can't put you in jeopardy just to make myself feel a little better."

"Yeah, you can," he says in a soothing voice. "You're always telling me that rich guys end up on top. It's pretty much true. Nothing in this divorce is really going to hurt me. I can take it, Charli. Especially if there's a chance you'll come back to me afterwards."

My heart practically bursts to hear that. And for a long moment, I can't say anything at all. I just close my eyes and breathe through my confusion.

A hug from Neil would be nice right now. Now there's a thought I never used to entertain.

"Charli, look at me."

I open my eyes. "What are you talking about? It's a phone call, Neil."

He chuckles. "Come over to the window."

Oh. I take a few steps toward the window, and there he is, three stories up. The silhouette of Neil stands there, backlit by the warm lighting in his fancy living room. One hand holds the phone, one strong arm is braced against the window sash.

My tummy flips at the familiar sight of him.

He raises his hand and waves. "Hi, wifey. Long time no see. I miss you."

Suddenly there's a lump in my throat. "I miss you, too," I whisper. "But when I said I couldn't do this, I wasn't lying. I tried. But I can't be your fake wife and your real...whatever. Not at the same time. It's doing my head in."

"Hey, it's okay," he says softly. "I keep complaining that you won't talk to me, but I haven't been honest, either. I want more from you than just a party date. But I did a shit job of explaining myself."

"You're..." I clear my throat. "Not *so* bad."

I hear laughter in stereo—from Neil and my teammates. "*You* shut up," I say over my shoulder. "No eavesdropping." As if they have a choice. I'm in the center of their home.

"You're hard on my ego, baby," Neil says sweetly.

"I don't mean to be," I say, looking up at him. "I'm not good at this."

"Yeah, well I thought I was, and it turns out I'm not. So we have that in common. What did your crew think of the roasted cauliflower gratin?"

"Major hit," I say. "If you're looking for another fake wife anytime soon, I think there'd be takers."

"I won't be," he promises. "Now you take care of yourself, okay? Sign that document. Divorce my ass. Take me up on my offer to put down your security deposit. I need you calm and happy so you can figure out what a catch I am."

"Okay," I say with a shaky laugh. "I'll, uh, work on all that stuff."

"You do that. Then you come talk to me. I'm not going anywhere." He puts his palm on the glass, as if touching me. "Don't you lose my number."

"I won't," I say with a throat that seems to be closing up on itself. "Good night."

THIRTY-FIVE

JUST AN ORDINARY FRIDAY

Charli

We tie up our game against the Philadelphia Fillies. Then we lose in overtime. *Thanks, Philadelphia. You're a pal.*

That town was never good to me, and it doesn't want to start now. But at least the road trip gets me off of Fiona's couch and into a real bed.

After another week of serving omelets and apartment hunting, it's time to head to Boston. We gather behind the Brooklyn hockey facility at two o'clock. My teammates and I lean against the brick wall, waiting for the bus driver to open the doors. We huddle close together like ducklings under the overhang as a cold March drizzle pings down from the leaden sky.

And—as they often do—my thoughts turn to Neil.

That's a strong theme with me since I've signed our divorce papers. I've put them in a new envelope, carefully addressed to the lawyer. I've sealed them up and taken them to the post office for proper postage. I'm well on my way to a divorce.

Except for that last thing I haven't done—drop them in a mailbox.

I'm planning to. I swear. But every time I walk past the mailbox, I can't make myself stop and throw the envelope in.

Neil has already sent me two gentle texts asking if there are any problems, or if I have any last questions. *It will turn out okay, kitten. You can file. I'll be fine.*

Those messages made me feel all gooey inside. But I'm pretty sure I'm going to have to get up in front of a judge and claim that Neil was cruel to me. Out loud.

I'm a tough person. I can do this.

Soon.

Just not today.

Neil is constantly on my mind, but it's even worse today, because I know that damn meeting is happening without me in a couple hours.

He'd never said another word about it. He hadn't pressed me about trying to show up this afternoon to help him conquer his controlling uncle.

Maybe if I'd actually managed to be helpful to Neil, I wouldn't feel so shitty about our divorce proceedings. Maybe…

"What are they doing?" Sylvie grumbles beside me. "My hands are icicles. Shouldn't we be on the bus already?"

I glance up to see the bus driver kneeling beside the bus's wheel while Coach Sasha and Bess try to talk to him.

"Flat tire?" I guess.

"No, he's trying to put chains on the tires," Samantha says. "This rain is supposed to freeze over in the next hour."

"And it's snowing in Boston," Fiona says, scrolling through her phone.

"Pffft," Sylvie says dismissively. "In Canada, that's just an ordinary Friday. If we could just get on the road, we could be there before it turns ugly." She stomps off.

"Is Sylvie in goal tonight?" I wonder aloud.

"You guessed it," our other goalie, Scarlet, says. "She's raring to go."

Bess pulls up the hood of her Brooklyn jacket then crosses

the asphalt to talk to us. "Just a few more minutes, ladies. The bus is almost ready."

"Okay," Fiona says. "Should have brought my mittens. Do you mind if we wait inside?"

Bess checks her watch. "Sure. Stay close, though. This will only take a second. And leave your bags—I'll watch them."

"Thanks." Fiona takes my forearm. "Let's go. I'm freezing."

I follow her into the corridor, because I need a moment of her time. "Guess who has a new plan to stop sleeping on your couch?"

"Yeah?" She brightens. "I knew something would come through for you."

"That hasn't exactly worked yet," I say carefully. "I'm still hoping to find somebody who needs a roommate. But I found a youth hostel I can stay in for a while, if I could leave just one large box in your apartment for safekeeping."

"A youth hostel." Fiona frowns. "Like, bunkbeds? With a bunch of college kids from Europe?"

"With whoever." I shrug. "It's cheap, but I don't want to leave any valuables there while I'm at work or at practice."

"No way," she says. "You can't move to a youth hostel! Where is it?"

"Um, the Bronx."

"Why would you ever *do* that?" Sylvie asks, rubbing her cold hands together. "Do we snore?"

"No!" I say through a clenched jaw. "But I don't want to be that friend who won't leave. It's rude."

Fiona looks at me like I'm the world's biggest idiot. She opens her backpack and pulls out a single key, shiny, like it was just cut at the hardware store. "You know what else is rude? Assuming that we don't want you there, even after we said we did. Look, I made you a key this morning." She presses it into my hand.

"Thank you," I say quietly. "But I don't like owing favors."

She rolls her eyes. "So what if you owe me one? I'm hoping

to cash in someday when you invite me to stay at your Italian villa on Lake Como." She shrugs. "But don't be a twatwaffle, Charli. You're not going to a damn youth hostel."

"My Italian villa?" I snort. "You must be confusing me with another girl."

"Nah, I've been googling your husband." She leans back against the wall and gets a dreamy look in her eye. "He has a seven-bedroom villa with a travertine hot tub on the patio. Don't tell me you haven't found that article."

Slowly, I shake my head. "I spent the last few years avoiding the Drake family." Once I verified that Neil was Paisley's brother, I never looked him up again.

"Wow." Sylvie shakes her head. "There is nobody quite like you."

"So I hear." I take up a position against the wall beside her, and my thoughts go to Neil. Again. I can finally admit that Neil is not at all what I expected. When this is all over, I'm going to tell him that.

I unlock my phone and check my messages. There's a bank notification, and those always make me queasy. But since it's Friday, the update announces that my paycheck from the diner has landed. So that's awesome.

In less exciting news, there are three increasingly urgent text messages from my brother Denny. From this morning: *I need to ask you a question*, he says. *I'm not asking for money, I swear*.

I don't trust it, though, so I haven't replied.

He subsequently wrote: *I got a job, Charli. I've stayed away from the poker table. I'm doing what I need to do. But I still have to talk to you about something*.

That does sound promising, and if I don't talk to him about whatever it is that's so pressing, I can stay here in my happy place and believe that he's pulled himself together. My optimism is a fragile thing. I'm trying to hold onto it without crushing it.

Lastly, I check the time. It's 2:02, time to ride the bus to Boston.

Coach Sasha comes into the hallway after a couple more long minutes and claps her hands. "Gather round, guys. Let's go! Team huddle."

I'm sorry, Neil. I really am.

THIRTY-SIX

LOOK IT UP

Neil

File this under first-world problems.

It's only a twenty-foot trek from the car to the entrance of the New York headquarters of Drake Enterprises. But the leather soles of my Ferragamos are no match for the slick sidewalk, and I nearly fall on my ass trying to cross the pavement.

A hockey player who almost slips on the ice? It's not a good look.

Nothing about this meeting will be fun. Mom and Paisley and I will sit across the table from Harmon, his wife Christina, and my cousin Fred. With the help of the foundation's CEO, we will compromise our way through another quarter's contributions and expenditures.

Philanthropy can make a guy more cynical than you'd think.

I take the elevator up to the 32nd floor. The doors part into a plush reception area, draped in thick imported carpets and dark wood. A polished receptionist straightens up in her chair the moment she sees me. "Hello, Mr. Drake, you're right on time. The boardroom is all set up for you. Can I bring you a coffee drink or a cocktail?"

"A cappuccino would be lovely, thank you." Although I'm half tempted to ask for a cocktail. I wonder if they'd actually bring me one.

I show myself into the meeting room, which is situated in the corner of the building. Most days it has a killer view of midtown. But today, gray clouds hug the plate-glass windows, giving the room an aura of a damp cave with very expensive furniture.

Christina is seated and waiting, as is my sister, on the opposite side of the table. They aren't conversing, because the chasm between us all runs pretty deep. Christina gives me a stoic nod, though.

Paisley gets up. "Hi Neil. How have you been? Long time no see." She lifts her pretty eyes to me. She's looking for forgiveness.

But there's a reason I haven't spoken to her since the evening of the gala. "I'm fine, Paise. But I haven't felt like hanging out with you."

Her chin dips. "I'm sorry. I know I was out of line that night. But Iris was so upset. You strung her along for years."

I want to argue with her, but the truth is that I was lazy where it came to Iris. It was easier to date her on and off than to acknowledge my real feelings. "Maybe I could have been quicker to figure out that she and I were a disaster, but that's between her and me. You owe my wife an apology."

Paisley eyes the door. "Where is she?"

"Well..."

Before I can explain, my mother sweeps through the door, counts the number of people in the room, and stops dead in front of me. "Where is Charli?"

"On a bus to Boston," I say tightly. "Like I told you she would be."

A scowl takes over her face. "Oh, Neil. This is a disaster. How could you let this happen?"

"Yeah, it's my fault for not noticing the meeting date had changed. But Charli can't help her game schedule."

With a dramatic sigh, my mother melts into a chair like a character in a Victorian novel, and I half expect her to call for smelling salts. She's wearing an expression of devastation.

It's nothing I can help, though.

I sit down just as my uncle and his son breeze through the door, followed by Jacobs, the elderly CEO of our foundation. "We can get started," Harmon says with the manner of someone who's terribly important.

At the head of the table, Jacobs opens his leather folder. Then he reads the same spiel he uses at every single meeting. "The agenda shall proceed as follows: I will provide a summary of results for last quarter. Then we will move on to considering proposals for next quarter."

I zone out for a few minutes while he lists some facts and figures. I picture Charli on her bus with all her teammates. That's my happy thought. I hear the team has a solid chance against Boston, and that they're a lock for the playoffs.

When my phone buzzes with a text, Charli is the first person I think of. Even though I know better, I pull it out for a peek.

But the two-word message is from Vera. *You're welcome.*

Hmm. I don't remember asking Vera for anything.

"Neil?"

I sit up straight in my chair. "Sorry. Yes?"

"He's taking attendance," my mother says sourly.

"*Oh.* Present."

The CEO checks me off. "Paisley Drake?"

"Present," my sister chirps.

"Charlotte Fern Higgins Drake?" he drones. Then he waits, as if Charli might materialize before us.

It's like that Ferris Bueller movie. I sigh. "She is otherwise engaged."

"All right, then." The CEO lifts his pen. "Let the attendance record show that six of the seven eligible—"

The door opens, and I glance up, expecting to see the receptionist with a cappuccino. But that is not who steps through the door.

Maybe I'm having a very intense hallucination, because there's a beautiful doppelgänger for Charli standing there in a dead-sexy red suit, red lipstick, and smoky eyes. She's also wearing silky stockings and shiny black heels.

She's even wearing a dapper black hat, which she removes as she takes us in. She looks like a female sexpot from the *Mad Men* era.

She looks like a wet dream.

"Sorry I'm a few minutes late," Charli announces to a room full of gaping stares. "Where shall I sit?" She puts a hand on her hip and gives me an arch look.

I leap out of my chair as if my ass were on fire. "R-right here. I'll get another one."

She gives me a cat-like smile and waltzes around the table to stand before me. "Good afternoon, doll. Where's my kiss hello?"

Doll. I break out in a wide, stupid smile. And as the whole room watches, I lean in and take that perfect mouth.

Charli's green gaze hovers beneath me, a smile in her eyes as I press her with a significantly horny (yet PG) kiss. God, how I've missed her. It gives me physical pain to straighten up again instead of pulling her into my arms.

With a knowing smile, she reaches a hand up to my face. "Bit of lipstick," she says naughtily as her thumb slowly cruises my hungry mouth. "There. All set."

Then she winks.

Good thing my suit jacket conceals my boner. She is wearing some kind of perfume that intensifies her lemony scent. I just want to heft her over my shoulder and carry her out of here.

But first things first. "Sit, wifey." I offer my chair.

"Thank you," she says in a saucy voice. "Now somebody

pass me a set of papers, please. Let's do this philanthropy thing! My first board meeting. So exciting."

I want to shout with laughter, but I rein it in somehow as two executive assistants hurry in. One of them is pushing an extra chair, and the other carries a tray full of coffee cups and — is that a martini?

The drink is set in front of Charli. "Thank you. This looks delicious."

The CEO clears his throat. "Charlotte Fern Higgins Drake?" he calls.

Charli lifts her cocktail, takes a sip and then sets it down. "Present!" she says when she's good and ready.

God, I love her.

I really do love her.

That's going to scare the crap out of her when I admit it.

I take another long glance, drinking her in. On second thought, maybe it won't scare the crap out of her. Charli looks steady as a rock.

The CEO turns a page in his folder and starts the business part of the meeting. "First major contribution, proposed by Frederic Drake—a hundred thousand dollars to the Stanford Alumni Fund, earmarked for a new parking lot behind the business school. Naming rights guaranteed."

"I'll second it," my uncle says.

Charli holds up the proposal from her packet. "A parking lot? Am I to assume that someone in this room attended Stanford Business School?"

My cousin raises his hand. "I did. It's a worthy institution in California. You can look it up."

Charli sips her martini. "And you believe that a parking lot with your name over it is the *best* possible use of a hundred thousand dollars? I'll bet they'd name an entire university after you if you used that money to feed hungry children in Yemen. That's a worthy country on the Arabian Peninsula. You can look it up."

My mother claps a hand over her mouth, and my sister allows a snort of glee.

I bite the inside of my cheek to keep from laughing. "I think Charli's made a point. I'm not feeling the love for Stanford Business School today. Shall we vote?"

"All in favor!" the CEO says.

Three hands on the opposite side of the table go up. Four hands on our side of the table stay down.

"Motion fails to pass," the CEO says. "The next resolution concerns fifty thousand dollars for a horse-riding therapy program for disabled children in New York State. Proposal by Paisley Drake."

"I'll second it," my mother says.

Charli skims that page of the packet. "Huh. I think horses are terrifying. But you do you."

"Shall we vote?" I ask.

"All in favor!" the CEO calls.

Four hands on our side of the table go up. "This is super fun," Charli says as the other three hands stay down.

"Motion passes," the CEO says. "Next item —"

"We get it," my uncle snaps. "You made your point. Now let's compromise. What do you all want?"

My mother is ready for the question. She pulls a sheet of paper out of her leather folio. "I want full control of my trust. You'll resign as executor, appointing me. Here is the paperwork." She pushes it into the center of the table, in reach of my uncle.

My uncle doesn't reach for it. Not yet. Instead, he pulls another sheet from *his* folder. Then he points a finger at my wife. "If I sign that, *she* resigns. Then we'd be even again."

Charli glances at me. I give her a tiny nod.

She reaches for my uncle's paper. "On the count of three? I'll sign if you will."

Then? She curls her foot around mine under the table and slides her toe up my leg.

Yeah, there is a non-zero chance that this is all a fantastic dream. But I sure hope it's real.

"One problem," the CEO says. "There is a forty-eight-hour waiting period on board personnel changes. For the purposes of this meeting, Mrs. Charlotte Fern Higgins Drake is still a board member, even if she resigns right now."

My uncle sighs. "I guess we'll have to compromise the old-fashioned way for an hour?"

"Sign first," Charli prompts. "Then I'll approve your egotistical parking lot. Do we at least get a roof over this thing? I wouldn't want all those convertibles to get rained on."

With a glower, my uncle signs the paper. He hands it to the CEO. "You hold this. If the girl doesn't sign, tear it up."

"The *girl*," Charli says, her pen poised above the page. "*Excuse* me?"

Where is the popcorn when you need it?

"Pardon," my uncle says, his eyes on her pen. "Slip of the tongue."

With a shake of her bright hair, Charli signs the page. She passes it to the CEO for safekeeping. Then she picks up her martini and drains it. "Okay boys, let's finish up."

The CEO begins reading off the rest of the proposals, and we all dutifully vote for every single one. It's less interesting without Charli's acerbic commentary.

At least my proposal passes—a hundred-thousand-dollar grant to a laboratory that's trying to build batteries that are both powerful enough and light enough to fly an electric plane.

"This technology is only fifty years away from practical application," my uncle grumbles.

"You'll have devastated the planet by then," I agree. "But at least I tried."

He doesn't know that I've already invested millions in electrical tech. I want to fix the private-jet industry. This stray hundred thousand dollars is just to rub his nose in it.

"We've reached our last proposal," the CEO announces.

"Sixty-five thousand dollars for a sports complex to be shared between the Draper School and the boys of Parkhurst Prep."

"Can't imagine anyone objects to this one, since we all went to one or the other," Cousin Fred says. "Although we don't get naming rights. The complex will honor a retired soccer coach."

Charli straightens up in her seat. "Wait. Which coach?" She picks up the sheaf of papers in front of her and flips to the last page.

"Clint Hauser." My cousin smirks. "Who else? He coached more All-American athletes than any other coach in Parkhurst history."

I glance at Charli, and then I do a double take. She's going pale before my eyes.

"Shall we vote?" the CEO asks.

"Hold up." I reach for her hand. "What's the matter?"

"I don't like that man," she says softly.

"You don't have to like him," my cousin says. "He's just a name on a sports complex at a school *you* attended. And we have a deal on the table. Let's vote."

THIRTY-SEVEN

THE GUY IN YOUR CORNER

Charli

It took a lot to get me into this room. I find it easier to face down a bloodthirsty hockey team than Neil's family.

So the first person I'd called after our game got canceled was Vera the stylist. By quickly producing the red suit and the mean-girl heels, she'd given me the courage to walk in here and play this role.

I'd coolly handed over Neil's credit card, purchasing my armor. Treating this meeting like a military mission.

It had worked, too. I'd marched into this room feeling strong and happy to do my part helping Neil and his mom defeat the patriarchy.

The moment Neil looked up at me, I'd known how much it mattered, too. Nobody has ever looked at me with such love and gratitude. His glow of approval is more seductive to me than any drug will ever be.

Until now, when it's all come to a crashing halt. I can't vote to glorify Clint Hauser. I just can't do it.

"Hey," Neil whispers, stroking the back of my hand. "Tell me. What's wrong?"

Everything. Just everything. I sit very still, and I try to breathe. Neil waits. He doesn't push. He just strokes my hand. I make myself turn and look him in the eye. All his focus is on me. As if there's nobody else in this room.

It helps. It really does. I look into those steady eyes and feel a little tougher.

This is my Waterloo moment, whether I asked for it or not. Neil keeps asking me for the truth. I keep refusing to show it to him. I've always known that if Neil saw the real me—the scared kid and the hot mess—his infatuation would die a sudden death.

And now I guess I'll find out.

I clear my throat. A quick glance confirms I have everyone's attention. I start my tale. "When I was sixteen years old, I was a recruited player on the soccer team at Draper. It was my first semester there." My voice comes out scratchy, and my throat is suddenly dry. "My big dream was Team USA. I had that Mia Hamm poster on my wall."

Neil's eyes smile at me, and I manage to carry on by telling this story as if he's the only one in the room.

"Hauser was the boys' coach over at Parkhurst. But he was also on the committee for the national U18 teams. Sometimes he would come across the road and watch the girls' practice. I used to show off for him."

You'd think, given my history, that I would be the least naïve kid at Draper. But you'd be wrong. I loved the attention I got for being a star on the soccer team. And I felt like I'd finally arrived somewhere that wanted me.

Neil waits.

"That season, the girls made it all the way to the finals, but the boys didn't. Hauser watched all our playoffs games. The night before the final, I got called into his office…" I swallow hard, remembering my excitement. I'd wanted a chance at the U18. I'd showed up expecting to hear praise.

"Breathe," Neil whispers.

I fill up my lungs with air, and then I wheeze out the truth.

"He told me that if I gave him a blowjob, he'd add my name to the U18 long list."

"*Fuck*," Neil whispers.

Nobody else says a word. I have to wonder if the word *blowjob* has ever been uttered in this room before. Maybe not. Or maybe it has—by some corporate asshole asking his assistant for a favor. Does that kind of thing happen at Drake Enterprises?

Sometimes it's hard to tell whether the whole world is cracked, or if it's just your little slice of it. My slice has always had a lot of cracks.

Neal's mother is the first one to break the silence. "What happened?"

Ah. The age-old question. "You're asking whether or not I *did* it? Or whether I told anyone?"

She opens her mouth and the closes it again.

"Neither of those questions is fair. But because you asked —*no* and *no*. I walked out on Hauser, which was terrifying all by itself. You don't storm out of a coach's office and expect to live. Then I went back to my room, and I got into the bed with all my clothes on, and I stayed there for twenty-four hours. My team lost the final the next day, and I got kicked off the soccer team for failing to show up."

That seems like the end of the story. Hauser never sought me out again. But my troubles were only beginning, because no one on the soccer team ever spoke to me again. And the soccer girls were very popular. Which meant that nobody at Draper dared to be my friend, either.

Even my hockey teammates were chilly, in spite of the fact that I played hockey after that like I was starring in *The Hunger Games*.

It was a lonely three years. But my hockey game improved a lot. The female hockey coach appreciated it.

"And as for your second question," I continue, "there was nobody I trusted to tell. Men get away with things like this all the time. Every boarding school on the East Coast has had to reckon with mishandling a sexual predator or two. I never told a soul until right now, because I didn't think anyone would believe me."

Neil squeezes my hand. "I do."

I take a breath and just sit with that a moment. Because it feels really fucking good to hear it.

"So do I," Paisley chirps.

That's a surprise. I can't help but glance over at her. She gives me an apologetic smile and a tiny shrug.

Who knew that girl had a beating heart somewhere in her body?

"Regardless," Neil's uncle snaps. "We still have to vote. Don't forget—we had a deal."

Neil's mother twists her wedding ring around her finger nervously as the CEO rereads the motion. "All in favor of the donation to fund the Clint Hauser Sports Complex, raise your hand and be counted."

Three hands go up on the opposite side of the table.

My hand stays locked down, and so does Neil's.

Paisley shakes her head. "No way."

I'm just about to smile when Neil's mom slowly raises her hand.

"*Mom*," Neil barks. "Don't you dare!"

"We had a deal," she says.

"Motion passes," the CEO says.

Neil springs out of his seat. "*Fuck* the deal. Giving money to assholes is never the right call. I'm done with this."

"He doesn't get the money, even if he is a pervert! The school does," his uncle growls. "And you already registered your opinion with your vote."

"I don't think you understand. I'm *done* with this." Neil marches around the table. At first, I think he's going to storm out and leave me here with these crazy people and an empty martini glass.

But his progress stops right beside the CEO. Neil reaches down, plucks a piece of paper off the desk, and tears it in half. Twice.

Four pieces of my resignation letter fall to the boardroom table.

His uncle lets out a gasp of rage and then dives for *his* signed trustee transfer document.

The sound of tearing paper rents the air again. Another contract destroyed.

Paloma Drake gasps. "Neil! Look what you've done!"

"You don't get to lay this on me," he thunders. "Your issues are not my fault. Dad's estate provisions were not my doing. None of this is my problem. Fight your own battles." He nearly completes his circuit of the table but comes to a stop beside my chair. He holds out a hand and offers it to me. "Can we leave now, wifey?"

"We so can." I push back my chair. "Thanks for the martini, boys. It's been a pleasure. See you next quarter?" I give them a saucy wink, and they stare back with dead eyes.

Then I take Neil's waiting hand.

His long fingers close around mine, and satisfaction surges through me as I follow him out of the room.

Neil is silent as we make our way out of the corporate offices. He finds my suitcase and my hockey bag in the closet where the assistants stashed them and tosses one over each shoulder. "Come," he says in a growly voice.

I hurry along behind him. He's clearly upset.

As we enter the elevator, I realize that nothing good will come out of this. I could have just kept my trap shut. That damn sports complex will still get built, and that asshole's name will still be on it. In gold letters, probably.

Hell. All this drama for nothing. But I hadn't heard that

man's name in years, and when Neil's cousin had said it, I'd panicked.

I'd been triggered, plain and simple, and so I'd reacted.

Now Neil's scary mom wants to kill me.

It's a good thing she isn't really my mother-in-law. I don't think Thanksgiving would be very pleasant.

Outside, on the freezing, rain-slicked pavement, Neil steps to the curb and whistles. A car and driver appear. It's not the limo this time, it's merely a shiny black town car with the same female driver who'd picked us up at the airport the afternoon after Vegas.

Neil murmurs a greeting to her and puts my stuff in the trunk while I watch, dazed. "Get in, sweetheart," he practically growls. "You're not wearing a coat."

The car is warm and smells of leather. I lean back against the headrest and try to calm my galloping heart. When I open my eyes, we're cruising down Fifth, and Neil still looks like he wants to punch something.

But then he turns to me, and his expression softens. "Are you okay?"

"Yes," I say simply. I'm always okay.

"Look, I'm sorry. I'm sorry that happened to you. I'm just... sorry."

"Well, thanks? I don't see how it's your fault."

"Yeah, but you were *sixteen*. Jesus. And you didn't have anyone to talk to about it." He pinches the bridge of his nose. "That must have been scary as hell."

"It *was* scary," I surprise myself by admitting. Thinking about it causes a familiar knot of tension to gather behind my breastbone. It had been a dark day when I'd realized even my fancy new school couldn't save me from the same bullshit I'd faced at home. There had been no safe places. Anywhere. "But it was also humiliating. I went to this man expecting praise and a conversation about my future. All he'd wanted was to get his dick sucked."

"Shit," Neil curses. "I want to break him in half. And there's no way you were the only one, right? You can't be the only kid he ever propositioned."

"I doubt I was. But I was the scholarship kid. The kid with literally nowhere else to go. The kid they probably wouldn't have believed even if I had told."

His handsome frame bends as he puts his head in his hands. "And now he's getting a building named after him."

"That's how it works." *And that's why I'm always so angry.*

Except right now I'm just tired. I sag against the leather seat. Clint Hauser hadn't been the worst man in my life. People in my own family have done more damage than he'd managed.

And that's my real secret—the pattern. "You know…"

I chicken out.

Neil takes my hand and strokes it. "What, baby?"

"It wasn't the first time," I whisper.

His hand goes still. "He approached you before that?"

"No." I shake my head. "Not him. Other people did worse to me before that. And at some point you start to wonder if it's you."

That had been really hard to say, and I look away—out the car window. Rain smacks against the glass as we glide toward the east side of town.

Neil strokes my hand again. Then he lifts it to his mouth and kisses my palm. "Thank you for telling me that," he whispers.

I can't say anything at all. I have to hold very still and breathe through the familiar shame.

The car moves on through midtown traffic, and eventually I start to relax. When I risk a glance at Neil, he's staring out the window. Thoughtful. When he catches me watching him, he laces his fingers through mine and gives me a cautious smile.

"I can't believe you ripped up my resignation," I say. "We

finally got what you wanted. What if I signed it again? He still thinks the foundation vote is lopsided."

Neil is already shaking his head. "No way. I only *thought* that deal was what I wanted. But I was so wrong." He turns his body, so he can look me right in the eye. "I told you our marriage could be useful to me."

"Well, it *was* until you ripped that thing in half."

"Not quite." He smiles again. "Our marriage actually gave me everything I wanted, because it brought you all the way into my life. *That's* what I needed. And I'm so damn sorry I was too dumb to own that before."

My jaw actually flops open as I try to process that statement.

Neil reaches over and cups it. "You're it for me, kitten. If I could go back in time and do it over, I'd ask you out, instead of drunk-marrying you. I'd go slowly. I'd cook you a steak and invite you to hang out with me—so you'd see that I'm the guy who'll always be in your corner."

"But I..." I've basically lost the ability to speak. "I p-probably would have turned you down. I don't trust people. I'm too angry. But I'm not brave."

"Charli, you're the bravest person I've ever met. Besides, I'm angry too. But I always thought I had to hide it. Like, rich guys don't deserve to get angry. But thanks to you, I'm mad as heck at some people who deserve it. And I'm not sorry."

For another moment I just blink at him. This is a lot to take in. "What happens now?"

"I thought you'd never ask." He gives me another beautiful smile. "Now I get to take you home and cook you a steak. That's our arrangement—any time you put up with my family, you get a steak dinner."

That sounds dreamy. "And then?"

"And then we watch a movie on my new TV, sitting on the cayenne couch—together at the end with the chaise. And a big bowl of popcorn."

"Like a date?" In spite of everything that happened today, I'm smiling back at him.

"You can call it whatever you want. I want you in my life, Charli. I want a real chance with you. I want you in my kitchen. On my couch. And in my bed." At that, he scoops me into his lap. "This is a killer suit, by the way. Vera's getting a raise."

I rest my head on his shoulder. "I asked her if she could make me look both fierce and beautiful inside of ninety minutes. And she said, 'Oh honey, try me.'"

He laughs. "You always look fierce, baby. That's one reason why I love you. So much. And brace yourself, kitten. Because I have lots of other reasons, too."

My blood stops circulating as I play back his words in my head. He'd actually said it. Without any qualifiers.

"I love your smile, for example. I love to watch you play hockey. I love the way you don't take any shit from anyone. I love waking up with you. And I want all of those things."

My heart quietly detonates.

"Breathe," Neil commands.

And, yup, I'd forgotten to take on oxygen there for a minute. "Neil," I gasp.

"Yes, kitten?"

"But we're still married. We're still a mess."

He shrugs. "And you can decide what to do about that. To me, it's just details. If I don't get to have you in my life until our divorce is final, then I'll wait. You'll have to let me know when that's going to happen. I noticed you've never filed the papers."

"I couldn't do it," I breathe against his collar. "I just can't get up in front of a judge and say that you were cruel."

"That is your choice," he says, stroking my hair. "We could just run down the clock on a no-fault divorce and worry about it again in four months. The lawyer will take your call when you're ready to decide."

"Wow," I say. That's it. That's my whole response.

"Yeah, I know. But I've had some time to myself to really get my priorities in order. Like I said, I want to be the guy in your corner." He runs a finger down my nose. "But I can't do it unless you let me be that guy. If you don't feel the same—if you don't want to be the girl in my corner—you'd better let me down easy."

"You…" I take a deep breath. "You terrify me."

It's the truest thing I've ever said.

"I know," he whispers. "But I'm kind of worth it once you get to know me. Can I cook you a steak while you think it over?"

"Okay," I whisper back. "Yes, please."

He presses a single, slow kiss to my cheekbone while the car eases its way toward Brooklyn, and I relax in his strong arms.

THIRTY-EIGHT

I DIDN'T KNOW I WAS HAVING A PARTY

Neil

"Hello, Ms. Higgins," the concierge says as we enter the building. "It's so good to see you again."

"Thank you," my wife says as a blush stains her cheeks.

"Say, Miguel?" I lean against the counter. "Is there anyone on staff who's got a minute to make a quick run to the grocery store for me?"

"If she's staying for dinner, I guess I could find someone." He puts a pad and pen on the counter. "Write down what you want. I'll phone the break room."

"Thank you, sir."

After that's done, I take Charlie upstairs and set down her bags in my foyer. I'd just as soon carry them into the bedroom, but I don't want to make assumptions. "You're welcome to wear this killer outfit repeatedly and continuously in my presence. But you've had a long day, and if you wanted to go change into sweats, I would totally understand.

"You know I do." She gives me a smile that's a little shy. Like maybe we're out of practice.

"Well, get on it, girl. I'm gonna go pour you a glass of wine."

I shoo her toward the bedroom, and she grabs her suitcase and disappears.

I'm just taking my first sip of Bordeaux when she reappears in leggings and a flannel shirt from my own closet. "Oh, so it's going to be like that is it?" I say even though no sight has ever made me happier.

"I guess so." She smiles, but it's still shy.

"You know..." I set my wine glass down and nudge hers closer to her side of the kitchen island. "When you smile at me, it's all worth it. Every fucking thing. You make me happy just standing here in my kitchen."

Charli walks around the kitchen island, a solemn look on her face. She reaches up and strokes the stubble on my jaw, and the friction makes my body hum. "Neil," she whispers. "I'm sorry I scare so easily sometimes."

"You have your reasons, kitten. I just need to learn to be more patient."

She stands up on her tiptoes and kisses me. Just like that. Easy as rolling off a log.

I catch her and pull her in slowly. I don't want to advertise how badly I need her in my arms. How desperate I am to feel her heartbeat close to mine.

But Charli melts against me anyway. I catch her lip between my teeth and give her a nip that was supposed to seem playful. But I shoot past that, because there's no way to disguise how needy I am for this. I catch her face in my hands, tilting my head to kiss her again.

And again. And a hundred more times until we're hardcore making out against the fridge and her hands are unbuttoning my shirt and my thigh is wedged between hers.

The buzzer rings, of course. My groceries are here.

Charli pushes me away with a laugh. "You want me to get it?"

I look down at the tent in my trousers and my rumpled shirt, half unbuttoned. "That would be great, kitten. I need to change

before I cook for you." I pull open my menu drawer and hand
her a ten for the tip. "Be right back."

She gives me a saucy grin, and I finally feel like we're going
to be okay.

The dinner I throw together is simpler than the first one I ever
cooked for her. I'm too impatient to make the cauliflower gratin.
I use the microwave to jump start a couple of cheesy baked
potatoes, which I finish under the broiler. I grill the steaks on
my gas Weber and make coleslaw from a bag. The whole thing
takes twenty minutes, tops.

Skipping the dining table, I set two places side by side at the
kitchen counter. I put on some music by Justin B. which is, let's
face it, a chick pleaser. I'm not above using a few cheap tricks to
put Charli in a mellow mood.

It works, too. She sits on a stool, sipping her wine, the color
slowly returning to her cheeks. When I set down a plate of
steak, potatoes, and coleslaw in front of her, she makes a happy
sigh. Then she moans on the first bite of her filet.

I feel—no exaggeration—as victorious as the night my team
won the Cup. Having her here in my kitchen, feeding her some
excellent food... I've missed this.

"Even that horror show of a meeting is worth it if I get to
eat this afterwards," she says after a few bites.

"The end sure was ugly, but earlier on, it was the best
meeting ever. When you told my cousin where to find
Yemen..." I have to set down my wine glass and laugh.

She gives me a big, catty smile. "Fine. That part was fun.
But Neil, your family is not my favorite group of people."

"Not mine either," I agree. My mother and I are going to
have a *very* uncomfortable discussion. That's for damn sure.

There's a loud knock on the front door.

"Who's that?" Charli asks, a furrow reappearing between

her eyes.

Uh-oh. Until right this minute, I'd totally forgotten that I'd agreed to watch —

"Drake! Puck drops in three minutes. Come open this door!" Trevi yells through the door.

"Shit. Sorry," I say, sliding off my stool to head for the foyer. "I'll get rid of him."

But when I open the door a moment later, Leo Trevi shoves a pizza box against my chest. "Do you have beer? My sister and her friend are drinking all of mine."

"Actually, it turns out that tonight is not the best time..."

"Dude, *no.* I need to get out of there. And you owe me for trying to cheer up your grumpy ass all month after you got dumped by... Hey Charli!"

I look over my shoulder and see Charli standing there, her wine glass in her hand. "Hi, Leo."

He pushes past me and gives her a kiss on the cheek. "You have *no idea* how happy I am to see you. You're gonna watch the game with us?"

"Sure," she says, flashing me a quick smile. "Washington versus Philly, right?"

I'm quickly losing control of the situation. That much is obvious. "Just don't take our seat in the corner of the sofa."

Trevi just chuckles and heads for the living room.

At least I have a kick-ass couch. Charlie and I have claimed our rightful seat, our feet extended on the comfortable chaise. I have a glass of wine in my hand. Most importantly my girl is happy. She's tucked against me, unabashedly rooting for Philly.

"That's it, boys!" she says as they rough up a New Jersey player. "That's how we do it in Philly."

"Cut it out," Trevi whines. "We need New Jersey to clinch because they'll stink it up in the first round of the playoffs."

"That's your problem," Charli says gleefully. "You can take the girl out of Philly, but you can't take the team out of the girl."

I honestly don't care who wins this game so long as it doesn't go to overtime. I want my apartment and my date all to myself.

Someone knocks on the door. "Now who could that be?" I ask on a grumble.

"Oh, I told the other guys we were watching the game." Trevi shrugs.

"What? Doesn't anyone have their own TV?"

"I'll get it," Charli says as she tries to hand me her glass of wine.

"Oh no you *won't*. Trevi, answer the damn door yourself."

"Some host you are." He gets off the couch.

"You're drinking my beer!" I point out. "Make yourself useful."

Charli just shakes her head and watches the next play.

A moment later four more people enter the living room.

First up are Castro and Heidi Jo. Then Sylvie and Anton bring up the rear. "Hey guys! Charli—so good to have you back."

"Funny, I didn't know I was missing?"

"Babe," Anton says. "I don't think you understand how blue our man Drake has been. This is a guy who always used to beg me to go out dancing. He never even went out for a beer with us on the last road trip. None of my efforts to cheer him up worked. I took my life in my hands drawing a Sharpie moustache on O'Doul just to get a rise out of Drake. But nope. Just a sad panda face."

Charli turns to give me a sideways glance. "Wow. Not even a smile for shenanigans on the team jet?"

"No, baby." Sometimes you just have to lean into your own embarrassment. "The only shenanigans I'm interested in are with you. Unfortunately, my apartment is full of hockey players."

She laughs, and Castro asks where he should put the sixpack he brought.

"How about in your own apartment?" I try.

No such luck. My new sofa accommodates everyone, with Anton on the rug. But it's a tight fit. It's not exactly the romantic evening I'd been planning.

Philly takes the lead in the game, and I have to laugh as my boys get upset. "I'm not superstitious, but I won't be offended if you decide I'm bad luck," Charli says with a laugh after they score a third goal.

"No way, girly." Anton reaches up to give her ankle a squeeze. "We need our man Drake energized. And I guess we can handle New Jersey missing the playoffs. For you."

"That's so generous of you," Charli says while sharing an eyeroll with me. "I'm honored."

I just shake my head. And then the damn doorbell rings again.

Sylvie gets up to admit Fiona, who says she was feeling left out across the street. "There isn't any of that cauliflower dish, is there?" she asks hopefully.

"Sorry," I say with a shrug. "I didn't even know I was having a party."

"Let me guess—they heard Charli was here. And they had to see it for themselves?" She drags an upholstered dining chair away from the table and positions it where she can prop her feet on the chaise near ours.

"Go go go!" Trevi yells at the screen. New Jersey has a breakaway. There are only a few minutes left in regulation play.

Jesus Lord, please do not let this game go into overtime.

New Jersey shoots. The lamp lights, and all the hockey players on the sofa holler with victory.

Overtime is almost guaranteed now. "I'm so screwed," I whisper into Charli's ear.

"You wish," she whispers back.

And that is one hundred percent true.

THIRTY-NINE

SOME QUALITY WORK

Charli

My brother calls during the overtime period. I'm a little drunk on wine and emotional overload, but I answer it, moving over to Neil's piano bench for a moment of privacy. "Dennis, don't kill my mood. What is it that you need to ask me?"

"It's about your place, Charli. Robert got us jobs at a club. But I need to know if I can stay in this apartment. Robert said it was okay, but I didn't want to assume."

"Oh," I breathe. "You really got a job?"

"Yeah. I work in the stock room. He works security. I've stayed clear of the poker, Charli."

"Well… the place is paid up for another week. But then you'll have to pay the rent. On the fifteenth." I'm proud of Dennis, but I can't let him bleed me dry. Not anymore.

"How much?" he asks.

"Nine hundred and fifty."

"Hey—I can do that!" he says, his voice giddy.

"Yeah?" My mind is blown.

"Yeah. I'll get Robert to kick in some."

Good luck with that.

"Can I pay cash, you think?"

"You can. The landlord manages that check-cashing store on the ground floor. His name is Roy—I wouldn't hand it to anyone else. And Dennis, get a receipt."

"Okay, okay. Good plan. But Charli—you're not coming back?"

"No," I say softly. "It's all yours if you want it."

He chuckles. "Movin' up, huh? Always knew you would. Maybe I will too someday."

"I hope so."

The guys behind me roar at some play on the screen.

"You gotta go," Dennis says. "Sounds like you're havin' fun. Talk soon?"

"Sure. Good luck, Denn."

"You too!"

He hangs up, and I make my way back to the couch.

Neil lifts his arm, beckoning me to curl up next to him again, and I go right in like a heat-seeking missile.

I've realized a few important things tonight. First of all, Neil missed me. Really missed me. And he missed *me*—not the idea of me. Not just my naked body. He actually missed the redheaded, hot mess, angry girl who verbally spars with him at every opportunity.

He'd told me so several times. He'd even said *I love you*.

I hadn't really believed him until his goofy friends showed up to razz him.

Until now, I couldn't picture Neil needing me like I need him. The idea of him moping around Brooklyn for a few weeks didn't compute.

That's on me. I've spent the last decade yelling about how underappreciated women are, especially female athletes, but the person who did the best job of underappreciating me was... me.

Yup. My bad.

The other thing I'm realizing is that I like Neil's taste in sofas. And also red wine. It's super comfortable here with the weight of his arm around me.

"I'm sleepy. And I may have a super-low tolerance for alcohol," I say to Neil's shoulder.

"I'm getting that impression," he says, petting my hair. "It was a really stressful day. But don't conk out yet, baby. Your team is about to win this thing."

Two minutes later, Philly scores to end the overtime period. My whoop of joy has barely ended when Neil announces that the party is over.

Everybody laughs as they rise to clean up the empty glasses and bottles and discard the pizza box.

"You're coming home tonight, right?" Fiona says.

"Umm..." I say from where I'm practically draped over Neil. "Maybe not?"

"I'm joking, honey. See you in the morning. You can expect lots of nosy questions."

"Oh goody," I say with a sigh. "I love nosy questions."

"Night, Drake," Leo Trevi says. "Thanks for barely hosting."

"You're barely welcome," Neil says cheerfully. "See you on the plane."

"Later."

I glance at Neil as everyone files out of the living room. "You have to travel tomorrow?"

"Yeah, but not until late morning." Neil scoops his arm under my knees, stands, and heads toward the bedroom.

Oh goody!

Unfortunately, he makes a stop in the bathroom. "Wash up, hot stuff. Need a T-shirt to sleep in?"

"No," I say.

"Suit yourself." He leaves me to brush my teeth, which I accomplish with absolutely zero finesse. Then I remove all my clothing. Every stitch. And I waltz into Neil's bedroom.

"Well, hello dolly!" Neil says. "I like your outfit."

"Thanks," I say, sliding into the bed. "This is my side," I say, patting the mattress. "Did you sleep on it when I was gone?"

"No, I did not," he insists. "Back in a sec." He disappears into the bathroom, and I snuggle under the comforter, delightfully naked. We are going to have so much fun now. I've earned it.

Neil returns a few minutes later wearing flannel shorts and a T-shirt. He shuts off the lights and then slides into his side of the bed.

Turning to him, I purr. He pulls me into his arms and kisses me.

Yesssssss. I throw a knee over his leg and kiss him like the world will self-destruct in the next sixty seconds.

It doesn't. Neil breaks our kiss and rubs my back in gentle circles. "Good night, sexy. I'll see you in the morning."

"But..." A yawn stops me before I can get the rest out. "But we get to have make-up sex now. I always wanted to have make-up sex."

His smile feels stubbly against my cheek. "It's still make-up sex if we have it tomorrow. After you relax and sober up."

"I *am* relaxed," I insist. "Very, very relaxed. And very ready to show you how much I missed you."

He lets out a very low groan. "And you can. Tomorrow. You're finally back, right where I want you. But you told me today that people have tried to take advantage of you. And I will not be that guy. If I ever was, I can't be again."

"You are *not* that guy," I argue, pressing myself up on an elbow to make my point. "You were never that guy. I want you. I probably always have! That's why I was so angry at you."

His smile is beautiful in the moonlight. "You'll still want me in the morning, then. Now put your head down right here..." He pats the pillow. "And go to sleep."

I put my head down right where he's indicating, and sleep takes me before I can argue any further.

I wake up in the middle of the night, as is my habit, snapping into wakefulness and checking my surroundings.

This time it only takes me a half second to know that I'm safe. Neil is sleeping peacefully beside me. Each slow breath reminds me that all is well.

I sneak out of bed and tiptoe to the bathroom, where I use the facilities and take a cool drink of water.

Neil has tidied up the counter, dropping my toothbrush into the holder beside his. I don't know why this small gesture tugs at me, but it does.

It took me a really long time to picture myself as a part of Neil's life. But I can see it now. I can be here with him, and it won't be a game we're playing, and it won't be an illusion.

The chilly air chases me back to bed. I tuck my naked self back under the covers. I'm sober now and wide awake.

I roll over and gaze at Neil. He looks young and untroubled when he's sleeping. Long eyelashes point down at his aristocratic cheekbones. Full lips relax into sleep.

He's so beautiful. Maybe it's okay to feel a little stunned that someone with a face that handsome could turn to me and say, "I love you." I hope the surprise never entirely wears off. I wouldn't want to take him for granted. There's nobody else like Neil.

I ease forward and kiss the tattoo on his biceps. It's *right* there. Who could resist? Then I kiss his neck. And his throat. The stubble brushes against my lips. I kiss the inch of soft skin right in front of his ear.

"Baby," he whispers.

"Neil," I answer, kissing him again.

"Is it morning?"

"No," I admit. "But I can't fall back asleep. I'm too happy."

A sleepy arm reaches out and pulls my body close to his. "And you're still naked."

"Yeah, I noticed that too."

He smiles without opening his eyes. "Am I getting lucky?"

"Not as lucky as I am."

His beautiful eyes open and he pulls me in for a kiss. An ambitious kiss, especially for a guy who was asleep a minute ago.

But athletes have great reflexes, and Neil is already rolling on top of me, kissing my neck, his thumb circling my nipple with bossy accuracy.

I thread my fingers through his soft hair and down his neck until he shivers. "Fuck, I missed this," he whispers, tonguing my earlobe. "You're so sexy it breaks my brain."

My reply is incoherent, because his skillful hands are wandering everywhere. My body softens like butter in the sunshine. The way I feel when I'm underneath him is magic. Like I was born for pleasure.

We kiss, and then we kiss some more, until I'm desperate. "Please," I beg.

He's still wearing those damn boxers. I slide a hand under the waistband and stroke his cock until he moans.

"Patience."

"No," I argue.

He laughs. "Insulin pump is on my side." He removes my hand from his shorts and brushes my fingers across the plastic edge of the medical device, so I'll know not to accidentally scrape it off.

"Noted. Now get to it."

He kicks off his boxers, thank God. He kisses his way down my body, worshipping each breast, stippling my belly, and teasing my hips.

"Neil," I prompt, because patience is not my strong suit.

"Shh," he says, a hand on each knee. He parts my legs. "I need to taste you."

A shimmy of pleasure zings through me as he brushes his

lips across my clit. I've always been too self-conscious to enjoy this. I open my mouth to argue.

Then Neil mutters, "Fuck yes. I've been dreaming about this."

Well, then.

He lowers his mouth to my core with patient determination. His tongue makes a slow journey, and he hums happily.

And, yup, I'm shaking with need. If he doesn't get up here and do me, I might cry. And I never cry. "Okay, Neil, that's..."

He presses his lips against my flesh as he teases my entrance with blunt fingers.

"Oh God," I pant. *"Baby."*

With a deep groan, he finally swings up my body and kisses me as he fills me.

Yesss. This feels so right. It always has. And I'm finally ready to stop fighting it.

Neil moves, his athlete's body more graceful than a man has a right to be. I'm just settling in to enjoy the ride when he suddenly rolls us over. I find myself staring down into his clear-eyed smile.

Then he does an impressive ab curl, sitting us up so I'm astride his lap. "Giddy-up, kitten. You woke me up for this. Better finish what you started."

Without hesitation, I go for it. I don't hold back — I ride him until we're both groaning and desperate. The friction of his skin on mine and the heavy-lidded desire in his eyes are making me crazy. Strong hands lock onto my hips, urging me on.

I can't look away from those beautiful eyes. Now I know why it's so good with him every time. Now I know why sex got easier for me when I started having it with Neil — because that blissed-out look on his face is *love.*

I hadn't recognized it at first, because I'd never seen it before.

I recognize it now, and it takes me right over the edge. Before long, I sink down onto him with a shivery cry.

With a satisfied grunt, he jacks his hips beneath mine and attacks my mouth in one more kiss. We ride it out together, before I collapse in a sweaty heap on his chest.

"Good grief," I try to say, but it comes out as a sigh. His watch beeps with a blood-sugar warning. "Uh-oh."

He slaps my ass with a tired motion. "Up, kitten."

I disengage slowly and with great effort.

Neil reaches into the bedside table and pulls out a pack of peanut M&Ms. He rips open the bag and shoves a few into his mouth. Then he catches my hand and pours a few into my palm. "Here, baby. Keep up your strength. That was some quality work."

We eat the whole bag. Then we curl up together in the messy bed and fall asleep.

FORTY

REALLY AWKWARD HOLIDAYS

Neil

I wake up to my alarm at eight o'clock. Charli is right beside me, passed out on her face, her red hair a snarl on the pillow.

She's still the most beautiful thing I've ever seen.

Leaning down, I kiss her shoulder.

She twitches but doesn't wake up.

Ah, well. I suppose I'll have to do the grownup thing and get up quietly to start the coffee. I sneak away from the bed, grabbing my bathrobe before Charli can steal it.

I look at the robe's tag, finding the name of the brand. Then I locate my phone, take a picture of the tag and a selfie of me wearing it, and send it to Vera. *Please find me another one of these at your earliest convenience. It's the only way I'll ever get to wear it myself. Charli likes to steal it.*

She replies quickly, even though it's early on a Saturday morning. *No problem. Time for a haircut, though.*

It's true. But I can never quite find the time, and the salon at the store where Vera works is too far away. *You don't know any barbers who make house calls, do you?*

Negative, she says. *But I wish I did. Hey Neil—if I quit this job at the department store and go out on my own, will you still work with me? I'd be able to solve more of my clients' problems.*

What a question. *Of course! Get on that, girl. I know a bunch of professional athletes who don't know how badly they need a style upgrade.*

She sends me a smiley face emoji.

I haven't checked my messages since yesterday's fiasco of a meeting, and there are quite a few piled up. The team group text is full of congratulations to me. *Great to hear you're back with Charli*, etc. Some of them make lewd references to my multi-hour disappearance from the group chat, but it's harmless virtual catcalling.

Then there are the messages from my mother and sister. I wait until the coffee is brewed before I make myself face them. Paisley first.

Is Charli okay? That was really rough yesterday. I feel terrible. I always knew her as that girl who screwed up the soccer championship. But I never knew why. Can you give me her number or her email? I would like to apologize.

Man, you'd think that high school crap would be over by now. But I guess it never goes away. We all carry our sixteen-year-old insecurities around wherever we go.

Charli is okay, I tell her. And then I look up her email address and send it to my sister.

After that, I read the texts from my mother. They are not what I'm expecting.

Neil, Paisley yelled at me for an hour after the meeting.

She says she won't speak to me until I apologize to Charli.

It's hard to believe that a school I went to as a girl would tolerate that kind of behavior from a coach. I didn't want to believe it.

I didn't want to believe that it could have happened to your sister, too. And I might never have known.

When I think about how much money this family has given that school over the years, it's a lot. I didn't want to think that they might not deserve it. I didn't want to hear that they let some of their students down so badly.

I wanted to be proud of the Draper School.

I'm still not sure what to do. I think I made a mess of everything.

Please tell me how to reach Charli. So I can tell her I'm sorry.

Wow. That's a lot of word vomit from mom. She's obviously struggling. It's easier to believe that everything is okay and that you trusted the right people.

I get it, but her struggle doesn't let her off the hook. I send her Charli's email address, too, and tell her that I appreciate her efforts here. *Charli isn't going anywhere*, I tell her. *Please make your best apology, or holidays are going to be really awkward from here on out.*

When I'm just finishing my first cup of coffee, my mom replies. *At least we still control the foundation.*

I roll my eyes at an empty kitchen.

Then I tiptoe into the bathroom to brush my teeth and start the shower. Before I get in, I cross the bedroom to perch on the edge of the bed. I put a hand on Charli's bare back and massage the freckles I find there. "Wake up, kitten. It's time to shower with me. I have to leave in ninety minutes."

She rolls over with a smile. "You have the best ideas."

I lean down to kiss her. Because she's right. I do.

FORTY-ONE

WORLD CLASS APOLOGY

Charli

I float through the next three days. Even though Neil is out of town, I'm riding a high that just will not die.

"You'd better not be moving into a hostel," Fiona says when I stop by to fetch more of my things. "Or I will hunt you down and drag you home myself."

"It's a really nice hostel," I tease her. "Right across the street."

"Fine," she says, muting the TV. "I expect you to live there forever like a fairy tale character in the castle. But if anything goes wrong, I expect to see you right here." She pats the sofa cushion. "And use your key."

"Okay, thank you," I say, humbled by the knowledge that my friends are more amazing than I'd given them credit for. "I really appreciate it."

"Lake Como," she says with a shrug. "I want to eat Italian food and hit on Italian lesbians."

"Roger dodger. See you at practice."

Several hours later, I'm staring into Neil's refrigerator when I get an unexpected food delivery from the Turkish place. It's accompanied by a text: *Wish I were there to spoil you in person. It's my new favorite hobby.*

There is really no easy response to such loveliness, except to send him a kissy face selfie. The first such selfie I've ever taken in my life.

But maybe not the last.

We'll see.

A half hour later, the buzzer rings again, and a doorman tells me he's sending flowers up.

Am I with the right guy, or what? Nobody has ever sent me flowers. The delivery guy appears, and I let him carry them in and put them on the new coffee table. The vase is enormous. It's full of tulips in two shades of yellow.

I tip the delivery guy, close the door behind him, and pluck the full-sized card from the giant bouquet, where *Charlotte* is written on the envelope. And—hold on—these flowers are not from Neil. The thick paper stationery inside is embossed with *Mrs. Paloma Drake.*

His *mother* sent me flowers? Really?

Standing there in the middle of the living room, I read the handwritten letter from top to bottom.

Dear Charlotte,

After a good tongue lashing from both my son and daughter, I am ready to admit that I was far too caught up in my own drama to be properly empathetic to yours.

Darling, I made a grave error. I let a little thing like money get in the way of compassion and good sense. I wish I'd made a different choice. I apologize for my poor behavior. If I could go back in time and undo my vote, I would.

I am sorry.

With regard to that awful sports complex, Neil and I are trying to think of a practical way to undo the damage I have done.

If we come upon a solution, I'll let Neil tell you. But in the meantime, I humbly ask your forgiveness.

I can already tell that you are a smart, talented young woman who loves my son very much. And I will be proud to spend the next thirty years posing beside you in publicity photos at various charity events where we are both bored off our arses and wearing uncomfortable shoes.

With much love,

P.D.

You could knock me over with a feather. I read the letter twice more in rapid succession. It's not merely an apology, it's a *world-class* apology.

If I were someone who cried, this letter might get me going.

Gazing down at the tulips, I can hardly believe my turn of fortune. It's a rare thing when someone reverses course and does the right thing, even when she didn't have to.

Maybe Neil's mother isn't so terrifying after all. I might have to notch her down from eight and a half to a six.

But now it's time to watch some hockey. So I hurry back to the kitchen to finish my meal before Neil's game comes on TV.

The Bruisers win in Tampa before heading down to Miami. Neil and I stay in touch with a long-running text conversation that has me smiling at inappropriate moments—such as behind the counter at the diner.

Sal catches me, and he rolls his eyes. "Thought you weren't the kind of employee I had to yell at to put away her phone. Is it that handsome husband of yours?"

"Of course, it is," I say, dropping the phone in my apron

pocket. "I like hockey, coffee, and three people in the whole world."

"Am I one of them?"

"Sometimes."

He just grunts. But for his sake, I don't resume chatting with Neil until my shift is over. I call him on my way home, catching him after the morning skate.

"So what kind of date should we have when I come home?" he asks me.

"Well, we did the watching-sports-with-friends date already. Is it time for a movie?"

"Hmm." His low voice in my ear makes me happy. "How about a comedy club? Those are fun."

"I've never been."

"It's not glamorous," he says. "The tables are too close together, and the drinks are watery. But if you sit up front, the comedians will make fun of you."

"And that's a good thing?"

"Oh, totally. I'll look around and see who's playing. Thursday night, right? I checked your schedule."

Warmth curls through my chest. "That's right, and there's a goalie clinic. So I'll be done early."

"Smashing."

"Are comedy clubs dressy?" I have to ask.

"Not at all. But you're required to wear a low-cut top and do those smoky eyes. It's part of the dress code."

"Interesting. Can't wait to see you in a low-cut top with smoky eyes."

He cracks up. "Wear whatever you want. And if the comics bomb, we can sneak off and find a pool table somewhere. Oh — wait. Bad news, babe. My sister hit me with another gala fundraiser for next month. And you won't have any excuses, because the women's playoffs will already be over."

"Ouch. Another benefit? For what?"

"A children's hospital. My sister is on the board."

"Huh. I guess you can't say no to a children's hospital."

"No, you really can't. And I was once a patient there. You might even get to see a picture of fourteen-year-old me in a hospital johnny."

"You should've led with that. Now I'm looking forward to this."

"Better send that blue dress to the cleaners, then. I better run—there's a team lunch, and then we're doing video."

"Send me the deets on that comedy club."

"You bet, baby. I love you and miss you."

I stop walking. *I love you, too.* I could say it right now. Just four little words.

But nope. I chicken out. "Come home safe to me," I say instead.

"I will." Neil's voice is a scrape. "See you Thursday."

We hang up, and I start mentally cataloguing my inventory of tops, which is not vast. None of them are low cut.

I'll just have to borrow something from Fiona, then.

Totally worth it.

I'm still wandering around like a dreamy-eyed schoolgirl as I leave the rink on Thursday evening. My plan is to hurry over to Fiona's, let myself in with her key, and grab one of the tops she and Sylvie left out for me to choose from.

"Try the velvet one first," Sylvie had said. "It looks sexier on the body than it does on the hanger."

After that, I'll have a half hour to do my makeup before I take the train into Manhattan to meet Neil.

These are my deep, important thoughts as I round the corner of the training facility and head towards Water Street. For once in my life, I'm feeling happy-go-lucky.

Which means that for once in my life I don't scan my surroundings.

Which proves to be a mistake.

Two hands punch at my shoulders and shove me against the corner of the building. My back slams against the bricks. My reaction is a half second slower than it ought to be, so when I knee my assailant in the balls, he has just enough time to swerve his hips and dodge.

"Fuck you," Robert spits. "Hold fucking still."

As if. My heart is all the way up in my throat. "Get your hands off me!"

"Shut up," comes another man's jeer. "Robby, let go. People will stare."

Robert removes his hands from my body, but it doesn't help. All my blood vessels constrict at once. I know that voice. I'm scared shitless of that voice.

Then my living nightmare looms in my peripheral vision. It's Gianni—Robert's father.

Oh no.

Oh no no no.

"Hey, Charli," he says in his two-pack-a-day voice. "Long time no see."

Sweat pools under my arms. "This is my place of business," I say in what ought to be a calm voice. But it's shaking. "Robert, I told you to leave me the hell alone. You got what you wanted —a free month's rent."

He laughs. "You think that's all I wanted? Think again."

"We need something from you," Gianni says.

"Can't get blood from a stone," I try. But I'm already trembling.

"Cut the crap," Gianni says. "You're married to a goddamn billionaire."

"I already explained that's a lie. It's a stunt," I manage to say.

"Sure looks real," Robert says with a smirk. "We saw you taking groceries into his pad."

They *watched* me? My hands are icy, and yet a drop of sweat runs down between my breasts.

"How did you pay for his stuff?" Robert asks.

I summon a little zap of much needed anger. "What do you care? Don't you have anything better to do than watch me shop for groceries? I did him a favor."

"Like you married him for a favor?" Gianni says.

"Yes!" I hiss. "Exactly like that."

"You dirty little whore," he whispers, looming so close that I can smell the stale cigarette smoke on his jacket. "What other favors do you do for him?"

My mouth is so dry that I can barely make my next threat. "Take two steps back, or else I'm going to scream."

"The fuck you will," he snarls. "Better not scare us off until you hear what we got to say. You'll be sorry."

"This guy—Drake. You have access to his money," Robert says. "You get us ten grand, Charli. And then ten more next month."

"You're *high*," I gasp. "I don't have his checkbook."

"Get. It." Gianni bites out. "He won't even miss it. You don't do it, we have naked pictures of you to show around town."

"You do not," I spit. "*Fuck* you."

Gianni slaps me. It's just a quick, open-hand slap, but I am already so scared that I stop breathing as the sting sets in.

"Look, you little bitch. Here." He thrusts a piece of printer paper at me, with a single photo centered in the middle.

It's me behind the bar at the strip club, my hair teased, my breasts bare save for the little pasties they made us put on our nipples. I've got a bottle of liquor in each hand, and I'm pouring a drink. A Long Island Iced Tea, maybe.

"H-how'd you get this?" I stammer, too shocked to hold the question in.

Robert actually laughs. "I thought Dennis told you we got jobs at a club. I work security. Do you know what else they still got? Video. I can get video of you behind that bar. I'm going to sell it to TMZ unless you do as I say."

"Nice tits," Gianni says, his voice a mean scrape. "I mean, I seen 'em before. But they're bigger now."

My vision swims. I make myself look away from the picture by cramming it into my coat pocket. As if that would help at all.

I can barely breathe, but self-preservation is a strong force, so I know what to say. "It doesn't matter. None of it matters. We're getting divorced."

"That's what you said last time," Robert grunts.

With a hand that's still shaking, I unzip my bag and pull out the envelope. "This is the paperwork, asshole. I'm sending it to the lawyer right now. It's done. It was just a joke. Never meant to last."

Even as I say this, I know it was always true. You can take the girl out of the slums, but you can never get the slums out of the girl.

"So what?" Robert says. "You can still get the money."

"I never could have," I say. "Go ahead. Show that picture to whoever you want. It's not Neil in that photo. Nobody cares if I worked in that club. Nobody cares what I do. Just like nobody cares about *you*, either. So how about you both fuck off?"

I couldn't even tell you how the conversation ends. I keep talking, and then I start walking. There's a mailbox on the corner, and I pull down the handle and throw the divorce papers in.

My body is shaky and too loose. I have the worst urge to look over my shoulder to see if they're following me. I don't think they are. I head up the street, where there are plenty of pedestrians on the sidewalk with me, so I'm no longer in danger.

But I feel like I am. Like I'll never be safe again.

When I put my hands in my coat pockets, the rumpled

picture is in one, and Fiona's key is in the other. My feet point me toward their apartment on Water Street.

As I approach the front door, I finally give in to the urge to look over my shoulder. I don't see my cousin or his father. But that doesn't mean they can't see me.

I'd better never forget that.

I hastily open the door, and I climb the stairs like a zombie. I insert the key into the deadbolt on the apartment's door, and I let myself in.

"Charli!" Sylvie calls from her bedroom. "Is that you? I'm still here. Come see these tops!"

But I only make it as far as the sofa, where I sink down onto the cushion. I weigh a thousand pounds.

"Charli?"

I open my mouth to greet her, but the oddest sound comes out. It's like the bark of a seal. My ribs contract painfully.

It's a *sob*. I take a gasping breath, trying to hold myself together. But it's like a dam bursting. My chest heaves again. My eyes spout like fountains.

It *hurts*. It hurts so bad. My head is a boulder. Tears stream down my face, and I can barely breathe.

Everything hurts. And nothing will ever be right again.

FORTY-TWO

THE ONE WITH ALL THE BAGGAGE

Neil

It turns out that comedy clubs aren't that much fun if you've been stood up.

My texts to Charli go unanswered. At first, I assume she's just late. She probably took the subway. Maybe there's a delay.

But then I start to worry. Can she not get inside? Did they screw up her ticket at Will Call?

Is she hurt? Did something happen?

And now I'm that asshole sitting in the front row, looking at his phone.

"Dude, am I boring you?" the comic says, miming a kick at my head. "Oh no! There's an empty chair here. Looks like he got stood up. Was it a guy or girl?"

Yeah, I don't know why I thought this would be fun. "My wife," I say drily, and the whole room laughs.

"Look, I know a good divorce lawyer," the comic says. "I've been divorced. I sat across that pricey table from my ex while they explained the terms to me, and I said, 'Hey honey, I wish you'd tried to screw me this much when we were still married.'"

More laughter.

My phone finally pings with a text. It says only: *I can't. I'm sorry.*

I get up and thread my way through a hundred tables on my way out of the room.

By the time my taxi crosses the bridge, I've tried calling Charli fifty times. She doesn't pick up.

I see an incoming call from Anton, and I pounce. "Bro," he says. "Something is the matter with Charli, but she won't say. She wouldn't want me telling you."

"What do you mean? Is she hurt?"

"Not that Sylvie can tell. But she's a crying mess on their sofa. She won't say why."

"Shit. I'm almost there." We hang up, and I try to imagine what's wrong. I come up with nothing. She sounded fine when we were texting this morning. And yesterday, too.

What the hell?

I hit Sylvie's buzzer with an impatient finger until somebody unlocks the door for me. I take the stairs two at a time, unable to shake a feeling of dread.

Sylvie opens the door. And there's Charli—tipped over on the couch, still wearing her jacket, her face red and puffy and hardly recognizable.

She squeezes her eyes shut when I walk into the room. "Baby?" I plead. "What is it?"

"I'm sorry," is all she says. "I really am."

I walk over to the sofa and lift her feet, so I can sit at the end of the couch. I put a cautious hand on her knee. "Charli. Can you come here, please?"

"No," she says in a hoarse whisper. "I filed the papers."

It takes me a second. "The divorce papers?"

She gives a jerky nod.

"You going to tell me why?"

"No."

I sigh. "I want to hear it, Charli. Whatever it is."

"There's always something to drag me back down. This time it's so, so bad."

Glancing up at Sylvie, I give her a pointed look.

After hesitating a moment—after all, I'm shooing her out of her own living room—she turns and heads for the bedroom. The door clicks shut.

"There is nothing you can't tell me," I say quietly.

"I'm tired, Neil. So tired of being the one with all the baggage."

"Men like carrying your luggage around, doll."

She picks up her head and turns her angry eyes my way. "It's not funny, Neil. Not everything can be laughed away."

"Are you sick? Are you hurt?"

She shakes her head.

"Then it can't be that bad. Come on." I drop my hand on her hip, and something crinkles under my hand. There's something in Charli's pocket.

Her hand whips back and shoves mine off, then clamps down on the pocket.

I always let Charli win these fights, but not tonight. I wait until her arm relaxes and perform a ninja move where I nudge her hand and yank out whatever's in her pocket. It's a piece of paper with a photo printed on it.

"Neil!" she shrieks, lunging for it.

I see the picture before she grabs it. "Jesus. Is that you?"

She crunches up the paper tightly, then covers her face with her hands and cries.

Fuck. "I'm sorry! Hell. I was just... surprised. You gotta fill me in." I try to pull her into my arms. "Start from the beginning."

To my surprise, she lets me hold her. "It's b-b-bad, Neil."

"Okay. I'm not scared. Where was this photo taken? In a

strip club?" It's not like I've never seen a topless bartender before.

"Y-yes. Last year."

"All right. So what? I am working really hard not to say the wrong thing right now. But I've *been* to bachelor parties, Charli. I know titty bars exist. This isn't the end of the world."

"Yes, it IS!" she shrieks. "This p-picture is going to end up everywhere. In the tabloids. With your name attached. And I can't let that happen, Neil. I can't. Because I *love you*!" She glares at me. "I love you, and I really, really wanted to be the girl in your c-corner. And not embarrass your family."

"Oh, honey. You're already that girl. And you're so much more than one unflattering photo."

"I know," she bites out. "But he said he can also get video. Neil, I'm being blackmailed."

"Oh." *Oh shit.* "By who?"

Instead of answering, she just sobs.

I wise up and stop trying to pry answers out of her. I just hold her, stroking her hair, rubbing her back. And I tell her everything is going to be okay. That she and I are a team, and we're stronger than this.

After a while, she listens. She finally calms down. I bring her a glass of ice water, and I ask if she trusts me enough to explain the situation to me.

"I do trust you," she whispers.

Then she tells me the story.

And I almost lose my shit.

It takes me an entire day to calm down enough to make a plan.

We're coming up on the playoffs, my schedule is crazy. So the plan waits a few more days. I won't be telling Charli the details ahead of time.

"You have to let me take care of it," I insist. "My way. This is just one of those times."

I expect an argument. But Charli is so afraid of her mother's cousin that she doesn't even put up a fight.

This man had hurt her when she was a teenager. One night while staying in his home, she'd awakened to find him naked and on top of her. She'd had to fight him off.

"I haven't really slept well for almost ten years," she told me. I want to kill him. I really do.

But I'm not going to. I'm just going to scare him a little bit. Which is why I'm driving a rental car deep into Brooklyn on my day off in the company of a young bodyguard named Duff.

"You have to let me go in first," Duff insists. He works for the security company that protects the team. "What if this guy is packing? I'm wearing a vest."

"Fine," I say, parking in front of the dingy, old apartment building. "You can go in first. I don't need to get shot."

"And we leave no marks on these guys," Duff adds.

"That's a taller order," I grumble.

"I bet it is. But neither of us is going to jail. You can scare a man half to death without punching him."

"Castration was more in my line of thinking."

Duff shakes his head. "Do you need to stay in the car?"

"No."

We get out together, and Duff picks the lock on the building's door in about four seconds flat. Even as we climb the stairs, we can hear the TV playing behind the door to Charli's old place. It's so loud that Duff picks that lock, too, and the people inside don't notice until he flings open the door and steps inside.

"Don't fucking move," he says, his hand on his piece. "Keep your hands where I can see them."

Two doughy men on the sofa raise their hands. They both look baffled. And they both look like they're about to pee themselves.

"You're right," I say to Duff. "Big danger."

He grins.

Then I turn my attention to the asswipes on the sofa. "I'm Neil. I'm a guy you never want to cross."

The older creep seems to gather himself. He lowers his hands to his thighs and sneers at me. "Yeah, you're tough. You had to get *another* guy to bust in here for you like Rambo?"

I put a foot on the milk crate they're using as a coffee table and look down at the two of them. "Yeah, yeah. Say what you will. Do either one of you want to fight me? I'm available right now, and my day job is hockey. I enjoy it when things get a little rough."

There are no volunteers, so I move on.

"First up, I don't give a crap about that picture of Charli. As far as I'm concerned, you can cover the Goodyear blimp with that photo and fly it over New York. So Charli worked in a titty bar. Who cares? My family doesn't."

The men on the couch scowl.

"But I'll tell you who cares—Charli," I continue. "And I love Charli. So that's why I need you to know something. If those pictures leak, I'm coming for you. I don't care if it's this year or a decade from now. I don't even care if it was you who leaked it. I'm coming for you *both*."

"Bring him, tough guy." The older turd points at Duff.

"Oh, I won't have to," I say easily. "I've got your rap sheet. Possession of unregistered firearms. Possession of illegal substances. I got a feel for your tastes. So if you do something I don't like, the police are going to get a tip. Your house gets searched. Your mother's house gets searched. And maybe they find some extra-special drugs there. I'm sure my team can think of something."

Suddenly the dude doesn't look so brave any more.

"And if I'm feeling extra cranky, maybe your car gets forced off the road after dark. Maybe you get called in for a lineup at the police station when they're looking for a murderer. Who knows what I'll come up with?"

Both men glance at each other. But neither of them moves.

"I guess I'll decide later. But I have a lot of money. Nearly infinite resources. I have a lot of friends in high places—and low ones, too. And when I hold a grudge, it's gonna sting. If you want to find out how bad, you leak that picture. Meanwhile, don't contact Charli. Don't call her. Don't visit. Don't come within two hundred feet. Don't reach out to her in any manner in the present, or in one invented in the future."

"Jesus, we get it," the younger asshole says.

"Excellent. Now I just need each of you to tell me the rules. Once you clarify your understanding, I'm done here. You first." I point to the older punk.

He gives me a scathing look.

I wait.

Duff unholsters his gun and inspects it. He blows some invisible dust off the barrel.

The punk sighs. "I will never share the picture."

"In any format, ever," I add.

"In any format, ever," he says.

"And?"

"And I won't contact Charli."

"Excellent. Your turn." I point at his asshole of a son.

"What he said. We won't contact Charli or ever share her picture. Or a video."

I dust my hands like a movie gangster. "That's all, boys. Have a nice day."

We leave the way we came. "You got it, right?" I ask on the sidewalk.

"I got it. Let me drive? You can see."

"Sure." Duff and I climb into the rental car, but this time he drives. He hands me his phone at the first red light.

I edit the video to delete the part where I'm threatening them. And then I send it to myself and my new personal lawyer.

Then I call Charli. "Hey, baby. What are you doing?"

"Just finished a shift at the diner. Sal was happy to see me."

"I bet." I break out in a huge grin. If Charli's working, it means she's feeling better. "Sorry I couldn't make it in there today, but I had a piece of business to take care of."

"What kind of business?"

"Well, I'm about to send you a video. You don't have to watch it if the sight of your cousins is triggering. But if you did watch it, you'd see both of them promise never to contact you or share that photo or video."

There is a silence on the phone for a second, and I worry. But then she says, "Really?" in a happy gasp. "Seriously? That's incredible. Show me!"

"Okay, I'm going to hang up and hit send. Call me back after you watch it."

The wait to hear from her again is just three minutes. When I answer her call, the first thing she says is: "I've waited my whole life for someone to put them in their place. And you... This is..." She sucks in a breath. "Wow. I don't even know what to say."

"Say you're free for dinner after practice. That's all I need from you, my love."

Another beat of silence. "I love you," Charli says.

"I know, baby. Turkish? Chinese? Sushi?"

"I *love* you."

"And I love you, doll." Yeah, I had to throw that in there just for old time's sake. I wait for her to yell.

But nope. "I love you! Thank you for being in my corner."

"Aw." I grab my heart, even though she can't see me. "You're welcome. Thank you for being in mine."

"Always," she says. "You pick the restaurant. Just text me a location. I'll wear a low-cut shirt and smoky eyes."

"You really do love me," I murmur.

She finally laughs.

FORTY-THREE

EPILOGUE
LAKE COMO, ITALY

Late July

Neil

It's a beautiful evening about a half hour before sunset, and I'm carrying a tray through our family home on the lake. It's loaded down with servings of gelato in brightly decorated cups. "Are you coming outside, guys?" I call to my teammate in the living room and the woman he's arguing with. "You don't want to miss dessert. The flavor of the day is rosemary and olive oil."

Crikey's head turns in my direction. "Did you say olive oil? In *ice cream*? Gross."

"I think it sounds *amazing*," snaps Vera, who is on this jaunt with us as Charli's guest. Vera and Crikey have been squabbling like children since the minute we all arrived. "Can I have one?"

"Of course." I meet her in the center of the airy room, and she helps herself to a cup and a spoon.

"Thanks." She spins around and she and Crikey go right back to arguing, as if they'd never even stopped. "You should never wear Chuck T's with a suit," she says. "That looks childish."

"Nah, it looks hip," he argues. "You're the one who said that hipness is nothing but whimsy."

"The right *kind* of whimsy," she argues. "Sneakers with a suit just looks like you forgot to pack your shoes."

"Why do *you* get to decide which is the right kind of whimsy? Because you went to some kind of expensive design school? Kinda snobby of you, no?"

Vera lets out a little shriek of rage, and I hurry toward the veranda, so I don't have to listen. Outside, nobody is arguing. Several of our friends are stretched out on deck chairs, while Charli and Fiona drink flutes of prosecco in the hot tub together.

"Gelato delivery," I announce, and two of my teammates pop up out of their chairs and come running. "Olive oil and rosemary."

"That sounds really fucking weird," Castro says. "But I'm in." He takes two—one for him and one for Heidi Jo.

"Sounds amazing," Anton mutters. "I'm gonna weigh twice as much when we get on the plane to go home."

"Not my problem," I say, carrying the tray to the hot tub. "Ladies?"

They both look up with joy on their faces. "Dessert in the hot tub? I'm in *heaven*," Fiona declares. "I knew this place would be magical." She hands a cup to Charli before reaching for her own. "Just admit it," Fiona says. "I was right when I said you'd end up here with Neil."

"Nobody likes to hear an *I told you so*," Charli says, rising out of the water to set her glass down in a safe spot.

I get a full-on view of Charli in a tiny red bikini. "Damn, wifey. Love the new bathing suit. It's... boobalicious."

Fiona snorts. "Subtle, Drake."

Who needs subtlety? I have the serious urge to kiss all the places those tiny straps touch her skin and then remove it with my teeth.

"The suit is Vera's work, as usual," she says, with a glance down at her amazing rack. "That girl is dangerous to my pocketbook. But at least I get the corporate discount now."

To Sal's dismay, Charli finally quit the diner this spring. Now she works a few mornings a week on Vera's new personal-styling venture. Charli is the cosmetics guru. She helps Vera's clients find the right products and does makeup for special events.

"Vera's clients interpret the idea of a *special event* very broadly," Charli had laughingly told me right after she'd started. "We're not talking weddings, here. Today's client had me do all her makeup for an afternoon tea she was attending."

"Maybe the queen was gonna be there?" I'd guessed.

Charli had just shaken her head. She loves her new job. "I can't believe I am paid to play with makeup," she says. "It feels like cheating."

She and Vera have been brainstorming a line of cosmetics, but the whole thing is still new.

As for us, we're still new, too, I guess. But our connection doesn't feel tentative to me anymore. We're enjoying every moment. Charli has fully moved into my apartment and has a closet of her own and her own drawers in the bathroom. Her makeup case isn't shoved against the bathroom wall anymore — the products are spread end-to-end on the counter now.

Whatever. I need Charli far more than I need countertop space.

I give myself a little insulin boost and then take the last gelato cup for myself. I slide into the hot tub next to my girl, and she immediately captures my feet with hers.

"It's poker night," she says. "Get ready to cry."

"You wish, wifey."

"This could be amusing," Fiona says.

"You know it." Charli beams at me.

I eat my gelato and watch the sun start to dip. The Italian sunsets are always breathtaking, and tonight's had better not be any exception. "Hey, Charli? We got some mail today. Can I talk to you upstairs for a few minutes?"

She looks up quickly, putting her spoon back in the cup. "Right now? It's almost sunset time."

"Yeah, but we can stand by a window. Come with me a sec?" I step out of the tub and put our empty cups on the tray. "You can even bring your drink." I hold out a towel insistently.

She looks like she wants to argue, but then gives in. "Sure, hubby. Why not." She takes my hand and steps out of the tub, and I wrap her in a towel. I wrap another one around my own waist, grab her glass of prosecco, and then lead her toward the house.

We pass Vera and Crikey, who have moved on to arguing about drink mixers. Or something. It's a little hard to say.

"It will be quieter upstairs," I point out. "Come."

Charli follows me up the grand staircase and into the master bedroom we're sharing. She stops in the middle of the rug. "Is everything okay?"

"Everything is fine. But I need to wish you a happy half anniversary."

Charli blinks. "Six months?"

"That's right. Six months ago, yesterday, you won that medal in Vegas. Then we went out drinking and got married sometime early the next day."

"Wow, you're right," she says. "Italy made me forget what day it is."

"I forgot, too," I admit. "But the lawyer didn't forget, and this just arrived while you and Sylvie were out biking." I hold up a FedEx envelope from New York. "New paperwork."

"Six months," she repeats. "Now we can get divorced without cause."

"That's right."

Charli meets my eyes, and everything stops for a moment. We just take each other in. These have been some of the best months of my life. Our relationship has finally found its groove. I can't even remember the last time we discussed our divorce.

But now Charli rips the strip off the envelope and pulls out a set of papers. She stares at the cover letter and doesn't turn the pages. "Wow. That woman is super prompt. How much is she costing you?" She laughs awkwardly. "Do you want to do this right here?"

"Well, only if you want to," I say carefully.

She looks down at the papers in her hand. "Up to you, hubby. On the one hand, why not? But on the other hand, why bring down our vacation vibe? It could, uh, wait a couple days?" She tips her green eyes up to mine.

I break out into a huge smile. If Charli went sprinting for a pen, I don't know what I would have done. "I don't see any reason to bring down our vacation vibe."

Her shoulders relax. "Okay, good. It's not just me. Missing the sunset to sign off on a divorce is kind of a bad call."

"Right." I cross to the French doors and open them. There's a little balcony facing the lake. "Come on, then. This sunset isn't going to watch itself."

Charli drops the papers on the bed and follows me onto the balcony. The sun is a huge orange ball sinking toward the mountains in the distance. They're turning more purple with each passing second.

"Oh look, another bottle of prosecco," I say.

Charli glances down at the ice bucket I'd left out on a tiny, tile-topped table. "Where'd that come from?"

"Happy half anniversary, wifey." I give the cork a twist and it pops into my hand. She holds out her glass, and I refill it. Then I pour an inch for myself into another glass.

"To, um, six really crazy months," she says, her smile going shy.

"Six incredible months," I echo. We touch glasses and take a sip. Then I loop an arm around her and watch the sunset for a moment.

The prosecco bursts over my tongue with its bright, acidic flare. And I know there's only one way this moment could be better. I set down my glass on the little table, and I slowly sink down onto one knee.

Charli turns. She looks down at me, her eyes widening in surprise. "Neil?" she whispers.

"Charli," I whisper back. Then I reach behind the ice bucket and retrieve the little velvet box holding my grandmother's ring. I open it up. "I would like to know if you'd do me the honor of not divorcing me."

She actually grabs the railing with her free hand, as if she needs the support. Then she tosses back her prosecco and drains it. "Jesus Christ, Neil. Way to stun a girl. Are you for real?" She's blinking rapidly now.

"So real," I say.

"Oh my *God. Yes.* I'm in if you are." She bends over and grabs her knees, like they tell you to do if you feel faint.

I set the ring down and throw my arms around her. "I love you."

"And I love *you*," she repeats. "I just need a minute to get my head around this. You want to do this for real."

"So much." I kiss her neck. "And I swear I'm not under the influence this time."

"I know," she says, laughing. "You barely had a sip of prosecco."

"That bikini is pretty potent, though. It could turn a guy's head."

She laughs and hugs me. We're in an awkward crouch, so I grab the ring and pull her up to stand next to me. "I think it's high time you put this back on. And not just ceremonially."

She waves a hand in front of her face rapidly. "That ring still scares me. I'm afraid to lose your family heirloom. But that is my only reservation."

"Put it on already."

Sliding it onto her finger, she lets out a little squeal and then hugs me again. "This is super exciting, and I am so surprised I can barely form a sentence. I can't believe that just happened."

"Believe it." I carefully get to my feet, bringing her along with me. "Why not now? There is nobody like you, wifey. I found the craziest, prettiest, most competitive one. And I'm keeping her."

Then I lay a kiss on her. Because there's a sunset and we're in Italy and she's wearing a bikini.

And she just said yes.

Charli kisses me like a woman who knows what she wants. But then she pulls back. "What would you have done if I had wanted to sign those divorce papers?"

"I'm not sure," I admit. "But I had to show them to you. It's only fair. Our marriage can't be an accident. I still maintain that drunk Neil knew what he was doing."

She presses her forehead against mine. "Drunk Charli doesn't get enough credit, I guess. She sure can pick 'em."

I kiss her on the forehead. "Hey, look quick. The sunset is almost over."

She turns to admire the horizon. It's deep purple now. "Life is short, and it happens fast," she says.

I hug her to my side. "That's right. You have to be ready to catch the beauty however it comes to you. Even if you're drunk off your ass in Vegas."

We fall silent as the last lip of the sun sinks beside Monte San Primo.

"This is also for you," I say when the spectacle is over. I hold out the ring box. "There are actually two compartments in here."

She turns to me, eyes shining. "Sorry, what?"

"Lift off the ring holder."

Charli does, revealing a necklace in the bottom of the box. "What is...*oh.*" She holds up the choker-length necklace made of many tiny stones in black and bright rainbow colors. "Neil!

This is badass. Are the colored stones from…?" She raises curious eyes to mine.

"Yup. From the Vegas ring. The other stones are called black spinel. I asked Vera to find a designer who could make the ugly ring into something cool."

"Damn," Charli whispers. "I'd have bet that couldn't be done. But wow. This is amazing."

"Let's put it on you." I put the box onto the table, and Charli turns around so I can clip the necklace around her creamy neck.

"I need a mirror," she says.

I beckon her inside, where she looks into the mirror on the bedroom wall. "Hubby, it's amazing. *You're* amazing."

Behind her, I wrap my arms around her waist and kiss her neck. "You know we're going to have to let my mother throw us that party now, right?"

She laughs. "Fine. I'm not wearing a fluffy white dress, though. That ship has sailed."

"Whatever you want." I kiss her neck again. "I love you."

She turns around and hugs me. "Not as much as I love you."

"If you say so. But…" I pull away and grab the divorce papers off the bed. I offer them to Charli. "You want to do the honors?"

She grabs them and then gets ready to tear. "Never tell me how many billable hours this woman charged us for."

"Deal."

She rips the papers, and they flutter to the bedroom floor.

On the way home, we use one of the larger Drake jets to accommodate all our friends. Charli and I sit side by side holding hands. "So, I got you an engagement present, but it's a little weird."

She rolls her head against the leather seat to look at me. "Now I'm nervous. I hope it didn't cost more than a hundred bucks, Drake. You know I get antsy when you spend a fortune. And I'm already wearing a fortune in jewelry."

"Hmm. This cost a little more than the jewelry. And you can't even use it."

"Great pick then, hubby. What did you do?"

I tap my fingers nervously on the tray table. Charli looks pointedly down at them, so I stop. "The sports complex for Draper and Parkhurst. The one that was going to be named for a child molester?"

"Yes," Charli says slowly. "What about it?"

"I got them to drop his name. In fact, I got them to promise they would never name any building or any part of the campus or the curriculum after him."

She leans toward me, eyes wide. "Really? *How?*"

"By donating a little more than sixty-five thousand dollars. Well, a lot more. Actually, it was—"

She clamps her hands over her ears. "I don't want to know. I probably wouldn't think it was a great investment."

At two million bucks, she probably wouldn't. So I guess I'll just keep that figure to myself. "It's going to be a really nice facility."

She removes her hands. "But you and I had to change in those dank old locker rooms. We lived."

"You, meanie." I squeeze her knee. "Do you really want to deprive the teens of wooden locker cubbies and new carpeting in the team colors? There's an indoor soccer field for wintertime practice, too."

"Ooh." Her eyes light up. "Okay, so I guess it sounds cool. But keeping that asshole's name off it sounds even better. I can't believe you got them to agree to it."

"It was a really interesting conversation. But here's the thing —we got naming rights. So now we have to decide what to call it."

Charli sits back in her seat. "Naming rights? Like—the Drake Family Gymnasium?"

"Baby, no. I was thinking the Charli Fern Higgins Gymnasium."

"You'd really name it after me?" she squeaks.

"In big-ass gold letters, doll. What better way to get back at that asshole? Splash your name all over the entrance."

Her smile is enormous as she leans in and puts her chin on my shoulder. "That's... wow. I like your style. But I have a better naming idea. I like—the Charli and Neil Drake Gymnasium."

"That does have a certain ring to it," I whisper.

"In big-ass gold letters," she agrees. "I'm totally sold."

THE END

ALSO BY SARINA BOWEN

ACKNOWLEDGMENTS

Thank you so much to Sue Moss, attorney at law, for straightening out my understanding of New York divorce law. Who knew the law was so bonkers?

Also, thank you to Anna Schlissel for your expert advice on Neil's diabetes.

Thank you K.J. Dell'Antonia and Jess Lahey for your constant support and company!

Thanks to Jenn Gaffney and Natasha Leskiw for your tireless efforts to make these books shine and reach their full potential.

As always, thank you to Edie Danford for your insightful edits, and to Claudia F. Stahl for your impeccable proofreading.